Johnny Glass has had it with Nashvill[...] politicians preyed on him for four diffic[...] talented, struggling singer-songwriter, h[...] still wants to make a living doing what he loves, writing and singing songs. A former band mate lives in a broken down Airstream camper on the Florida-Alabama State line near the sparkling Gulf of Mexico—for free. Playing music and singing songs at the world-famous Flora-Bama Lounge and Package Store on the beach is his everyday gig. Johnny has a standing offer to join his buddy anytime, as the owner of the place is a lover of singer-songwriters, and could certainly use someone with his skills.

Lucy Whitman is a sophomore debutante at the University of South Alabama and the privileged daughter of an Alabama State Senator. Uninterested in her life as a university student and sorority girl, Lucy tilts to the wild side on the weekends where she sings, unbeknownst to her overbearing parents, in a bona fide honky-tonk band at America's Last Great American Roadhouse, the Flora-Bama. Instead of planned summer school, she has decided to spend the entire tourist season singing; and if it goes well, she likely won't go back to South.

For Johnny and Lucy, it's love at first sight. Through joined artistry their relationship grows, and they become a popular on-stage duo. They enjoy each other and the creative fulfillment the partnership brings. However, Lucy's mother and powerful father want nothing of their daughter playing a honky-tonk joint in Orange Beach. After gently trying to win her favor, they make their strongest, connected attempt toward altering her brazen life path; and it has devastating consequences—not only for Lucy's music, but for everyone living on Pleasure Island: The beloved Flora-Bama may be shuttered—for good.

Lucy's father uses his political connections to deploy an army of state government agents against the beach bar, trumping up dozens of unfounded charges resulting in its indefinite closure. Already in financial trouble stemming from bad outside investments, a great recession and an unprecedented manmade environmental disaster, the bar cannot afford to be closed during the lucrative tourist season.

Johnny and Lucy, the locals and the rest of the musicians join forces with the Flora-Bama's loveable owner and come up with a plan to save the quintessential beach bar, and the community it faithfully supports. In doing so, Johnny and Lucy realize the grand futility of commercial success, and the bountiful wealth they already possess—from living and enjoying life, making music and many friends, in a beautiful, unforgettable place like no other.

Saved at the Alabama-Florida Line is a romantic, satirical tale of forbidden love that seeks to draw semblance to Southern living, art, failed politics and pop culture.

A Double Novel
By Chris Warner

Copyright 2014 & 2021

CEW/Wagon Publishing

ISBN # 978-0-9884880-1-4

Layout and Design: Jamie Welch
Cover Illustrations: Susan Nugent Clark

"Blessed are the weird people: poets, misfits, writers,
mystics, painters, troubadours: for they see the world
through different eyes."
– Jacob Nordby

Acknowledgments
Many people have supported me in this effort. However, Joe Gilchrist has been most instrumental in this regard. Thank you, Joe, for motivating me and helping me realize the principal business of life. You are a true mentor and friend—the best a guy could have. Also, thanks to my many friends of the extended Flora-Bama community. All of you are vivacious, beautiful, creative, loving people and it is you who truly make the Flora-Bama the special, unforgettable place it is, and hopefully always will be.

BOOK 1

1

Early May 2010

King-sized sheets of rain pelted the 2002 Dodge truck's cracked windshield as the vehicle lumbered south down the Tennessee highway. In the waning twilight, visibility was low. Driving conditions were awful, especially with balding tires. A motivated Johnny Glass, hunched over the steering wheel, and focused intently on the road, had never seen such rain; and neither had Nashville. Lucky for him, he was leaving the Music City—and hopefully the stormy weather, behind. His truck was packed tight with his worldly possessions; two prized Martin guitars, sentimental personal effects and some old clothes, most of which were wrinkled.

The face of the thin black cell phone perched on the dashboard lit up like a small candle in the dark cab. It rang loudly over the heavy pitter patter of rain and the low volume George Strait hit playing. Johnny turned off the radio and picked up the device. He recognized the 850 area code. He was expecting the call. He left an earlier message for his old band mate, Jake Justice—a fine singer-songwriter, that he was heading down to see him. They spent their first two years in Nashville playing in a band that eventually broke up as they all tried to make their way. On a whim, Jake headed south with a new girlfriend to her sunny home of Perdido Key, Florida. Johnny instead opted to stick it out, chasing that neon rainbow of country music fame and fortune.

Two years later, Johnny had had enough of Music Row. He was finally ready to bail. He hoped to follow Jake, as he had not heard from him much, and figured he had to be doing well if he was still playing the same honky-tonk joint on the Florida-Alabama State line. But in reality, Johnny had few options. He had no place else to go—and no other ideas.

The last time Johnny spoke to Jake, two years before—Jake told him to come down anytime, that he didn't even have to call, and that he would love it, as there were, as he put it, "as many gigs down here as there are loose women and change." Johnny didn't really know what to think of that statement, or the place he was now headed to work and live. He did, however, find much solace in the fact it was on the beach.

"Jake!" answered Johnny with youthful enthusiasm.

"Johnny Glass! Is that you?" he yelled into the flip cell phone on his end. A cacophony of loud females and boisterous, high-pitched laughter made it difficult to hear him. Johnny pulled over on the shoulder of the road and put the truck in park. He placed his free hand on his open ear. Outside, the rain fell harder, and louder.

"Jake! Yes, it's me! What's going on bro?"

"Johhnny Glass—I got your message! Get your sorry ass down here you sonofabitch...come on!" he barely made out. His voice was drowned by the surrounding noise. It got much worse when the band in the background began playing the undeniable first few notes of "Sweet Home Alabama." The crowd went nuts and the decibels rose.

"I'm driving down now. I should be there tomorrow afternoon."

But there was no response from Jake; there were only screams of ecstasy, and the continued cover of the legendary Lynyrd Skynyrd favorite. Shortly thereafter, the line went dead.

Johnny sat in silence on the side of the highway pondering his near future, wondering about the mystery and adventure that awaited him. The deluge continued unabated, wipers flapping.

"Jake hasn't changed much," he thought. "I seriously doubt he is still dating the same girl."

As hard as he tried, Johnny couldn't remember the name of the place where Jake was. He remembered it was on the Gulf of

Mexico where Florida and Alabama meet, and that the owner loved singer-songwriters. But that's about all he really knew of where he was headed. Like when he left home four years earlier for Nashville, it was a big move for the 22-year old Johnny Glass.

Johnny put on his left blinker, entered the highway and continued south, over the billowing Cumberland River. He made it to Birmingham, Alabama around midnight. Low on funds, he stopped at a truck stop and slept in his cab for five chilly, difficult hours before resuming driving in the dark early morning when the road is less traveled. By his estimation, he would make it to Perdido Key, Florida around lunch time.

***

During the weekend of May 1st and 2nd 2010, torrential downpours in the Southeastern United States flooded the Tennessee capital of Nashville, elevating the Cumberland River 13 feet above its flood stage, causing an estimated $1 billion in property damage, and killing more than 30 people, making it one of the more expensive natural disasters in American history. More rain fell on Nashville over that long weekend than has ever been recorded.

Singer-songwriters and musicians who made a living on Nashville's popular music row were forced to vacate their beloved home and workplace. Regular music and entertainment tourism came to a screeching halt as a result of the destructive damage. Retail and hotel receipts were non-existent, as everyone headed for higher, dryer ground.

But for Johnny Glass, things were stormy even before the deluge. Days earlier, he vacated a dingy, drafty, one bedroom apartment. Life in Nashville was never what he envisioned when he left French Lick, Indiana an 18-year old full of hope and promise. Four years of songwriting with little notice and low-paying one night gigs had taken their psychological toll. The money and notoriety he sought in Nashville never came; but it wasn't because he didn't try.

To his credit, Johnny Glass was as talented and hard-working as he was good-looking. Of medium, athletic build and height with dark, pompadour hair and hazel eyes, he was what the ladies called, "Hot." It was just his luck—or apparent lack of it, it seemed. Like so many artists, he simply needed a break—that one performance or connected person who could or would make a difference in their careers. His story was as common as they come. Making it in the music business is a lofty aspiration. Johnny knew the industry had eaten up and spit out stronger, more talented people than him. Nevertheless, he was determined to continue his art. In his mind, it was too late to look back. He'd already set his course. Although he was basically broke, the bright fires of his imaginations fueled him; that and the undying hope that one day he would make it in the music business.

***

Lucy Whitman stood next to the gleaming black Steinway Baby Grand piano in the expansive, posh den of her parents' home on Mobile Bay on Highway 1 just outside Fairhope, Alabama. The setting sun's marmalade light shined through the long horizontal windows facing a wooden pier that ran 100 yards into the bay toward the setting sun and ended under a rusted orange tin roof. Lucy, with her hair in a pony tail and wearing sandals, running shorts and a Delta Zeta Sorority party tee shirt, squared her shoulders and took a deep breath as the dark horizon split the sinking sun.

"Go a little slower this time. Don't rush it. You are oh so close!" instructed her smiling, erudite veteran voice coach, Dr. Jim Smith, a retired music professor from UC Berkeley. Lucy nodded in affirmation. Jim began playing on the piano John Lennon's Imagine. Lucy's soothing voice followed. While she sang, her mother, Mary Whitman, an attractive, impeccably-dressed matron, quietly entered the threshold of the doorway behind her daughter. Barefoot in her dazzling black sequined evening dress, she leaned on the door frame and listened intently to the performance. Having rehearsed the song countless times, Lucy's pitch and tone were excellent. Like Dr. Smith, Mrs. Whitman was impressed.

When Lucy finished, Dr. Smith enthusiastically praised the effort.

"That was your best yet, Lucy! You have improved a great deal, and you continue to improve. I am proud of you young lady."

He wore a smile as warm as the exploding Western sky.

"And so am I," blurted Mrs. Whitman, making her presence known. Lucy whipped her head around in surprise.

"Thank you Dr. Smith," Lucy replied, turning back to him. She spun her body around and faced her mother.

"Hello Mother," said a blushing Lucy. She thought her mom was still playing doubles tennis at the nearby Grand Hotel Racquet Club in Point Clear, like she did every Thursday afternoon.

"That was excellent. In fact, it was so good, we may have to ask you to headline one of your father's fundraisers," she joked.

Lucy shuddered.

While Lucy had long demonstrated a creative flair and an obvious singing ability, her parents had never encouraged the nurturing and development of her talents. Active in the Fairhope High School play production throughout her high school days, and on the Alabama Junior Miss pageant circuit, she never had professional voice training until recently. Nevertheless, the lack of formal instruction never kept her from winning numerous local singing competitions. Lucy had talent; and she felt it. After begging her parents for lessons from Dr. Smith, they finally relented, realizing that they could schedule them at their home, providing an opportunity to see their beautiful daughter; and more importantly, to keep careful tabs on her.

Like her mother, Lucy Whitman was a blessed female. Her thick, shiny, shoulder-length, ebony hair had a gorgeous cobalt tint that was most noticeable in direct sunlight. A former cheerleader and soccer player, she was athletic as she was busty, possessing a toned upper and lower torso, the by-product of years of regular stretching, aerobics and cardio training. Lucy's mother, Mary, was a former track star at the University of Alabama in Tuscaloosa. Lucy was not quite as tall and lean as her mom, or as athletically gifted, but she was prettier, and her hair was much darker, like her father's.

Senator Dee "Slip" Whitman was a controversial public figure. One of the area's avowed "good ole boys," his dubious reputation preceded him. The prodigal son of a local farmer who grew up plowin' and plantin' local crops like sweet potatoes, new potatoes, pecans and silver corn, he was one of the most powerful men in Montgomery, Alabama, the State Capital. Like his wife, he was a graduate of the University of Alabama in Tuscaloosa.

A former fraternity officer and lieutenant in the notorious machine that controlled campus politics, Dee Whitman was groomed for blood sport. At the University of Alabama he convened and led underground, candle-lit meetings in guarded, fraternity house basements, ensuring a continued stranglehold on university, local and even state politics that had gone unabated for decades. Along with his pedigree, Slip was large, easily six foot five and nearly three hundred pounds; and he wielded that uncommon political stature and physical might over his Lower Alabama fiefdom with an iron fist.

By using his vast political connections and clout, and the deft of a bull in a china house, the senator unethically secured a number of annual public contracts totaling millions of dollars with municipalities across coastal Baldwin County Alabama. While objective media coverage of his questionable business activities was predictably scant, many in the community were nevertheless aware of how he made a lavish living feeding off the public trust. And of course, there is no such thing as a secret in a small Alabama town.

"Mama I thought you would still be playing tennis." Lucy announced.

"We played this morning instead, dear. Your father and I are having dinner tonight with Governor Finchley at the Grand Hotel, and I needed the extra time to get ready. We will be leaving in a bit. Our reservation is for 8:00. What are your plans for the weekend?"

While she spoke, Mrs. Whitman adorned each of her pierced ears with one-carat diamond earrings, a fiftieth birthday present from her doting husband.

Lucy shifted her weight. Since she left for college in Mobile she rarely slept at her parent's house, which was not the home she grew up in. Her parents had recently moved into their dream home on the bay, after they had it designed and custom built to their liking.

"I'll be staying on Ono Island with Michelle. Her parents are out there. They invited a bunch of us."

"Alright darling. Tell Fred and Tammy hello for us. Will you be passing through on your way back to Mobile on Sunday? Maybe we can have a late lunch? Your father and I will be attending service at eleven."

"I will Mama. And yes, let's plan to get together Sunday afternoon. I'll text you."

"Dr. Smith, thank you for your time. I left a check on the kitchen counter for you."

"Thank you Mrs. Whitman," he replied. "Good evening."

***

The uniformed black valet driver at the luxurious Grand Hotel in Point Clear, Alabama opened the driver's door of the shiny black 2010 Cadillac Escalade, allowing for Senator Dee Whitman's exit. Another valet opened the passenger door for his wife. A large man wearing a dark brown suit and a canary tie emerged and stood tall, dwarfing the attendant.

"Good evening Senator Whitman!" the smiling valet announced, looking up. How are you and the Mrs., Sir?"

Slip didn't bother to acknowledge the welcome.

"Now boys, I don't want y'all joy ridin' in my new vehicle, now…" he loudly proclaimed, gesticulating.

The senator spoke not only to the valet in front of him, but also to his partner, at the podium under the awning. Both black men's shiny faces wore a peculiar, puzzled look.

"This is a brand new Cadillac Escalade. It still has the new car smell!" the senator exclaimed.

Slip paused for effect.

"Let's keep it that way, gentlemen."

The senator raised the intonation of his voice at the end for added emphasis, punctuating the word "gentlemen."

The two men just shook their heads.

Senator Whitman joined his waiting wife and walked into the lavish hotel's main entrance, through the Fred Nall art-adorned, high ceiling area preceding the main dining room. Moments later, they were joined by another couple, similarly dressed. It was State Representative Blaine McElroy, of Gulf Shores, and his wife Jane.

"Hey Slip!" said Blaine, extending a handshake and a smile. The two men locked and shook hands. They both turned their attention to the ladies.

"Jane, you look lovely tonight," said Senator Whitman, with a manufactured smile as wide as his waistline.

"Thank you, Slip."

"Mary, what a beautiful dress! You look so pretty tonight," said Blaine.

"Oh Blaine, thank you."

The well-dressed maitre' d spoke up.

"Excuse me, Senator, Governor Finchley phoned us moments ago and said he was running late. He asked us to seat you and State Representative McElroy and your wives. He insisted he will be here shortly."

The two couples were seated near panoramic windows overlooking Mobile Bay. The ruby orb had minutes earlier slipped below the western horizon, leaving only the timid, reflecting light of a thin crescent moon.

"You know why we're here, don't you?" the senator asked, sipping on a doubled up bourbon and coke.

State Representative McElroy glanced to his right at the women, who were engaged in a cocktail conversation of their own.

"No, I don't. What's up?"

The senator spoke softly.

"The Governor was contacted by the CEO of British Petroleum, Tony Stewart. BP wants to give the State of Alabama $100 million to make restitution for the oil spill...but get this—it has to be spent down here on the coast."

"I'll help em' spend it!" Blaine answered with a boyish grin. He sat up straight in his chair.

Slip laughed. "I bet you would!"

They both laughed and rocked back and forth in their seats.

The senator continued, "Tonight he's gonna let on what he has planned on how to spend the money."

The senator looked up. The maitre d reappeared. He led Governor Bob Finchley and his wife, Dorothy, to their table. Everyone stood to greet him.

"Governor!" announced Senator Whitman, "You made it!"

"Good evening, Governor, Mrs. Finchley," said Representative McElroy, fawning their arrival.

The men exchanged handshakes; the women traded pleasantries. The Governor, after ordering their food and receiving a sweet tea without lemon, got down to business. He asked the men if they would like step outside to "get some of that good Alabama salt air" with him. They of course said yes, and they politely excused themselves.

Once outside, the governor walked to the edge of the bay and stood near a wrought iron guard rail. He looked out over the water, where the faint light of the sliver moon danced like ancient fireflies on the dull horizon. A faint breeze lifted the governor's combed over gray hair gently up and down. With his back to the men, he lit a freshly-cut Cuban cigar and puffed it hard three times through his right thumb and forefingers. He retrieved a ready flask from his coat pocket. He removed the screw cap, took two quick pulls and reversed the sequence, returning the black leather bound chrome container neatly to its hiding place.

This was a huge surprise to the legislators. Governor Finchley was a preacher of his own church in Montgomery, Alabama. Further, he had run for office on a strict, Southern Baptist ideology that included him being a devout teetotaler. The Governor, during the campaign, had even impugned his democratic opponent's well-known drinking and smoking habits.

The men just looked at each other, stunned; but neither said a thing.

Senator Whitman broke the ice.

"What's up, Governor?"

Governor Finchley let the white lightning filter through his bloodstream, slowly making its way back to his brain. When the desired, calming effect set in, he spoke.

"Senator, did you fill Representative McElroy in on why we're here?"

"Yes Sir, I did."

The governor puffed on his cigar.

"Good. Gentlemen, the money must be spent in your district. It has to be spent here on the coast, because of the proximity of the spill."

There was a moment of silence. The eager legislators hung on his every word.

"I have decided to build a five star hotel at the Gulf State Park. I figure for a hundred million dollars we can build something that many generations of Alabamians will enjoy and be proud of."

The wheels tumbled in Senator Whitman's brain. He swallowed hard.

The governor continued.

"We are not going to bid this out. I want and need legislation written that states I "may" bid the project out. I don't want to have to. Therefore, my office will control everything—all contracting and subcontracting, material purchases, etc. It provides a rare opportunity for us to help the business community, the very people who have helped us so much in the past. There will be plenty to go around, gentlemen."

Senator Whitman smiled.

"I understand, Governor. I will gladly sponsor the bill for the building of the park. Blaine can co-author it with me."

"Certainly, Sir!" Blaine chimed in.

"Excellent, Slip," the governor replied, puffing on his cigar. He grinned and instinctively went again for his flask.

2

Late Friday morning Johnny Glass exited Interstate 65 onto Highway 59 south in Bay Minette, Alabama. His smart phone Global Positioning System map told him to take 59 all the way down to where it ended at the Gulf of Mexico in Gulf Shores, Alabama. From there he'd take a left down the beach highway and drive east another 18 miles to the Alabama-Florida state line. He distinctly remembered Jake telling him that half the joint rested in Alabama and the other half in the State of Florida; and that he slept in a camper only a few yards away. He knew he would find this fabled place Jake claimed was "paradise." He was almost there.

The Alabama/Florida gulf coast is paradise; or at least it usually is. Its quartz sand beaches and emerald surf are legendary for sun and fun, making it a popular vacation destination for the entire Deep South. However, in late April 2010, just two weeks before Johnny Glass arrived, that all changed.

On April 20, 2010, British Petroleum, known more commonly as "BP," Halliburton & other misguided oil exploration subcontractors allowed the occurrence of one of the worst man-made oil spills in modern history. A single blowout protector on the rig failed to do its intended job, and as a result, jettisoned millions of gallons of unrefined crude into the theretofore gulf's foamy, turquoise waters.

Fortuitous headwinds kept the huge, dark brown spill offshore for almost two weeks before it finally began making an unavoidable approach along the Louisiana, Mississippi and Alabama coastlines during that first week of May. The impending oil landfall did little to encourage vacationers and tourism. Cancellations were predictably high, while tax receipts slowed to a trickle. Pleasure Island was in economic peril; unfortunately, it was where Johnny Glass wanted to find a new gig playing his music for tourists. Johnny had heard about the oil spill, but thought it was off the coast of Louisiana—and not three states over in Florida. He was clueless; just relieved to be out of dreary Nashville.

The weather was pleasant that morning as Johnny drove past the "Forward City" sign in Foley, Alabama, the boyhood home of Kenny "The Snake" Stabler of Crimson Tide and Oakland Raiders fame. Thin, symmetrical bands of cirrus clouds blinded an otherwise clear, gentian sky. At 75 degrees, with low humidity, it was a gorgeous day for driving. Johnny listened to Cash's Folsom Prison Blues and a bootleg live Billy Joe Shaver CD a friend pirated and gave him. He rolled the windows down and inhaled the brine-filled air. He knew he was close. He could smell the Gulf of Mexico.

As he motored through Gulf Shores Johnny encountered a village of family tourist attractions. Goofy golf, wacky water parks and a host of tee shirt, trash and trinket shops dotted the low-lying coastal zone. He crossed the Intracoastal Waterway and turned left at the "T" where Highway 59 ended at the beach road and headed east. He spotted the sparkling Gulf of Mexico.

"Sweet!" he thought. He checked his fuel gauge and noticed the tank was close to empty. On fumes, he rolled into the first gas station he came across.

Johnny began filling up, taking notice of the beautiful weather and the scenery. Wearing blue jeans, two days of stubble, a tee shirt and a pair of well-worn, gray snakeskin cowboy boots, he was comfortable, as the unrelenting summer humidity had not yet enveloped the island. He looked across the beach highway at the rolling turquoise battering the foamy shoreline. Behind him he heard a mess of young females.

He looked back and noticed a six pack of college-aged girls in bikinis, shades and tops leaving the convenience store of the gas station. The girls strutted like peacocks past Johnny, who continued pumping gas. Johnny's hair and svelte profile caught the roaming eye of one of the girls, who carried a small foam ice chest containing cold beer, wine coolers and bottled water.

"Hey good-looking! Want to lay out with us?" A blonde in a red bikini and a white, see-through pullover yelled amidst the pack. She giggled.

Johnny gulped. "Think on your feet!" he thought.

"Sounds wonderful," he managed. He pulled his sunglasses down on his nose, to get a better view. When he answered the pack slowed to a stop, and turned to him, giving him a much better look of the lot.

"These girls are gorgeous," he thought. He swallowed hard.

"Well come meet us then!" answered the blonde who started it. "We are gonna set up right across the street. Right in front of the water. Where are you from?"

"I just drove in from Nashville. I am originally from Indiana, though."

"Where in Indiana?" asked one of the other girls, a sandy-haired peach in Daisy Dukes, pigtails and a Crimson Tide tee shirt.

Johnny smiled.

"French Lick."

There was a moment of silence. A couple of the girls laughed, and their smiles were contagious. The spokesperson for the group quickly recovered.

Johnny chuckled but said nothing. He wore a wide grin.

"What is your name?"

"Johnny Glass."

"Nice to meet you, Johnny Glass. I am Michelle. These are my friends from school. We all go to South Alabama."

The petite brunette stepped forward and extended her hand. Johnny shook it.

"I see," he said. "Cool."

He paused and continued. "I am a singer and a songwriter and I came down here looking for work. I'm trying to find this place that has live music on the Florida and Alabama state line. Have y'all heard about it? I hear it's popular."

Michelle laughed.

"You mean the Flora-Bama?" she asked, like he was kidding.

It finally registered with Johnny.

"Yes, I believe that's it!" he said, pointing his index finger into the air.

"Well, yeah, everybody knows The Bama! It's where everybody goes almost every night." Michelle added. "We're going tonight. Are you gonna be there?"

"I guess I will be," said a beaming Johnny, his white teeth gleaming. "I'll see you ladies there. I need to get down to the Flora-Bama right now."

"Nice meeting you, Johnny!" Michelle answered. "Good luck!"

She and the other girls waved goodbye and made their way across the beach road into the cascading midday sun, their tiny shadows stirring after them.

"We'll be there around nine!" one of the other girls yelled back.

Johnny smiled and shook his head as he topped off the tank. He looked over his shoulder and watched their bouncing hourglass figures scurry across toward the glistening talc.

"This may be Paradise after all, Jake," he thought to himself.

He checked his watch. It was noon.

"Time to find Jake," he thought, as he entered his truck and made it back onto the beach road. He continued east, grabbed his cell phone and dialed Jake's number.

***

Lucy Whitman parked her candy apple red convertible Volkswagen Beetle in the parking lot off the beach highway. She got the vehicle a year before as a high school graduation present from her parents.

It was noon and the weather was fabulous. Lucy didn't schedule Friday classes for a reason. Anxious to meet her girlfriends, she removed her white cotton top revealing a curvaceous, taut torso, a golden tan and an athletic cut white bikini, an obvious, sharp contrast to her thick, dusky hair. She grabbed a straw-handled satchel and darted barefoot over the powder sand toward the water's edge, leaving the top down on the bug. Her freshly cut and curled shoulder length hair danced on her head as she sauntered over toward her friends. As she did, she caught the roaming eyes of a dozen or more Louisiana guys sunning themselves nearby.

Michelle Carter and her friends were laid out on beach towels, in seriatim, supine across the dry white talc, facing the gleaming sun and surf that reflected on them like an endless ultramarine mirror.

"Hey y'all!" Lucy shouted as she reached the water's edge. All of the girls quickly sat up to greet her.

Michelle popped up and hugged her.

"Lucy! Oh my God! I love your hair! It is so pretty!" Michelle doted.

One of the others agreed.

"It is so cute Lucy!"

"Do y'all think so?" Lucy asked, blushing through her tanned face.

"God yes, child!" squealed Michelle. "Let me see! Turn around!"

Lucy pirouetted, giving everyone a glimpse of the rear length of her hair, and the gawking male throng nearby, a full view.

"Too cute girl!" said one of the others.

Lucy donned her shades and joined the girls in resuming their sun worship. Michelle updated Lucy on the evening plans.

"It's Friday. Everybody's going to the Bama tonight!"

"I can't wait," chimed one of the others. "I'm craving a bushwhacker!"

"Who is playing tonight?" Lucy asked.

"I think Jake Justice's band may be playing the main stage. I don't know who is under the tent outside." Michelle answered.

"What's the name of Jake's band?" asked the blonde.

"Hung Jury," Lucy answered. She was a fan of the Flora-Bama music scene.

"Jake is really hot," blurted the blonde who earlier told Johnny hello.

"Dangerously," added Michelle. She knew Jake—well. "I hear he's screwed half the island."

"Another dog?" the blonde retorted.

"They're all dogs!" Michelle yelled.

They all laughed.

"Hey, speaking of hot guys, Lucy you missed this musician guy we just met at the gas station across the street. He has a funky hairdo, but he is so yummy! He said he just drove in from Nashville."

Lucy was intrigued.

"Did he say what kind of music he plays?" Lucy asked.

"Girl, you ain't gonna care about that! Wait till you see him! He said he would be there tonight," stated the blonde.

***

Johnny's cell phone rang Jake's number. Johnny checked his watch. It was 12:20 on a Saturday. His phone continued to ring, but there was no answer. He got his voice mail. Johnny left a message.

"Jake, it's me, Johnny! I'm down here man! And I am close to the Flora-Bama! Call me back, brother!"

Johnny ended the call and placed his phone on the dash, continuing east on the beach highway toward the Florida-Alabama line.

"He's likely shacked up with some broad," Johnny thought.

***

Without opening his eyes, or rolling over, Jake Justice reached behind him for a loud, vibrating cell phone on the metal bedside table inside his small Airstream Camper. Bright white light splashed through the ineffective blind on the rectangular side window, bathing the spooning, naked couple. A small, dusty oscillating fan pointed at them ran on high mode. Jake finally found the phone and brought it to his right ear. It had stopped ringing—unlike his head. He looked at the number. He recognized it.

"Johnny Glass!" he thought. "I forgot he was coming down! He called me yesterday!" Jake barely remembered. After a typically wild first night of the weekend—a Thursday, it was all coming back to him. Then he remembered the cute blonde he was curled up with, as she turned to him, getting his full attention.

"Who is that?" she asked, pulling herself on top of him. Big round blue eyes stared into his tanned, unshaven face.

"My friend Johnny, he's coming in today from Nashville, and I think he is looking for me." He smiled.

"Well, he's gonna have to come find you, baby. I'm not lettin' you outta here just yet..."

***

Mrs. Whitman, wearing a white athletic skirt and top, matching visor and low cut socks with spiked shoes, addressed her tiny white ball. After a practice swing she made solid contact and bounced the orb along the ground 90 yards onto the green, about ten feet from the pin.

"That'll play," groaned her husband, Senator Whitman, who was seated behind the wheel of the electric golf cart. She returned her club to the bag and sat next to him. They drove to his ball, only paces away.

The senator wore baggy khaki pants, a pastel madras shirt, aviator shades and a wide-brimmed Panamanian style straw hat with a thick, black, nylon band. He chewed an unlit cigar as he addressed the dimpled sphere lying in light rough.

"What's Lucy doing this weekend?" he asked, squaring his shoulders across the ball, perpendicular to his target.

"She's on Ono with Michelle and the Henderson's. Fred and Tammy are out there."

"Is she going to summer school?" he asked. He didn't let her answer.

"I won't have her going to college longer than four years, I tell you. She is going to graduate in four years! She ain't gonna be no slacker!"

Unlike his wife, the senator did not use a practice swing. After a slow drawback and an unnatural, quick, jerking motion with no follow through, he topped the ball, weakly spinning it into the air. The shot dribbled and stopped thirty yards from the green.

"Shit!" screamed the senator. "God Damnit!"

"She has two summer school classes scheduled," commented Mary, trying to avoid the obvious.

"Mary, give me another damn ball!"

Her blood pressure spiked. Her throat turned beet red.

She reluctantly grabbed the new ball on the dash and threw it to him.

"Hurry up!" She answered.

She looked behind them at the tee box perched on a hill. A smartly-dressed coed foursome waited to tee off. The realization that they were being closely watched turned her stomach. Lakewood was a prestigious club. Worse, they were likely voters.

Senator Whitman dropped his new ball, improving his lie. Mary winced and glanced again behind her. She felt like a fish in a bowl.

In a near repeat of what happened before, the senator topped the ball a touch harder, forcing it to within twenty yards of the green. Although it was a slight improvement, he was nevertheless livid.

"Jesus! Give me another God-damned ball, Mary!"

Mary Whitman was petrified. She pleaded with her husband.

"No Slip! We can't! Come on! Play one of those balls! We can't cheat! This is a tournament!"

It was the Point Clear Rotary Club's annual fundraiser.

"Give me that God-damned ball, Mary!" he bellowed.

There was one left.

She reluctantly grabbed and threw it at his feet. It bounced and hit his shin. In a rush, he gently foot-wedged the ball and shot, landing it near her ball on the green before rolling to the edge into a soft tuft of Bermuda grass.

"I guess I'll take that one," said Slip. He replaced his club and drove off, picking up each of his previous shots with his left hand while driving the cart with his right.

"Let's see...one, two...I'm hitting three here on the side of the green," said Senator Whitman, smiling.

Mary rolled her eyes in disgust.

***

"Who is that guy?" asked one of the puzzled men on the tee box above. The foursome had witnessed everything.

"That's our Senator," replied the other sarcastically.

"That's Senator Whitman?" asked his wife.

"Yep. Ain't that some shit? I wouldn't trust him with a dime," said the other woman, vigorously shaking her head. She bent and pushed her teed ball into the ground. She stood and surveyed the fairway, sizing up her shot.

"I don't know how he was ever elected, to tell you the truth," she finished.

3

Johnny Glass traversed the Alabama Point Inlet via the Pass Bridge. At the top of the span he slowed his roll and enjoyed a gorgeous, sparkling, panoramic view. Ahead of him, the island's narrow, vertical strip was surrounded by teeming emerald-blue waters on the right and left; and dozens upon dozens of watercraft—pontoon pleasure boats, jet skis, sailboats and party barges. Hundreds of playful tourists dotted the blue-green water's edge on both sides of the bridge. To his left he saw two small islands surrounded by a floatilla of boats and half-naked people. To his right, he saw the expansive, beckoning, deep blue hue of the Gulf of Mexico. The sun blared high atop a cloudless sky. He was awestruck.

"Jake wasn't kidding…this is paradise! Whew!"

"Unbelievable!" Johnny thought. "I am here! I made it."

As he traversed the down slope of the gentle span Johnny glanced at the map on his cell phone. It looked like the state line was within a mile or two of the Pass Bridge. Like a kid on Christmas morning, he was ecstatic. His blood pressure rose and he noticed the beating of his heart under his tee shirt.

High-rise condominiums lined the beach road on both sides. He saw several joggers and cyclists, followed by a blue sign with white lettering that read, "Welcome to the Sunshine State…Florida welcomes you!"

"I need to pull over here," Johnny thought. Before he crossed the state line he veered left, towards a sign that read, "Flora-Bama Parking." He pulled into a white oyster and clam shell lot half full of various makes and models of cars and trucks.

Johnny exited his pick-up and looked across the beach road toward the Gulf of Mexico. What he saw surprised him.

The place's façade was in complete disarray. Large, treated pylons—once sturdy trees, were being driven loudly into the ground by a giant hydraulic jack hammer in front of what looked like a makeshift entrance to the ramshackle place he now knew was called the Flora-Bama. Johnny, along with a group of eager tourists, made his way across the black asphalt of the gulf beach highway.

"Please pardon our progress" read a handmade sign, followed by another that said, "Enter this way," trailed by a large, hand-painted red, pointing arrow. Johnny followed the placards to a small wooden shack where a gray-haired, pony-tailed woman with multi-colored tattoos was checking I.D.'s.

Johnny noticed another sign placed prominently in view before the shack, at eye level. It read, "Welcome to the World-Famous Flora-Bama. We raise taxes for a livin' and sell whiskey as a sideline!"

The line moved fast. Johnny's turn came. He smiled politely at the mature woman and spoke.

"M'am, I'm looking for Jake Justice. He told me he lives in his Airstream Camper not far from here."

The pony-tailed woman tightened with both hands one of the many rubber bands that bound her long, graying locks. She returned a bigger smile.

"You are even cuter than Jake," she replied.

Not expecting it, Johnny blushed.

"Lookie here," she said. She pointed in the direction behind him. "That building across the street is the Silver Moon Package Store and Lounge. Jake's Airstream is behind it."

"Thank you, M'am."

"No problem, sweetie!" she smiled.

Johnny turned and made his way back over the white-washed double-lined walkway crossing the beach highway. The old gal with tattoos taking money marveled at his butt as he walked away.

A passing motorist slowed to a crawl, allowing Johnny to get across the beach highway. As he walked around the left side of the Silver Moon, a package liquor store and makeshift lounge with live entertainment, he noticed a spectacle at the drive-in window.

A long, faded red, white top-down, Cadillac convertible with a massive set of cream-colored Texas Longhorns bolted to the hood purred as it sat in park. Behind the wheel was local architect Brad Masterson, an early fifty-something, heavy-set, hairy-chested, brown curly-haired, unshaven fellow with thick glasses, wearing Crimson Tide P.E. gym shorts and a red and white flowered Hawaiian shirt. A lit cigarette with a quarter-inch ash hung precariously from his thin lips. He stared directly at Johnny and smiled as wide as his unusual hood ornament.

"You need to trade in them cowboy boots for a pair of flip flops, partner!" he yelled, pointing at Johnny's feet with his index finger. He surprised Johnny.

Johnny stopped walking and acknowledged him. He looked down at his boots and turned one up.

"I reckon you're right. I guess I need a swimsuit too." He smiled.

"Where abouts you from?" Brad asked.

Before Johnny could answer, a young brunette flung open the tinted drive-thru window of what was once a Kentucky Fried Chicken Restaurant. In her arms she held a large, bulging brown paper sack.

"Here you go honey. A fifth of Crown Reserve, a twelve pack of Coors Lite and a carton of Marlboro Lights. That'll be $48.35 darlin'."

"Thanks sweetie. I appreciate it, baby." He replied. "Keep the change."

The girl smiled and thanked him. She disappeared with the cash behind the closed window.

The curly-haired fellow turned to Johnny, smiled and spoke in his best Caribbean accent.

"Where you from, mon?" He playfully asked.

Johnny chuckled.

"Indiana originally. I just got here from Nashville. I am a singer-songwriter, and I'm trying to get a gig down here. I'm looking for work. Jake Justice and I used to play together."

A shiny black Hummer pulled up behind the Cadillac. Brad saw its approach in the rearview mirror.

"Ah…so you used to run with Jake, huh? Well, you should have no problem around here! Jake and his band have done well."

"I hope so," Johnny answered.

"I gotta run, boss man. My name is Brad Masterson. I'm an architect. I designed most of the bigger homes back here on Ono Island. I'll be at the Bama tonight. Look for me. I'll buy you a beer!"

"Nice meeting you, Sir. I'm sure I'll run into you later," said Johnny.

"What's your name?" Brad asked. The bright red Caddy rolled him slowly away onto the asphalt beach road. He maintained his stare.

"Johnny Glass," he replied with a grin.

"Smooth," Brad thought.

"Later on Johnny Glass!"

He nodded and popped a beer tab and lit another smoke into the gulf wind.

Johnny shook his head.

"What a character," he thought, as he continued walking toward Jake's place.

***

The inauspicious Flora-Bama Lounge and Package Store was founded in 1964, after the construction of the Alabama Point Inlet Bridge in Orange Beach, Alabama. The span, funded and constructed completely by the State Government of Alabama, due to a lack of coastline on their part, connected by road for the first time the no-man's land between the Alabama Gulf Coast and the greater Western Pensacola area, known also as Perdido Key.

Nearby Perdido Bay, which is accessed by water through the Alabama Point Inlet, takes its name from Spanish explorers who found difficulty finding the narrow, coastal cut to the protecting backwater; they aptly named it the "lost" bay, in their dialect.

By funding and building the Alabama Pass Inlet Bridge the State of Alabama gained from the State of Florida two miles of coastline and all of nearby Ono Island, greatly expanding its Gulf Coast footprint. Further, the bridging of the two states and their coastal communities created an overnight market for serious adult fun and frolic in an area that was enough removed from civilization to allow it to flourish.

In the sleepy years prior to the construction of the Alabama Point Inlet Bridge, a bona fide riverboat honky-tonk, The River Queen, existed just over the state line in Florida, on Old River, an ancient tributary that today runs for miles parallel to the gulf beach road between Alabama State Line and Perdido Key. In its heyday, this dilapidated river boat served up gambling, prostitution and drinking—in varying and sundry doses to an ever-willing patronage. In fact, it was the ruffian proprietors of this thriving early honky tonk who allegedly burned down the Flora-Bama the night before it was supposed to open on July 4, 1964—to make sure there was no area competition on liquor and good times. As a result of the Flora Bama's razing, their monopoly on vice continued.

The owners of the Flora-Bama, undaunted, immediately re-built and reopened within months, by the fall of 1964. However, they were once bitten and twice shy. For the much-anticipated reopening they introduced to the thirsty public their new night watchman, Mr. Frank Brown, an extremely large and imposing black man who was at one time in his youth a Golden Gloves boxer. Mr. Frank had a deep voice and wore two six shooters in a leather holster and a five-gallon, black cowboy hat that made him look even more ominous. His deep, bellowing voice was his preferred implement, however, as he never had to draw his weapons. "Now boys, what would y'all mamas think?" was all he usually had to say to diffuse a difficult moment.

And the River Queen? In the weeks during the Flora-Bama's rebuilding, the River Queen was shuttered by scrambling Escambia County Florida politicians who decided their under-the-table stake in the operation wasn't worth the political embarrassment and headache the vessel had become. As a result, the Flora-Bama inherited the coveted cultural monopoly on area fun and frolic.

With a perfect location benefitting from a new bridge and road, and Mr. Frank's help, over the next dozen or more years the Flora-Bama evolved into a favored destination for thirsty locals, Navy fly boys and tourists from neighboring states in the proverbial know. These reveling rednecks and thirsty Cajuns were attracted to the homespun, anything goes feel of the endearing one-room watering hole on the Alabama and Florida state line—far away from the dreaded, real world they left behind. Those early days at the original Flora-Bama were pretty tame. There were no regular live music acts. A few local amateur musicians would occasionally pick a guitar and sing. But, in 1978, that all changed, for the better; the Flora-Bama was sold.

In 1978, when he purchased the Flora-Bama, Joe Gideon, a nearby native of Gulf Breeze, was a 36-year old former high school chemistry teacher, experienced bar manager, a lover of singer-songwriters and a self-proclaimed music aficionado. With the help of a $10,000 loan from his parents and another $10,000 loan from an affluent Auburn University fraternity brother, Gideon became the sole proprietor of an eventual global tourism icon, a revered Mecca for aspiring American singer-songwriters and—a legendary cash cow; making him a unique American success story; and veritable prince of the Redneck Riviera; a bona fide living legend to locals and repeat tourists in the proverbial know.

The first crooning character Joe found to play at his fledgling, state-line watering hole was Ken Lambert, a rough-edged singer-songwriter chasing gigs and tail in Pensacola's lively, historic, downtown music district, Seville Quarters. After Ken, the firebrand Jimmy Louis hit the scene.

Louis, like his predecessor, was discovered by Joe in nearby Pensacola. Jimmy Louis was playing a gig on his birthday one evening and Joe was really impressed with his performance— which included a full moon of the crowd, after he had a few beverages. Louis, like Lambert, quickly built a following. However, they were soon joined by another outlaw country singer-songwriter, pony-tail wearing Jay Hawkins, and later on by the incredible comedic crooning talent of Rusty McHugh, and the ingredients of this seaside experiment of music, laughter and song were firmly in place.

Gideon built his business from the ground-up on a customer-first philosophy with a personal touch and by creating calendar events on the beach that filled otherwise dead travel time. Like clockwork, cultural happenings cropped up. Amazing annual marketing stunts were born. Events like the Polar Bear Dip on New Year's Day, the Chili Bowl Cookoff preceding Mardi Gras, the infamous Mullet Toss during the third weekend in April, the summertime Mullet Triathlon and the Frank Brown Songwriter's Festival in November, which began in 1984. Mr. Frank passed away four years after the festival began, in 1988, but his legacy lives on in the annual event that bears his name.

By the early 1990's the Flora-Bama hit its zenith, its many cash receipts reaching their historical peak. The robust economy that typified the Clinton Presidency made a beach trip to the beloved Flora-Bama the preferred option for successful Southerners bent on letting their hair down and passing a good time. "Do it with Us on the Line" became the quintessential beach bar's universal party pitch—and it stuck, as many have through the years; and there are armies of thankful children to prove it.

Twenty mostly successful years later, in 2010, Joe was nearing 70. Instead of retiring and enjoying his grandchildren like most his age, Gideon was in the fight of his entrepreneurial life. Six years earlier, in 2004, his beloved beach bar was nearly destroyed after Hurricane Ivan scored a direct hit, leaving in its wake untold devastation and property damage. It was the first of many tests for Joe, unbeknownst to him.

Like many wealthy Floridians, Joe invested heavily in the highly speculative real estate market. By 2005, after the hurricane, the market began to show signs of a serious correction. The real estate bubble, driven by questionable home loans and inflated prices driven by out-of-control demand, had finally burst. Five years later, after a simultaneous stock market crash and a floundering national economy, Joe was nearing the incomprehensible end of his cash reserves. For years he had used a pile of money earned from earlier successful real estate deals to pay the many notes he'd written for failing new real estate deals. The day he feared had finally come: He could no longer maintain his payments. Bankruptcy was now a real consideration.

It turned out that a devastating hurricane and financial Armageddon weren't enough to challenge the aging Gideon, as he would soon have to deal with one of the largest manmade environmental disasters in history, the BP oil spill. For the first time in his business career, he was unable to meet his obligations. Everything he had, everything he had worked for in life, his business, and more importantly to him—his reputation, hung precariously in the balance. But aside from his personal assistant and his attorney, no one knew how bad off his financial situation was. It was still a secret, for now.

4

Johnny Glass knocked three times on the thin metal door of the silver, egg-shaped camper. Moments later the Airstream metal shell shook and creaked; the knob turned and the door slightly opened. A wide-eyed and bushy-tailed Jake Justice stuck his head out the thin crease. Johnny barely recognized him with almost a full beard. Jake turned his head, saw Johnny and smiled.

"Jake! It's me, Johnny!"

"Give me a second, bro. I'll be right back!" Jake exclaimed with a boyish grin.

The night before at the Flora-Bama was typically raucous. Jake fortuitously ran into a hyped-up bachelorette party from Biloxi, Mississippi—eight 20 and 21-year old girls dressed identically in bright pink stripper outfits with revealing bikini tops, black fish net stockings and matching nurse's caps. During a break from playing he introduced himself to the blonde, who wore a large pink penis balloon, replete with a large pair of testicles, on the top of her head. It was lust at first sight.

Moments later Jake emerged from the camper wearing only a tattered, sun-bleached bathing suit, and leather sandals. He held a soft pack of Marlboro Lights and a disposable lighter. His thin physique was accentuated by his bony rib cage and rippling stomach muscles.

"What's up brother?" Jake asked. He opened his arms wide and hugged his friend.

"I made it!" Johnny exclaimed.

Jake lit a cigarette, stood up straight and took a good look at Johnny. He laughed.

"It's about time! How long has it been? Two years?" Jake asked.

"Right at I believe," said Johnny.

The camper rocked slightly and stirred. The door cracked open.

A pretty young blonde poked her head out.

"Jake?"

"Yeah baby?"

"Will you walk me across the street to my room? I don't want to walk by myself."

"Yeah, sure."

She disappeared into the silver bullet.

Jake smiled at Johnny.

"The walk of Shame," he whispered.

Johnny chuckled.

"Give me fifteen minutes to get her across the street. I'll come back and buy you breakfast here at the Waffle House," Jake said, motioning to the building only paces away.

Johnny was hungry.

"Sounds good, man. I guess I'll see you in a bit, then."

The blonde reemerged—wearing her makeup from the night before and the bright pink, slightly-loved stripper outfit and pointed, black high heels. She carried the crumpled up nurse's hat and the popped penis balloon and still-inflated testicles, in her hand.

"Hey Johnny," said Jake, "I've got extra shorts in my camper. Take your pick. There are flip-flops, too. Make yourself at home, man. I'll be right back. I'll see you at the Waffle House."

Johnny watched the two as they walked away. Jake was now barefoot, having flipped off his sandals. He wore only his bathing suit, a messed up hairdo and a killer tan. He puffed hard on his cigarette and placed his arm around the blonde, who leaned into him.

"He hasn't changed a bit," thought Johnny.

***

Johnny rummaged through Jake's tiny, crowded closet inside the cramped camper. He found and donned a pair of old cotton workout shorts and some braided leather sandals. He was much more comfortable. He walked to the Waffle House and sat in a corner booth and waited for Jake, who arrived shortly after. They ordered breakfast, coffee and ice water.

"I almost didn't recognize you with the beard," Johnny said.

"It's low maintenance, man. That's the way things are here. It's really laid back. You'll see! Wait until you get into 'island mode.' Soon you'll be on island time. It's altogether different."

Jake continued.

"How you been, man? You finally decided to just say 'screw it' huh?" Jake sipped his coffee black.

"Yeah, Nashville wore me down. I need something new. I hope I can find a job around here. I don't have much money." Johnny answered matter-of-factly.

"Don't sweat it, man. I'm gonna introduce you to Big Daddy Joe G. tonight. He's the owner and he calls all the shots around here. He makes this whole island tick. He'll be hanging out next door at the Silver Moon around five or so. We'll introduce you and let you sing a song or two for him and it'll be a done deal, no questions asked. Don't worry about it!"

Jake shook his forefinger for emphasis. He paused and stared at his friend. He saw the uncertainty in Johnny's face, the concern for the unknown.

"Johnny, look at me—this ain't Nashville, brother. I promise."

"Thanks for the vote of confidence, but are you sure? You think he'll just hire me on the spot?"

Before he could answer, their food arrived. They thanked the waitress and started eating. Jake chewed it with vigor and gesticulated with fork and knife-bearing hands as he spoke.

"Look, you are much better than more than half the players we got here now. He'll hire you! I've seen him do it before—and yes—on the spot."

Jake knew nothing of Joe's dismal financial condition; and like Johnny and everyone else, he was unaware of the looming threat the BP oil spill posed. To Jake Justice, everything was fine. He was working his dream job in one of the nation's coolest hot spots. He was living the dream—doing what he absolutely loved to do; and life really couldn't be any better for him.

"What happened to Ella?" Johnny asked.

Ella was the girl Jake moved to Perdido Key with two years before. Jake's countenance briefly changed. He finished chewing his food before he spoke.

"Ella is in med school in Birmingham. We still talk." Jake answered.

By the way he reacted Johnny could tell he still had feelings for her.

"She's a keeper." Johnny said. "I'd stay in touch with her."

"Well, she's a career girl...and I'm in a band living down here in paradise. There ain't no med schools in Orange Beach; and I'll be damned if I ever leave. I've got it too good here."

Johnny listened intently.

"This is the deal...I play three or four regular gigs a week and they sell my CD's at the gift shop inside the trailer out front for an extra hundred or so per week during the season. It's steady money with all the tips, a lot better than Nashville, really. Plus, I live rent free...at the beach! All the babes come here! There is a new crop every week during the summer! You can't beat it, I'm telling you bro! Money for nothin' and your chicks for free! I'm living proof of livin' the dream!"

His meal finished, a contented Jake leaned back with his arms stretched out and pulled wide apart. Johnny wanted badly to meet Joe Gideon; this man who had made his friend's life so much fun and worth living. Johnny had not really ever suffered since he left home, but at times he definitely struggled. He was ready to move up and move on so that would never happen again. But more importantly, he wanted to feel like Jake did, to have his outlook, as he could tell he hadn't a care in the world.

5

J
ake and Johnny spent the afternoon on the satin white beach behind the Flora-Bama. They drained a few cold canned light beers and Johnny began working on a much-needed tan. With Jake's money they rented fast jet skis and rode foaming turquoise waves until the fading white light turned baby blue and lilac across the Western sky, signaling the end of what Johnny thought was a beautiful day, and what Jake thought was the coming of another classic Gulf Coast Saturday night.

Johnny too sensed the prospect of an exciting evening ahead. He was eager to hear some of the local singer-songwriting talent, and of course, to meet the establishment owner, Joe Gideon; and to play for him, if he could, so that he might award him with a regular, paying gig. Johnny wasn't kidding when he told Jake he didn't have much money. He had just under $300 cash. Finding a job was his chief concern.

Jake and Johnny cleaned up in the music community's makeshift, outdoor shower located in the area known as "Boy's Town" across the street from the Flora-Bama, on Old River. The adequate facilities, which included a protected bathroom and sink, were just a few paces from Jake's camper. A pink-faced, clean-shaven Johnny donned his blue jeans, boots and a clean cotton tee shirt. He pulled on a short-sleeved Western shirt and left it unbuttoned and un-tucked. He slicked his hair back on both sides and puffed up and combed into a cresting wave the longer hair on the crown of his head. He grabbed his favorite Martin guitar, a couple of picks and a working capo. He was ready to perform.

A wet-haired Jake, wearing faded, torn blue jeans, sandals and a psychedelic, tie-dyed, V-neck, long-sleeved, cotton shirt, lit a cigarette as he stepped out of his camper. A smiling Johnny stood nearby in the cascading light of a large evening lamp, his guitar slung over his left shoulder.

"You look ready," Jake said, checking his watch, toking on a half-smoked Marlboro Light.

It was just after 7:00 p.m. The lilac beach sky faded fast beneath a visible crescent moon.

"Me and the band were supposed to play the Bama Dome tonight. After you called yesterday I swapped the gig out for Saturday night with Lee Yankee's Band. He's a cool young cat—a mean guitar player; you'll like him. There's a bunch of great players here."

Jake finished the cig and crushed it into the pavement.

"Let's roll," he said.

The two turned and strutted fifty paces into the East entrance of the place that was originally built as a Kentucky Fried Chicken Restaurant. The KFC eventually gave way to the Silver Moon, which prior to Hurricane Ivan in 2004, was primarily a popular package liquor store. After the violent storm, the old main room at the Flora-Bama, where the singer-songwriters performed, was no longer intact. The Silver Moon Lounge was born out of necessity, as they needed an intimate setting for artists to perform. A tiny stage on one side of the main room allowed for three or four musicians. The place was small and simple, yet functional; as the sound quality and ambiance was as good as the drinks and regular characters that created interesting company.

Johnny followed Jake into the Silver Moon. The low-ceiling place was cool and dark. Its thin black carpet reeked of stale beer, spilled whiskey and smoked cigarettes. Black and white and color pictures of artists and musicians adorned the panel wall behind the stage. Roxy Hart, a raven-haired, guitar-picking, Grammy-winning singer-songwriter/cowgirl from Oregon was playing and singing solo on stage. As she sang she made eye contact with Jake and winked and smiled. Jake waved to her.

"Hey Jake!" muttered one of the regulars.

"Hey man!" Jake turned and whispered, trying to be discreet while Roxy performed.

Jake and Johnny found two bar stools and ordered beers. Jake surveyed the room. There were about two dozen people there, including the staff. In the back he spotted Joe G. sitting with his long-time girlfriend, Mandy Baird, another singer-songwriter. Jake paid for the beers and leaned close to Johnny so he could hear him when he spoke.

"Joe is over in the back corner with the blonde. Follow me."

Jake slipped off the bar stool and walked in their direction, with Johnny right behind him. As he got closer, a seated Joe recognized them and stood. Jake shook his outreached hand, placing his left hand on Joe's right shoulder at the same time.

"Hey Joe! Hey Mandy!"

"Hi guy!" was Joe's pleasant reply. Roxy had finished her song and was making small talk with the regulars seated in front of the stage.

"What's cooking tonight?" Joe asked.

Jake answered. "Joe, I want you to meet a good friend of mine, Johnny Glass. He and I used to play together in Nashville."

He continued, "Johnny, this is Mr. Joe Gideon, the owner of the Flora-Bama and the Silver Moon."

Johnny stepped in and first tipped his hat to Mandy, a sandy blonde with deep dimples and blue eyes. He shook her hand and then Joe's, making sure to square his shoulders and to look him in the eye, like his daddy always said.

"Johnny is an extremely talented man, Joe. He's got his guitar and would love to sit in and play for a short set. Is that okay?" Jake asked.

"I believe we can arrange that," said Joe. "I think Roxy is nearing a break. That may work out perfectly."

Joe turned his body and complete focus to his newest guest.

"Johnny, welcome to the Flora-Bama! It should be a fun night tonight! Are you ready to have a little fun?"

"Always," Johnny replied with a smile that belied his nerves.

"Excellent!" exclaimed Joe. He beamed with excitement.

Roxy Hart, who had announced to the crowd that she was taking a break, made her way off the stage and over to where Jake and Johnny were next to Joe. She walked right up to Jake and put her arm around him and kissed him on the cheek.

"How y'all doing?" she playfully asked.

"Good evening Roxy!" said Joe. "Roxy, have you met Jake's friend, Johnny? He's down from Nashville."

"No, I haven't," replied Roxy. She removed her right arm from around Jake's waist and squeezed Johnny's hand.

After getting a closer look, she added, "And I obviously needed to."

She conspicuously winked at Johnny.

Johnny saw it, and blushed. He thought Roxy was as attractive as she was forward.

Rhonda "Roxy" Hart was a smoking hot forty-something, but she acted more like the teenager she looked like in her low-cut white satin blouse, black leather skirt, black fishnet stockings and matching heels. She loved attention.

"You a singer?" Roxy asked.

"I am," Johnny confidently replied.

"He was gonna sing a song or two for us, right Johnny?" Joe asked.

"I gladly will," said Johnny, even more confident than before.

Roxy looked a bit surprised.

"Well alright," she said.

Jake settled in next to a watching Joe, Sandy and Roxy as Johnny grabbed his nearby guitar and walked onto the stage. He settled on the padded black leather-topped stool resting before the standing microphone and slung his guitar into playing position. He adjusted the capo on the acoustic neck and strummed a few test cords.

Johnny felt a tinge of nervousness. He had auditioned countless times, in certainly much more difficult settings. But something—a déjà vu, more specifically, told him this one was more important than the others. He took a deep breath, exhaled and panned the watchful crowd, relishing the moment, the opportunity before him.

"I want to thank my good friend, Jake Justice, for getting me down here. He's been tryin' to get me to move here—or at least visit, for a couple years now, and I'm really glad to be here. This place is absolutely beautiful, I can't tell you enough. As you can see I got some sun today. Me and Jake went jet skiing out in the surf, and man, it's just amazing down here. I'm still trying to process it all, to tell you the truth, but I'm loving it! It's really, really pretty here."

He paused and sipped his beer. He returned the can to the rail and got comfortable.

"I'm gonna sing three songs, if y'all don't mind, while the lovely Ms. Hart is on break."

He looked over to Roxy, who was doing her best not to spill a vodka soda. She smiled and raised her glass in appreciation.

He continued, "The first song is for our host, Mr. Joe Gideon. It's a Beatles tune. I imagine you like the Beatles, huh Mr. Joe?"

Joe nodded his approval, punctuating it with the raising of his shiny, aluminum Coors Lite can.

"The second song was written by a guy from Georgia I met while I was playing a gig three years ago, after I had lived in Nashville for only a few months. He's a great songwriter and singer and a really nice person, too—very deserving of the success he's having. I think he's gonna continue to do really well for himself. Y'all mighta' heard of him. His name is Jason Aldean…"

The small crowd chattered, snapped and clapped with approval.

"And the third song I'm gonna sing is by a guy who is not as well known, but who was just as talented, if not certainly more talented, since he was inducted into the American Songwriter's Hall of Fame at the young age of 40…he is a personal favorite of mine and someone I look up to a great deal as a writer…and that would be Mr. Mickey Newbury."

Johnny paused for effect. He looked to his friends in the

back. Joe G. wore a pensive expression and sat still in anticipation. Jake smiled and leaned back.

"I'm gonna sing all three songs and then give this stage back to Ms. Hart. Like I said, this one's for you, Mr. Joe. It's called 'Rocky Raccoon.'"

The melodic sound of Johnny's Martin guitar preceded the words:

"Now somewhere in the black mountain hills of Dakota
There lived a young boy named Rocky Raccoon..."

The song went over well, drawing a solid round of applause from everyone watching, even the bartenders and staff. Johnny sounded great. His soothing voice never faltered; and the performance was full of emotion.

"This second song is titled, 'Big Green Tractor...'
She had a shiny little beamer with the ragtop down
sitting in the drive but she wouldn't get out..."

After the second song was over, the crowd again positively responded. Everyone clapped and there were several loud whistles and female shrieks amidst a few hoots and hollers.

"And finally, for my last song, I'm gonna sing Mickey Newbury's "Frisco Mabel Joy..."

"Lord, his Daddy was an honest man, just a red dirt Georgia farmer
His momma lived her short life having kids and baling hay
He had fifteen years and an ache inside to wander
So he hopped a freight in Waycross and wound up in L.A. ..."

When he finished another emotional performance everyone in the small room stood and clapped. Sandy and Roxy each wiped tears from their eyes. Goosebumps riddled Joe G's forearms.

Jake yelled, "Great job Johnny! Well done, Son!"

"Thank y'all so much," Johnny said, stepping off of the stage, guitar in hand.

Jake walked up to Johnny and gave him a big high five.

"Super job, brother! You're a superstar now, huh? Damn, son, I didn't remember you being that good!"

Johnny appreciated the fine compliments.

"Thanks Jake."

Roxy Hart walked past Johnny and grabbed the microphone.

"And I have to follow that?" she asked the crowd. "Seriously, that was great, Johnny. It was great meeting you and having you play. Welcome to paradise!"

Johnny waved and thanked her and everyone else in the audience once again.

"Yeah, that was really something, Johnny," said Mandy.

"One of the best impromptu performances I've seen," commented Joe.

"Thank you kindly—both of you," Johnny nodded, his soul temporarily redeemed.

"Well Johnny, what do you say we head on over across the street to the Bama and see what's shaking? There is a guy over there playing right now that you just gotta' see to believe."

"Who's playing over there right now?" Mandy asked.

"Earl the Pearl," Jake answered.

"Oh God!" laughed Joe. "Johnny'll love it! Y'all get on over there before he's finished."

Johnny could only wonder.

"What are you guys doing tomorrow afternoon?" Joe asked. "I am having a few guys over for a guitar pull. Y'all are certainly welcome. We'll be getting together over at my place on Old River around four or so. Bring something to cook and the beverage of your choice."

"We don't have any plans, yet, Joe. We'll probably come by, thanks." Jake answered.

"Alright then, I hope to see you tomorrow. We may head across the street later, we're gonna hang here for a while and finish watching Roxy. Johnny, it was great meeting you and hearing you play. You were terrific, thanks," Joe added.

"It was my pleasure, Mr. Joe. Thank you," Johnny answered.

Jake led Johnny out the doors opposite of those they entered. Jake lit a cigarette as they paced towards the Flora-Bama. The sun had faded and it was dark outside, but the front of the property was well lit with multiple, large outdoor lamps and floodlights. There was a line of thirty or more people waiting to show their I.D.'s and to pay a $5 cover. Traffic along the beach road was bumper-to-bumper looking west. There was a smorgasbord of utility vehicles, cars and trucks parked everywhere.

"You did good in there, Johnny. Real good, brother. I was impressed. Joe was too. I could tell. Everybody was—big time. You have really improved. All that pickin' has made a difference!" Jake said. "Tomorrow afternoon we are gonna go over to Joe's for that guitar pull. I'll talk to him about bringing you on into the regular rotation. We'll feel him out on it."

"Thanks bro!" Johnny answered. He truly felt things were looking up for him. He liked the vibe inside the Silver Moon.

"I've been playing hard for four years. You know the drill. Most people go to college or learn a trade. Me and you, we went to Nashville. Can you believe it?" Johnny asked, thinking they were a bit crazy.

Jake exhaled and smiled.

"But now, I'm in Perdido Key, Florida!" Johnny exclaimed, raising his closed fists high above his head, like his good friend had earlier. He was starting to decompress. The performance and the beer, and his changing outlook, helped him relax.

"And you deserve it, my brother!" Jake answered. "We all do!"

The two briefly embraced arm-in-arm, side-by-side, and after assuming their spot in line in front of the Flora-Bama, Jake finished his cigarette and Johnny checked the time on his cell phone. It was 7:55.

Jake got in free but he paid Johnny's five dollar cover for him.

"Thanks man," Johnny said.

"No sweat," answered Jake.

6

Once inside the Flora-Bama compound, Johnny listened but could not hear any music. They made their way along the cracked pavement, through the ongoing construction, into the bulk of the wooden structure, past the vertically-perforated, visqueen-lined entrance into a large, dark room with a high wooden ceiling with rafters.

The air inside the Flora-Bama was damp and cool. A large, leaky air conditioning unit labored overhead. Southeastern Conference school pennants and flags hung haphazardly from the rafters high above. Two long ropes transected above the crowd in the middle of the large space. Each rope was encumbered by hundreds of brassieres of every shape, size, color and conception. They served as an everyday reminder of the type of adult activities that regularly happened on the line. There were easily five or six hundred of them hanging in plain view.

On the wide, ship-rope lined stage a four piece band was setting up to play. There was an aging black drummer in Ray-Bans with a large afro, a brunette with short hair wearing a blue bandana and cheap shades playing bass, a blonde, curly-haired male keyboard player and a balding, cheesy moustache-wearing, guitar-playing, late forty-something lead singer who wore a tight white muscle shirt and Richard Simmons-style, tiny red and white-lined jogging shorts and cheap flip-flops. The puny muscle shirt read: "Arkansas: The Natural State." It was apparent that they were still on a break.

The band wasn't playing any music, but the place still buzzed. It was early on a Friday night. There were people everywhere. A gamut of humanity filled the wooden booths with table tops along the walls. The scantily-clad were sprawled across the tops of the many wooden picnic tables and benches strewn about on one side of the large dance floor. Both young and old—many still in swimsuits and tee shirts, were represented among the conversing, laughing crowd. Two bars with long lines and two busy cocktail waitresses filled an endless stream of canned beer and cocktail orders. Everywhere you looked, folks were making time.

Jake caught the eye of one of the waitresses and quickly got them served canned light beers.

"Come with me," Jake said, pulling Johnny into the crowd toward the front of the stage. The balding guy in the really short shorts and super-tight white tank top slung his guitar over his shoulder. Jake and Johnny appeared below him, right up in front of the stage.

"Earl the Pearl! Earl the Pearl!" Jake yelled, with a beer in one hand, his other arm around Johnny.

"What's up Jake?" Earl stated from above. He stopped what he was doing and rested both elbows across the acoustic guitar and smiled from ear-to-ear, giving them his full attention.

"Earl, this here is my friend, Johnny Glass. We used to play together up in Nashville. He's a singer-songwriter and just moved down here today. I told him he had to see your show!"

Earl knelt and offered a handshake to Johnny, which he thought was mighty kind.

Johnny squared up and firmly shook Earl's hand.

"Good to meet you, Johnny Glass," said Earl, in a way Johnny felt belied his ridiculous outfit.

"Good to meet you, Earl."

Earl stood back up and strummed a few test chords. The sound indicated to the crowd that it was again time for the show to start. Everyone looked to the stage. Earl spoke directly into the microphone.

"Alright everybody, I think it is due time now that we get serious in here."

"Screw you, Earl!" yelled a badly sunburned, large-breasted, middle-aged woman on the side of the stage. Barefooted, she wore only a small denim skirt and an orange bikini top. She held her vodka tonic high.

"Would you?" Earl retorted.

"I'd do you, baby, for sure!" he added.

"Right behind the Waffle House, there, too! I'd tap that ass, bitch!"

He slowly strummed his guitar. The crowd loved it. They jeered and cheered.

"Why don't you show us them big ole titties, darlin'?" Earl asked, surprising no one.

The crowd went wild.

"Show your tits! Show your tits! Show your tits!" they yelled in unison, from every corner of the quintessential beach bar.

Expectedly, in one quick motion the gal released her bosom. The unclasped boulder holders fell apart and two large, creamy white orbs with dark, silver dollar-sized areolas with erect nipples bounced out with what seemed like a life of their own. Turning to the crowd, she placed a hand on each and smashed them together and squeezed them like they owed her money. She kissed the top of each tit and placed them back into her top and clasped it once again. The charade was over as fast as it had begun. The crowd went nuts. People hooted and hollered and laughed and carried on like high school kids. It was a wild scene.

"This place is nuts," thought Johnny. He had never seen anything like the spectacle before him.

"Wooo-hooo!" Yelled Jake, amidst an avalanche of childlike laughter and screams.

He bounced up and down like a pogo stick and elbowed Johnny hard. "This sonofabitch cracks me up!"

Earl commented, "Goodness, honey. That was quite a show. You are one talented woman, I wanna tell you. I will be done with this show in about an hour or so. We ought to do the Waffle House thing I was talkin' about...damn you got some nice big ole titties, let me tell you, dadgummit! Ooh wee!"

Earl vigorously massaged his crotch for added effect. Everyone enjoyed another big laugh.

"Alright, that got me so riled up and horny I'm gonna have to sing this here song. I'm dedicating it to our newest singer-songwriting resident on the island, Mr. Johnny Glass, down here on the front row. Johnny just moved here from Nashville, Tennessee."

Earl motioned toward Johnny, down in front of him. Jake pointed to him and everyone clapped and cheered.

Earl continued, "Nashville is a fine place—if you like Yankee pricks who fuck up country music. But anyway, this is for you, Johnny. Welcome to paradise! This song is also for anybody who has ever made love out on the water. I call it, "Poontang on a Pontoon.""

The band cranked up and Earl sang.

"Me and my baby wanted to go out on the bay…
We rented us a boat for the whole damn day.
Big pontoon, loaded up with beer,
Plannin' on havin' sex as soon as we left the pier.
We're headed toward the pass
I'm spanking that ass
I got the throttle pushed down
I'm givin' her the gas
I'm getting poontang on a pontoon.
Poontang on a pontoon…"

***

After Earl the Pearl completed his final set around nine or so, Jake and Johnny mingled amidst the growing crowd, right near the bar closest to the stage, in front of the entranceway they had earlier used. When Lucy and Michelle and the rest of their adorable friends entered the chamber nearly every warm-blooded male in the place turned and stared at the fertile pack. Eight knockouts were on display.

Lucy and her well-tanned friends wore the latest fashion trend: colorful sundresses, wide, shiny belts and leather cowboy boots. They were a shapely, lovely lot. The well-tanned throng stood in front of the entrance together for a moment, unable to really move through the maddening crowd. Like fawns in the crosshairs they huddled, and then, led by Michelle, turned and moved toward the bar, where Jake and Johnny were.

"Here they come, Johnny," Jake said, elbowing him hard. "Are you ready for this?"

Johnny knew exactly what he was talking about. He stared over Jake's shoulder, in disbelief. He had never seen so many pretty girls. Upon second glance he realized they were the girls he had earlier met at the gas station. He swallowed hard, letting Jake take the lead. Moments later, the girls were upon them.

Jake made eye contact with Michelle, who was in the lead. She was followed by Lucy and the rest.

"Good evening ladies," said Jake, lifting his gleaming, silver canned beer.

"And you too, Michelle," he added, lunging and hugging her tight before she could react.

"Oh really, Jake?" she laughed, going along with his teasing. She hugged him back.

"Hey Johnny!" said a waving Michelle, recognizing him from the gas station.

"Hey!" he answered. "How y'all doin' tonight?" He smiled.

"Well, thanks! Just getting here," she answered.

Michelle looked to her friend, Lucy. She noticed she was busy checking Johnny out.

"Let's get drinks!" Michelle suggested.

"To the bar!" Jake insisted. "Everyone, this way!" He pointed toward the bar with both hands.

Johnny didn't hear Jake. He was too busy looking at Lucy. Their eyes met and they smiled simultaneously. Butterflies rumbled in Johnny's stomach. He was a sucker for brunettes, but she was unlike any he'd seen. He knew he hadn't seen her earlier in the day.

"Oh my," he thought. "She is stunning."

Lucy couldn't get over how cute he looked with his pompadour hairdo. "He even looks like a Nashville singer," she thought.

Johnny, maintaining eye contact, stepped toward her and extended his hand.

"Hi, I'm Johnny—Johnny Glass."

Lucy firmly clasped his open hand and shook it.

"I'm Lucy—Lucy Whitman," she answered with an inviting smile.

Johnny's canned beer had less than a swallow left and he noticed her hand was empty.

"Let's follow the others to the bar," Johnny suggested, motioning the way the others had gone.

"Sure," she said. She grabbed and squeezed his hand with her other, and spoke into his ear.

"Lead the way."

Johnny found her Lower Alabama accent as inviting as her shapely figure and symmetrical face. His stomach again rumbled and he squeezed back and made his way through the crowded mass of inhumanity toward the bar, with Lucy in tow. He couldn't believe the day he was having.

"This is almost too good to be true," Johnny thought. In Nashville he never really found time to have a steady girlfriend. He was always too consumed with "making it" in the music business.

When they reached the bar Jake was already at the front of the line. He was busy taking orders from the girls and relaying them to the tall, smiling, broad-shouldered, moustache-wearing bartender, Phil, who stood at eye level behind the dugout bar.

"Okay, Phil. I got four bushwhackers, two vodka sodas, a screwdriver and a Coors Lite, for me," Jake declared to the girls. Johnny walked up with Lucy.

"Johnny, my boy—have y'all met Johnny?" Jake asked the group.

"Yes, we met him earlier." Michelle answered.

Jake glanced at Johnny's left hand clasped with Lucy's right. He smirked.

"Damn son, you work fast! Whattaya wanna drink, you two love birds? Come on, what's it gonna be?" Jake demanded.

"I want a bushwhacker," said Lucy.

"What's a bushwhacker?" Johnny asked.

"You'll be getting a Coors Lite, along with me, son." Jake answered, matter-of-factly.

"It's like a spiked chocolate milk shake," said Lucy. "It's delicious—but strong."

The group got their drinks and headed outdoors, as inside the crowd was now elbow-to-elbow. Once outside they spread out and relaxed under the two large, adjoined wedding tents. Big white vinyl tarps spread across metal poles protected an outdoor stage and enough room for three or four hundred people, or more. Weathered picnic tables situated throughout, served as makeshift seating and dancing platforms.

Johnny and Lucy found a lone empty picnic table in the rear near the open beach, and sat down. The gang followed and crowded around, the ten of them taking up the entire table. The band, The Lucky Doggs, returned to the stage and played true honky tonk music. It again became loud.

"So you just got here?" Lucy asked Johnny.

"Yeah, earlier today. Drove in from Nashville."

Johnny sipped his beer. He offered a toast.

"Here's to meeting you here!" Johnny said, holding up his beer.

"To the Flora-Bama!" Lucy answered, touching her clear plastic bushwhacker cup to his Coors Light can.

"So, I hear you're a singer?" she asked.

"And a songwriter," Johnny answered with a grin.

"Impressive," Lucy replied, returning a smile.

"Well, it's not as easy as you think. I spent four years in Nashville and didn't get anywhere. Jake played with me before he moved here. He's been here for a couple years and always said that I should come down if I ever got tired of it up there. Well, I did—and here I am. I met the owner of the Flora-Bama, Mr. Joe Gideon, a little while ago. I played and sang three songs for him across the street at the Silver Moon Lounge. I think he likes me. Hopefully I can get a working gig here. I need it."

Lucy momentarily took it all in, before speaking.

"I am a singer. But I don't write songs. I haven't ever been in a band or anything, either. I've just sung in local competitions."

She paused.

"But lately I started taking voice lessons, and I think they're really helping."

She sipped her bushwhacker through a straw. It had a bright red cherry and stem on top.

Johnny was surprised that this gorgeous creature also sang. It was difficult for him to fathom.

"Really? That's great! Wow—you are a big-time double threat—looks and talent! Look out!"

Lucy blushed.

"I am just like you, then," she reciprocated, proudly beaming while returning the compliment.

Johnny blushed. Although he was a looker, he was hardly a player. He genuinely appreciated the compliment.

"Thanks Lucy," he answered.

The group was busy conversing amongst themselves when Big Daddy Joe G., the owner of the Flora-Bama, along with his girlfriend Mandy, made his way out under the tent to where they were seated.

"Good evening everyone! Anybody having any fun, yet?" Joe G. implored with a smile as captivating as his quintessential beach club.

"Hey Joe!" yelled Jake, who acted as the group spokesman. He stood to greet him and Mandy.

"We are well on our way, Joe. Well on our way."

"Excellent!" replied Joe. "Looks like we have a few new victims here. Let's see, I recognize Michelle..."

Joe waved to her and she waved back.

"Hey Mr. Joe!"

"Who are these other lovely friends of yours, young lady? I am thoroughly impressed. You girls look absolutely gorgeous this evening!"

"They are my friends from South." Michelle answered.

She introduced each of them to Joe, ending with Lucy, who was still seated across from Johnny, at the end. Joe shook each of their hands and thanked them for coming to his club.

"Guys come to the Flora-Bama to meet lovely ladies like you girls. Without gorgeous females like you we wouldn't be half as exciting. Thank you so much for coming. Here is a free drink ticket for each of you."

Everyone thanked Joe for his kindness, chiming their appreciation.

Jake again spoke for the group.

"Joe, you didn't have to. Thanks, man."

"Oh, no problem. We love having you guys. Thanks again for being here."

There was a brief pause. Joe now stood behind Johnny, at the end of the picnic bench. He placed a hand on Johnny's shoulder, which of course, surprised Johnny.

"Johnny, do you have a minute? I would like to chat with you," Joe asked.

Johnny immediately stood, as he needed to talk to Joe about a job.

"Sure, Joe."

He stood and turned to Lucy.

"Lucy, please excuse me. I will be right back." Johnny said, smiling in anticipation.

Lucy understood. She smiled and nodded her head, encouraging him.

"See you in a bit," she said, looking directly into his eyes.

"Walk with me out here, toward the beach, where it's not as loud," Joe said to Johnny.

Johnny followed him to a wooden boardwalk that ran from the back area of the outside bar all the way to the middle of the beach, past the protected dunes. Halfway across the boardwalk Joe stopped and turned to Johnny and spoke. The music still blared underneath the tent, but because of the distance covered, they could now hear each other well.

Johnny stopped and listened. His heart beat fast.

"Your performance earlier was fantastic," Joe said, speaking in a noticeably lower tone. "Mickey Newbury was a friend of mine. He came here in the early 1990's and he fell in love with the place."

Johnny couldn't believe it.

"THE Mickey Newbury? He used to hang out here?"

"Yes," said Joe. "For several years, until he passed, just a few years ago. He was such a great writer, and a much better artist than he was given credit for. He left a lot of friends here, including me. He is greatly missed by a lot of people who really appreciated him and his rare ability to put words together."

There was a brief pause. Johnny was awestruck.

"Johnny, I know you are probably a little low on cash. Here's an advance. Once you start playing on a regular basis, and you have a little more money, you can pay me back."

He handed Johnny three one hundred dollar bills with the big picture of Benjamin Franklin on them. Johnny couldn't believe it. He was stunned. The money anxiety that had tormented him for the past several hours left him like he had just awakened from a bad dream. Joe had just doubled his wealth.

"Mr. Joe, you are too kind. I really appreciate it. Thanks so much. I promise to pay you back and I promise I will be one of your best players. Just like I did in Nashville, I'll put my heart into my music here at the Flora-Bama," Johnny said with conviction.

"You are already one of my best players, Johnny. Just be yourself."

Johnny was truly humbled by his compliment; he immediately wondered how good he really was.

"Thanks, Mr. Joe. That means so much to me. You just don't know."

"You're welcome. I mean that."

There was a pause.

"Hold out your other hand." Joe said.

Johnny obliged, extending his left hand, wondering what else he had in store.

Joe placed a single key in his open palm.

"That's the key to the penthouse condo right next door at the Phoenix Ten. I own it. It's all the way on the top floor. There are a couple of guys up there right now, but the master bedroom and suite next to the gulf view, my room, is open. I don't know if you had made any sleeping arrangements, but you can stay there for the next week or so until you find a regular place. Just take the elevator all the way to the top floor. It is the first door off the elevator, to the right."

By now, Johnny felt like everything was a dream, that all of this surely wasn't happening to him. He was moved by Joe's generosity as much as he was by his love and respect for songwriters and musicians. He wondered if Joe G. was his Guardian Angel incarnated. Nashville never treated him like this. He could only muster a few words.

"Mr. Joe, thank you so much. I don't know what else to say."

"You don't have to say anything, Johnny. However, I do want you to promise me something, going forward."

"Sure, Mr. Joe. What's that?"

"I want you to promise me that you will have fun. I want you to fully embrace the concept. Act like a kid again—if you can; you'll be better off for it. Always remember, Johnny, the principle business of life is to enjoy it. The sad thing is most of us never realize it until it's too late."

He paused.

"Can you promise me that, Johnny—that you will try and have fun here?"

"Yes Sir, Mr. Joe. I promise," Johnny answered, not really fully understanding what was happening. It all seemed like something out of a fairy tale.

"Great! Because, you could be a lot more useless in life, Johnny. A lot more useless…"

Johnny tried to wrap his head around the oxymoronic statement, but couldn't.

"I've got to get back inside to Mandy. You had a real cutie pie sitting across from you over there, Johnny. She is likely wondering where you are. You need to get back to her."

Joe turned and began walking along the boardwalk, tracing his earlier steps back to the bar. Johnny followed alongside him.

"Oh and again, I'm having a guitar pull tomorrow at my

house on Old River, just east down the beach road a couple miles or so. I told Jake y'all are invited. You can bring a guest if you like. Maybe the brunette back there would like to come along with you? We are getting together in the late afternoon around four or so. Just bring a swimsuit, something to cook on the grill, and a beverage or two, if you are so inclined."

"I'm sure we will make it, Joe. Thanks again."

***

Johnny went back to the picnic table area under the tents where the group was when he left them. However, when he got back out there, they were no longer around. He panned the scene, and noticed Brad Masterson, the architect he'd met earlier in the day. They made eye contact.

"Johnny Glass!" yelled Brad. He was now wearing a navy blue Hawaiian shirt, khakis and flip-flops.

Johnny recognized him and walked toward him, near the outside bar.

"Hey man," Johnny said, shaking his hand. "Brad, right?"

"That's it Mon! Let me get you a drink. What would you like?"

"Coors Light," answered Johnny. "Thanks."

Brad purchased a bushwhacker for himself and handed Johnny a cold, slim, silver can.

"What's up brother Mon?" Brad asked.

"I'm looking for Jake and a mess of pretty girls."

"I haven't seen Jake. But I just got here," Brad answered, looking around. "As far as pretty girls,

check this one out, walking this way."

Johnny panned the crowd in the direction Brad pointed. There were people everywhere.

Coming at them through the crowd was Lucy, alone. They saw each other and smiled.

"Hey," she said to Johnny when she came upon them. "We are all inside, listening to the music. I thought I would look for you."

"Thanks," Johnny answered, smiling. He resumed holding her left hand with his right.

"Lucy, this is Brad," I met him earlier today.

"How are you Miss Lucy," Brad said, extending his hand.

"Fine, thanks. Nice to meet you." She smiled and shook his hand.

"What's your last name, darlin'?" Brad probed.

"Whitman, I'm Lucy Whitman."

"Are you related to Senator Whitman from Fairhope?" he asked.

"Yes Sir," she answered. "He's my dad."

Johnny took notice of the comment, particularly the way she reluctantly answered. They made their way back into the large front room the locals called "the Bama Dome."

A young fellow named Lee Yankie was playing with his righteous band, Hell Yeahz, and he sounded really good, Johnny thought. It was bluesy with a little funk, and the crowd really dug it. The place was in full swing. Johnny and Lucy caught up with Jake and Michelle and Johnny told them about Joe giving him cash, a regular gig and a key to his luxury condo.

"I told you, son! I told you everything was gonna be alright!" Jake exclaimed with a high five. He placed his right hand firmly on Johnny's left shoulder.

"And, you already hooked up with a real looker! Damn son, I'm gonna call you butter, cuz you're on a roll!"

"Shooters at the bar on me! This calls for a celebration!" Jake exclaimed.

After a couple more hours of music, dancing, laughter and fun, after midnight, Johnny asked Lucy if she wanted to take a walk on the beach. He wanted to kiss her.

She said yes, and they made their way hand-in-hand onto the wooden boardwalk he and Joe had earlier used. Each had enjoyed several drinks, and they were feeling the normal effects. At the end of the boardwalk Johnny removed his boots and socks and Lucy removed her sandals, stashing them behind a nearby trash receptacle. They walked, still hand-in-hand, toward the water and sat on one of many wooden reclining chaises that were available to touring sun worshipers during the day.

And there they kissed, sweetly, for the first time, under the faint light of the crescent moon and gleaming stars on the edge of the murmuring gulf surf and soft sand where Alabama and Florida meet. Johnny was in bliss. The day had gone unimaginably well for him—meeting Joe and playing for him was his short-term dream; but being with Lucy was completely unexpected. In between long kisses, he confided in her, still clutching her hand.

"Today was an amazing day for me, Lucy. I got a job doing what I love to do, a place to lay my head on this beautiful island—for the time being; and the most amazing thing of it all—I met you," Johnny said.

Lucy blushed, so much so that he could see it, despite the dimness. He squeezed her hand. She squeezed back and smiled. They again kissed. Johnny was starting to feel tired, as he didn't sleep much the night before.

"Where are you staying tonight?" he asked.

"At Michelle's supposedly. Her parents have a place out here on Ono...the little island across Old River. They aren't out here tonight, though. They are coming out tomorrow."

Johnny turned and looked up at the tower next to the Flora-Bama.

"Joe gave me the key to his penthouse condo up there. You wanna check it out with me?"

"Sure," she said, without hesitation.

After a long elevator ride all the way to the top of the tower, Johnny and Lucy entered the condo. The overhead light in the large living area was on, but no one was in sight. Johnny recognized one of his favorites, "Pancho and Lefty" by Townes Van Zandt playing faintly from a portable CD player nearby. There was a standing electronic keyboard and a bass and an acoustic guitar on stands stationed next to two large sliding glass doors in the corner overlooking the gulf. There were red solo drink cups and beer bottles scattered everywhere, like people had been partying.

Joe told Johnny that his room was the one with the gulf view. He opened the red corner door to find a large, posh bedroom with a made king-sized bed, a sofa and coffee table with assorted magazines, a walk-in closet and a large, mirrored bathroom with a Jacuzzi and standing shower. It looked like the maid had been there earlier. The plush carpet was immaculate. It still had vacuum lines. The space also had its own private balcony overlooking the gulf. Johnny and Lucy made their way into the bedroom, Johnny shutting the door behind them. They surveyed the pretty place.

"This is really nice," Lucy said, admiring the tub and shower.

"I'd say," Johnny answered.

"Excuse me," she said, winking and closing the bathroom door behind her.

Johnny smiled at her until she was no longer in sight. He turned and stepped onto the balcony where he admired the moonlight cascading on the continuous, rolling water.

Johnny and Lucy, feeling a deep connection, stayed up talking to the wee hours of the morning. Johnny wanted to know how Lucy didn't have a boyfriend. Lucy wanted to know why in the world he didn't have a girlfriend. As far as they could tell, it seemed that time and circumstance had allowed them to meet. Both felt so lucky, so excited to meet the other.

Johnny explained his working class upbringing, his long-time goal of songwriting and singing success via the Nashville circuit, and the way he especially missed his departed maternal grandmother's love and guiding influence, after losing her to cancer two years earlier. After listening, Lucy felt that in addition to being extremely talented and handsome, Johnny was also gentle and kind.

Lucy explained as best as she could her privileged upbringing on the Eastern Shore of Mobile Bay, her father's obnoxious political standing and clout; and her utter disdain for all it did to her family. Mostly though, she talked wantonly about her unfulfilled love of music and song.

"I am in college right now, but it's not my choice. Over the last couple years I've realized that music is what I want to do. It's what makes me happy."

She paused. "But I know my parents wouldn't want me to pursue music as a career. They want me to get a degree, and I don't know if that's for me. I've never sung in a band before, and I really want to," Lucy said. "I've been taking lessons from a former college music professor. He has helped me a lot. I know I am getting better, but I really want to sing with a band."

A smiling Johnny replied, "Well, I am looking for a band, too. Maybe we could work together and form our own band?"

The two again embraced. They eventually made their way inside, onto the large bed, where they slept in a spooning position on top of the covers, with an Afghan throw covering them.

7

At 7:00 a.m. white sunlight crept around the dark curtains in Joe's master bedroom and interrupted Johnny's resting eyes. Johnny woke and noticed Lucy next to him. He smelled her shiny black hair, and the lovely perfume that complemented her so well. A flood of unprecedented, fond memories from the night before buoyed him; he could almost again feel the excitement he had so enjoyed while at the Flora-Bama, just hours earlier. He wanted to do it all again, as he had not had that kind of fun in a long, long time.

He remembered what Joe G. had asked him to do... "Have some fun," so he didn't feel guilty for it. He remembered he was in Joe's posh penthouse condo overlooking the water.

"This place is really something," Johnny thought. He felt like he was light years from Nashville, Tennessee, which had been only a burden for him, compared to this. The moment's reflections filled him with much hope and promise for the new day, and what else exciting and fun was ahead of him in his new life on the gulf coast.

Johnny's wonderful thoughts were interrupted by the sound of an acoustic guitar in the main room. To his trained ear, it was clearly the workings of a melody. He went to the bathroom and washed his face. He emerged from the bedroom, where Lucy still slept, into the living room, opening and closing the door behind him.

The curly blond-haired dude in his late twenties with an unlit Marlboro Light between his lips strummed the chords in sequence, repeatedly. Johnny walked to the large kitchen area and found a clean glass in the above cabinetry. He used the ice and water dispenser in the refrigerator door. Dehydrated, he sipped the ice water and walked to the living room area and stood facing the player, behind the large sectional between them. The blond strummed a few more chords before he finally gave pause. He looked up and smiled.

"Good mornin.' You gotta light?"

Johnny didn't smoke.

"Nah man, I don't," Johnny apologized. "But if you give me the cig I can light it on the stove for you. Hold on."

Johnny walked to the electric range and turned the front right coil controller on high. Within seconds, the black coils turned a bright glowing orange. Johnny walked and grabbed the cigarette from the guy and walked back and lit it, puffing it neatly once without inhaling to get it going. He handed it back to the much-appreciative bloke.

Johnny remembered Joe told him that there was someone else staying up there.

"I'm Johnny Glass," Johnny said, offering his hand.

"Sam Holiday," he answered, standing and gripping Johnny's right hand with his own, dragging hard all the while.

"Wanna step outside while I smoke this here cigarette?" he asked.

The two stepped onto the spacious balcony with a table and four chairs and enjoyed a panoramic view of bright white, baby and royal blue. To their left the bright yellow dot climbed in the east; a flock of gulls squawked and glided along the beach airspace. Johnny noticed a tinge of humidity in the air, as he eyeballed a couple walking barefoot along the foamy, rolling shoreline. The vast Gulf of Mexico shimmered in the early light. Johnny thought it was breathtaking.

They sat down across from one another.

"What brings you down here, brother?" A cool Sam asked, puffing nonchalantly on the cig. His curly blonde locks lifted up and down in the high breeze.

"I'm just down from Nashville. I'm friends with a guy who plays at the Flora-Bama—Jake Justice, do you know him?"

"I do," Sam nodded.

Johnny continued, "I write songs and sing. I couldn't make it in Nashville. But, looking back now I don't know if I'm cut out for their kind a' success, anyway, you know? I tried really hard to do all the right things, I played the game, but it never came to be for me."

Sam nodded. He understood.

Johnny continued.

"So, I'm gonna give Perdido Key a chance. I'm gonna start playing down here. I talked to Mr. Joe Gideon, the owner, last night, after I played for him at the Silver Moon Lounge…and he gave me a gig after that—and the key to his place. I can't believe it. I am really stoked about living and playing here. This place is beautiful. Look at this!"

Johnny pointed to the rising sun, a radiant, red-yellow ball of fire and light climbing in the eastern sky. A wide band of symmetrical cirrus clouds dotted the cobalt horizon transected by a pale blue sky. It was a picture postcard moment.

"I'm from Nashville, man. I grew up there. My dad's a player; has been forever. He's staying up here with me. He's sleeping in the other bedroom. Our bus is parked across the street, near the River House. Joe is cool to let us stay here for a few days. The AC on the bus is broken and we're trying to get it fixed."

Sam continued.

"That's all I've ever known, really; is writing and singing songs. My dad has a seasonal gig here right now for a few weeks through the summer and I am on the road with him. I sit in sometimes. He's on the keys, mainly by himself, though. I don't know what my Dad wants to do long-term, but I told him I'd like to stay in this area for a while."

Sam extinguished his cigarette in the ashtray and continued.

"I like to write more than I do playing, but I play bass and guitar and a little keyboard. I also dabble in acting and screenwriting. I'm working on a script right now, as a matter of fact…"

The sliding glass door rumbled along its corralling base.

Sam and Johnny both turned to Lucy, who made her way onto the deck. She wore her hair up and it was obvious she had just washed her face, as she wore no makeup. She walked over to Johnny and kissed him on the cheek, and then squeezed his hand.

"Good morning," she sweetly whispered.

Sam stood and offered his hand. They shook and Lucy joined them around the table, next to Johnny.

They talked about the unforgiving Nashville music scene — Crazy Town, as it is often called, the contrarian, slower, laid back pace of life in Perdido Key, and ultimately, of forming a band if they could find a drummer, as Johnny already had an in with Joe and the Flora-Bama. The three agreed, on the spot, to find a drummer, and then to name the band and then — to start playing. They were excited.

***

It was mid morning on a near placid Mobile Bay, before the sun was high in the gentian sky and the air thick with humidity. The bay area was clear of any other people — an oddity for a Saturday. Senator Slip Whitman and Representative Blaine McElroy sipped Kentucky bourbon and ice water with orange peel and smoked fake Cuban cigars rolled in Nicaragua on the end of the Senator's long pier. There was a large section of shiny Kelly green outdoor carpeting — the stuff like shredded plastic, and a permanent black plastic golf tee set up at the end of the long wooden structure overlooking the bay. A gray five gallon bucket nearby was half full of golf balls.

Representative McElroy, wearing shorts, a dress shirt and a nifty cream colored straw hat with a black leather band, was seated in the awning shade in a relaxing wicker chair behind and above the Senator, who was busy addressing the ball on the tee.

Senator Whitman, wearing an Alabama golf shirt, nylon golfing shorts and spiked shoes, reared back and swung the driver hard through the small dimpled sphere. The tiny bright white circle flew fast like a rocket taking off; it quickly disappeared into the vastness of Mobile Bay. It came down, but the splash was much too far away to see or hear.

"Woo wee! I got all of that one, Blaine. Did you see that? I nailed that sonofabitch!"

"Damn straight you did, Slip. You crushed it." A sipping Blaine returned matter-of-factly.

The senator stood and postured, savoring the moment, leaning hard on his massive metal graphite driver, bending it.

"Yeah, I'm getting better. I've been hittin' a lot more. I really needed the work, too. My game was suffering. Mary has really been kicking my ass."

He paused, but continued.

"This here driver is hot—like that young thing you got stashed in Pratville, Blaine."

The senator paused for effect. He saw he had Blaine's full attention. Blaine perked up in his seat. The senator waved the huge club in the air above his head with both hands.

"Yep," he continued. "It's barely legal," he laughed uncontrollably.

Blaine answered, "That's not funny, Slip. You gotta keep quiet about her! Come on now, we promised."

His face bore a look of grave concern, as he thought no one knew.

"Slip has fantastic intel," thought Blaine. He couldn't believe it.

"He must have tailed me," he thought.

"Man oh man, that's some sweet stuff, partner…yes siree! Just turned 21! Tell me that ain't nice!"

The senator saw the concern on Blaine's face. He knew he had pushed his button. He relented.

"I know. I'm just having a lil' fun! The last thing I want is for your wife to find out about her. Because if that happens, Mary is gonna be all over me like a hound on a June bug, and that's the last thing I want, because we all know…what happens in Montgomery, stays in Montgomery."

Senator Whitman placed another ball on the tee, addressed it and swung hard, producing the same, desired result.

"Nice," Blaine said. "Another goodie!"

Startled, he changed the subject.

"Slip, those balls you hittin' into the water, are they biodegradable?"

Senator Whitman sipped his bourbon and water and laughed.

"Are you kidding? The City of Fairhope pumps sewage into this bay. You think a few golf balls are gonna make a bit of difference in our water quality? Gimme a break! You're joking, right?"

Blaine said nothing. He looked away and sipped his drink. As a kid he fished the same bay every summer with his now deceased father, who had done the same with his father.

Representative McElroy continued, "Let me get this straight, Slip. I'm having trouble understanding it all...BP says they're giving us $100 million as just part of total reparations for the spill, right? I mean, there are some serious cleanup costs involved. That well is still gushing oil and it's all gonna come ashore somewhere! According to reports, a lot of it is headed our way! Who is gonna pick up the tab on the cleanup? What about the long term impacts to our sea life?"

"Blaine, this first $100 million is just the beginning. It's a start. These British assholes are gonna be on the hook for a long, long time. And as far as cleanup, according to the governor, they are gonna set up grants for boom and oil retrieval and cleanup for the entire coastal area, from Fairhope all the way to Perdido Key. It's all coming down the pike, my boy, just give it some time. Be patient."

The senator lined up, squared his shoulders perpendicular once again and shot. Like the others, this one went far, but it sliced hard to the right after a couple hundred yards.

"Did you get the legislation drafted for the state park?" the senator asked.

Blaine, an attorney, reached down into a brief case at his side and retrieved a long brown legal folder with strap bindings.

"It's all here." He stood and handed it to the senator. Slip briefly looked at the bound package and placed it on the nearby table holding his nearly empty drink.

"Excellent. I will get it filed immediately and we will start pushing it through this week," said the senator. "Also, I'll fill the governor in on the good job you did here. We appreciate it."

The senator took a long pull of the remaining light brown liquid in the glass, finishing it off. He returned the melting ice to the table. He placed another ball on the tee. He squared up and swung hard. This time the ball hooked terribly.

"God dammit!" he screamed.

Blaine jumped uncomfortably in his seat at the outburst.

Slip spun completely around and faced him.

"When you heading back up to Montgomery?" asked the smiling senator, in a hushed tone.

8

A clean-shaved and combed Joe Giddeon, wearing a plush dark blue robe over pajamas and matching slippers, stood in front of the gas stove in his kitchen. On one burner was a frying pan with three eggs sunny side up, sizzling bacon strips and two sausage patties the size of hockey pucks. Fluffy homemade biscuits baked in the oven, filling the entire house with a wonderful, nourishing aroma. A pot of Quaker oatmeal and another of grits occupied two other burners. The kitchen reeked citrus, as Joe had just squeezed a dozen navel oranges. The stainless steel coffee maker percolated bold Community Coffee.

A few feet away, seated at Joe's dining room table, was John Penn, his longtime attorney. Badly balding and wearing thick glasses, he wore an out-of-style dress shirt and a velour coat without a tie. John was not in a good mood. Joe insisted he meet him on a Saturday, at Joe's house on Old River, instead of regular business hours during the week, in downtown Pensacola, thirty minutes away. It was one of many odd concessions that came with the job of legally representing Joe Gideon.

"Would you like oatmeal or grits, bacon or sausage?" Joe asked, his back to the counselor.

"I'll take grits and bacon," he answered. "Joe, I don't have a lot of time. Let's talk."

A female voice emanated from Joe's bedroom.

"Joe where are the extra vacuum cleaner bags?"

"I think they are somewhere in there," Joe answered in a higher tone.

He placed a full breakfast plate and a glass of orange juice in front of John Penn and walked out of sight into the bedroom, where his former girlfriend and current assistant, Connie Blum, was, as usual, trying to clean up his fraternity house mess. Connie also handled Joe's finances, and she knew better than anyone how dire his money situation was. She pretty much knew everything about him.

"Forget about the vacuuming, for now. John is here and I need you to sit in on this." Joe softly stated.

She followed him back into the dining area, where John sat. She sat to his left, at the end of the table, and to Joe's right.

"John, you remember Connie, my assistant, don't you?"

"Good morning, Connie," he blandly stated, remembering her as Joe's girlfriend.

"Connie, this is John Penn, my bankruptcy attorney."

"Good morning," she said, remembering John as one of the few pleasant attorneys.

Joe served Connie a plate and then poured coffee for everyone, before sitting down to join them. John didn't waste time. He ate his egg, took a bite of his biscuit and savored the coffee, before speaking.

"Joe, I am sending a press release to the *Pensacola News Journal* on Monday morning. It will be short. It will announce your bankruptcy filing, stating your many liabilities in excess of assets and appreciable income and properties, as well as your intention to save the Flora-Bama by paying all bad debts associated with the Flora-Bama Corporation, as well as dealing with the ongoing issue of back taxes, both state and federal, moving forward."

Joe slowly chewed the end of a biscuit. He removed the makeshift paper towel bib he'd made for himself and flipped the biscuit onto the plate.

"Well, that's it," Joe stated. "It's out there, now. Everyone will know my business."

"You agreed that we should issue the release before appearing in bankruptcy court," Penn answered, matter-of-factly.

"I know, John, I know," Joe answered.

"I also added in the release that you will be losing to the lending institutions a number of your financed properties, including your home—this place."

"Terrific. I am a failure." Joe stated. He pushed his plate away and turned in his chair. He looked outside, past his swimming pool and hot tub, to Old River and across it, to Ono Island, and off far into the distance, beyond Perdido Bay, below a cloudless, pale blue sky.

Penn continued, "Of course, you still have the principal issue of the $8 million loan collateralized by the Flora-Bama parking lot. It must be paid off. If not, the bank can come after the Flora-Bama. It could be theirs if you don't pay that debt."

Connie sat in silence. She saw all of this coming years ago, when Joe, against her repeated warnings, decided to put so many of his financial eggs in the real estate basket. For months and even years, it was her who wrote the debt service checks to the banks for the many huge commercial and residential real estate deals he cut. She begged him to let her buy in cash and manage small rent houses with his money, but to no avail. The day she dreaded and knew was coming was finally upon them. She was scared for Joe; she knew it was a nightmare for him in so many ways. She fought back tears.

"I need a White Knight," Joe said. "Somebody who can bail me out of this mess and be a partner with me moving forward."

*****

At around ten that same morning, Lucy decided to head to Michelle's parents' place on nearby Ono Island so she could shower and change while Johnny caught up with his stuff back at his truck, which was parked by Jake's camper. After walking Lucy to her vehicle and kissing her goodbye, he paced a few hundred feet to his truck, right past the silver, egg-shaped compartment with wheels Jake called home. He opened the truck door, grabbed a change of clothes and a towel, and hit the outdoor shower Jake showed him the day before. Upon returning to his vehicle, he saw Jake and Michelle embraced outside the tiny camper door.

"Get a room!" Johnny squawked.

The two stopped kissing and stared in his direction.

"Not everybody is rock star like you, Johnny Glass! You damn devil!" Jake answered, still clutching Michelle's tiny waist.

They all smiled.

Johnny told Jake about Sam wanting in on the band they were forming. Jake suggested Johnny invite him along to the guitar pull at Joe's river house, that Joe certainly would not mind, as most were always welcome. Johnny and Lucy and Sam and Michelle and Jake made it to Joe's house around four o'clock.

9

Unbeknownst to anyone, the guitar pull that afternoon was probably going to be the last at Joe's river pad. It would be a matter of days until bankruptcy court, and after that the house would no longer be his. He was determined to enjoy it one last time with his dearest friends.

When Johnny and Jake and the girls walked up there were already several people at the party. Some mingled on the screened in porch area. Some sunbathed. Some relaxed in the pool and still more in the bubbling hot tub.

"Jake and Johnny!" exclaimed Joe. "More victims! Thank you for coming along gentlemen…and ladies."

"Hey Joe!" Jake answered. Johnny waved behind Jake, taking in the scene.

"Put your drinks and food upstairs, get your suits on and come back and join us down here where all the fun is," Joe said, laughing and smiling while holding up his drink. He was seated inside the hot tub with three ladies in string bikinis managing beverages of their own.

They spent the rest of the available sunlight time frolicking in the pool and the hot tub, with Joe and his other friends, many of which were musicians. They made several new friends and heard many stories that afternoon. Johnny was introduced to a drummer named Preston, who was also looking for a band. They traded numbers. After the sun set and everybody had dinner and cleaned up for the most part the monumental mess that had been made, the group gathered in Joe's austere living room, forming a seated circle around the living space.

A well-tanned, well-shaved, salt and pepper haired, blue-eyed fellow with a thin moustache confidently strummed an acoustic guitar. His name was Mark Sherrill. He wore only a plain white Flora-Bama tee shirt and a bathing suit. Along with the other new faces, he had been introduced to Johnny and Lucy earlier.

"What y'all wanna hear?" he asked, slowly strumming.

"Ol' Red," said the smiling older guy next to him.

"Yeah, Ol Red," chimed another behind them.

"Okay, I'll sing Ol Red," he answered, satisfactorily.

The song, "Ol' Red," written by Sherrill, and two others, James "Bo" Bohan and Don Goodman, in the early 1990's, was originally cut by George Jones and then Kenny Rogers for separate albums, but was never released as a single until Blake Shelton did in 2002, on his self-titled debut album. Shelton calls it one of his signature songs, and certainly, one of his most requested. Like all truly great songs, it tells a fascinating story.

The song is about a convict doing time for murdering the man who was sleeping with his wife. He gets a job tending the prison dog named Ol' Red, an old bloodhound who is known for tracking escaped prisoners. So renowned is Ol' Red that in the chorus the warden dares the prisoners to attempt a run, so that Ol' Red "can have a little fun." He brags that no prisoner ever escaped on Ol' Red's watch.

The convict writes his cousin a letter. His cousin delivers a female Blue Tick hound inside the prison. The Blue Tick befriends Ol' Red and the dogs, well, do what dogs do. The convict then keeps Ol' Red separated from his new female friend for several days, making Ol' Red extremely excited to see her. The convict escapes, knowing that Ol' Red will track down the Blue Tick, instead of him. The song's final lyrics explain that the escape was successful with Red and the bitch even having puppies.

Mark tapped his foot three times and started strumming. He sang:

"Well I caught my wife with another man
And it cost me ninety nine

On a prison farm in Georgia
Close to the Florida line
Well I'd been here for two long years
I finally made the warden my friend
And so he sentenced me to a life of ease
Taking care of Ol' Red
Now Ol' Red he's the damnedest dog that I've ever seen
Got a nose that can smell a two day trail
He's a four legged tracking machine
You can consider yourself mighty lucky
To get past the gators and the quicksand beds
But all these years that I've been here
Ain't nobody got past Red
And the warden sang
Come on somebody
Why don't you run
Ol' Red's itchin' to have a little fun
Get my lantern
Get my gun
Red'll have you treed before the mornin' comes
Well I paid off the guard and I slipped out a letter
To my cousin up in Tennessee
Oh and he brought down a blue tick hound
She was pretty as she could be
Well they penned her up in the swampland
'Bout a mile just south of the gate
And I'd take Ol' Red for his evening run
I'd just drop him off and wait
And the warden sang
Come on somebody
Why don't you run
Ol' Red's itchin' to have a little fun
Get my lantern
Get my gun
Red'll have you treed before the mornin' comes
Now Ol' Red got real used to seeing
His lady every night

And so I kept him away for three or four days
And waited till the time got right
Well I made my run with the evenin' sun
And I smiled when I heard 'em turn Red out
'Cause I was headed north to Tennessee
And Ol' Red was headed south
And the warden sang
Come on somebody
Why don't you run
Ol' Red's itchin' to have a little fun
Get my lantern
Get my gun
Red'll have you treed before the mornin' comes
Now there's red haired blue ticks all in the South
Love got me in here and love got me out."

When he was done, and the last chord had been strummed, a solitary silent moment preceded a serious round of prolonged applause. Everyone clapped and several whistled.

"What a great song," said the sandy-haired woman seated twice over to his right, a non-assuming gal in her forties. She wore cutoff blue jeans and a cotton shirt—and was barefoot, like everyone else.

"Thank you," said Mark, wearing a wide smile.

He passed the acoustic guitar to the conspicuous fellow sitting to his right, Bo Roberts. Roberts, with an unlit cigarette behind his ear, wore cutoff blue jeans and a tee shirt. His graying hair was a mess and his unshaven face was sunburned to a peel. An experienced Nashville songwriter and performer, even half drunk, Bo Roberts could still play the guitar and sing with anyone, as he had his own style and presence, and he was always as entertaining as he was fun to be around.

"Y'all wanna hear "Ten With a Two?" he implored.

A resounding "Yeah" echoed throughout the room, followed by anticipating silence. The song suggested by the group was another popular chart hit. Originally cut by Willie Nelson, it was Kenny Chesney who later made it more commonplace. The punch line of the song is its undeniable title. "Last night I came home at two with a ten, and I woke up at ten with a two. I never went to bed with an ugly woman but I sure woke up with a few."

Bo sang his song and everyone applauded, just as before.

"That's an all-timer right there," said Jake, commenting afterward on the song.

Johnny and Lucy just sat next to each other and took it all in. They were in awe of the talent around them. Neither had seen that many prominent songwriters perform in person before.

Bo handed the guitar to the woman on his right, Beverly Jo Scott, the Mobile, Alabama native and singer songwriter who found mega fame in France and Belgium. She was in town for a rare, coveted visit. She too had been earlier introduced to Johnny and Lucy.

Beverly Jo sang a rendition of "Ol' Alabam'" that brought tears to Lucy's face. There were others who cried. The emotion Beverly Joe wielded was powerful—like dynamite, Johnny thought, as she truly grabbed his heart with her lovely, haunting voice, lyrics and unmatched tenor.

When she was done everyone applauded like before. Afterward there was discussion. Several commented on how uniquely Alabama the song is, and how well it portrays the Southern gulf coast state, as well as how wonderful Beverly Jo was in presenting her rendition. She was fabulous.

Jake took the guitar next. He strummed it and asked the group.

"How about I do a Keith Whitley song?"

"Oh yes," Joe exclaimed. "I liked him a lot."

"Alright then. This one, this song, they found among Keith Whitley's possessions after he drank himself to death. He recorded it on a cassette tape. He wrote it for his love, Lorrie Morgan." Jake answered. It's called, "Tell Lorrie I love her."

Jake sang the beautiful, emotional song; one laden with symbolism and imagery, with great conviction. Johnny sensed a visceral connection, and he felt like Jake was singing the song thinking of Ella, the one who got away.

After Jake sang and everyone applauded, Johnny got his

chance to sing. He sang another Mickey Newbury song, "Just Dropped In," and like his performance at the Silver Moon, it was extremely well-received. During and after the performance, Lucy was smitten. She was so proud of Johnny; he did so well. He looked and sounded like the pros who sang before him, and she thought he was notably better than Jake.

The first to comment on Johnny's performance was Beverly Jo. "You are special. That was possibly the best cover of Mickey Newbury I've seen."

"Why thank you M'am."

"I'll be looking out for you," she added, shaking her finger at him.

Johnny blushed.

After the guitar pull was over, around nine or so, the party broke up and Joe thanked everyone for coming. Some left for the Flora-Bama, as it was Saturday night. Jake looked to Johnny.

"What are you doing tonight, big spender?" Jake asked.

Johnny looked to Lucy. She held his hand and smiled.

"I think we're gonna get a bottle of wine and listen to the gulf." Johnny answered. "We're gonna head back to the penthouse."

Jake laughed. "It's already going to your head! You're already a superstar!"

Johnny blushed. "Whatever, Jake! What are y'all gonna do?"

"I've got a gig at the Bama, tonight. We start at ten."

***

Curiosity got the best of them and Johnny and Lucy opted to go to the Flora-Bama—at least for a little while, to hear Jake and his band. They enjoyed the first set of Jake and Hung Jury's 10:00 p.m. Bama Dome performance. At the break, as the place was really starting to get obnoxiously crowded, they told Michelle and Jake goodbye.

"Are we gonna see y'all at service tomorrow morning?" Jake asked.

"Service?" Johnny answered.

"Yeah, Worship on the Water, outside underneath the tents, tomorrow at 10:00 a.m. You coming?"

"You mean Church?" Johnny asked.

"Yes, we call it service," Jake added.

"We can go if you want, Johnny. I have been with Michelle before," Lucy commented. "There's music."

"I guess so, then. We'll see you here a little before ten." Johnny said.

Johnny and Lucy went back up to the penthouse condo. They talked briefly in the living room with Sam, who was still up and had a guitar across his lap. He was working on a song. They were both tired, so they only said hello and good night.

Lucy had earlier gathered a few things in an overnight bag. She brought it with her into the bathroom and readied for bed. Johnny slid the glass door slightly open. He removed his clothes, except for his underwear, and jumped under the covers of the huge, comfortable bed. Supine, with his arms over his head, he relaxed and listened to the undulations of the surf down below.

Lucy, wearing pajamas, opened the bathroom door and flipped the light off. She crept into bed with Johnny and found the warmth of his closeness. They passionately kissed.

"Remember now Johnny," she said.

"What's that?" he asked, in between breaths.

"We're going to service tomorrow. We have to behave ourselves," she insisted.

"I'm Catholic. We can just ask for forgiveness."

10

Johnny and Lucy walked over to the Flora-Bama around 9:55 a.m. They went out back under the tent, and to their surprise, there was standing room only. Johnny made eye contact with Jake, who was up front on stage at the dais. Jake waved them over and pointed in front where Michelle sat waiting with two empty chairs for them. They made their way and sat down.

Jake's band behind him, made up of volunteer musicians, cranked up. To get things started, Jake sang "Peace in the Valley" the way Elvis did, followed by "Amazing Grace." Jake's voice was clearer than it had ever been, Johnny thought, and he was impressed with the way the band arranged the music for him. He could tell they had practiced.

After the introductory songs, everyone sat and Jake welcomed the sizable congregation. He went into his message for the day, which was as simple as it was direct—that all of us are God's children—and that he didn't make trash. To the contrary, Jake said that he made each of us in His own likeness, and that he has a plan for us, no matter how difficult things at times seem. He finished by promising that God loves each and every one of us—and that he wants us to be happy and to have a life full of love and contentment. Finding that happiness—"is the biggest challenge for all of us," Jake finished.

The service ended with a much faster number—a Billy Joe Shaver tune, "You Can't Beat Jesus Christ," and everyone stood and danced to it. A devout Catholic, Johnny found the entire ceremony fascinating. When it was over, he walked up to Jake, who was busy shaking hands. After a minute or two he pulled him aside.

"Jake!" he said.

"Yes brother?" he answered.

"Well—which is it?"

"Which is what?" he asked.

"Music, or Jesus?" Johnny quipped.

Jake smiled.

"It's music and Jesus, brother! Music and Jesus!"

***

After Worship on the Water Lucy gathered her things and drove nearly an hour to Fairhope to meet with her parents. She had promised her mom she would get in touch with her, but she hadn't. She called her once she got into her car, around 11:45 a.m., and let her know that she was on her way to see her and her father.

During the drive she contemplated the message during service, and what the lesson held for her, and her life.

She arrived at her parents' place on Mobile Bay at around 12:40 p.m. Her mother fixed chicken salad sandwiches and fresh-brewed iced tea with fresh cut lemon and potato chips. She greeted and kissed her mom on the cheek and grabbed one of the made sandwiches cut diagonally in half and stacked neatly into a pyramid on a silver platter. She grabbed a paper plate and a handful of potato chips and poured herself a glass of tea, before sitting down at the glass breakfast table in the kitchen situated next to the large bay windows.

"Where's Dad?" Lucy asked. Her mom cleaned the kitchen counter with a dish towel and spray gun.

"He is playing golf. We went to service together and then he went to Lakewood to meet friends."

There was a pause. Mary Whitman removed the rubber gloves and placed them on the counter.

"Did you go to service today?" She asked Lucy.

"Yes." Lucy answered.

"Where?"

"We went to Worship on the Water at the Flora-Bama under the tent this morning. It was a great service."

"You went to church at the Flora-Bama, the bar?" her mother asked in a heightened tone.

"Yes mom. There were over 800 people there this morning. They were standing everywhere because they didn't have enough seats. The preacher is really young but everybody likes him."

Mrs. Whitman was perplexed. She had not heard of such a thing. It was difficult to grasp such a ridiculous notion—of people worshiping God at a dive bar on the beach.

"Well did you manage to have a nice time this weekend?" her mother asked, having a seat across from her daughter. She wore a tight-fitting warm-up suit and brand new running shoes. Her hair was perfect. She sipped unsweetened tea with lemon and watched her daughter's every move, her every reaction.

"Yes, we did," Lucy said. "There were some good bands at the Flora-Bama. It was so packed."

Lucy's neck and face were flustered. Her mother noticed.

"I understand you spent a LOT of time at the Flora-Bama this weekend." Her mother said.

The way she emphasized LOT was clearly a red flag to Lucy. Her tone was unprecedented and she knew she was on to her.

"What do you mean?" she asked, standing her ground.

"I talked to Ms. Tammy a little while ago. She told me that she and Fred weren't out there with y'all on Friday night like you said. You lied to me young lady!"

Lucy was overcome with anxiety. Her mother continued, pointing at her.

"Also, she told me that you didn't even sleep there last night!"

Lucy shuddered.

"You have some serious explaining to do young lady!"

Mrs. Whitman, arms folded, stared at her with piercing eyes and a furrowed brow.

This was uncharted territory for Lucy. She had never challenged her parents. She swallowed hard and took a sip of tea.

"Mom, I thought Mr. Fred and Ms. Tammy were going to be out there on Friday! I didn't know they made other plans.

Michelle said they were going to be there when she invited me, because that's what she thought. We are older now…in college, we can't keep up with everything y'all do!"

Her mother listened intently. "And last night?" she pressed.

Lucy swallowed hard.

"Last night I did not make it back to Ono with Michelle and the girls. I went to an after party with one of the musicians I met, this singer-songwriter from Nashville." Lucy managed, not offering the whole truth.

"So I guess this was an 'all-night' after party?" Mom continued.

Lucy said nothing. Her head down, she stared at her neat leather sandals, tanned feet and painted cherry toenails through the transparent table.

"This is the surest way to be seen as a whore, Lucy. How do you think your father will feel when he hears that his daughter is running around and sleeping with hippy musicians at the Flora-Bama?"

Lucy was stunned. Her heart felt like it was in her stomach. She couldn't believe what she heard. Her mother had never talked to her like this. She said nothing, but felt like she was going to die in her seat. Her mom rambled.

"Not only will it embarrass him, but it's gonna break his heart—knowing that his baby girl—despite doing everything for her and giving her everything a girl could want bringing her up—still became a whore!"

Lucy lost it. She flew into an unprecedented rage. She screamed.

"I am not a whore mother! That is totally unfair! You obviously don't trust my better judgment, because I am NOT like that! I am absolutely not a whore—because I haven't slept with anyone!"

Lucy stood and the conversation quickly digressed into a shouting match. Mrs. Whitman pressed her about school.

"How many classes do you have scheduled this summer?" she asked.

"I have two classes scheduled, and one has a lab!" Lucy answered, feeling threatened.

"Good, then get busy with it! Get back to South and stay away from the beach! There is nothing out there for you, young lady. The men out there at that club are trashy with a capital T! That is NOT where you will find a decent husband! In fact, it is the LAST place you want to look! So stay away from that Godforsaken place! The Flora-Bama is full of low-lifes and it is only going to bring you misery, child, believe me!"

The shock was beginning to register with Lucy. She felt like she had fought enough. It was time to flee. She pushed her plate away, grabbed her keys and purse, and stormed out the sanitized kitchen.

"Goodbye, mother! I'm going back to school! Just where you and Dad want me!"

Lucy fled the home through the garage door, hurriedly entered her car and drove away; before her mother, who'd gone after her, could catch up. The brand new Volkswagen Beetle tires screeched and left thick black rubber marks on the pavement as she sped off. Her mother stood in the driveway, her inverted hand over her mouth, sobbing, tear rivulets running down her face.

***

Johnny headed back to the Phoenix X Penthouse in the early afternoon. As usual, Sam was seated in the bright white living room on the sectional, lightly picking a guitar, working the same melody as before. All the curtains were pulled open. Sunlight filled the large, panoramic living space with glorious white light. The majestic, royal blue of the gulf beckoned with a shimmering sheen.

An unshaved older fellow with graying curly black hair and pink tinted prescription glasses sat in a plush, cushioned chair across from Sam. He held a 16-ounce red Solo cup wrapped in a napkin. He was dark-skinned and a little thin, and looked like he had been around the block and back a few times, as he appeared tattered. His hair and clothes were an equal mess. He looked kinda' like a bum to Johnny, in his dirty, cuffed blue jeans and tee shirt; and there was really no resemblance, as far as he could tell, between the two.

"Johnny Glass!" Sam exclaimed, greeting him. He placed his guitar on the seat next to him and stood.

"What's up brother?" Sam asked. He was glad to see Johnny.

"Nothing much," Johnny answered from the edge of the living room, behind the sectional. "Who is this?" Johnny asked.

"Johnny Glass, this is my dad, "Mike Barker.""

Mike made no effort to stand. He did offer his hand up to Johnny. Johnny stepped forward and shook it.

"Nice to meet you, Sir."

Mike nodded and sipped his drink.

Sam's enthusiasm was evident.

"Dad, Johnny is the guy I just told you about, the one living up here in Joe's room. We are gonna try and start up a band, me and him and his girl, Lucy. Lucy's a singer and me and Johnny are gonna play bass and guitar. We're looking for a drummer, but we may have met a guy on Saturday who is interested—an experienced player, so we may be close to being on our way!"

"Well that sounds great. You play guitar and sing, Johnny?" Mike asked, perking up.

"Yes Sir. I write a little, too. I try anyway."

"I see," he said, shaking his head.

"I hear you have been playing a long time," Johnny asked.

"You could say that. I've been playing piano since I was six. Later I learned guitar, saxophone and harp."

"You learned to play the harp?" Johnny asked.

"Yeah. Doesn't do me much good, though, because nobody listens to it."

Johnny was intrigued. They talked and picked songs for a couple hours, sharing a few that each of them had been working on. They talked about the inherent power of story, and marveled how a good story always captures our attention. The time passed quickly, and before long, it was almost three o'clock.

"Dad has an interesting story involving his music," don't you, Pop?" Sam asked his dad.

Mike didn't answer. He gave his son a blank stare and looked away. He stood and went outside to the balcony and lit a cigarette, leaving the room without a word. Sam followed him out, closing the sliding door behind him, and began talking to him, as he lit his own smoke.

Johnny felt awkward. He could tell it was a sore subject— whatever it was. He sat silently, picking his guitar, until the two men returned and sat down where they were before.

Mike spoke without being prompted.

"In 1978, I was 21 years old. At the time, I was living in Austin, Texas, playing the regular Sixth Street haunts for a decent nickel, just enough to get by. Back then I wasn't hitting the keys and singing. I was mainly a guitar player; and I was really good, too. But, being young like I was, I was also brash, and unfortunately, really stupid.

"A buddy of mine I knew from the music and party scene there asked me if I wanted to make what he called 'easy money.' I couldn't resist. I ate a lot of beanie weenies at the time, so I said yes. He said that I could make $30,000 for transporting a suit case of cocaine and heroin to Morocco, through the airports. He said that it had been done countless times by him and his friends, and that it was really no big deal. Keep in mind, now, that this was long before the TSA was ever conceived.

"So, like a dumbass, I went ahead and signed up for the deal. They gave me $10,000 in cash up front and said that they would give me another $20,000 after delivery, when I got back home. The stuff, a full kilo of coke, and several grams of black tar heroin, was neatly packed under the liner on both sides of the suitcase, which had been meticulously unthreaded and resewn to hide their handiwork. I was impressed. It looked and felt like a regular Samsonite suitcase.

"I made it through Houston and flew into Atlanta where I switched planes without a hitch. From there we flew into Morocco. At the airport I got nabbed in what I later learned was simply a random contraband search. Unfortunately for me, I was the unlucky lottery winner that day—and to make matters worse—there was a drug dog. Of course, the dog did its job.

The liners of the suitcase were ripped open by his handlers, the drugs were found and within a matter of hours I found myself sitting bound and cuffed before a Moroccan magistrate, trying to fathom spending forty years in a Moroccan jail, which was what I was told I was facing for smuggling illegal drugs."

Johnny listened intently. He swallowed hard and took a sip of water.

Mike continued.

"I had no legal representation, no one to call, nowhere to turn. It was a bleak situation. The jail they put me in was pretty bad. It was overcrowded and the food was horrid. I lost a good bit of weight. I slept on the floor and in general, it was hell.

"After a couple of months I was visited by a representative of the U.S. Embassy. The guy told me there was little that he could do outside of begging for a reduced sentence, but he said it was extremely political. I gave him my parents' contact information and he phoned them and told them of my situation. After that I started getting letters, but it was of course, still hell.

"I was there for about six months, trying my best to survive, to keep my head and wits about me in a difficult situation, when one day one of the guards came to work with an acoustic guitar. The guard, who got the guitar as a birthday gift, did not know how to play, but he wanted to. I told him that if he gave me the guitar, I would entertain him and everyone else, for hours. He didn't believe me. He called me "The Lying American."

"It took me a while but after three or four days I finally was able to persuade the guard to let me play the guitar for him. When I did, everyone on the cell block perked up, because we never had any music. And, I did what I promised. I played for hours. Every day after that the same guard brought his guitar, and I would play for his entire shift. Everyone loved it, especially me, as it gave me something I loved to do to help pass the time. In prison, that's really important."

"So what happened? How did you get out of prison?" Johnny asked.

"I'm getting to that," he answered, with a smile.

"The prison guard who owned the guitar didn't show up

one day for work. He missed a day. The next day he came to work, as usual; but he didn't bring his guitar. I asked him where it was and he said he didn't bring it, and that I needed to come with him. Outside of procedure, he removed me from my cell. I was scared. I thought I had done something wrong. I didn't know what was going to happen to me.

"The guard, along with other much bigger guards, took me by military truck to a big palace. We had to drive through a heavily fortified gate at the front entrance. We were allowed through and I was led into this huge, lavish space, which appeared to be a castle. We came to a large opening that led to what looked almost like an altar inside of a cavernous room with all sorts of lavish accoutrements and decor. At the top of a flight of about twenty steps was the Moroccan Prince, seated on a throne, just like you see in the movies. He had sent for me."

"As it turned out, the guard with the guitar was the youngest brother of the favorite young wife of the Prince of Morocco! The guard told his sister about this American who could so wonderfully play the guitar, and how well he entertained everyone with his magnificent playing. She eventually mentioned it to her husband. His curiosity was piqued. The Prince was about 35. He was older than me, but still young. He wore extravagant, silky looking robes and a magnificent gold turban adorned with jewels."

They led me before him and made me kneel. I couldn't look at him until he asked me to. One of the guards pushed my head down so I would not prematurely look at him. Once the Prince asked to speak to me, he pulled my head back up—and the Prince addressed me.

"'Lowly American—you will play for me!" the Prince stated. "If I like your music, I will release you. If I do not, you will die on Moroccan soil!"

"They handed me the guard's guitar, and of course, I did play for the prince. I played better than you could ever imagine, too. Knowing I had to play perfectly for my freedom motivated me something awful—because I nailed it. I played him everything great I could think of...you name it. I was there for over three hours! He absolutely loved it. He even filmed and recorded a large part of it with a camera and microphone, after he realized he liked it. And to his credit, the next day I was on a plane bound for Atlanta. But I spent the last night there in the castle, and not in that prison cell, which was really nice."

"Unreal!" Johnny answered.

"That's the unbelievable power of music!" Mike answered.

"Man, I can't even begin tell you how good it felt to leave that palace unshackled, a free man. True to his word, the Prince's guards brought me straight to the airport and I was put on the first flight out to the states. When you lose your freedom, you have nothing left. I felt born again and it really was absolutely amazing. It completely changed my life. I have taken little for granted since."

Johnny noticed a change in Mike's countenance. He seemed much different to him now. He really respected the man. There was much more to him than what he saw. He felt bad for judging Mike the way he did initially.

There was a knock on the condo door.

"I wonder who that is?" Sam asked. He walked to the door and opened it.

Lucy Whitman stood in the doorway, her jet black hair up in a bob and an overnight bag draped over her shoulder.

"Is Johnny here?" She asked.

11

L ucy explained to Johnny what happened with her mom back in Fairhope. She told him that she couldn't bear to go back to Mobile, to the University of South Alabama, for summer school.

"I called and cancelled my classes and got a full refund," she said. "I want to take the summer off and concentrate on music, on our band..." she said.

Johnny was of course ecstatic, as he would get to see her more. He clasped her hand in his.

"And on us," she finished.

Johnny smiled and hugged her tight for several long seconds, and kissed her.

Johnny, Lucy and Sam phoned the drummer interested in joining their band. They asked him to meet them at "the Bama" later that afternoon so that they could talk business. The three were raring to go. They wanted to form the band and start practicing as soon as possible.

The three strolled over to the Flora-Bama around four on Sunday afternoon. There was a reggae band, Rhythm Intervention, playing on the deck outside, and they were really grooving. They sat on one of the picnic tables and listened while they waited for the guy they hoped would be their drummer.

Preston Stanfill was an experienced drummer who, like Johnny, moved from Nashville to Perdido Key to find work. He was older than Sam, in his late thirties, but he looked much younger than his age, obviously the result of good genetics, because Preston lived life to the fullest. He was always up for a good time. But, like the others, he was serious about his craft; and of course, he needed the work.

Preston showed up at four and they ordered a round of light beers. The relaxing beat of the reggae band served as a great meeting backdrop. After brief introductions the group discussed the prospect of forming their own band. They agreed that they wanted to play classic and modern American country; and that they would pick songs that would accentuate both Johnny and Lucy's singing talents. They also agreed that having two voices would be an asset, since the Flora-Bama lacked a band that had both a male and a female singer.

After a few minutes it was pretty much understood that Preston would be their drummer. He had played in many bands, could read music, and knew a ton of songs. About fifteen minutes into the conversation, Johnny spoke for the group.

"Well, is everyone in agreement that we should form this band? If there is anyone who objects, speak now, or forever hold your tongue."

Everyone laughed and shook hands, solidifying the deal. The next question was obvious.

"What will we call ourselves?" asked Sam.

There was a moment of silence while everyone pondered. Sam overheard a group of young surfers at the picnic table next to them. They had spent the early afternoon riding unseasonably large waves caused by a fast rising tide and a stiff south wind.

"Those waves were bitchin'!" one of the uber-tanned, athletic bleach blonds emphatically stated, raising his beer in the air for emphasis.

"Yeah, but so was the undertow! It actually scared me a couple times!" answered another, before taking a swallow of his cold beer.

"What about Undertow?" Sam asked the group. "Like a riptide, you know?"

"I like Riptide even better," said Lucy, being raised an Alabama Crimson Tide fan.

"I do too," agreed Johnny.

"I dig it," said Preston. "Riptide!" he echoed.

"Let's go with it!" Sam said.

"Riptide it is then," Johnny stated. He raised his Coors Lite can in a toast.

"To Riptide's roaring success!" Johnny confidently stated.

Their four aluminum beer cans touched in unison, symbolizing a union moving forward. They finished their beers and excitedly talked about practicing, and when they might start playing.

"Let's go back up to the penthouse and get started on a song list!" Sam suggested.

They agreed and headed out.

***

On Monday morning Pensacola and Perdido Key residents awoke to a startling *Pensacola News Journal* front page headline: "Owner of Iconic bar in the red." The first line of the front and center featured article read, "The owner of the Flora-Bama Lounge on Perdido Key has filed for personal bankruptcy, but expects the iconic haunt to survive."

Sam's dad, Mike, was up early that morning at Waffle House, having his usual coffee and eggs, when he picked up the paper and read the detailed story that revealed Joe's financial challenges in a most public way. It stated Joe's impending day in United States bankruptcy court, listing more than $40 million in unpaid debts resulting from his many varied real estate investments in condos and other developments gone bad. The article stated that Joe's listed assets were around $11 million, and that he would likely have to give them back to the banks that financed them.

Joe's attorney, John Penn, clarified in the news article that Joe's assets were actually much more when the value of his Flora-Bama stock was taken into consideration. However, the problem was placing an accurate value on that stock, as the popular business was mainly a cash one, and had never been fully appraised for such an impromptu stock sale.

"It's a question of getting experts to look into them (the stock) and value them. The plan we would propose will provide for him (Joe) retaining his interest in Flora-Bama and paying his creditors out of income from it," Penn added.

Johnny and Lucy and Sam were up and back working on a song list when Mike returned to the penthouse with the somber news. Everyone was of course shocked, particularly Johnny. He thought Joe would be the last to have money problems. He wondered what this meant for him, and whether or not he would be able to really start his new dream job of playing at the World-Famous Flora-Bama, now that its future was up in the air. It scared him; returning ringing doubts and fears of failure that for so long had been his traveling companions.

The utter shock and dismay at the sobering news resonated throughout Pleasure Island and across the entire gulf coast region. Long-time fans of the Flora-Bama deluged the bar with calls, wanting to know if they could help in some way. Some even suggested a benefit concert to help Joe, just like the one that had been done for Willie Nelson during his financial troubles. The thought of losing the Flora-Bama made many of the regulars inconsolable, while most of them were clearly in denial. Everyone wondered if Joe would be able to find the white knight he spoke of—that person or persons who could provide the capital necessary to pay his bad debts—so he could save the beloved Flora-Bama.

The news of Joe's bankruptcy on the front page of the newspaper stunned everyone; but the news of the massive oil flow from the BP oil spill 50 miles South of the Mississippi River slowly making its insidious way to the pristine Alabama coastline, was equally, if not more stunning, and harrowing for residents of Perdido Key. Appearing on the same front page, just below the featured story of Joe's money problems was a piece about the ominous, gigantic, black blob of oil deliberately making its way to Alabama's sugar-white beaches. According to the segment, the oil would be there within a week. This meant that the summer season could be completely lost to an unthinkable, manmade disaster.

Everyone who worked and played on the island was in a terribly somber mood, as the summer was usually a make or break time. Most island workers collected unemployment during the offseason and worked doubles during the season. The reality was that an unmitigated financial disaster loomed just as large as the impending environmental nightmare unfolding on the gulf coast. The area faced total devastation.

As can be expected, Joe laid low for a couple days. He refused to leave his house on Monday, never removing his pajamas, and dreading the thought of facing the world in lieu of the front page article embarrassing him in what he felt was the worst way possible. It was bad enough losing his wealth, but losing his business reputation, and quite possibly his Magnum Opus, the Flora-Bama, was physically debilitating. By Wednesday, though, he was back to his old self after soul-searching. He was determined to save his place, and ultimately, his reputation.

12

Aweek passed. Johnny and Lucy and Sam and Preston practiced nearly all day, every day that first week together, amassing a play list. It wasn't until Monday of the second week that they found out that they would be playing the regular 9:00 p.m. gig under the tent on Wednesday nights. It was to be expected, as the older bands that had been playing there for years had already locked up the busier weekend nights of Thursday, Friday and Saturday. Nevertheless, for Riptide it was a good start. Sam also got them a Thursday night gig at The Reef, a popular hot spot down the beach—with another in the works, so things were definitely looking up, despite the turmoil associated with the BP oil spill and Joe's unexpected bankruptcy.

Lucy did not speak to her mother or father after the Sunday episode. She had purposefully avoided her mother's repeated phone calls and texts. She was firm in her decisions that she wasn't going back to South for summer school, and that she was going to give herself the summer to see how things went with the band, and of course, Johnny.

She and Johnny spent every waking and slumber filled moment together and naturally grew closer. They soon became a couple in every way. Although they had known each other only for a few days, the romance between them was real; and they adored each other. Both admitted that they had never felt that way about anyone in their young lives. Further, each worked hard to help the other become better at their craft through affirmation, positive reinforcement and honest criticism, when needed. They were good for one another, as each brought out the best in the other.

Lucy was not accomplished in playing an instrument, but her voice was a tremendous asset to the group. Johnny and the guys were really impressed with her range and tone; it was just a matter of getting comfortable working together, and letting her learn the words to the songs they already knew how to play. Johnny tried to encourage Lucy and make her feel needed and appreciated as much as he could, because he knew she felt somewhat inadequate being only a singer, and not having much experience playing live gigs. In all though, the band came together quickly, as the three guys were basically pros, having played for so long. Also, Lucy worked hard, and in short time she was more than pulling her weight.

Their first show at the Flora-Bama was fairly well attended. However, it was mostly regulars—loyal locals who paid most of the overhead at the Flora-Bama with their devout patronage. The oil spill and the resulting bad press had taken a noticeable toll on the tourist trade.

Unfortunately, on Monday, a week after Joe's bankruptcy announcement, the *Associated Press* ran a story about the oil and tar balls beginning to wash up on the Alabama and Florida panhandle coastlines. The AP sent a reporter to the Flora-Bama to cover the spill's many harmful effects. The reporter spoke to more than one of the fabled beach bar's workers, asking each about the oil spill and its apparent impact on the area. One of the bartenders gave the reporter exactly what he was looking for—a particularly juicy quote about the awful smell of the oil in the gulf. The bartender, after the fact, claimed he was misquoted. The huge backlash from locals was predictably ire-filled.

Joe was terribly upset that one of his workers had even entertained what he considered off-the-record as a "classless reporter." However, he was equally if not more upset with the so-called journalist for writing the article the way that he did. It read:

"Perdido Key, a Florida barrier island between Pensacola and the State of Alabama lined with sugar-white sand and studded with condominiums, could be the first place affected by the

BP oil spill. "You could smell it, a real heavy petroleum base," said the bartender. "It's sad because I grew up out here. I went to the beach all the time as a kid, and as an adult I probably go just as much. A lot of people are watching and crying right now."

Since it was an AP story, many daily newspapers across the country picked up the piece, and just like that, the damage was done. Most vacation goers with room reservations in Perdido Key and Gulf Shores cancelled them and made plans for other, less tumultuous, beach destinations, like in South Carolina and across the rest of the Atlantic Seaboard. Within a few days of the damaging article, it was apparent by the ever-dwindling sales receipts that the summer was going to be a bust. It was tough to stomach, but everyone who worked on the coast was going to suffer as a result of the oil spill, which really was not nearly as bad as the media described.

While there were certainly tar balls and oil washing up on the nearby beaches, BP cleanup workers toiled daily at the water's edge and in the surrounding waters, soaking up the spill, and therefore the beaches day-to-day looked pretty much the same as they did before the onslaught. Nevertheless, the negative press and subsequent fallout was real, as most of the condos on the beach ran at less than fifty percent of their normal occupancy for the beginning of the summer season.

Amidst this uncanny confluence of financial and environmental disasters was the birth of a debacle of a different kind — a political one.

Two days after the negative AP story ran, on the second page of the Mobile *Press-Register*, buried underneath a human interest story about a 90-year old Alabama graduate who had attended every Crimson Tide football game for the last fifty years, was a story detailing the passage of the enabling legislation for the building of a Gulf State Park and Convention Center in Gulf Shores with $100 million in BP reparation money. The article, which was short on actual details, said that the legislation was sponsored by Senator Whitman of Fairhope and provided a quote from the governor.

"Alabama doesn't have a five-star hotel and convention center. We need one to be competitive with Louisiana, Mississippi and Florida." The article also said that the $100 million from BP had already been received by the State of Alabama, and that a groundbreaking ceremony was scheduled for Gulf Shores the following week.

13

Senator Dee "Slip" Whitman stood at the microphone on the makeshift outdoor podium under a large white wedding tent at the site of the old Gulf Shores State Park on the beach in Gulf Shores, Alabama—the one destroyed by a Cat 4 storm several years before. Dressed in baggy Wrangler blue jean overalls, scuffed steel-toe work boots, a dingy, collared white work shirt and a navy baseball cap with gold scrambled eggs on the bill and matching, conspicuous gold lettering—W-T-F, representing "Whitman Tractor & Farms" across the front, the state senator looked every bit like a working man from Lower Alabama. Unfortunately for him, it was a bad day for acting, as he had been tabbed, as the author of the enabling legislation, to introduce the governor for the ground-breaking ceremony. He looked out of place, but was oblivious to it, as he hadn't been challenged in years and he no longer cared or was even bothered by what he considered, "the little things."

Before the ceremony began Senator Whitman mingled with the other dignitaries present, which included the Lieutenant Governor, two previous governors, two congressmen, and a slew of connected local politicians and able contractors and friends ready to help build the new multi-million dollar Gulf State Park Hotel and Conference Center. At the time he thought it was strange that he was getting so many picture requests, especially from the younger folks in attendance.

The Governor's aides got a shot with the senator, and so did the Lieutenant Governor's aide, who was a freshman at Alabama; as did the Mayor of Foley's daughters. Senator Whitman simply figured they all dug his contrived "working man" look, and wanted a shot with him—a veritable rising star in Alabama State politics, for their facebook timelines; or so he thought. In reality, the younger generation saw "WTF" as representative of "What the fuck?" a commonly used texting abbreviation. The kids thought he looked like an idiot, and they indeed wanted to share the moment of hilarity on social media with their countless friends.

When the ceremony began Senator Whitman sat all the way on the left of the platform, closest to the dais. Seated to his left were nine other dignitaries impeccably dressed in coat and tie or suit. He was introduced by one of the four Baldwin County Commissioners as the person who would introduce Alabama Governor Robert Finchley. After a brief round of applause, the senator spoke.

"Thank you, thank you. I appreciate that. I do. I really do. Thank you very, very much. I am proud to be here today. I am proud because we live in a great state. This is surely a wonderful place to live, in case you didn't notice. Just look behind you there at that pretty water—it's absolutely beautiful! We are truly lucky to be citizens of this great state, this place we call home, Alabama, the beautiful."

The crowd was phlegmatic. Senator Whitman saw this, and decided to try and perk them up.

"I am a lucky guy. I have been extremely fortunate in life. As a younger man, I was married to the fastest white woman in the State of Alabama…and she is still fast, don't get me wrong, but she is no longer the fastest."

He paused for effect. The crowd murmured. He continued.

"But as lucky as I am for that blessing in life, I feel even luckier to introduce our next presenter here on the panel, our very own governor of the great State of Alabama—a fine Christian man, a good man, an honest man, and an even finer governor—Governor Roger Finchley."

The commissioner who introduced Slip tried to quickly correct him. He spoke softly, trying not to alert the crowd.

"It's ROBERT Finchley, not Roger, senator!"

The senator quickly corrected himself, speaking louder into the mic.

"I mean Robert—Robert Finchley," he reiterated. "Governor ROBERT Finchley, everybody. Let's hear it!"

Slip turned and made room for the governor at the podium. The governor shook hands with the senator, assumed the large space he vacated and took the microphone. A smattering of placating applause quickly subsided. It was an awkward moment.

"Thank you, Slip, thank you so much. Slip, you are a great introducer. Has anyone ever told you that? I need to take you with me across the state so you can introduce me at every single function I attend!" the Governor quipped. There was an obsequious smattering of light laughter and faint applause from the crowd, ending in a sigh. Senator Whitman could only smile like the Cheshire Cat underneath his ridiculous hat.

After the Governor and the other dignitaries spoke about how great the new hotel and convention center was going to be for the people of Alabama, when the ceremony was over, and the media had moved in and out and gotten the footage they needed for a rushed, minute-long segment they could air on the five, six and ten o'clock news, Senator Whitman was approached by his aide, Tommy Wilson, a recent Troy University graduate and the son of one of the contractors earlier in attendance. Unlike his boss, Tommy was smartly dressed in a navy coat and red bowtie over a starched white dress shirt and pleated khaki dress pants, with shined penny loafers.

When the moment was right, Tommy grabbed the senator by the arm and gently pulled him to the side. By now, everyone was walking to their vehicles.

"What's with the outfit, Senator? What was going on here? You didn't mention this to me when we spoke earlier."

"What, this—this outfit?" he answered. "These are my overalls that I use sometimes when I work outside, that's all. I just thought I would try and look like my constituents for TV. You know, Tommy, most of the folks in Baldwin County are working people. I thought they would relate to this."

Tommy could only stare at the outdated scrambled eggs and the matching WTF on the navy baseball hat.

"Okay. I see. But what about the hat, Senator? What does it mean?"

The senator looked strangely at him.

"What?" he asked.

"The hat—the W-T-F—what does it mean? What does it stand for? I am confused."

"Whitman Tractor and Farms," replied the exasperated senator, in a deprecating tone.

"I had a handful of these printed up. Pretty sweet, huh? I'll get you one, Tommy."

Tommy placed his right palm squarely across his own face and slowly pulled it down to his chin, wiping the perspiration that had beaded on his tanned forehead and cheeks.

He lowered his voice before he spoke, almost whispering.

"Senator, W-T-F, on the Internet, and especially in phone texting, means 'What the Fuck.'"

The senator's countenance changed. He went from being confident, to slightly puzzled. He said nothing for several seconds. He pulled off the hat and looked at it, revealing a terrible hat head.

"Well, what the fuck!?" he incredulously stated, placing the hat into his front right pocket while scanning the remaining people under the tent to see who was still there, and if they were looking.

14

As it turned out, the local nightly news coverage in Mobile had no video footage of Senator Whitman, which was a huge relief to both he and his aide, Tommy Wilson. However, exactly like the Senator earlier envisioned, the photos of him with the young aides of the Governor and Lieutenant Governor were already on facebook by the time the Senator took the stage to introduce the Governor. An hour later, by the time the ceremony was ending, the pictures had been shared over a hundred times each, to an audience of over 80,000 people. In only minutes, it had gone viral. Across the State of Alabama, media outlets and radio and TV scrambled their management, wondering what they should do—if they should cover it. Everybody genuinely thought, "What the fuck?"

By the following day the damaging image of Senator Whitman had made national websites like *Deadspin.com, Upworthy. com, Salon.com* and even the *Huffington Post*. Comments under the online segments depicting the senator were harsh; and he quickly became the backwoods poster boy for Alabama Politics. It was a distinction he loathed, as he hated the many jokes via email coming from his colleagues in Montgomery and even more—the humbling embarrassment of it all. Slip wasn't used to that drill, and it stung. The whole sordid affair put him in a terrible funk, as he knew he brought it all upon himself.

***

Later that afternoon, after hitting the sauna and steam room at the spa and then catching two double high balls at the Birdcage Lounge at the Grand Hotel Marriott Resort, Senator Whitman rolled in his shiny Escalade down Highway 1 for the short ride to his long, gravel-filled driveway on dusky Mobile Bay. He no longer wore the overalls he'd earlier sported at the press conference. Instead, he wore khaki pants, a madras summer dress shirt and deck shoes with no socks.

To the west, the mercurochrome sphere met the steely horizon below a cloudless, star-studded cobalt sky. It was the end of a difficult day for the senator. He had really tripped up. It was his own fault, though; he knew well he had no one else to blame. Nevertheless, he was not looking forward to the ridicule that awaited him back in Montgomery; and that burden hung over him like a sharpened Sword of Damocles.

The senator made his way into the house and went straight to the loaded wet bar in the living room and turned on the overhead light so he could operate. The commotion alerted his wife, Mary, who was reading on the back porch with one of the dogs. She walked back into the house.

"I thought I heard someone," Mary said.

Slip stood at the wet bar, his back to his wife. He placed two perfect ice cubes from the ice maker into a clear crystal high ball glass. He took a fifth of Maker's Mark whiskey and poured liberally, quickly filling it to two fingers. He grabbed the glass and turned to Mary.

"How was your day?" she asked, walking up to him. She opened her arms for a hug but he didn't flinch. She could tell something was definitely wrong. Slip brushed off her attempt to hug him. He sat down on the plush, pillow-filled couch and sipped hard on his drink. At first, he said nothing.

"Slip! What happened?"

"I had a shitty day is all!" he bellowed. He didn't want to talk about it. He knew she was going to find out, although neither of them was really even on facebook. However, he knew she would hear it from her gossiping friends. It was just a matter of time.

"Any particular reason why your day was so shitty?" she asked, trying to be funny.

"I don't want to talk about it!" he insisted. In a single pull, he finished his drink.

"Mary, make me another, please." He begged.

She obliged. Moments later she brought him another, without saying a word. By then, the third caramel colored elixir had begun making its certain way into his vast bloodstream. With the help of the previous two, it calmed him significantly.

Mary, who had been silently worried about Lucy the past several days, started rubbing her husband's broad shoulders as she stood behind him seated on the sofa. He had been so busy lately. She wanted to talk to him about her, but wondered if it was the right time.

"Just relax, Slip," she insisted. She rubbed some more and coupled with the good booze, it felt great to him. He sipped his fourth drink. After a couple minutes of relaxing massage, he spoke.

"What's going on with Lucy? Is she in summer school? She has been awful quiet," he said with closed eyes. Mary kneaded his shoulders with her aching fingers. She realized that now was the time to talk about it.

"I don't know. I haven't spoken to her in several days," she answered, her tone noticeably lowered, like something was certainly wrong.

Slip noticed. "What's going on?" he asked. "Is she okay?"

"I'm not sure," Mary said.

"What do you mean 'you're not sure?'" he asked. "What's going on?"

She thought hard about what she said next. She didn't know how he'd take the news. She stopped rubbing. She turned and began making a cocktail of her own—a vodka tonic.

"I'm afraid to tell you. You are already in a bad mood," she answered, sipping on her drink.

"Mary, come sit down here and tell me!" he insisted, turning to her. His face became red, his brow furrowed.

She sat next to him.

"I wanted to tell you about this earlier but you've been running the roads to Montgomery and back and it's just so hard to keep up with you, you know."

Skip intently listened.

"Last weekend Lucy said she was staying at the Carter's place out on Ono. She said that Fred and Tammy were gonna be out there, so I said no big deal, have fun, right. Well, she said that she would call me Sunday and come by before heading back to Mobile. You were playing golf that afternoon."

He nodded in affirmation.

She sipped her drink. Slip listened.

"Well, I spoke to Tammy on Sunday, after lunch. She said that she and Fred were not out there at their house on Friday night and that on Saturday she stayed up late for all the girls and Lucy wasn't with them when they came in after 2:00 a.m.; but that she came by and got her things on Sunday after lunch."

She paused. Skip stared at his feet. He was no longer looking at her.

"I confronted her when she got here that Sunday afternoon. She knew she was caught. She told me that she was with some musician at the Flora-Bama, and that she went home with him on Saturday night, instead of going back to Fred and Tammy's."

Slip was crushed. The thought of his daughter sleeping with some lowlife, tattooed, mangy redneck musician on the Alabama-Florida line made him cringe. He'd had an unbelievably bad day, but this bit of news ruined it for him. This was the kind of thing—that if it got out, could hurt his reputation. It could be used against him, as Alabama was full of family-value driven religious zealots. He said nothing. Mary could tell that he was hurt. She still knew nothing about the press conference debacle. She was clueless.

She continued.

"I told her that those men out there on that island were not good for her and that she was never gonna meet a husband out at the Flora-Bama!" Mary continued.

Skip finished his drink in one long pull.

"Where is she?" he asked, grimacing from the take.

"She's in Mobile at her apartment, I guess. She hasn't re-turned my texts. She said summer school started, and that she has two classes and a lab."

"So she never went back to Fred and Tammy's?" he asked.

"Only to get her things on Sunday."

Skip looked outside, past the manicured lawn and wooden pier, to a shimmering Mobile Bay and across it, to downtown Mobile and its high rises, and beyond; off far into the distance below a twinkling charcoal sky.

He said nothing.

"What are you thinking?" Mary asked.

"I'm thinking we need to have a 'Come to Jesus' with her," he said, almost slurring.

"That's what I was thinking. We just can't have this," she said, finishing her cocktail.

"And we won't." He finished.

"Make me another please," he added, handing her the emp-ty crystal container.

15

In late May Johnny got a call from Big Daddy Joe G. saying he needed to reclaim his penthouse condo for the summer season, as he always used it to entertain guests during the peak visitation time. He asked Johnny to please clear his things out in a couple days, but that on a positive note he also had an idea for a place where he could stay after that.

Joe asked Johnny to meet him around lunchtime at the marina below the Theo Baar Bridge, about six miles east of the Flora-Bama, where the Intracoastal Canal makes its meandering way through the Perdido Bay area. Joe said that they would meet up and talk more about his idea and that he would take Johnny to lunch.

Johnny, with all his things again packed neatly into his Dodge, drove to the marina. He lowered his tailgate, sat and waited. Joe showed up about ten minutes later in his faded 1990 Red Ford pickup. Joe exited his vehicle, smiled and shook Johnny's hand.

It was much warmer now and both men wore shorts, tee shirts and sandals.

"Hey guy! How goes it?" Joe delightfully asked.

Johnny thought he was mighty chipper, and that he hardly seemed like a guy facing federal bankruptcy court.

"Pretty good, Mr. Joe. Pretty good, Sir. Just trying to keep my head above water."

Joe chuckled.

"It's funny you should say that!" he answered.

Johnny wore a puzzled look.

Joe explained.

"Follow me. I want to show you my idea regarding a possibility for your new living arrangements."

Joe turned and trudged along a cinder walkway toward the Intracoastal waterway, where several sailboats of differing length and configuration were moored by twisted white ropes against a fully equipped pier. Joe walked onto the wharf, past two sailed watercraft, before turning and boarding a third sailing vessel, a 1976, 32-foot Olander, with brand new sails and riggings. Its particularly thick, white fiberglass hull was built beyond modern specifications, making it an extremely durable and popular boat for beginning sailors. Although it was pushing forty years, it was still in remarkable shape, as the previous owners had taken good care of it. The inside was a little dingy, but it had potential, Joe thought, as a place where Johnny could lay his head at night.

Joe stood on the top of the deck, near the entry into the lower inside compartment that led to the tiny, crammed living, forward and rear birthing areas. Johnny stood on the dock, looking toward Joe, only a few feet from the vessel. It was then and there that he had a strange déjà vu, much like the one he'd had inside the Silver Moon the first time he played for Joe. It was significant; he felt it, and it registered with him.

It's not a penthouse, but I think this might work as a place for you to crash for a while," Joe said. "With a little love the cabin could be quite comfortable. I had the power turned on this morning, so all we have to do is plug in the cable and you'll have power throughout. I bought a small window unit air conditioner for you. It's in the box in the back of my truck. We'll get it in a minute. We'll set it up next to one of these smaller windows and it will cool this space off pretty quick. You'll be surprised. After that, it's just about getting your bedding area situated."

Eager to see for himself, Johnny jumped on the boat and stepped down into the cabin. There was a small rear sleeping area to the right and behind him. To his left and behind him was a small sink beside the engine cover. Ahead of him were regular sofa foam seating on both sides and wooden storage cabinets above. He walked forward. There was a tiny shower and toilet in the middle on the left. Past that space, in what was actually the front part of the vessel, was a larger, elevated sleeping platform with a hatch door above it leading to the deck. It looked comfortable, as Johnny noticed it was plenty large enough for him and Lucy.

"Kinda cozy," he thought.

Joe explained, "I got a deal on it. A young sailor from down at the Naval Base was getting transferred. He needed to sell. He was living here as recently as two days ago. Yesterday I paid the rent at the marina office for six months to keep it here. If you do choose to live here I will only ask that you take care of it, run the engine every now and then to keep it in working order and pay the power bill every month. What do you think?" Joe asked.

"I think you are right," Johnny answered, somewhat surprised. Joe was so kind to him, he couldn't believe it. "With a little love, this place could be comfortable—especially with an air conditioner," he added, wiping the sweat from his brow.

Joe and Johnny got the air conditioning unit from the back of Joe's truck and brought it to the sailboat. They found a suitable window for it, and set it up so that it worked. Like Joe said, it quickly cooled the inside of the small craft.

They wiped everything down and made a short list of other items Johnny might need, like a lamp, some paper towels and some bottled water. Johnny noted that there was a small refrigerator in the corner, the kind you find in dorm rooms, and also a small hot plate with two electric burners. The previous owner had even left an aluminum pot to cook in. The whole thing was really funky.

"But it's free," he thought, and that was what he found most appealing, as money was always a deciding issue.

Joe and Johnny got in Joe's truck and drove east over the Theo Baar Bridge to the New Orleans Creole style restaurant on the other side of the Intracoastal Canal. They parked in the shaded area underneath the bridge span in front of the restaurant, which was located next to a fresh seafood stand where many local fishermen sold their fish; so it always had the best of the day's fresh catch for their menu ingredients. It was well-known as a great place to grab a bite, and for its specialty—grilled oysters.

After they ordered and spoke to the owner about the business downturn, Joe asked Johnny how the band was coming along, and whether or not they'd had any luck getting other gigs in the area. Johnny explained that they just had their first Thursday night gig at the Reef, and that Hub Stacey's at the Point on nearby Inerarity Island was interested in having them play on Friday nights, and that if they got that job it would give them a full three day rotation of gigs.

"Once you guys play a while you may want to cut a simple CD and sell it in the tee shirt trailer out front. When you walk up to the trailer there's a CD section on the left. Check it out. If you do get one cut, let me know and we'll add it to the CD section. During the summer season they do a ton of business out there."

There was a pause.

"At least they normally do," Joe added, an obvious reference to the BP oil spill and obvious other challenges the community faced.

Joe's weakened tone and body language communicated to Johnny that he was still struggling with the unthinkable happenings in his world; and that he was trying to deal with it the best way he knew how—by being his normal, upbeat and jovial self.

"I had no idea about the oil spill when I left Nashville," Johnny said. I had heard about it, but I thought it was in Louisiana—not three states over in Florida. And of course, I knew nothing about your financial situation."

Joe said nothing. It pained him to think that his ability to give and provide for others was diminished by his money problems—problems he had brought about because of his own business decisions. Over the years many had become accustomed to his benevolence, his selflessness, his unmatched generosity. It was Joe who was always there to cushion the blow, to make things easier, for everyone; or at least anyone who asked or whom he felt needed something. That's just how he was. Not being able to do for everyone like he always had greatly affected Joe. For so long he had been the complete master of his own destiny. Now—not so much.

"Sometimes I think what is going on is like 'Global Wierding,'" Joe muttered. "The Nashville flood, the BP oil spill, my financial problems...I am wondering when the pestilence and disease will be upon us."

He and Johnny could only laugh, as it was certainly better than crying. They had no idea how prescient the statement was, however.

"Mr. Joe, I really appreciate all that you have done for me. I'm just getting started out here, and I want you to know that I'm still gonna be one of your better players. Our band is gonna' do well. We are really working hard."

"I know you are. I'm not worried about that. And you can just call me Joe."

He paused.

"Johnny, do you remember what I asked you to promise me that first night I met you?"

"Yes sir, I do."

"What was it that I asked?"

"That I have a little fun." Johnny answered.

"That's right," Joe said. He seemed relieved that Johnny had not forgotten.

"I saw that you and the multi-talented brunette—Lucy, I think her name is, are a couple. She is lovely. That's a great start, don't get me wrong, but what else have you been up to? What else have you enjoyed about living here?" he asked, probing.

Johnny thought hard. He sipped his ice water before he spoke.

"I like the water all around us. It has a calming effect. I like the weather. The sunshine is great. Didn't have it like this in Nashville."

He hesitated.

"But, really, I just like the Flora-Bama."

Joe smirked and furrowed his brow in anticipation.

"Every time I go there I meet somebody new; and I always laugh like a teenager and have fun. It's sort of like a make-believe world, really. I've tried to figure it out, to put my finger on it, Joe—this great, necessary, fun place you've created."

Joe listened intently.

"It's the exact type of place we all need as humans—a place where we can go to escape from reality, to let loose and be ourselves...where nobody cares."

Joe was flattered. The aging sage smiled and continued to listen, lifting his graying eyebrows in affirmation as Johnny spoke.

Johnny continued.

"It's the perfect place to entertain, because the audience is always eager to be entertained—and to have fun. They understand this coming in—that they are going to have a great time, and that makes all the difference. It makes my job much easier, and much more enjoyable."

Joe snacked on a buttered cracker and sipped his ice water with lemon.

"Johnny, I really appreciate that you would say those things about the Flora-Bama. I've always tried to make a place where characters from all walks of life and from anywhere could come together and enjoy good music, laughter and song. Music and song are so important. Being a songwriter, I know you can appreciate that statement. You understand as much as anyone how important the right words are and can be."

"I can appreciate that, Joe," he answered. "And I do appreciate it."

"Songs stay with us. They can define a generation and they are a true indicator and reflection of the times. They tell us how we are, and eventually, how we were." Joe added.

Johnny nodded in agreement and listened intently to Joe, whom he found so compelling.

"I love people, Johnny. One of my most memorable experiences was when I traveled to Africa and I sat inside a mud hut and talked to the indigenous people living in a remote village. To see how this primitive tribe lived was such an interesting experience.

This particular tribe in Africa practices that the actual birth day of a child is counted not from when they are born, not from when they are conceived, but from the day that the child was an original thought in its mother's mind."

Johnny was amazed. Joe continued.

"When a woman in this village decides that she will have a child, she goes off and sits under a tree, by herself, and she listens until she can hear the song of the child that wants to come into the world. After she's heard the song of this child, she comes back to the man who will be the child's father, and teaches it to him. And then, when they make love to physically conceive the child, sometimes they sing the song of the child, as a way to invite it. And then, when the mother is pregnant, the mother teaches that child's song to the midwives and the old women of the village, so that when the child is born, the old women and the people around her sing the child's song to welcome it.

"As the child grows up, the other villagers are taught the child's song. If the child falls, or hurts its knee, someone picks it up and sings its song to it. Or perhaps the child does something wonderful, or goes through puberty, then as a way of honoring this individual, the people of the village sing his or her song.

"There is one other occasion upon which the villagers sing to the child. If at any time during his or her life, the person commits a crime or aberrant social act, the individual is called to the center of the village and the people in the community form a circle around them. Then they sing their song to them. The tribe recognizes that the correction for antisocial or errant behavior is not punishment; it is love and the remembrance of identity.

"When you recognize your own song, you have no desire or need to do anything that would hurt another. And it goes this way through their life. In marriage, the songs are sung, together. And finally, when this child is lying in bed, ready to die, all the villagers know his or her song, and they sing—for the last time—the song to that person."

Johnny was blown away. He had never heard of anything so beautiful. Goosebumps riddled his forearms and his bleach-blond arm hairs stood on end.

"Is that not amazing?" Joe asked.

"Unbelievable! It really makes you think about the infinite power of song."

"I like to think that here at the Flora-Bama, we tap into that power a little bit; and that's what makes it such a special place," Joe said.

16

Lucy put off her voice lessons at her mom and dad's house for two weeks. She received a demanding text from her mother insisting that she not continue to skip the voice lessons they agreed to. She said that she had continued to pay Dr. Smith, who faithfully showed up the last two Thursdays, despite her absence. She knew if she went that she would likely have to confront both of her parents. However, she also knew she needed to see Dr. Smith. She wanted to work with him again.

When Johnny cleaned his stuff out of the penthouse condo, so did Lucy. After seeing Johnny off to his lunch date with Joe, she tossed her clothes onto the backseat of her car and drove off, deciding she would run on the beach and get some sun before she headed back to Fairhope for her 4:30 p.m. lesson and what she knew would be a difficult meeting with her parents, afterward.

While she ran barefoot along the water's shifting edge in a pair of red nylon jogging shorts and a Flora-Bama beefy tee shirt that read, "Come do it with us on the Line!" Lucy thought about her life, and what she really wanted for her future.

She loved her parents, but she also knew they were not perfect. She also knew they loved her. But beyond that, she really didn't identify with their warped world view. She couldn't stand the contrived, pretentious way they operated and how every single facet of their family lives was examined, politicized and basically distilled to the question, "What will people think?"

She didn't want to live like that. She abhorred it all...the name dropping, the grandstanding, the backslapping, backwoods, barbaric, insidious nature of it all. She knew she didn't want that for a life, and she was determined that she was not going to get trapped into it.

What Lucy did badly want was a life full of music and love...with Johnny Glass. She loved Johnny. She was not going to give him, or her new life, up, just to please her parents' jaded worldview driven by her father's blind political ambition.

"I can't live a lie like that," she thought. "I have to be true to myself."

***

Lucy made it home around 4:15. Her mom was not around. Dr. Smith showed up ten minutes later and they got started. They had a great 90 minute session. After their regular lesson material was covered, Lucy sang a couple of the new songs she had learned, with Dr. Smith playing along on the piano. Afterward they talked about the summer decision she had made to pursue singing in a band that played at the Flora-Bama. Dr. Smith was a bit surprised, but he could tell that she was serious in her pursuit, as he thoughtfully noted her continued progress and development as a singer. He told her he was happy for her, and that he could tell she was happy with the decision. Like any good teacher, he was wholly positive and he wished her well.

"I think it's a wonderful idea, Lucy," Dr. Smith said. All you need to do is to keep practicing. Keep singing. You have grown considerably in these few months we've worked together, and you continue to grow. Making music for a living, and preparing for that, is going to only elevate your abilities. You are on your way young lady! Stay focused!"

"I appreciate that, Dr. Smith. Thank you so much for your help. I have learned a lot from you," she said.

"You are most welcome young lady!" he answered.

Lucy reluctantly explained to Dr. Smith that because of her decision she would no longer be taking lessons from him at her parents' house. He understood and again wished her well.

"You were a joy to work with. I'll be looking out for you Lucy!" he assured her, walking out.

"Thanks Dr. Smith!" she answered. "Thanks for everything!"

***

Lucy's parents weren't home yet. The sun was setting so she walked down to the end of the long wooden pier. She stared off into the distance, following the bright orange marble as it made its predictable descent and disappearance below the western horizon. She inhaled the rejuvenating salt air and sang the songs she'd been working on with the group. She got through three of them before sunset, just before her father drove up in a loud, rolling spectacle. He pulled into the front driveway and honked the horn repeatedly on a brand new gleaming white Chevy Pickup truck pulling two shiny new royal blue and white Kawasaki jet skis on top of a silver trailer.

The truck came to a noisy stop in the wide front driveway that passed across the front of the house like a giant horseshoe. Lucy saw her mother following the truck in the family Escalade. Her father jumped out of the fancy 2011 truck and yelled to her, bubbling with enthusiasm.

"Lucy girl—get down here, now! I got something to show you! Come here girl! Get on over here!"

Lucy cringed. She heard him loud and clear. She turned and began walking toward the house, still concentrating on the song she had been singing. After a couple minutes she made it to the front yard where her father and mother stood admiring their newly-purchased toys. Slip had been bringing in some serious bucks lately. His many public heavy equipment rental contracts with municipalities across his district were making him an extremely wealthy man; and of course, that only fueled his greed for more money, and power.

"Whatta ya think, Lucy?" We got some brand new toys for the summer!" the senator proudly exclaimed, gesticulating wildly.

"They are nice, Dad. Really nice." Lucy managed.

"That they are, darlin'! These are actually the best kind of jet skis you can buy! You ain't gonna believe how much fun these new models are. They have brakes and they tell me they're like Harleys on the water! They certainly cost as much…heh, heh, heh."

Lucy smiled pretty. She tried her best to look grateful, but she could care less about a couple of expensive new jet skis. The song she was earlier working on was stuck firmly in her head, along with intermittent thoughts of Johnny, which had become the norm in recent days.

"I've got supper here for us," said Mrs. Whitman. She held a large brown paper sack with grease stains on the side. "Hot fried chicken, fixings and biscuits from Danny's! Let's sit down in the kitchen where we can visit," she insisted.

Mrs. Whitman made eye contact with Lucy as she walked past her into the house. Lucy saw from the dogged look that she was still aggravated, and that made her nervous. She followed her mother into the home, past the large living area to the kitchen table, where she set down the greasy brown paper sack. Her father followed her and immediately sat down and started making himself a plate of fried chicken and generous fixings, which included baked beans, mashed potatoes and dirty rice.

"You want dark or white meat, Lucy?"

"She prefers white meat, Slip." Mary answered for her daughter, eyeballing him.

"Please, just a little bit, Daddy. I'm not that hungry, really. I'm just gonna eat a bite or two, is all," she answered.

"Now, you gotta keep your strength up young lady," he said.

He heaped a large breast, a generous scoop of mashed potatoes with gravy, baked beans, cole slaw and a buttermilk biscuit onto a plate and handed it across the table to her. She thanked him and placed it before her and picked at the cole slaw while her parents made their plates. Moments later, they were seated together, the three of them. They held hands around the circular glass table and bowed their heads. Mary said the "Bless us

O' Lord" version of Grace Before Meals and the three of them ended the prayer of thanks with a resounding "Amen," spoken in unison.

The sun had set and it was now dark outside, keeping the focus on the well-lit breakfast area where the Whitmans sat with their gorgeous 19-year old daughter. Like the other intelligent, promising young women her age from Fairhope, Lucy had her sights set on bigger things than South. Her grades and ACT score were good enough to get her into the University of Alabama in Tuscaloosa as a true freshman, but her parents wouldn't allow it. They preferred that she spend the first two years closer to them, at South, and then transfer to Alabama after she completed two years. At least that was the plan, as they were intent on keeping close tabs on her. Lucy had no say in this earlier decision.

"Mom tells me you got two summer school classes?" Slip asked, while cleaning a chicken leg with his front teeth.

"Yes Sir. And a lab," she lied.

The refund money was already deposited into her checking account. She figured she had no other option but to lie. She couldn't tell them the truth; at least not at this time and certainly not in this setting. But, she could definitely tell her dad was getting ready to schmooze her. She sensed a forthcoming pitch.

"That's a heavy load for summer school, isn't it?" he inquired.

"It's not too bad," she answered.

Lucy wondered what was coming next. She dreaded having to talk about Johnny to her father. She was ashamed.

"Well, your mom and I have been talking and we think that you should drop out of summer school and enjoy yourself this summer."

Lucy was perplexed. She wasn't expecting the suggestion; but is sounded great to her. Slip continued.

"We want you to drop out of summer school, since you still can with no penalty and no withdrawal on your record. We want you to forget about Mobile for the summer and come home and stay with us, here at the new house. You and all of your friends can ride the new jet skis, lay out on the pier and just have fun here in Fairhope—all summer long. It will be great, just like old times—don't you think?"

Lucy's blood pressure spiked. She saw clearly what her father and mother had in mind, and it incensed her. She tried her best to contain her anger; but it was difficult. For the first time she saw her father in a much different light. Now that she was beginning to plan her own life and seek her own happiness, she enjoyed a different perspective. She noticed how manipulative and controlling her father was; and she was beginning to really dislike him and his tactics, and of course, the way her mother always fell perfectly in line and did everything he told her.

The fact was that Lucy didn't even have a designated bedroom at the "new house." Her mom boxed up all of her stuff in her old room at the "old house" and stored it, so all she had was a choice of two "guest bedrooms." Her mother and father were no longer geared to raising her as much as they were controlling her, and she knew it. She was just a small part of the master plan.

Lucy knew her dad was a political animal, and that she, as the only child, was a critical part of the story line. She saw clearly that she couldn't be construed by her father's conservative, evangelical voting base as some liberal slut who gave up the University of Alabama in Tuscaloosa and a charmed, protected life within the shadow of the Machine to sing in a band and hang out with hippies at the Flora-Bama. It just wouldn't work.

Slip had his sights set on much bigger things than the state senate. He firmly believed the "rising star" label pinned on him by the media and his colleagues. Lucy could not be a problem for him. He knew it was time for him to squarely nip it in the bud. However, Lucy was a step ahead of him. She thought quickly. Her wheels turned, and on the fly she developed a plan of her own.

"That sounds good, Dad. I've been thinking I need a break from school anyway. I'll drop my classes and get together my things at the apartment over the next couple of days."

And just like that, Slip and Mary were relieved. They got the answer they badly wanted and needed.

"That's great, baby! Momma and I are really looking forward to having you back around the house again. You're gonna have fun, baby. You're gonna love those new machines I bought!"

"I know I will, Daddy. I'm gonna head back to Mobile and start getting my things together. I'll call y'all tomorrow, okay?"

"Alright darling," answered Slip.

She hurriedly hugged and kissed them both on the cheek, and left. Slip smiled and walked to the beckoning wet bar for a celebratory punch; as he felt he had won another battle. However, unbeknownst to him, the war had not even started.

***

That night Lucy drove to her condo in Mobile near the campus of South Alabama. On the way there she spoke to Johnny via cell and he told her about their new digs on the sailboat located under the Baar Bridge on the Intracoastal. He was excited about it; so she was too, and she was not worried in the least. She was just as excited about being with him—and about them having their own place.

Johnny told her to bring whatever she thought would make the place more comfortable, and that they needed bedding. She went through her fully furnished apartment and picked a few things. In addition to her favorite casual clothes and other necessities, she grabbed a 20-inch Visio high definition color television, a small Bose radio and CD player with built in speakers, a huge down comforter, Egyptian cotton sheets, a wool blanket and two down pillows with matching cases. She also brought along some CD's, a small microwave, a can opener, a couple of bowls and plates, and a handful of utensils.

After packing everything into her Volkswagen, she drove straight to Perdido Key to be with Johnny. In her eyes, things in her life would never be the same. During the drive down to the beach she thought about how the many material things she left behind in the condo meant nothing to her now. She longed for the island life—she and Johnny both did; and she knew the next few months of singing in a band at the Flora-Bama and surrounding parts, and living on a sailboat with the guy she loved in Perdido Key, Florida, was infinitely more promising and potentially fulfilling than the predictable future her parents had in mind for her. Besides, she was no longer a child. She loved Johnny, and wanted to be with him, and to make her own decisions.

Lucy decided that she would not contact and would just wait to hear from her parents. Once they contacted her about the move she would explain her real decision to them. She would apologize to them. She would tell them that she is in love with Johnny Glass, a singer-songwriter. She would explain that they formed a band, Riptide, and that they are playing three regular gigs every week and are close to getting a fourth, and that she is now living with Johnny. She wasn't going to tell them where. She figured that this would never go over well with her parents, but that there was really no other way but to tell them the truth. It was going to be a bitter pill, as in the short run they would be losing control, and in the long run the ongoing, all-important public opinion battle. She knew well her decision could hurt her father politically; and that his enemies could and certainly would use her chosen path against him. Nevertheless, she felt it was time for her to start her own life, her own pursuit of happiness—away from her parents.

17

Johnny and Lucy fixed up the sailboat to the best of their liking. Johnny hooked up the power and the cable television and Internet feed from the portal connection at the dock. He bought a wireless transmitter and set it up inside the boat so that they could use the Internet on their phones and portable computing devices. They stocked the fridge with bottled water, designer chocolate, white wine and a six pack of beer. They made their bed with the comforter and other nice bedding items Lucy brought from her apartment, mounting the small flat screen television neatly above their feet in the forward sleeping area. Lucy made a closet out of the rear birthing area for her many clothes and shoes. After it was all in place, Johnny rested in a supine position, crossed his legs, clasped his hands behind his head, and relaxed, surveying his humble resting place.

"You've made us a happy home, Lucy!" Johnny teased, smiling.

She stood in the main part of the cabin, looking beautiful as always, staring at him. Her shiny, dark hair and curvaceous figure beckoned him. The window unit hummed lightly in the background, competing with Tracy Lawrence's "Paint me a Birmingham" emanating from the Bose radio nearby.

"That looks kinda comfortable," she noted, eyeballing him.

"Oh it is," he replied. "Come and see for yourself."

He pulled the comforter aside revealing a cozy, empty spot by his side.

***

Lucy did not talk to her parents for 48 hours. On Saturday evening, around 6:00 p.m., she got a call from her mother's cell phone. She was in the sailboat relaxing, casually watching TV, net surfing and checking email alone, so she answered it. The sun was beginning its quick descent in the western sky, but it was still hot and humid, a regular end to a typical summer day. The window unit air conditioner across from Lucy hummed and blasted cold air between its plastic dividers, lifting Lucy's bangs rhythmically up and down. She sipped a cold light blue plastic bottle of Dasani drinking water.

"Hi Mom," she said. Her Iphone4 was on speaker mode. She held a working Ipad on her lap.

"Hello Lucy! What are you doing? Your father and I were wondering where you were! We thought you would have rolled up here with all of your stuff by now. Where are you?"

Lucy took a deep breath.

"Mom, I dropped out of summer school, like y'all suggested; and I got all my things together at the condo that I needed."

"Oh great, honey. Are you on your way here now?"

"No, Mom. I'm not," she answered, matter-of-factly, her mother noticing a certain difference in her tone.

"Well what are you doing? Where are you?"

"I'm in Perdido Key," she answered.

Her mother's blood pressure spiked. Her breath quickened.

"Whatever for? Why are you out there? I told you to stay away from that God awful place, young lady!" Mary raged.

"I am taking the summer off, Mom. I'm going to live out here at the beach and concentrate on my music. I have joined a band with a great guy I am dating. I love him, Mom. His name is Johnny Glass," Lucy honestly answered, her heart racing. She pushed the Ipad aside and sat up straight, her legs crossed Indian style.

Mary seethed with anger.

"You are what? No you are not young lady! Your father and I will not support you! We will cut you off before that happens! Lucy, don't try us!"

Lucy fought back. She had already wiped out her checking

and savings accounts, netting her a cool $4,500. Plus, she still had her credit cards, which she had used exclusively the past two days.

"Mother, go ahead and cut me off! Everything in the condo is yours and daddy's anyways! All of it was bought with your money. Sell it! I don't want or need it anymore! I have everything I want here. I can take care of myself. Don't y'all worry about me! All I want you and Daddy to do is to let me pursue my singing. It is really important to me and that's all I really ask."

"That's all you ask? Little girl, when everybody in Fairhope and Montgomery finds out that Slip Whitman's debutante daughter is sluttin' and slummin' around with a Flora-Bama musician, it's gonna sting. You can't put your Daddy through that, honey! What are you thinking? Have you lost your damn mind? Good God child!"

Lucy was devastated. She thought her mother would at least be somewhat sympathetic to her feelings, but she was being a total cold hard bitch.

"Mom, I am in love with this guy!" Lucy emphatically stated.

"I told you to don't go looking to get married to some guy out there! Why are you not listening to me Lucy? Are you deaf? What is wrong with you girl? Are you on drugs? Tell me if you need some help. We can get you some help, Lucy, if we need to. Are you pregnant?"

Lucy was now madder than hell.

"Mother, I am not on drugs! Pregnant? Are you kidding me? Oh my God!"

Lucy caught her breath and continued.

"I am so done with the sorority girl thing, Mother! I hate it! It's all so phony and it's not my gig. I love music, and I love Johnny, and right now, that's what I want in my life. I promise to stay in touch with you and Daddy, but please don't worry about me, Mother. I love you and I love Daddy, but it's time for me to make my own life! Goodbye!"

Lucy hung up the phone. Her feelings went from anger to

fear; although she did feel somewhat relieved. She had dreaded talking to either of her parents. Nevertheless, she cried. She sobbed alone in the tiny cabin, as it was difficult, and she knew she still had to deal with her father.

***

While Lucy was starting World War III during a cell phone call from her mother, Johnny was visiting Joe at his house on Old River. The day before Joe had asked him to stop by and drop off copies of the debut CD Riptide had cut. Joe promised he would get them up for sale in the souvenir trailer out in front of the Flora-Bama and that 50 percent of all subsequent sales would go back to him and the group, and that they would get paid every two weeks on those. Potentially, when coupled with their regular gig money for each show and tips from reveling patrons, the CD sales could be a financial difference maker for everyone. Every little bit certainly helped, and Johnny wanted to do everything he could to get ahead. Besides, it was also good to have a CD so that people could listen to them. He was eager to get Joe a copy, as he knew he would be proud of him for getting the band formed and up and running so fast.

Although the tourist season had been adversely affected by the BP oil spill—by late June beach occupancy was running just under fifty percent—Johnny soon realized that a regular summer season was a profitable span for musicians like Jake who basically lived for free. The constant jam of fun-loving tourists brought their hard-earned vacation money they loved to blow having a good time on the island. Even with fewer tourists, Johnny felt he was making decent money in tips every time he played, although that was coming from the many locals living nearby whose loyal everyday patronage paid most of the overhead at the Flora-Bama and the other local watering holes. However, Johnny could easily see that with twice as many tourists he could expect twice as many tips; and of course with that came the possibility of getting more regular gigs during the busiest time of the year.

It was now late June. The day before Joe had attended his much-dreaded bankruptcy hearing in Pensacola, and it had drained him. Johnny drove up to Joe's place on Old River, which was on stilts, and walked past the pool and hot tub, up the steep stairs coated in thick, gray outdoor paint. He opened the screen door and knocked on the wooden door with a bronze knob. Moments later, Joe, wearing a burgundy robe and slippers, appeared in the side window. He recognized Johnny and opened up.

"Hey guy," Joe said. "Come on in."

Johnny held an open shoe box with 20 CD's in his hand.

"Hey Joe, I got those CD's you asked for. I hope I didn't wake you."

"Wake me? No. But yes, come on in, Johnny. I'll take those from you." Joe answered, grabbing the box. "Have a seat."

Johnny entered the living area. The place was a wreck. There were leftover red solo cups and styrofoam plates, white plastic utensils and opened and unopened mail and magazines and receipts and handwritten notes and all kinds of other shit everywhere you looked. There were clothes strewn all about, and they all looked crumpled and dirty. Johnny pushed a pile of wrinkled tee shirts, gripper style boxer Fruit of the Loom underwear and dress socks resting on a leather chair back into a nearby dark green plastic wash basket and sat down.

"Don't worry about that stuff," Joe said. "Yeah, just put it in there. I'm gonna fold it up later."

Joe took the box of CD's and put them on his dining room table. He examined the CD cover. It was a recent picture of Johnny and Lucy and Sam and Preston together in front of the Flora-Bama. He liked it. He walked back to the living room and sat across from Johnny, on his sofa.

"Thanks for getting the CD's to me. I'll make sure they go on sale tomorrow," Joe said. "How are things going? Did y'all get that gig over at Hub Stacey's on the Point?"

"We did," Johnny answered. "I found out a little while ago as a matter of fact. I haven't even told everybody else. That means we are busy three nights a week, now. Wednesdays at the Bama, Thursdays at the Reef and Fridays at Hub Stacey's."

"You'll probably find another gig soon. In fact, I may be able to help you. I know a guy who is getting ready to start a new place on July 1st. He may want entertainment. I'll look into it for you."

"Thanks Joe," Johnny said. "We appreciate your help."

"You guys are just getting started and you're a new group on the scene. People are gonna start calling you, and that's good because you want to work as much as you can during the season. What sucks is that our numbers are down. Our sales are half of what they normally are this time of year. This BP oil spill and media cluster is just so disgusting, Johnny. I feel bad for you, because you had no idea all this shit was gonna happen either. You just came down here to write and play songs."

He paused.

"I'm sorry, Johnny."

Johnny felt really bad that Joe even said anything like that. It wasn't because of him.

"Joe, it's not your fault. Come on, man. You didn't know all of this was gonna happen! That's nonsense! I'm gonna be okay. We're gonna all get through this together! I can feel it!"

Johnny saw Joe was tired and troubled, and that he was not really fazed by his impromptu pep talk. Joe had recently showered and neatly parted his hair, but the bags under his eyes told the true story of his concern for the future. Joe still needed to find an investor or investors to save him from his financial troubles. He needed a real infusion of outside cash to save the Flora-Bama. It was difficult, however, because he knew he had to find the right person, or persons. He didn't want to do business with people who wouldn't appreciate what he'd created. It was a difficult and tricky situation; a true life challenge for the spry 70-year old.

"Yesterday I was with lawyers all morning and into the early afternoon," Joe said and paused. He continued, "I felt like they were gorging on me."

Johnny saw Joe's posture slowly sink and his noble countenance change. The color in his cheeks faded. Johnny wanted to say something, but couldn't. He wondered if they really would get through it all.

"I have only a few days left in this place. I have to be out by next week. They are going to take my house," Joe said.

"I'm sorry Joe," said Johnny. It was feeble, but it was all he could muster. It was difficult for him to fathom, but Joe was now in the position he was weeks prior—without a place. Johnny dealt with his own guilty feelings.

Joe confided to Johnny that he needed to find a white knight, someone who could come along with a cash injection to save the fabled place by purchasing a portion of its stock and allowing him and his attorney to pay his bad debts tied to the Flora-Bama Corporation. It was a sobering talk.

Johnny left Joe to rest that afternoon with the firm realization that if Joe made it, they would all make it; but also that nothing was certain regarding the outcome. It was all still very much in the balance.

***

Johnny drove the two or three miles east back to the marina under the Baar's Bridge. He parked his pickup next to Lucy's Volkswagen and walked to the sailboat. He found Lucy lying in a fetal position. Her face and eyes were red, and he could tell she had been crying. He immediately consoled and hugged her, wanting to know what had happened.

She explained the call from her mom, her threatening to cut her off financially and how going forward she saw no way of returning to her old life. They talked about how she had made a huge life decision—like it or not; and worse—that they still had to deal with her normally inconsolable father.

"Johnny, I'm scared," she said, holding him. She wiped a tear from her eye.

Johnny squeezed her tight and slowly rocked her back and forth.

"It's gonna be okay, baby. It's gonna be okay," he assured her.

But alas, he didn't know Slip Whitman; and Lucy knew this.

"I've got some good news! Do you wanna hear it?" Johnny asked with a grin.

"Yes!" she said, pulling away so she could look at him. "What is it?"

Johnny smiled. "We got the Friday night gig at Hub's!"

"Really?" she squealed. "That's awesome!"

"Ain't it though? Baby, we don't need much. It's all here for us! Hey, look, we are just about booked except for Saturdays, and Joe told me a little while ago that he has a buddy opening up a new place and that he may want live entertainment. So, we've got a new lead! "

"That is exciting!" Lucy said, bristling with the adventure of it all.

Johnny's enthusiasm was contagious. They hugged and kissed for two or three minutes. He reassured her, and whispered to her not to worry. He promised her that they were going to be fine. He opened the hatch above their bedding and they held each other, enjoying the pastel palette created by the setting summer sun.

18

That Saturday evening Johnny and Lucy went to the Flora-Bama around 6:00 p.m. to catch the Earl the Pearl Show. Johnny was a huge fan of Earl. Joe planted a few of his CD's in one of the storage compartments in the sailboat and he had listened and laughed to all of them several times. Johnny felt his songs were really funny; and besides, he packed the place with a loyal following every Friday and Saturday afternoon. It was always a fun time full of music, laughter and song. Lucy thought Earl was nuts; and she had every right.

Johnny and Lucy got drinks and enjoyed the beginning of the show. Earl, dressed in shorts and a tee shirt that read Earl-thepearl.com, got through his first two songs—"Made Love to Your Mother at the Motel Six" and "Beauty is a Light Switch Away," before he surprised everyone. Once it was quiet, he explained.

"I'm gonna take a small break from our regular program tonight to introduce to all of you lucky folks a really famous singer-songwriter and honky tonk musician. Let me tell you what—y'all are some lucky SOB's being able to hear this man and see him here today. And that's exactly why you need to consistently come to the Flora-Bama, folks—because you never know who is gonna show up!"

Earl pulled a note from his pocket. He began to read from the crumpled piece of paper.

"This man I am fixing to introduce to you is a bonafide living legend. He was the inspiration for the movie "Crazy Heart" with Jeff Bridges and has written tons of great songs, including

"Georgia on a Fast Train," "Old Chunk of Coal" and "Old Five and Dimers Like Me," among others. He is a native of Corsicana, Texas, I give you none other than the biggest country music outlaw there is—Mr. Billy Joe Shaver!"

The crowd, genuinely surprised, erupted in applause and thanks. Everybody wondered where he was. They looked all around.

A white haired fellow wearing a cream-colored Stetson hat, a dark blue jean shirt, light blue wrangler blue jeans, a wide, gleaming silver belt buckle and brown cowboy boots came through the crowd and entered the main stage to Earl's left. Earl shook his hand and handed him the microphone. Billy Joe addressed the crowd.

"Thank you Earl. I appreciate that introduction. That was pretty good, but you forgot one important thing."

Billy Joe paused and looked directly at Earl. People in the crowd were on their cell phones texting others and taking pictures as proof of the outlaw country legend's visit.

"And what was that?" Earl asked, going along, leaning into the microphone.

"That I'm a great lay!" Billy Joe exclaimed, much to the laughter of the now-boisterous crowd. In jest, Jack slapped himself upside his own head and everyone cracked up.

Billy Joe Shaver was great that afternoon. During the impromptu set he sang with Earl's band "Georgia on a Fast Train," "Whacko from Waco" and "Live Forever." He was fantastic, Johnny thought, as he had always admired Billy Joe's supreme songwriting talent—Shaver's unique ability to use such simple words to paint a picturesque story. He had a chance to shake his hand after the show and it was a great moment.

"I love your songs Mr. Shaver." Johnny said.

"Thank you, Son. I appreciate that." Billy Joe answered.

"You use such simple imagery. You leave a lot up to the listener's imagination," Johnny commented.

"That's right," Billy Joe answered. "Give em' a little bit and let them figure out the rest," he added. He was then rushed by a small mob of autograph and picture seekers, obliging them all.

Joe G. showed up after Earl's second set, and was sorry to learn that he had missed Billy Joe's extemporaneous, three-song performance. Joe too was a big fan of Billy Joe.

"Hey Mr. Joe! Good to see ya! You just missed Billy Joe Shaver!" said Johnny, shaking Joe's hand.

"You're kidding?" Joe answered. "Well darnit I would have enjoyed that! Oh well, guess I should have got out here a little earlier tonight. It's just that I've had a few more challenges than usual, lately, is all."

Johnny knew exactly what he meant. He looked around and noticed that Lucy was no longer by his side. "She must be in the bathroom," he thought. He looked over toward the bathrooms and saw her standing in line behind two other women in their early thirties. He winked at her and she winked back.

Lucy heard her Iphone ping, notifying her of a received text message. She reached into her tiny purse and retrieved it. She checked the lit up face after pushing the button twice with her thumb. It was a message from her mother. It read.

"I told your father about your revised summer plans."

Moments later, another message came through.

"He said you better come back to Fairhope tomorrow or you'll forever wish you'd never pulled this ridiculous stunt."

Lucy was mortified. Her stomach rumbled. She knew her father was Machiavellian by design, and would go to any length to prove a point. She could only wonder, and fear, what he had in store for them, as she knew he played to win.

Johnny made his way back to Joe, who was now standing next to a gentleman he had not met.

"Johnny, I want you to meet Eddie Boy! Eddie Boy, this is Johnny Glass. Johnny, this is Eddie Boy Werner. Eddie is a business associate of mine—we have lost a ton of money together."

Johnny and Eddie Boy shook hands. Johnny squared his shoulders and looked him in the eyes.

Everybody chuckled. It was a funny introduction.

"Just kidding—well really I am not, but we are still friends!" Joe laughed. He continued.

"Johnny, Eddie Boy is opening a place called Flippers on the other side of Orange Beach—down toward the end of Canal Road. He's been working on it for a while and wants to open this weekend. I told him that Riptide might be a good Saturday night gig for his new place. I told him about your pretty co-star, Lucy, and he thinks that y'all would probably work out well for Saturdays, because he wants to feature live music on the weekends."

"That sounds great!" Johnny said. "We'd love to play for you, Mr. Eddie."

"Call me Eddie Boy!" he insisted, smiling from ear-to-ear. "Y'all wanna start next Saturday?" he asked.

"Absolutely!" he answered. "Thank you Eddie Boy!"

"You're welcome, Johnny!"

Jake showed up a few minutes later. Hung Jury had the 9:00 p.m. gig in the Bama Dome. Johnny caught up with him, and Sam and Preston, who were out and about like everyone else on a summer Saturday night. He surprised Sam and Preston with the news of getting two more gigs on Friday and Saturday nights, giving them a full four-day work week for the summer season. They were stoked.

"No way!?" Sam replied.

"Killer news!" said Preston. "Let's do a shooter!"

The guys lined up four shots of chilled Patron at the bar. Johnny, Sam, Preston and Jake raised the small, cool, clear containers in a ceremonial toast and threw them back. Johnny sucked on a lime the bartender offered on a small white napkin. The rest grimaced without.

"Wooie!" yelled Preston. "Damn fine news, Johnny boy!"

"Things are looking good!" Sam chimed in. "We just may make lemonade out of lemons after all!"

Lucy returned and Johnny shared the good news with her. She was excited and she hugged him tight. For a moment, she forgot about her fear of her father.

Despite the oil spill, the crowd was always at its peak on Saturday nights in June and July. By nine o'clock three bands were playing simultaneously and by ten it was standing room only.

Roxy Hart and Elaine Petty, who went by The Smoking Elvises, played at the Silver Moon Lounge across the street to a crowded room, Hung Jury jammed inside the Bama Dome and the Newbury Syndicate, made up of Chris Newbury, Mickey's talented progeny; Mike Locklin, Buzz Kiefer, Mel Knapp and for the night, Preston Stanfill, entertained under the tent outside. Preston was sitting in for their regular drummer, who needed a night off.

Johnny and Lucy enjoyed Jake's band for a set and then stepped outside to enjoy the Newbury Syndicate. They had a good time listening to the music and spending time with their island-dwelling friends. Although wholly preoccupied with the concern of her father's impending wrath, Lucy never mentioned to Johnny her father's crude ultimatum.

19

On Sunday Johnny and Lucy attended the 10:00 a.m. Flora-Bama-sponsored Worship on the Water service outside underneath the tent. Jake had enthusiastically invited them the night before. Given her predicament, Lucy felt like praying wouldn't hurt, so she rallied Johnny to get up and shower in the communal male and female bathroom facility near the outdoor pool and manager's office only paces away from their floating living quarters. Not having a ready bathroom or a shower in the boat was a drawback, but to youngsters like them it was fun and funky, and more importantly, it was free.

It was a regular, humid midsummer morning. The worship service was predictably well-attended. The large electric fans that had been set up on each side of the billowing, worshiping crowd buzzed on high mode, trying to provide a semblance of wafting relief to the pious, fun-loving lot. Strangely, some of them gripped cold canned beers, cocktails and frothy bushwhackers during the service, as the Flora-Bama always insists it was first a bar that spawned a church service and not vice versa; and that in life Jesus too regularly enjoyed the spiritual benefits of wine, laughter and song.

After the service Johnny asked Lucy if she would mind if he went fishing. The night before, at the Flora-Bama, Jake was offered by local charter boat captain, Max Pace, to go out on the salt to catch their limit of red snapper. Max Pace lived life as fast as his namesake. He was one of the more popular and successful captains in Orange Beach, and was also a bona fide Flora-Bama regular. Everybody knew "Captain Max," the smiling, blonde-haired, fun-loving fellow you could always count on to put you on the fish. He had a couple of extra spots on his boat on Sunday afternoon, so after the service he told Jake he could also bring a friend, prompting the impromptu invite to Johnny. Lucy of course said she didn't mind, although she dreaded waiting alone for her father's next move. Her intuition told her to be afraid; and she was duly scared.

***

On Sunday morning, after the early service at the First Baptist Church on Alabama Highway 98 just south of Fairhope, Senator Whitman and his wife Mary re-entered their Escalade. Slip used his Iphone to check his email. He was expecting a communication from a private detective he hired to find out where Lucy was living in Perdido Key. The hand held device indicated with a tiny, glowing symbol that he had a new message. He opened it with a forefinger. It read:

"Your daughter is living on a sailboat under the Baar's Bridge in Perdido Key with a long-haired young man close to her age. The boat is the fourth from the base of the bridge...slip number 106."

20

The assignment for the experienced private Dick was easy money. He had a current picture of Lucy and there were so many people at the Flora-Bama on Saturday night that it was easy to blend into the crowd and not be noticed. All he did was inconspicuously follow Lucy and Johnny back to the Marina after they left the Flora-Bama around midnight, and his mission was accomplished. He could have called or emailed the Senator when he had the information, at around one o'clock in the morning; but he decided to wait until later, as he didn't want to wake him—or ruin a good Alabama Saturday night.

Mary Whitman noticed by the direction they were heading leaving the First Baptist Church that they weren't going back to their home on Mobile Bay.

"Where are we going?" she asked her husband.

"To see Lucy," he answered. He sounded as serious as a heart attack.

"Where is she?" she implored.

"Shacked up with some hippie on a fucking sailboat under the Theo Baar's Bridge!" he yelled.

Mary was shocked, but not surprised, as she knew more than him.

"We're gonna pay them a little surprise visit." He added, pressing down hard on the accelerator as he pushed the Escalade south toward the beach road.

***

Unbeknownst to the Senator or his doting wife was the fact that Slip had that morning, once again, made the Mobile *Press-*

Register. After a late night of cocktailing and playing cards with friends on the end of their pier, they both slept late and missed their regular coffee and news time during breakfast. In a tiny, three paragraph story buried at the bottom of the second page was the title, "Fairhope Citizen Files Ethics Complaint against Senator Whitman for Local Contracts."

The first graph read: "Francis P. Tripp, 64, of Fairhope, a retired Marine sniper who served in Viet Nam, has filed an ethics complaint with the Alabama Ethics Commission, citing Senator Whitman's lucrative heavy equipment contracts with multiple municipalities in his district. "The Senator is violating a basic tenet of good government—that he should never use his public position for personal financial gain. I ask that the Ethics Commission conduct a full investigation of his considerable business with the local governments inside his senate district," Tripp said in a certified letter addressed to the Commission offices in Montgomery. "We cannot continue to tolerate public corruption at any level. I went to war to support freedom at home, not tyranny. Mr. Whitman is the worst kind of public official, and he should be stopped."

Half way down to the beach the Senator heard his phone ping again. It was the notification that he had a new email. He retrieved his cell and saw that the message was from his assistant, Tommy Wilson. The subject of the email read: "Article about you in the Mobile *Press-Register* today..." The body of the email was the pasted text from the online version of the article, along with the web address linking the article hosted on the metro area newspaper's website. The senator opened the email and viewed the text of the article. His blood pressure rose and his face turned beet red.

"Who the hell is Francis Tripp?" he thought, "And what is his problem with me?" Senator Whitman didn't understand, thinking it was possibly personal, whatever it was that compelled him to file the complaint. The senator had long rationalized his unethical behavior as "honest graft," and in his twisted mind, was completely justified in taking the many lucrative public contracts with municipalities inside his district.

The senator wondered who this man was, and if he had ulterior motives—and more importantly, if others were helping him. While he drove, he texted Tommy: "Find out everything you can on this Francis Tripp guy and report back to me."

***

Captain Max, behind the wheel of his trusty, 1968 Buddy Davis Sportfish—a long and sleek craft that cut quickly through the surf, took Jake and Johnny on a 45-minute ride due south to a specific GPS spot he had been fishing for years. They dropped anchor and got down to business.

It was a partly cloudy afternoon. Puffy cumulus clouds dotted an azure sky that almost matched in color the water they fished with weighted hooks baited with squid and fresh shrimp. The experience was a first for Johnny. He had never been deep sea fishing. He found the deep blue hue of the offshore water breathtaking.

Captain Max baited Johnny's peculiar, curved hook and showed him how to release the spool so that his weighted and baited leader could sink to the bottom fifty feet below. He explained that the curved hook they used fit perfectly in the Red Snapper's mouth, and that he only had to start reeling the line to set the hook once he got a nibble.

Excited to try his luck, Johnny took control of the rod containing 25 pound test monofilament line. He released the spool and the leader disappeared into the dark blue below. About four or five seconds later the line stopped moving. Johnny cranked the reel and brought up the slack, allowing him to feel tension. Seconds later he felt a quick, deliberate tap-tap-tap on the line. Captain Max saw the tip of the rod bend slightly three times.

"Reel! You got one Johnny! Reel him in!"

Johnny did as instructed. He reeled furiously and the rod bent over, nearly in half. He felt a stiff resistance and he strained to continue reeling. His body jerked against the side of the boat, and his heart pounded in his chest.

"Holy shit!" yelled Jake. "Whoa! You got one brother!" Jake pulled in his line after missing his attempt to land a fish. He tried to get out of Johnny's way, as it looked like he had something more than decent. Minutes passed and Johnny still fought the fish he had not yet seen. He jettisoned his shirt and let the sweat run freely across his torso.

"Damn Johnny you might have a state record!" Captain Max joked. "I'm pretty sure it's a snapper, too, because of the way it took the bait."

Johnny's arms grew stiff from the workout. His right bicep burned and his shoulder and back ached. The midday summer sun beat down upon him like a desert smile, and he could feel the whiskers of another sunburn tickling the back of his neck.

Johnny finally managed to reel the line in just enough that Captain Max caught a glimpse of the catch.

"You hooked two snapper, Johnny! And they are big un's! Keep reeling em' in! We have to net them one at a time. Just take it easy!" Captain Max coached, grabbing a huge black rubber net on the end of a long aluminum pole with a gripping handle.

Like a pro, Johnny maneuvered the first large snapper—the one on top of the other on the line, into netting position. Captain Max netted the gorgeous, broad, red and pink-colored fish and removed the hook.

"She's a beaut' Johnny!" Jake yelled. He high-fived Johnny.

"Damn right!" said Captain Max. "Whooie!"

Johnny brought the second fish, nearly identical in size and strength, alongside the boat, and Captain Max nabbed him. Seconds later, Johnny and Captain Max posed between the two monster snapper in the back of the boat while Jake snapped pictures with Johnny's phone.

"That's your limit, Johnny." Captain Max stated. "The limit is two per person." Stand back and let me and Jake get a couple and we'll head back in and have us some cold beer."

That sounded great to Johnny, as it was hotter than Hades out there where there was no reprieve from the sun's powerful rays. The fish were really biting. It took Jake and Max ten minutes to each catch two "keeper" snappers. None of the four were as big as Johnny's, however, which Captain Max said were easily 25 pounds. On the ride back to Perdido Key Jake attributed the win to "beginner's luck." Captain Max disagreed.

"Johnny held his mouth right, is all," Max said with a grin. They all laughed as the boat's engines roared and the craft shuttled them back to paradise—or so they thought.

***

Senator Whitman and his wife stopped on their way to the beach in Foley at Lambert's for lunch. After skipping breakfast, they were both starved, and while Slip badly wanted to get to the spot underneath the Baar's Bridge where he now knew Lucy was hiding, he relented to Mary's pleading to stop and get something to eat.

After enjoying good fried and smothered Southern cooking and the world-famous "throwed rolls," they left the tourist-packed restaurant and continued south along Highway 59. It was 1:45 by the time they left, as Lambert's was crowded, and it took them forever to be seated, much to the senator's chagrin.

They finally made it to the Marina underneath the Baar's Bridge around 2:30. The sun was still high in the summer sky. It roasted everything in sight; the temperature was a harsh 93 degrees—102 with the heat index, making their church clothes quite uncomfortable.

Senator Whitman pulled into the entrance of the marina parking lot and drove to the other end of the property near the bridge spanning the Intracoastal Canal.

"According to my guy she is in the fourth sailboat over there," Slip said, pointing.

"That little ole bitty thing?" Mary asked. "My Lord!"

Slip pulled into a vacant parking spot in front of a large, black, customized RV bus, the kind professional musicians and actors use. It was a brand new model and looked really expensive.

"Come with me," Slip insisted. He turned off the engine and removed the key from the ignition. He and Mary stepped out into the frying rays of the sun. Moments later, as they walked toward the sailboat, a big black SUV pulled up and blocked their path. A white magnetic sign with black lettering on the side of the dark vehicle read: "Marina Security."

The lone driver of the vehicle, a white male about 30, lowered the automatic driver's side window. He wore a dark blue uniform, a matching unmarked baseball cap and dark designer sunglasses.

"I'm sorry Sir, but you cannot park in that there spot. It belongs to a paying guest," said the security guard politely. "They will be coming back soon and they will want their spot. Please move your vehicle to the gravel overflow lot on the other side of the property." He pointed in the direction he wanted the senator to go.

By now it was really steamy. The sun blared high in the midday sky. The senator, wearing a coat and tie, was already sweating buckshot. The last thing he wanted to do was drive all the way over there and walk back. He would be soaking wet, and he knew it, as he was already sweating like a pig.

"I am not going to be here long, Sir. I need to be here right now! I have come to get my daughter!" Slip insisted. He walked away from the man, around the vehicle blocking his path.

The security guard, upset with his reaction, exited the SUV and walked around, following the senator and his wife.

"Sir, please stop!" blurted the young man. It was now apparent that the security guard was vertically challenged. He was maybe five foot two, with walking boots. He looked up to the senator and raised his voice again.

"Sir if you do not obey my request I will have you arrested! I am an off-duty Pensacola policeman," he said, puffing up his chest. This is a managed, private property. There are rules and regulations."

Slip was agitated by the much smaller man. He stopped, turned and puffed up his much larger chest.

"Sir, I said I have come to get my daughter!" insisted the senator, inflecting hard the "Sir" and gesticulating wildly. He purposely bellowed in an authoritarian voice. "Besides, I am an Alabama state senator! I represent all of Baldwin County, Alabama. Officer, I'm Slip Whitman."

Slip quickly stepped toward the tiny man and offered his right hand. The officer saw the advance as a potential threat, and he backed up like a sand crab, crouching and placing one hand on the mace holder on his belt, the other into the air in front of him to defend himself.

"I don't care who you are, Sir!" yelled the young man. "I am just trying to do my job!"

The guard was now pissed off big time. He continued, going back into procedure.

"I have politely asked you to move your vehicle. You have refused. I am asking you again, Sir."

Slip said nothing. He hesitated. He saw things escalating, and did not want a face full of mace. He was sweating profusely now. His lower back and underarms were drenched with perspiration, and he was getting uncomfortable fast.

"Slip, look—there she is!" Mary interjected. She pointed to the corner of the property, near the concrete base of the Baar's Bridge. Lucy, wearing a red bikini and tennis shoes with no socks, dark sunglasses, and a Flora-Bama Mullet Toss Fishing Rodeo baseball hat, pulled a bright yellow kayak by a small white rope. She had spent the past thirty minutes soaking up some sun and paddling up and down the Intracoastal Waterway for exercise. Once Lucy pulled the kayak up the embankment and was level with her parents, she saw them. She stopped momentarily, and stared. She was surprised; as she knew this wasn't a friendly visit.

"How did they find me?" she asked herself.

"A private eye?" she pondered. She knew she hadn't told anyone of her whereabouts.

Her blood pressure and heartbeat simultaneously spiked. She was ready to fight.

"There's our daughter!" Mary yelled to the security guard, momentarily diffusing the tense situation.

Lucy dragged the kayak within paces of her parents. Her face wore a disgusted look.

"What are y'all doing here?" she demanded.

"I've asked them to move their vehicle, Miss Whitman," the security guard stated, his dominant hand still on his mace, his torso slightly bent and poised for action. Lucy and Johnny both knew the security guard. His name was Shane.

"Tell them to move it back to Fairhope, Shane!" Lucy demanded.

"With you in it young lady! You are coming home with us!" Slip loudly insisted, his anger apparent, his finger pointing directly at her. Bubbles of perspiration dotted his forehead.

"I am going nowhere! I am an adult and I don't have to listen to you anymore! Get out of here and don't come back!" She pointed toward the exit, and back to Fairhope.

Lucy paused slightly.

"Shane, please ask them again to leave! They are harassing me!"

Shane did not hesitate.

"Sir, if you do not get in your vehicle and leave the property, I will arrest you for remaining after being forbidden and then phone for a cruiser to come and pick you up and bring you downtown. I am not going to say this again."

Just as the off-duty officer was taking control, Captain Max and Jake and Johnny drove into the front of the marina parking lot only fifty yards from the ongoing spectacle. Max and Jake and Johnny didn't notice the commotion only paces away. Each had enjoyed a couple of cold beers after being in the sun and surf; and Max and Jake were now geared toward getting down to the Flora-Bama so that they could continue their "Sunday fun day." Johnny was anxious to tell Lucy his amazing fishing story.

Johnny walked toward the sailboat. After a few steps he spotted Lucy in her tiny rose-colored bikini, standing with her arms folded and hip flexed. He saw the security guard between her and the couple, and realized it was her parents. As he stepped toward them, he saw that Lucy was terribly upset.

Senator Whitman's countenance and posture shifted. He silently acknowledged defeat. Lucy said nothing. She was surprised and then both happy and scared. She saw Johnny walking to her. He was now right behind her father. Johnny passed her mom and dad and walked up to Lucy and hugged her. He kissed her on the cheek and stood by her right side with his left arm around her, facing her parents.

"Who is this freak?" the senator derided. He scowled at Johnny.

"The man I love!" Lucy replied, defending herself. She squeezed Johnny close.

"My name is Johnny Glass, Sir," he said, pushing back his long locks on the front of his head with his right hand. His hair was a mess from the sun, wind and salt water and his face, arms and shoulders were sunburned. He wore only shorts and a ragged tee shirt and flip-flops, and he certainly looked and smelled like he had been deep sea fishing.

Johnny stepped forward, wiped his hand on his shorts and offered his hand to the Senator. Slip did not oblige him. He simply looked down upon him with further, evident disdain.

"No thanks, son. I don't have a wet wipe," he quipped with a vitriolic grin.

He continued, turning his attention to Lucy.

"You are officially cut off young lady!"

She fought back. "Good! Get out of here! You have twice been asked to leave!" Lucy reminded him, her arms still folded.

"Come on Mary, let's go!" the senator yelled.

Lucy said nothing. She just returned her mother's evil stare and watched them re-enter the Escalade and quickly drive off.

"You okay?" Shane asked.

"Yes, I'm fine," said Lucy, lying.

"What about you, Johnny?" she asked.

Johnny was startled. He never anticipated that Senator Whitman was such a vexatious soul. He now realized what—or more specifically—who, they were dealing with, and more importantly, why Lucy was so concerned.

"Yeah, I'm okay, baby. I'm okay," he said, squeezing her

close. Although he wondered what the senator would do next, as he seemed like the kind of guy who was going to cause them big trouble in the near future.

21

After Johnny showered and changed he joined Lucy at the small pool outside the shower area. He showed her the pictures and told her about his amazing fishing trip, how much fun he had and that he made 80 dollars cash by selling the two big fish he caught. He later used the money to take them out to eat at the seafood restaurant across the Intracoastal that Joe had brought him to. They enjoyed a wonderful meal—appropriately of blackened red snapper with lump white crab meat and stuffed shrimp with raw oyster appetizers. Over dinner they had time to talk about the earlier showdown.

"What do you think your dad will do next?" Johnny asked.

Lucy was somewhat startled, but she was willing to talk about it.

"I don't know. He hates to lose. I doubt if he will give up. I mean, he lost to a security guard today, so I think he'll be back. Had Shane not been there I don't know how it would have gone down. But I don't know what he is going to do. He is capable of anything. Who knows?"

"Well, it was inevitable. Sooner or later you knew he would object to this."

Johnny paused.

"All of this, it's not what he wants for you, you know?"

He seemed somewhat ashamed when he spoke, especially when he said, "this."

Lucy was emotionally distraught and she took it wrong.

"I know! But it's what I want, Johnny! It's not about me! As always, it's all about him!"

Johnny tried to recover, but it was futile.

"I know baby, I'm just saying. I'm not defending him!" he pleaded.

"Excuse me," she said, starting to sob. She abruptly rose and hurried to the women's room, upset and crying.

Johnny wondered what he did wrong and how they were going to handle the Senator Whitman problem.

***

"That long-haired, stinky-ass hippie tried to shake my hand, Mary! Did you see that shit back there? What did we do to deserve this assignment in life? We have given that girl everything—everything! And this is how she treats us—shacking up with a no-good degenerate on a broken down sailboat under a bridge in Florida? I think I saw a tattoo on his forearm! What a lowlife! This ain't gonna fly, Mary! I tell you this ain't gonna fly! I will not have it!" Slip raged while they drove west on the beach road.

"What are we gonna do, Slip?"

Slip stared off into the distance, far ahead of the column of weekend traffic ahead of him, past the towering white condominiums lining the beach.

"I don't know, Mary. I don't know just yet. But whatever I do, it's gonna be big. I'm gonna bust up her world!"

Mary could only wonder what he meant.

***

The next day, on Monday afternoon, Senator Whitman was getting a massage at the spa at the Grand Hotel when he noticed a call from his assistant, Tommy Wilson.

"I need to take this call," he told the masseur. "Give me a minute."

"Yes sir," said the tall, 23-year old Czech, one of many work exchange students from the former Soviet Bloc who had found work at the resort. He grabbed a hand towel and quietly left the small treatment room, shutting the door behind him.

The senator grabbed his cell and answered the call.

"Yeah Tommy, what's up?"

"I looked into this guy who filed the ethics complaint against you—this Francis Tripp."

"Yeah," answered the senator. "And what did you find out?"

"Well, he is a 64-year old former Marine sniper who served in Viet Nam, where he was awarded the Purple Heart. After Nam he lived in Birmingham where he ran a dive shop with his brother for a few years and then he moved to San Pedro, Belize, where he built and ran a tropical dive resort for 17 years. He retired to Fairhope 15 years ago."

"Okay," answered the senator. "But why is he after me?" he asked.

"Well, I'm getting to that, senator." Tommy answered.

He paused and continued. The senator grew silent.

"I called our guy at the City of Fairhope, your friend, Mr. Fred Timms, the city administrator. When I asked him about Mr. Tripp, he said that the guy is 'crazy like a fox.' He said he attends all the city council meetings and watches the mayor like a hawk. Apparently his dad was some big consumer advocate up in Birmingham where he grew up—a civil rights activist too, and a college professor. He likes to tell his dad's story of being an activist, and how he's just carrying on his public service. Timms said he has sued the city on three separate occasions and won judgments, and that the mayor and most of the council can't stand him because he reports on his homemade blog what the local newspapers won't about the city's politics. Timms said that we need to be worried, because the guy is smart, and that he knows what he is doing. He said he uses the Freedom of Information Act to get information he will use against you."

Senator Whitman said nothing. He pondered his next move.

"I'm not worried about him, Tommy." The senator said. "He isn't gonna get anywhere with the Ethics Commission complaint, and outside of that, I really don't have anything else to hide. He is harmless."

"Let's just be careful," Senator. "We don't want to do or say anything that would piss him off; but, I do think you should make a brief statement about his complaint, for your constituents' sake."

"I agree," said Senator Whitman. "Write this down: "

"Hold on Senator, let me record this."

"Okay. I'll wait."

"Go ahead."

There was an audible beep.

"The ethics complaint filed by Mr. Tripp is baseless. I was a heavy equipment contractor before I was elected to the Alabama State Senate. Also, I did not take a vow of poverty when I took my oath of office. I am operating entirely within the state's ethics laws, and I predict that the Ethics Commission will find accordingly in my favor."

Tommy was unsure.

"Are you sure you want to run this?"

"Send it out today. Blanket the state media with a release. Just like that!"

"Yes Sir."

"And Tommy—I need you to place a call to the Secretary of the Alabama Department of Environmental Management, a Mr. Sonny Hubert. Ask him to call me as soon as possible, please."

"Sure Senator. What's it about?"

"Don't worry about that. Just tell him it's urgent, and that I need to talk to him asap! Please, just do it."

"Yes Sir. I will."

The senator hung up on the call and dialed again.

He waited and a polite, female voice answered.

"Governor Finchley's Office...it's a great day in Alabama the Beautiful! How may I help you?"

"Yes, uh, this is Senator Slip Whitman. I am calling for Governor Finchley, please."

"Senator Whitman—good afternoon. Hold on please. I will patch you through. I believe he can take your call."

A few seconds passed and the Governor's voice appeared on the line.

"Slip! How are you? What can I do for you today?"

"Hey Governor! I am fine, Sir. Just fine. I am following up on the State Park initiative in Gulf Shores. I haven't spoken to you since the groundbreaking ceremony and I was wondering how things were going?"

"I appreciate that, Slip. It all looks good. I think they are getting really close to starting actual construction. I know it's all in motion now. You and Blaine did a great job with the legislation. I really appreciated that. Y'all did super!"

There was a brief pause.

"And I don't have it just yet, but in the next few days I hope to have an updated list of needed contractors for the project—you know, the kind of work we'll need done. I am going to send this list to you and others who have helped, for recommendations, so I will be welcoming your input, Slip. Also, BP is planning another round of grant money for floating boom to protect the Lower Alabama coastline. I was thinking you could be our 'go-to guy' for that project."

This was good news to Slip. He was always looking to get in on the action and this was going to be another big contract. However, at the moment, he had other business.

"Governor, I would love to take the lead. I greatly appreciate it. Thank you, Sir. Thank you so much, really. You know I am a team player, and that I am here to further assist—whatever you need down here...I am your mule...but there's something else I need your help with, Governor."

"Sure Slip. Anything for you, Son."

It was exactly what Slip wanted to hear.

"Governor, I placed a call to ADEM Secretary, Sonny Hubert, today. I'm having a little problem at home and now I really need your help, Governor."

"Like I said—anything. What can I do? I am at your service, Slip. I spoke to Sonny this morning about the BP Boom Grant program money they are planning for your area down on the coast."

Slip swallowed hard.

"It's about my daughter, Governor. She's gotten herself in a real jam..."

22

Persuading the Governor to help him shutter the Flora-Bama under the ruse of helping the environment was an easy sell for Slip. The Governor was also a Baptist preacher. Before he got into politics he established his own church and a willful flock. Despite his own weaknesses to the contrary, he was a reported teetotaler—and he usually did everything he could by look, word and deed to impugn the party lifestyle represented by the iconic beach bar down on the line. Plus, since his election three years earlier the environmental groups had assailed him tirelessly for his connections to and contributions from big business, and more specifically, big oil. The Governor saw this as an opportunity to feign that he really cared about the environment, while also helping a valued political ally.

The Governor convened a conference call that afternoon between him and Slip and the ADEM Secretary, Sonny Hubert. After briefly explaining the rather awkward situation, Sonny was instructed specifically by the Governor.

"Sonny, I want to look like an environmental advocate on this one. How do you think we should proceed?"

The Secretary of the Alabama Department of Environmental Management (ADEM), Sonny Hubert, like Slip, was a loyal lieutenant. Although he was an Auburn grad, Hubert had found a rare place in the political machine that ran the State of Alabama. His connections came from a former governor—the last Democrat to run the Southern state in more than two decades, to be exact. That former governor happened to also be his maternal grandfather; and they were both now republicans, as the republicans controlled every branch of government in the state. They held a majority in both the House and the Senate and they controlled the Governor's Office and the Supreme Court, through their controversial Justice, Coy Moor, who commissioned the construction of a monument honoring the Ten Commandments outside his Alabama Supreme Court offices after being elected in a landslide several years earlier.

Sonny spoke up, "Governor, down there in Orange Beach we've had the darndest time trying to manage the beach mouse—which is an endangered species." Of course, because of that special designation it is a favorite of the environmental groups. They have been complaining for years that all the condos and development on the beach have destroyed their natural habitat. They claim that their numbers are way down on the island. I imagine Hurricane Ivan in 2004 didn't help, either, but I do think the latest count indicates that the population has suffered."

"So what are you saying, Sonny?" asked Slip.

"I'm saying we issue an adverse environmental conditions citation stating that the bar must cease all business operations until an adequate environmental assessment and impact statement can be crafted and presented. This could take as long as you want it to take...several months if need be. He can fight it through the courts but it will take a while before a judge could hear the case. If the owner is truly hard up for cash like they say he is, well, then he won't make it through the end of the summer. I hear he is already trying to find a buyer. He's been shopping his interest across the state. He's in deep."

"Well, if you know somebody who's interested in buying that Godforsaken place, you may want to tell them to hold on before offering just yet—because it's gonna get really expensive to own without any customers!" Slip laughed out loud.

Governor Finchley and Sonny belly laughed right along with him. Before the conference call ended the three men agreed not to act on the matter until after the Fourth of July weekend, which was not far off. The fourth was on Friday, so it was already a shortened week. They agreed to let the Flora-Bama and its many employees have their hefty Independence

Day sales; but after that, they were going to indefinitely shut the place down.

***

The Fourth of July weekend was fast approaching. Everyone on the island readied for the big holiday and the many spend-thrift tourists it always brought to Orange Beach, Alabama. On Monday night Johnny and Lucy attended Open Mike night at the Flora-Bama. Monday was the only night of the week that the Flora-Bama did not schedule live entertainment. Instead, on Mondays anyone could come to the Bama and play a guitar and sing for the crowd. The Open Mike night was usually run by one of the local musicians who was paid by the Flora-Bama to serve as the host. That night Kathy Pace was the designated mistress of ceremonies.

Kathy Pace had been playing music at the Flora-Bama for over two decades. Like so many before and after her, she found a niche at the Bama and never gave it up. She'd played bass and sung in a number of bands—including at one time Earl the Pearl's—and she was loved by everyone in the community for her warm spirit, her undeniable talent and for her fantastic sense of humor.

"I heard you used to play with Earl the Pearl," Johnny asked Kathy, catching her off guard. She was surprised.

"I don't talk about that anymore, Johnny," she panned with a serious look. Johnny felt guilty.

Seconds later she laughed.

"Just kidding! I got you though, didn't I?" she smiled from ear-to-ear.

"You gotta love ole Earl, huh?" Kathy asked.

"You got to!" Johnny answered, matter-of-factly.

"That's what all the sheep say." She teased.

"Aw, that's wrong Miss Kathy! He's not here to defend himself!" Johnny squealed.

"Baaaaaaaa! Baaaaaaaaa!" she responded, giving her best sheep impression.

Johnny laughed out loud. She really had him going.

Johnny got up on stage and sang "Folsom Prison Blues," by Johnny Cash. After Johnny, Lucy sang "If I die young," by The Band Perry, while Johnny played guitar.

Shortly after Lucy sang the last note and a smattering of applause from the tiny crowd, they were interrupted by a much older, Auburn-haired woman wearing a lopsided gray beret. She wore aged red corduroy pants, a pink paisley long-sleeved shirt, and sandals with blue socks.

"Excuse me, but I am a little short on change, young man. I was wondering if you might lend me three dollars so that I can get a cold drink? My name is Harriet. They call me Hurricane Harriet around here—I guess cause I'm all over the place!" She laughed heartily.

"You're a handsome fellow...what's your name?" she asked with a wink.

Johnny stared and marveled at her energy; and her makeup and lipstick-smeared face.

"M'am, My name is Johnny Glass and I will be glad to buy you a drink!" he replied, smiling at Kathy. Kathy winked at him.

"Come with me to the bar, Harriet!"

He led her on his arm to the bar. He looked over his shoulder to a staring, smiling Lucy.

"Need anything Lucy?" he asked.

"No thanks!" Lucy answered, smiling.

She felt so lucky to be with Johnny, and not at her apartment back in Mobile, taking mindless courses and attending silly sorority parties with a bunch of immature fraternity boys. Later that night, back in the sailboat, with a Luke Bryan song playing low amidst the hum of the tiny window unit, Johnny confided to Lucy.

"You know baby, there is no other place I would rather be than with you, right here, right now. I know this is not much, but we are doing what we love and living in a beautiful place. We certainly have it good compared to most. I think it's all about perspective; all about one's point of view."

Lucy liked what she heard.

"I know! That's what I've been thinking all the time. So what if we don't have a ton of money, we live on the beach! We can worry about work, later. For now, why don't we just enjoy life—just like Mr. Joe says?"

Johnny kissed her and hugged her tight for several seconds.

***

On Tuesday night at the Flora-Bama Joe and the workers and players held a fundraiser for a young boy in the community who was struggling with what appeared to be terminal cancer. Dozens of people worked together for many days ahead of time to hold a silent and a live auction to raise money for his treatment and extended care.

That night over thirty musicians magically showed up and sang and donated their own hard-earned money and time to help a young man struggling to live. Among the many great players who showed and played were Rick Whaley and Lee Anne Creswell, Gove Scrivenor and his magical auto harp, Dave Caluger and his badass stand-up bass guitar with the Beach-billys, along with Mickey Springsten, Cowboy Johnson, Neil Dover, Jake Justice, Troy Brannon, John Cook, Roxy Hart, the Perdido Brothers, Johnny Barbados of the Lucky Doggs, guitar maestro Luther Wamble, Bo Roberts, Mike Locklin, Elaine Petty and many, many more; making for a memorable, fun and meaningful evening. It was a great community event that drew over 500 people and raised over $30,000 for a young man fighting for his life, and his family. It was just one of dozens of effective charitable fundraising events hosted by the Flora-Bama each year.

One of the musicians who showed up that night and played for the cause was a 42-year old self-proclaimed Outlaw Country musician named Wayne Mills. A native of tiny Arab, Alabama, Wayne was one of those exciting, young, fresh musicians who inevitably make their way to the Flora-Bama. However, Wayne was different. A former Alabama football walk-on, he was 6-3, with broad shoulders and a husky build. However, he had a heart as big as his thick, athletic frame and a soothing voice and presence. Wayne fit right in and everybody loved him and his great brand of music. Sadly, that night proved to be one of the last times Gerald Wayne Mills played at the Flora-Bama, as he was tragically murdered while on the road in Nashville, of all places, a few weeks later. Wayne Mills was snuffed out way too early in life, leaving everyone wondering what could have been. He is missed by many outside of his wife and surviving son, including all of his friends and family members left behind at the Flora-Bama.

Wednesday night before the Fourth was a big night at the Flora-Bama, as there were already a ton of people on the island. Despite the oil spill scare and the many real, worldly problems that hung over the place like a black cloud, many gulf coast residents—particularly those who still owned property on the island, still chose to flock to the beaches for the Fourth. Johnny and Lucy and Sam and Preston had to literally squeeze through the nine o'clock crowd just to get on stage.

The weekend was fantastic, with several magical impromptu music performances. Texas native Kim Carson stopped in to see what condition the Bama was in, and ended up playing a set with Jake and Hung Jury. The Mulligan Brothers also blew through town and turned some serious heads with their welcomed, newfangled Southern style.

Johnny and Lucy and the band had their best week ever—as the Flora-Bama invited them to play on Sunday underneath the tent after the Church service, giving them an extra gig to go with the many extra tips that came from the larger-than-normal, holiday crowds. As it turned out, it was a blessing; as it proved to be their last gig played at the Flora-Bama for a spell.

23

On early Monday afternoon a process server showed up at the Flora-Bama with a certified letter addressed to the owner, Joe Gideon. Joe hadn't made it by the club yet, as like most he was resting from the long weekend of music and festivities. The server said he would be glad to wait. Shortly thereafter Joe received a call from management saying that there was official business waiting for him—a certified piece of correspondence requiring his signature.

"Who is it from?" Joe asked his manager, Joanna.

Joanna covered the phone's receiver and asked the server, "Who is it from?"

"ADEM," replied the process server, when prompted.

"Adem, he said," she answered into the phone.

"Oh, great," Joe answered. He knew well about the agency he called, the "Alabama Department of Environmental Maniacs." He had been dealing with them and their anti-capitalist government types for years. But for some reason this one felt different. He begrudgingly jumped into his beat up red Ford and drove ten miles west to the Flora-Bama. What he found was his world turned effectively upside down.

***

Joe drove into the gravel parking lot adjacent to the Flora-Bama. He exited his truck and walked around to the front entrance. Walking in he saw two television news trucks—the kind with satellites on top—one from Mobile and the other from Pensacola, which made him extremely nervous. His sixth sense told him something bad was coming, and it was right.

He entered the makeshift front entrance area where his workers gathered. He saw a non-descript fellow holding a brown folder, smoking a cigarette. Joe saw two cameramen holding video cameras and two news people with microphones move in around him, focusing on his every move.

"I'm Joe Gideon," Joe said, much to the surprise of the oblivious fellow with the package.

The guy extinguished the cigarette. He retrieved the papers from the folder and handed Joe a pen. He instructed him to sign on the dotted line, testifying that he had received the citation. Joe signed it and took the two-page legal document into his hands and read it.

He got through the first paragraph about infringing on the indigenous beach mouse's habitat and cringed. He read the second graph regarding "immediately ceasing all sales and service operations at the Flora-Bama until otherwise notified," and he grew faint. He actually saw stars.

"I can't believe this," he muttered. "Why is all of this happening to me?" was all he could wonder, thinking that this was obviously the disease and pestilence he earlier joked of.

"Mr. Gideon—are you going to fight the Flora-Bama's closure, or are you going to put it up for sale?" the newswoman from Mobile asked.

"It's been up for sale!" Joe bellowed. "I was already busy trying to save the place before I got this—a citation saying that we have 'unduly encroached upon the pristine habitat of the endangered beach mouse'...this is the biggest bunch of crap I've ever seen! The same state government citing us today is building a $100 million state park and convention center with a massive footprint down the road in Gulf Shores! That too is the beach mouse's habitat! This is a complete joke! There are hundreds of condos bigger than us on the beach!" Joe pleaded.

"Will you fight it?" the other reporter asked.

"Yes, I intend to fight the citation," Joe stammered, "but at some point a business person has to ask himself if it's even worth it having to fight with government to stay afloat every time they turn around. Excuse me, I am going call my attorney," Joe said, pushing his way into the bowels of the Flora-Bama, into one of the administrative offices, where he sat and called his trusted counsel, John Penn.

***

After the call to his lawyer Joe gathered everyone comprising the early staff on hand for work that day and explained that for now they needed to secure all the doors and windows and lock the place up like they were preparing for a hurricane. In his own voice he taped an impassioned digital answering machine message for people calling incessantly from every corner of the globe to find out if the horrible news was true. Afterward, he ordered all employees to stop answering the phone, and to just let the message play.

The message Joe recorded for everyone calling went like this:

"This is Joe Gideon, the owner of the Flora-Bama. I have been here 33 years and have not been open for business a total of about a week during that span. I have always tried to create a place where people from all walks of life can come and enjoy the therapeutic wonders of laughter and song. Also, I always wanted to offer a place where people could come and meet people different than them. It was a good concept for a long time—until the Alabama government got involved. We have been cited by the Alabama Department of Environmental Management for disrupting the natural habitat of the endangered beach mouse. This included a cease and desist order of all service and business operations here at the Flora-Bama, until further notified. We of course, will abide by the order, but we also intend to fight it. If you are so inclined, please contact the Alabama Governor, Mr. Robert Finchley's office and the Alabama Department of Environmental Management and communicate to them your dissatisfaction with this despicable, disgusting example of over-regulation. ADEM doesn't realize it, but they just laid off 150 people during the peak of the tourist season—one we had basically lost because of the BP oil spill. At any rate, thank you for your call. Please call back later for more information. Thanks again, Joe."

Joe's voice faded in strength at the end when he mentioned his employees losing their livelihoods. It was a moving message. Before the end of the day the Alabama Governor's Office had been deluged with over 1,500 angry, blistering calls. They ranged from utter disgust and contempt to actual death threats. A couple of rednecks actually threatened to take out the governor, Robert Finchley. People everywhere across the Deep South and beyond were pissed. The Bama had been taken from them; as a result, a revolution was brewing. On the second day, the digital answering system received a staggering 19,000 calls, some ranging from faraway places like Australia, England, Alaska and even France.

By the time Joe stepped back outside Alabama Department of Environmental Management workers were busy placing signs on and adjacent to the Flora-Bama property. Each of the twenty signs posted was white with black lettering. Each, below the department crest and symbol for the State of Alabama, bore the words: "Beach Mouse Habitat: DO NOT DISTURB by order of ADEM."

News of the Flora-Bama's indefinite closure, by mid-afternoon, predictably hit social media and went viral. Although it was covered on the five, six and ten o'clock news segments in Pensacola and Mobile later that evening, by 4:30 p.m. Central Standard Time, the Flora-Bama's phone was ringing off the hook from former patrons across the United States and internationally. Die-hard Flora-Bama fans contemplated the unthinkable: That they had enjoyed their last frothy bushwhacker. Some of the messages left on the answering machine were gut-wrenching. One female caller from the Midwestern state of Wisconsin begged for the bushwhacker recipe, pleading that if the Flora-Bama closed she would "never have that feeling again." Of course, she was not alone.

The news of the Flora-Bama's closing was as confusing as it was shocking to fans everywhere. One of the local TV news outlets that caught footage of Joe outside the establishment, stated that the Flora-Bama was being closed to save an endangered species of beach mouse, and that the owner was now trying to sell it. The other correctly stated that the bar was under citation from ADEM and that it was now closed indefinitely until the property could be properly assessed for beach mouse habitat damage and re-designated. The second segment showed the clip of Joe saying that he was going to fight the closing, but that it was difficult to stay in business when you had to fight the government at every turn.

Joe had owned the Flora-Bama for over thirty years and only closed the bar three or four times, for impending hurricanes. However, after each of those threats from the unforgiving forces of Mother Nature, the Flora-Bama reopened as soon as it possibly could. This was different. The area's biggest cultural landmark and avowed epicenter of island fun was shuttered indefinitely. It took several painful hours for reality to kick in for the locals and regulars. Most of them were in denial. It was still just a Monday, albeit a particularly somber one; and predictably, there was no open mike night, like usual, on the Alabama-Florida Line.

Johnny woke to a text from Jake on Monday afternoon around 4:15.

"Dude—the Flora-Bama is closed for good! Call me asap!"

Lucy kayaked while Johnny relaxed poolside, enjoying a late afternoon snooze on a padded lounge chair. He sat up and dialed Jake.

"Yeah man, can you believe it?" Jake asked, answering the call.

"No, what is going on?"

Jake explained what he knew.

"They shut the Bama down because it is encroaching on a mouse's habitat?" Johnny asked.

"That's the word," Jake said. "Ain't that some shit?"

"It doesn't make any sense!" Johnny insisted. "What's really going on?"

***

Joe called a late Tuesday afternoon meeting of all employees inside the Bama Dome. The last month had been one of the toughest he'd endured as an entrepreneur. The embarrassing bankruptcy news, the bad press and poor tourist season stemming from the BP oil spill and now the forced closing, had pushed him to his emotional limits. For Joe it was bad enough dealing with the guilt he harbored over his bad business dealings. Now he had to also think of his saddened, disaffected employees.

Joe had the management open up the back bar downstairs and serve everyone whatever they wanted. Many of the support staff had already started self-medicating, as they were trying to cope with the unthinkable—losing their dream jobs at one of the South's coolest hot spots, and the realization of possibly having to find another way to pay the bills in the middle of tourist season.

Johnny and Lucy, Jake, Roxy and Earl the Pearl all walked into the Bama Dome together, joining about 40 or 50 others. One of them already there gave them a heads up.

"Joe opened up the back bar for us," Preston said.

Jake and Earl walked that way. They each ordered a whiskey and water. Johnny got Lucy a bushwhacker, as she had asked for it. She had said nothing to Johnny earlier in the day when she found out what happened. Johnny even thought that she was particularly somber.

Lucy knew immediately after she talked to Johnny, and before she read Internet reports, that her father was behind all of it. It had his signature. Plus, she knew that he was close with the Governor, and that he could easily get something like this done. She felt like a traitor to all of her new friends and family on the island—to Johnny, to Joe, to everyone. She felt that somehow she had brought all of this misery upon them.

"Earl do you know what the hell is really going on around here?" Johnny asked, sipping his drink.

Earl slammed half his drink in one gulp. He looked tired. Earl worked a day job as an instructor at a local community college and moonlighted at the Flora-Bama and other places that hired musicians for too little. He and his wife, a teacher, worked really hard to provide for their two college-bound girls.

"I don't know Johnny Glass, but I got a feeling it has nothing to do with a beach mouse, my friend," Earl said, finishing his drink. He ordered another.

Johnny saw Joe walk in with Mandy. He made his way back over to Lucy, handed her the bushwhacker and sat next to her on one of the picnic tables inside. Moments later, Joe got up on stage and addressed the crowd, which had grown to well over a hundred, and included some of the locals, like architect Brad Masterson, Captain Max and Hurricane Harriet, among others.

Dressed in his regular attire of worn, unpressed slacks, a softly wrinkled, collared, short-sleeved shirt and beat-up, loosely-tied white tennis shoes, Gideon addressed the people that for years had made it all possible. The words came deliberately, as if he were struggling to articulate; to get it over with. As the former chemistry teacher began to speak you could have heard a mouse peeing on cotton.

"Well, I have three things I want to talk to you guys about today. First, we are going to talk about your jobs. As long as I am owner you will still get a paycheck, regardless if we are closed or not. I don't know how long this is going to last, but I will get you a paycheck as long as I can. I know it isn't tips, but it's something.

Secondly, many of you have heard that I have been having financial difficulties. This is true. But, what I want you all to know is that this is not your fault. I brought these circumstances upon myself because of investment decisions I have made. You had nothing to do with this. This is not because of you."

Taking on the tenor of a father talking to his children, Gideon's eyes reddened and his speech slowed. By the hardest, he continued.

"Unfortunately, I invested most of my personal wealth in the highly speculative real estate market, and I'm upside down. The properties I own are worth a third of what I paid for them and there's no end in sight. I had no choice but to file for bankruptcy. I've lost over $40 million. Most of you already knew all of this from the newspapers, but I felt like I should address it while we are here together today."

The bitter news fell hard on the ears of his downtrodden troops. Their pale, expressionless faces reflected their worst fears. Many sat there motionless, holding half full beverages, mouths agape. However, Joe tried his best to find a silver lining amidst a growing cloud of doubt, to provide hope in an otherwise somber moment.

"The good news is that we are pretty sure the Flora-Bama and the Silver Moon (package liquor store and lounge across the street) are safe. They are profitable. They and you are not going to suffer because of my financial troubles, and that's the way it should be, because you guys have made it all possible. We have a great team of bankruptcy lawyers and we feel we are going to be able to survive this. We'll just have to wait and see, but I am pretty sure with a little help that we can save everything."

He continued.

"Now, the third thing I want to address is the latest fiasco with the State of Alabama's Department of Environmental Management. To tell you the truth I don't know what brought this on. I sense that it's political for one reason or another, because Alabama is building a huge convention center in Gulf Shores with $100 million in BP money. I don't see how they can't be encroaching on beach mouse habitat there, so it certainly looks dubious."

"I have already talked to my attorney and he has requested an emergency hearing before a judge to give us a temporary stay in the matter, which would hopefully allow us to continue doing business. Understand that we are going to fight this. It just pains me to think that someone is doing this for personal or political reasons. It's sickening," he finished, sounding strong despite the situation.

There was a moment of silence.

Lucy, her stomach in knots, unexpectedly spoke up.

"My father is responsible for this, Mr. Joe," she said. Her voice broke up at the end.

No one said a thing. A couple of seconds passed.

"My Dad—Senator Dee Whitman—did this! He does everything for Governor Finchley! He sponsored the bill for the construction of the state park and this is just payback for that! And they stand to make even more money off the subcontractor kickbacks after the state park is done. That's how it works in Alabama! "

Tears ran down Lucy's cheeks. She placed the more than half-drank bushwhacker and bar napkin on the bench to her right and wiped the rivulets from her face.

"You see, Mr. Joe, my Daddy won't have me singing out here at the Flora-Bama! It doesn't fit him and my mama's worldview. They think everybody out here is trash—but that is so not the case!"

She sobbed uncontrollably.

"They are so terrible! I am so sorry Mr. Joe—everyone! I'm so sorry!"

Lucy stood and ran outside toward the front of the property. Johnny ran after her.

Inside the Bama Dome, Joe felt terrible.

"Poor thing," Joe said.

"Poor thing is right," remarked Brad Masterson. "Her daddy is a real piece of shit."

Joe looked to Brad.

"What a jerk!" yelled Roxy, swigging her second dry martini. She looked even sexier when she was mad.

There was a moment of silence.

Earl the Pearl quipped, "I heard he's got a little dick."

Joe slightly smirked. A couple of people laughed out loud.

"Do you know the Senator, Brad?" Joe asked.

Everyone was quiet. They quit laughing and listened to their conversation.

"I don't know him well. But I do know about him, Joe. A number of my clients work with Slip and I have been introduced to him on more than one occasion. I've seen him speak at events and I've seen him at weddings and funerals."

Brad took a long pull on a frothy bushwhacker. It was his second. He knew it could be his last for a while. He continued.

"I also know that the senator is getting rich off of local contracts he has with several local governments inside his senate district. I think he even has contracts with Baldwin County itself. It's highly unethical, but he's been given a free pass by the Alabama Ethics Commission—which is a sham of course. The legislature pays their ridiculous salaries for looking out for them."

He took another sip and pushed his glasses up on his nose.

"And like little Lucy said, he sponsored the bill to fund and designate the $100 million in BP cash for the construction of a state park and convention center/hotel. He and the governor are absolutely thick as thieves. If Slip wanted this done I could see the governor saying sure just to throw the environmentalists a bone."

Joe spoke up. "Lovely." He shook his head and continued.

"Well guys, let's give all of this some thought and sleep on it. I want everyone to have fun this evening, join us across the street if you care to. We're gonna keep the bar open here a little while longer. Grab another drink or two as you filter out. If anybody needs anything, you know you can reach me on my cell—but remember that I am technology-challenged," he laughed, in the face of overwhelming adversity.

Joe caught up with Brad Masterson before he left.

"Brad, do you mind spending some time with me this evening? What you said got my wheels turning and I want to bounce a few things off of you. Do you feel like heading over to my place a little later? We can get comfortable and talk."

"Sure Joe," Brad answered. "No problem."

Brad knew that Joe, at 70, was fighting for everything. He was glad to help. Like to so many others in the community, Joe was a dear friend. He was also an amazing person; someone who had single-handedly made life in Perdido fascinating and fun for many years. Many more outside of Brad would be willing to fight for him and the place they all held dear to their hearts, the beloved Flora-Bama.

Johnny caught up with Lucy in the parking lot. They had traveled there together in Lucy's bug, so she had her own keys. She was already in her car and had it running when Johnny slid in front of the vehicle, temporarily preventing her escape. She sobbed inside the car. She cracked the automatic window.

"Move Johnny!" she loudly scowled, gesticulating with her left arm.

Johnny saw a frightful look on her face, and his instincts told him to move and to let her go.

"She's manic!" he thought.

He stepped aside and she drove off in a skid, ahead of a cloud of white clam shells, gravel and white powder sand. Johnny noticed she steered her Volkswagen west, in the direction opposite of their sailboat. He kicked an aluminum can with all his might and spit before returning inside to be with the rest of the guys.

24

After having a couple of beers at the Silver Moon, Joe and Brad Masterson drove to Joe's new place in West Pensacola off of South Loop near the Navy Base on Blue Angel Parkway. The ranch style house wasn't exactly a new place, as it had been built in the early 1980's, but to Joe it was new. He'd lost his place on Old River to the bank. However, he still owned the old ranch house that Bo Roberts and other musicians occasionally had lived in for some time. It was in a rustic, swampy swath of young timber off the thoroughfare leading to the military base. Joe had built the yard up by digging six different ponds on the acreage surrounding his home, and he was starting to settle into the place.

In the fading twilight Joe and Brad took a loaf of stale sandwich bread and threw it to the perch, bass, bream and goggle eye he'd stocked the ponds with, walking around the perimeter of the property to the various, dark water pools as they talked. Joe liked feeding the fish. It relaxed him, lowering his blood pressure.

"Joe, there's somebody in Fairhope I think we should talk to. I think he can really help us on this." Brad said.

"Who?" Joe asked, open to anything.

He flicked his wrist and threw a half slice of bread into the middle of the pond. Symmetrical wave circles radiated outward from the epicenter across the water. The bread popped up and down on the water as the fish devoured it from below the clear black water's surface.

"A Mr. Francis Tripp, of Fairhope. I read in the *Press-Register* a couple of weeks ago that he filed an ethics complaint against Senator Whitman. I know Francis Tripp. He and his brother Arnold ran a dive shop in Birmingham back in the 1980's. I made countless trips to Belize with them! They were fearless adventurers—really great guys. They even took me to the Blue Hole a few times. Arnie passed away a couple years back, but Francis is still alive—he is retired in Fairhope—and I'm certain that he knows everything we need to know about the senator."

"Call him and see if he will talk to us," Joe said.

"I have his number," Brad said. He reached for his wallet. "I still have his business card. I have kept it all these years. He is a hell of a guy—a former Marine."

Brad dialed the number and hit the speaker button. The number rang twice before there was an answer.

"Hello, can I help you?" asked the voice on the line.

"Francis!" yelled Brad into the speaker.

"Yes this is he," he answered.

"This is Brad—Brad Masterson—I used to run with you and Arnold back in Bham! Remember the trips to Belize, Mon?"

Brad inflected his voice like someone from the tropics.

"Yeah Mon. I remember you. I remember you, well! How are you, Mon?" Tripp returned in the same native Belizean English dialect they once spoke in an earlier, more carefree time.

"It's been a while, huh Tripp?"

"Yes Mon. It's been I'd say 20 or 25 years. You still in B-Ham?"

"No man—I'm on Ono. I'm an architect now. I went back and finished school after those two summers in San Pedro."

"No shit?" Tripp asked. "Well I'll be…"

"Hey Tripp, I saw in the paper that you filed an ethics complaint against the senator from Fairhope, Slip Whitman."

He laughed.

"Yeah, that was me. It's funny you ask. I was working on a second ethics complaint against him when you called. I take it you read the Mobile paper this morning?"

The truth was that Brad had not read the paper. All he had

done earlier was stare at the surreal headline stating that the Flora-Bama was closed indefinitely. It read: "Beach Mouse 1, Flora-Bama 0."

"No, I have not read the paper. What are you talking about?" Brad answered.

"It's Slip. He really slipped up this time!" Tripp stated emphatically.

"What happened?" Brad asked.

"Governor Finchley tapped Whitman to oversee the handing out of BP grant monies to the coastal cities in Baldwin County to place boom in the way of the encroaching oil. The senator tried to give two contracts—one for Fairhope and the other for Perdido Key—to himself—to his own company, Whitman Tractor and Farm! Apparently he's not only an expert in bullshit, he's also a boom expert!"

"He isn't that stupid, is he?" Brad asked.

"Of course he is! It's called arrogance!" Tripp yelled. The system is corrupted, Brad. It doesn't work anymore! There is no accountability."

Brad looked to Joe, who was much concerned.

"Tomorrow I'm filing this second complaint against the senator to the Ethics Commission—regarding the boom grants, and I am also meeting with an FBI agent."

Joe tapped Brad on the arm. Tripp continued.

"A guy I talked to in Fairhope, a former DEA agent, gave me the card of a female agent from the Bureau of Investigations in Mobile. She agreed to meet me at O'Charley's—tomorrow. I've got a file on Whitman a foot thick—he and the Mayor of Fairhope. She gets them both. You need to read the article in the paper so you can get the full story, but Whitman was told not to pursue the two local contracts by the county Emergency Management Director. He withdrew the contracts and re-submitted them under a different name—and still got paid by both Fairhope and Perdido Key. He's caught! I've got their asses this time!"

Brad and Joe were blown away by what they heard. Senator Whitman sounded like such a terrible person—certainly the worst kind of public official. They couldn't believe it. By this time Joe had picked up the newspaper, found the story on the third page and read it. He re-read the parts he found most disturbing while Brad talked.

"You are just like your old man!" Brad stated.

Tripp laughed. "I guess I am, huh?" he proudly asked.

"Man Tripp, this is crazy!"

"You better believe it, brother! This is Fairyhope! It's the most crooked city in Baldwin County. These fru-fru people are living in la-la Land! The locals like to brag that it's "not so Alabama," but have I got news for them! The mayor is an absolute sociopath. He lies constantly. He lies when the truth would serve him better. I hate to say it, Brad, but Belize's government wasn't this corrupt. Also, Louisiana gets a bad rap. Alabama is easily the most corrupt state! It's not even close!"

After Brad thanked Mr. Tripp and hung up the phone, Joe smiled from ear-to-ear.

He had a Eureka moment.

Brad saw the look.

"Brad, I have an idea!"

"Yeah?"

"Yeah!" Joe stated, smiling.

"I need you to create some drawings…"

25

Lucy woke inside her apartment in Mobile near the South Alabama campus. It was Wednesday morning, her second in as many mornings without waking up next to Johnny. She had ignored his repeated texts expressing his love for her, and to please come back, that everything was going to be alright.

Lucy had a hard time believing everything was gonna be alright. The Flora-Bama was closed down because of her father. She could not face anyone on the island until they opened back up. She just couldn't do it. It was too difficult to fathom, much less carry out. She was despondent. She loved and missed Johnny; but she had never been so scared and unsure about her future. She felt trapped, and confused.

***

Johnny woke inside the small forward berthing area inside the sailboat. He was a mess. The last two nights he'd drank heavily at the Silver Moon to forget about what he'd lost. The lounge and package store was not mentioned in the citation, so a few of the players had gotten together both nights and played for everyone who still wanted to have a little fun despite the circumstances.

It was not like Johnny to drink to excess. He missed Lucy terribly, and could only wonder why she would not talk to him. He imagined she must be hurting if she couldn't talk to him. He figured she blamed everything on herself. It saddened him.

It was Wednesday, and normally he would have been looking forward to playing the Flora-Bama that evening with Lucy and the guys. But, that was not the case. He had the night off. He wondered if Lucy would play with them at their other regular gigs the next three nights. He texted her again, but she didn't answer.

***

On Wednesday afternoon around five o'clock, after he got off work in Pensacola where he taught mostly young people how to use an ultrasound machine to look at babies, Earl the Pearl Roberts drove to the Flora-Bama parking lot in his beat up Toyota pickup truck. He opened the driver side door and stepped out of the vehicle, and stripped buck naked. He put on a tiny jockstrap that barely covered his goods. He put on flip flops and reached into the back of the truck and pulled out a huge, white sandwich board that a person could wear on their shoulders. On one side it read in black letters: "Senator Whitman has a TINY weenie." On the other it read: "Save the Flora-Bama!"

Wearing the apparatus, Earl crept to the edge of the beach highway in front of the Flora-Bama. It was the peak of tourist season. The road was thick with traffic. After he started waving he immediately started getting honks and waves from passersby.

"Woo-hoo baby!" said a hefty woman with a Louisiana accent and license plate. "Show it off, Big Earl! Wooie look at dem' legs!"

Since he wore only a miniscule athletic supporter, Earl from afar looked naked underneath the signs.

"Damn Right!" said a good ole boy in a blue Ford truck.

"Senator Whitman is a crook!" yelled a woman with an Alabama plate. "Screw him!"

Forty minutes later, an Alabama State Trooper showed up and politely asked Earl to put on some pants, quickly ending the charade. However, it was not before Earl had taken dozens of willing facebook pictures and a couple of choice videos, which had already gone viral. Within minutes, one of the locals had formed a "Save the Flora-Bama" facebook site, and it was mentioned on the Pensacola six o'clock news. By midnight it had over 5,000 likes, and it was obvious that the community was mobilizing politically in a way it never had before—to save the revered and fabled landmark everyone through the years had grown to love.

The Closing of the Flora-Bama story trended high on social media and the TV and radio community covered it incessantly. One Birmingham radio station offered hourly updates from the state line. It was apparent everyone across the State of Alabama felt that the beach bar—for whatever reason, had been unfairly targeted by ADEM. Fox's Shepard Smith even mentioned the shuttering of the Flora-Bama on his nightly national news broadcast, saying that it had disrupted many gulf coast vacation plans.

One of the Mobile, Alabama TV networks got a tip from a viewer that Senator Whitman was behind the citation, and that it was a favor done for him by the governor, Robert Finchley. One of the braver reporters caught Slip in between committee meetings at the Capitol in Montgomery; and put a microphone in his face. The young man asked him a single question.

"Did you ask Governor Finchley to get ADEM to shut down the Flora-Bama?"

The senator was caught completely off guard.

"No comment!" he said, moving away from the news people crowding him.

"Senator, please answer the question!" he tried again.

Slip Whitman said nothing and hurried into the temporary sanctuary of the Senate ante room, where media was strictly forbidden. Later that night, the reporter ran footage of the senator ducking the questioning.

***

On Wednesday, two days after the closing of the Flora-Bama, Joe and Brad Masterson stood in front of the Flora-Bama compound with several of the long-time employees. There were dozens of TV cameras facing them from stations across the globe and the Deep South covering the story. Joe, wearing a Flora-Bama collared shirt with a logo on his left chest, beige, frayed cotton shorts, white tube socks and tennis shoes, stepped up to the bank of microphones and addressed the crowd on hand.

"As many of you know, I have had my share of challenges. If it hasn't been a hurricane or an oil spill, it has been a financial or a political crisis. It certainly has not been an easy road!"

Joe smiled enthusiastically, and continued.

"Therefore, I have decided to get out of the bar business. I will not reopen the Flora-Bama. I repeat: I will not be re-opening the Flora-Bama. I am sorry to say that we have served our last bushwhacker."

The silence was deafening, as if E.F. Hutton himself had just spoken.

Joe deliberately waited three or more long seconds, demonstrating the uncanny timing of one of his veteran stage performers. He continued.

"I have decided, instead, to enter the hotel business. Yes—the hotel business. Governor Finchley recently said that Alabama does not have a first-rate hotel. I want to take him up on that challenge—and build one—with environmentally-friendly design elements—that will set a true standard for beach development. In fact, the entire bottom floor of our towers will remain white sand, except for its moorings, so as to preserve forever the beach mouse habitat. Not a single grain of sand will be displaced. Also, the current Flora-Bama structure will be completely razed and returned to its natural condition as prime beach mouse habitat. The hotel will operate high above the mouse sanctuary, as a true forerunner in eco-friendly, coastal hotel design and construction. We have tabbed it, "The Wayward Home for Lost Musicians.""

Joe paused again and kept a straight face. Cameras everywhere clicked and snapped. He continued.

"I would now like to show you a rendering of the project's feature design element—the two massive, 23-story towers—the "Flora" and the "Bama," as well as the connecting "Elvis Presley Sky Bridge," formed in the shape of an acoustic Martin guitar. I am going to turn it over to my partner on the $100 million project, local architect, Brad Masterson."

Joe stepped back and Brad took his place. Brad unfurled a rolled up document and placed it on a nearby easel one of the workers set up. He placed a piece of cardboard on the easel and clipped the corners of the rendering, allowing everyone, and the cameras, to view it. It depicted clearly the two massive towers and the guitar-shaped bridge adjoining the two monoliths.

After Brad answered a couple of questions and explained the inherent environmental merits of the design, he turned it back over to Joe, who closed out the press conference.

"I appreciate the media cooperation today. For your refreshment we are going to pop a few bottles of champagne. Please enjoy a tiny glass or two and share in our celebration. We will be building the gulf coast's finest luxury hotel here at the site of the old Flora-Bama. Oh…and did I tell you that a carousel bar on top will be a replica of the Old Flora-Bama main room? That's the plan, anyway! Thanks so much! We will keep you posted!"

***

After the press conference numerous environmental groups realized the sheer hypocrisy of the State of Alabama building a massive, 100,000 square foot hotel and convention center on the beach with $100 million in BP money, as it was going to certainly destroy additional beach mouse habitat. Further, there were thousands of daily calls pouring into the Governor's Office over the Flora-Bama's closing; and many more were taking a firm stand against the planned beach hotel and convention center, for obvious reasons.

"Give us back the Flora-Bama and Get Off our Beach!" became the battle cry of the self-proclaimed citizenry of the tiny gulf island republic. Late Thursday the Governor finally capitulated. He called Senator Whitman's cell phone.

Senator Whitman sat in the hot tub at the Grand Hotel. His Iphone, inside a waterproof OuterBox protective case, rang twice. He saw it was the Governor. Alone in the whirlpool, he tried to answer it, but fumbled. He mistakenly dropped it into the bubbling water. He quickly retrieved it and answered.

"Hey Governor!" Slip stated.

"Hey Slip," the governor answered. Slip could tell by his voice that this wasn't going to be a good call.

"What's up Guv?"

"Slip, ADEM Secretary Sonny Hubert is gonna reinstate the Flora-Bama's business license tomorrow. I'm sorry Slip, but unlike you, I have opposition—from both parties. I have to win re-election. You are unopposed, so I know you don't care about what your constituents think, but I am not afforded that luxury at this time! I am catching holy hell over this! This was NOT a good idea, Slip!"

As disappointing as it was, Slip understood.

"Okay Governor. I see. I understand where you are coming from. I see why you need to do it. Go ahead."

"Slip—I've gotten—my office has gotten, over 25,000 phone calls about the Flora-Bama! I have never gotten this many calls! Plus, now the environmentalists—led by the Sierra Club, are threatening a lawsuit on behalf of the beach mouse. It's over the Hotel and Convention Center project—they say its massive footprint is going to only hurt more mice...so you can see where all this is going—South—and fast! Now we are probably gonna have to adapt new design standards and have the thing completely redrawn before we can build it! And by the way, that Gideon is something else! I don't know why you ever messed with him! He kicked our ass up and down that beach on this!"

Slip could only listen in silence. For once, he was at a loss for words.

"I've gotta cut bait, Slip. Good luck with your daughter—and those boom grants."

The governor chuckled.

"Fairhope and Perdido, I'm sure, should keep y'all busy for a while."

***

Joe coordinated his Wednesday press conference with Mr. Francis Tripp's second ethics complaint against the Senator, on Thursday. As a result, Friday was a huge news day. At 10:00 a.m. Sonny Hubert, wearing a tan designer suit, yellow shirt, and silk Hermes neck tie, held a press conference in front of the Flora-Bama in front of over 500 hundred smiling workers, loyal locals and regulars. The good news everybody wanted to hear had already been leaked. The set-up was identical to Joe's two days prior, except there were hundreds more people in attendance. They all waited for the doors of the Flora-Bama to magically reopen.

"My name is Sonny Hubert, Secretary of the Alabama Department of Environmental Management. I am here today to announce that as of immediately, this place of business may resume all operations until a full habitat assessment and reconditioning plan can be conducted and formulated by our department. This is by official order of Alabama Governor Robert Finchley."

Sonny Hubert held in front of him—plainly for the cameras to see, the signed re-instatement. Joe, who was standing nearby with the keys to the front door, lunged in front of the cameras, taking advantage of a rare marketing opportunity. Like a kid, he yelled into the microphone:

"Two for one all day and night at the World-Famous Flora-Bama! Yipee!"

The crowd went nuts. It was pure pandemonium.

"Open up the Bama! Open up the Bama! Open up the Bama!" they chanted.

Several of the news stations ran Joe's last-second, two-for-one offer amidst the open up the Bama chants, and the news hit social media like a tsunami. Earl the Pearl updated his facebook page and said his 5:00 p.m. show was gonna be the greatest he'd ever had, and that he was "gonna give a 90 percent effort for the first time in his struggling career!"

In the newspaper that morning—this time on the front page, was an article about the second ethics complaint against Senator Whitman by Mr. Tripp, alleging that he conspired with the Mayors of Fairhope and Perdido Key to give the grants for boom deployment to his personal business, Whitman Tractor & Farm.

Surprisingly, the newspaper actually did some investigating and quoted the senator as saying, "In hindsight, I wouldn't do it again," but that he "had not yet had ethics training" at the time. He added that the Mayor of Fairhope actually asked him to do it, so he "just tried to help him out;" and that after everything was over, he "only got twelve percent of the grant money."

The article was damning, and the senator—already painted bad for being behind the closing of the Flora-Bama with the governor, was seen as a local pariah. That Saturday morning he failed to show for his tee time at Lakewood, and on Sunday he refused to attend church service at First Baptist. On Monday, he failed to show at the regular prayer meeting he chaired. Like his daughter, he was afraid to face the public.

**

It was late Friday afternoon. Brad Masterson was on his fourth bushwhacker, sitting next to Francis Tripp, who made the drive out to the Flora-Bama to celebrate its reopening, Senator Whitman's imminent demise, and to reconnect with Brad; as they hadn't seen each other in years.

A shoeless and shirtless, darkly-tanned Francis P. Tripp, wearing an ear ring, a toe ring, an ankle bracelet and a baby blue kerchief around his neck, drank chilled Patron with a lime wedge and chased it with cold draft beer in plastic cups. He'd had six or seven of the small, clear shooters and several beers, and was flying high.

"Drink what you want, Tripp, I got this!" Masterson noted, sipping on his bushwhacker.

"Thanks man. I appreciate it," he said, laughing uncontrollably.

He tried to talk, but couldn't. He was near delirious from the good Tequila and the calamity of events.

He composed himself.

"Guess what?" he asked Brad. He was still chuckling.

"What?" Brad said.

"Not only did I give the FBI everything on Senator Whitman and the mayor—over the last month I helped some fellow environmentalist/activists friends of mine recruit a woman to run against him as an independent. She only needed a few hundred signatures to get on the ballot and run against him as an independent. We busted our ass and got the signatures and filed it with the State. Whitman now has competition. He can't just go in like last time, when neither a democrat nor a republican signed up to run against him. This time he will have to run a campaign—and be held accountable for his crimes. I don't think he'll make it. Whattayou think?"

"I think you're definitely gonna help make sure he doesn't!" Brad laughed.

"You got that right, brother!" Tripp said, offering a toast.

Joe walked up and joined the two of them. He looked like a man who had been given a new lease on life. He beamed proudly and hugged his two friends. The mood at the club was indescribable. Everyone was hugging everyone—so thankful that their quintessential adult playroom had been restored. It was hard to fathom, but everyone seemed to appreciate the place even more in the wake of what had happened.

"Boy do I owe you guys a round of drinks!" Joe said, simultaneously wrangling each of them in by the neck, toward each other.

"Give me a Coors Lite, a chilled Patron and a bushwhacker, please Sir!" Joe told the bartender at the outdoor bar.

"Coming up, Joe!"

He lined them up and the men toasted.

"To a job well done my friends! I love it when a plan comes together!" said Joe. They touched beverages and took a powerful swig. He confided in them.

"You guys aren't gonna believe this! I just got off of the phone a little while ago with Jimmy Buffet. He called me when he got the news. He and his band are coming tomorrow to play in the afternoon for a Free Concert! I can't believe it. I've been a friend and a fan of Jimmy's for years, and for him to do this for us is just great, just super of him! I am so excited! We are getting the word out right now. It's a spur of the moment thing and we want everybody who can get here to come! The staff just sent out a release and updated the facebook page and the website saying Jimmy will be here tomorrow and that there will be no cover. We are gonna have him out on the beach so we can entertain more people."

***

Johnny and Sam and Preston hung out at the Flora-Bama and had a couple of beers before riding over to Hub's to do their Friday night gig. They had missed Lucy at the Reef the night before. They sung most of the same stuff, but it was certainly different without her.

Johnny sent Lucy a text early in the afternoon when the good news about the reopening was known. He told her he hoped that she would no longer hold herself responsible for what happened, now that it was all over. He told her about the Buffet concert the next day, and that he loved her and missed her, and hoped that she would come back to him. Hours later, as he worked on setting up their equipment on the deck outside at Hub's, he checked his messages and he still had not heard from her. It had been four difficult days in her absence.

Across the Intracoastal Waterway the sinking sun sprayed orange, maize, magenta and rose across the western sky, signaling the beautiful end of a momentous day on the island. Joe G. had managed to save the Flora-Bama. Everyone was in an upbeat, fancy mood. Although Johnny was relieved that the Bama was back open, he still longed for Lucy. He wanted her back.

"I heard y'all could use a singer," Lucy said, in her best Sweet Home Alabama dialect, interrupting Johnny's work setting up.

He looked up and saw her. She wore a catchy, stylish red and yellow sundress that accentuated her curvaceous figure.

He had never seen her in it before and he could tell her hair had been done. Curled to perfection, it shined like polished onyx in the dull twilight. She looked smoking hot.

"Absolutely!" Johnny said. He leapt from his knees and hugged and kissed her like there was no tomorrow.

"I told you everything was gonna be alright!" Johnny said, looking into her eyes.

She hugged him tight again and squeezed. He lifted her off her feet and spun her around.

"You ready to sing tonight?" he asked.

"Yes!" she squealed, clapping her hands together like a trained seal.

***

As promised, on Saturday morning, Jimmy Buffet's band and crew showed up at the Flora-Bama to start setting up on the beach for the free concert slated for the afternoon. It was a gorgeous, sunscreen-advisable July day—hot and clear with a slight breeze overhead. It was a great day for music and celebration; a confluence and rejoicing of many wonderful things.

The Flora-Bama and Jimmy Buffet used social media and the Internet to quickly promote the impromptu musical event slated to start at 4:00 p.m. Even though they had only 24 hours to promote the celebratory gig, by noon on Saturday there were over 4,000 people there, with more fast on their way. Two Flora-Bama buses shuttled people from Gulf Shores and West Pensacola from nearby supermarket parking lots, trying to get as many music lovers to the event as possible. By two o'clock, Joe estimated that there were around 7,000 in attendance. When Joe took the stage to introduce Jimmy, he was informed by staff that there were over 10,000 people there.

Wearing a bright orange and blue Hawaiian print, button-down short sleeved shirt and khaki shorts with white leather tennis shoes without socks, a cleaned and combed, beaming Joe G. stood before the massive, boisterous beach crowd. Buffet's band's equipment was set up behind him, framed by a large drum set, a keyboard and a couple of guitars on stands. He walked up to the microphone to light applause, as not many of the huge, excited crowd of Parrotheads even noticed.

"Anybody having fun yet?" Joe asked everyone in his best playful voice. The sound carried through the huge public address system tied to the massive black wall of speakers on both sides of the stage. He was heard clearly and the crowd yelled in approval. Joe was amazed at how loud they were. He had never addressed such a large group at the Flora-Bama.

"Hello! Today is a fantastic day here at the Flora-Bama! Good afternoon to all of you who have made it here. I know y'all are excited, like I am, to see Jimmy—but I wanted to say a few words about him before we let him get started."

He paused and continued.

"Jimmy Buffet was one of the first characters who used to come here after we opened. I knew him first as a patron and then as a singer-songwriter. I am proud to say that he played here when both of us were just getting started, so it's really neat to have him play for us today, in this context. I've seen Jimmy play in places as far away as New York City and Los Angeles, but I have a feeling that this show will be my all-time favorite! I hope y'all will agree!"

The crowd roared.

"Okay," Joe said. "Once again…are we ready to have some fun?"

The crowd roared louder.

"Alright, without further adieu, I give you Jimmy Buffet and the Coral Reefers!"

Four men walked onto the stage and took their positions. The drummer, the bass player, the keyboard player and guitar all settled in. The crowd buzzed with excitement and idle chatter. A balding, sun-tanned fellow in a red and white Hawaiian shirt, khakis and flip flops carrying a beige electric guitar walked onto the stage from the left. Buffet's entrance was met with wild applause; and then the music to "Cheeseburger in Paradise" began, and the crowd sang with Jimmy every single word.

Jimmy sang several longtime favorites during the first set, including "A Pirate Looks at Forty" and "Why don't we get drunk and screw." At the break after their first set, backstage, Joe introduced Johnny and Lucy to Jimmy. They had played hooky from their Saturday night gig along with the owner of Flipper's, Mr. Eddie Boy, who stood right behind them, next to Joe.

Meeting Buffet was a real treat for Johnny and Lucy. He was a living legend and it was great for them to always be able to say they met him. Plus, they both loved his music.

"Let's get a picture!" Joe insisted. "Gather everyone—all the players and employees—up here on stage!"

Five minutes later over 100 people crammed side-by-side on the stage, with Joe and Jimmy Buffet in the center of the throng. Some stood, some crouched and some kneeled—but everyone smiled. Ken Cooper of Orange Beach Online (OBA) got several high resolution shots of the pose and shared them on the worldwide web. The following week the finished product was hung in a special frame inside the main room, as a reminder of that wonderful day everyone celebrated with Jimmy Buffet the saving of the revered Flora-Bama.

After the Kodak moment Buffet played a much longer second set, which included favorites "Changes in Latitudes, Changes in Attitudes" and of course, "Margaritaville." After an ovation of ten minutes, he came back out and sang "God don't own a car" and for a fitting finale, "Come Monday."

Jimmy, Joe, Johnny, Lucy and the rest of the humongous crowd sang:

"Come Monday It'll be all right,

Come Monday I'll be holding you tight.

I spent four lonely days in a brown L.A. haze

And I just want you back by my side."

As the massive crowd began to disperse, Joe pulled Johnny aside. Lucy followed.

"So, Johnny, have you managed to honor my initial request?" Joe asked. "I've been wondering."

Johnny quipped, "You mean of course—am I having any fun?"

"Exactly!" Joe chuckled.

"Mr. Joe, if I am any more fulfilled as a human being and if I have any more fun I will most certainly be arrested for illegalities!"

"Ah-hah!" Joe laughed. He changed the sound of his voice. He was extremely enthusiastic and upbeat.

"You've done well here Johnny in a short time. We kind of put you through the ringer these past few weeks, but here we are, the both of us, better off for it, right?"

"Absolutely, Mr. Joe! I am certainly better off!" Johnny answered.

"At first I couldn't figure out what you meant about 'being more useless' in life, Mr. Joe. It was a mystery. But, I think I'm finally starting to see the light...to see that having fun is a state of mind — and a clear choice."

Joe was impressed, and duly encouraged.

"That's super, Johnny! You are a fast learner. Some people go their entire life working a dead end job, stuck in a bad marriage or living a complete lie, pretending to be someone they aren't. You don't have to be that person, Johnny. Always think to yourself, "Why shouldn't I be so lucky? In the end, it's not your luck — it's your choices. You must choose to live the life you love."

"That's really deep, Mr. Joe. You have saved me and Lucy from a lot of unhappiness in life, I think. And for that, we can't thank you enough. We are so excited about living and playing here! Ain't that right, Lucy?" he asked.

Lucy nodded. She squeezed Johnny close to her.

Joe was flattered. He explained:

"Johhny I found someone to partner with here at the Flora-Bama. I had been working on it for a while, and was close to inking the deal before we lost our license. It's an Alabama family who owns several businesses and I think that they will, in time, be good stewards of the place. At least I hope so. I can only hope that they'll honor the community, and all that we've always stood for. I finalized the deal this morning. I am now a minority owner in the Flora-Bama, but most importantly, I am debt free and my bankruptcy worries are over. I still have to deal with the IRS, but I should be able to clear that up too—BP is saying that they are going to make total restitution, so I'm gonna make a claim and just see what happens."

Johnny had mixed feelings. He was happy to see Joe relieved, but he also selfishly wanted Joe and the Flora-Bama to live forever—together. But he realized that Joe, at some point, needed to retire; and that he would have to turn it over at some point anyway. In this fashion, as a minority owner, Joe would hopefully, for a while still have a guiding influence over the fabled place he created.

"Joe, that's fantastic!" Johnny answered, hugging him. "Things are definitely looking up!"

Lucy, who was standing nearby, chimed in, "I'm so happy for you Mr. Joe!"

She hugged Joe and he tightly hugged her back.

As Joe and Lucy hugged, Johnny spotted his buddy, Jake—with the girl he'd left Nashville for—Ella. They walked up arm-in-arm, smiling. The couple looked extremely happy.

"Well, well, well," said Johnny. "What a fine sight, seeing you two here!"

Ella beamed up at Jake.

"Ella is transferring to South—they have a great program there. She's gonna commute to med school from out here at the beach. We've decided we're gonna make another go at it."

"In a condo! Right Jake?" Ella ribbed.

"What's wrong with the camper, baby?" Jake answered with a devilish grin.

"That's awesome!" Johnny said. He and Lucy smiled. They were happy for them.

***

In the wake of the Flora-Bama's glorious reopening, Senator Whitman found himself in a heated race for re-election from a female independent, Kim McClelland, of Foley, an environmental activist, mother and grandmother. Battered in image by the embarrassing WTF incident under the tent, for holding numerous lucrative public contracts with municipalities inside his district and for fraudulently securing two emergency boom grant contracts from the Fairhope and Perdido Key communities, Slip lost a surprisingly close election.

Ten days before the primary vote he was subpoenaed by a federal grand jury in Mobile, Alabama investigating him and the Mayor of Fairhope for boom grant fraud. But that was not all. Twenty-two months after the lost election, he was formally indicted, along with the Mayor of Fairhope, on 183 counts of conspiracy, perjury, gross malfeasance, witness tampering and grant fraud, among other related charges. After a lengthy, costly trial, the federal judge sentenced both men to twenty years in the Club Fed just outside the capital in Montgomery, Alabama.

***

On Sunday morning around 9:30 Johnny and Lucy went to nearby Johnson Beach. Johnny set up two folding lounge chairs, draping a dry beach towel across each. He stuck a large umbrella on the end of a wooden pole deep into damp powder sand. The white dot in the east gleamed endless rays of heat and cascading, bright, white light.

Johnny set the chairs up side-by-side and positioned the umbrella over Lucy, protecting her from the sun. He placed a small ice chest between them and they both sat down and enjoyed the panoramic view of the Gulf of Mexico. In the distance, a steely mirage tap danced on the horizon. It was another spectacular day for sun and fun, as there wasn't a cloud in the painted azure sky.

His favorite Martin guitar was beside him. He had started showing Lucy how to play and hoped he could continue teaching her the chords while they relaxed. Johnny cracked a beer and poured its contents into two red plastic solo cups, sharing one with Lucy. Johnny extended his cup to hers with his right. Lucy extended hers with her left, the two meeting in the middle.

"To a great life!" Lucy enthusiastically toasted.

"To the best life we've ever lived!" Johnny answered.

They both sipped.

"Joe always says that," he added.

"Joe's always right," she quipped.

They toasted again and finished their beers.

"Johnny?" Lucy asked.

"Yes, Lucy?"

"Can we get a condo?"

"Maybe, baby." He smiled.

"I love you, Johhny!" she cooed.

"I love you, Lucy. I love you too," he said, squeezing her hand.

Johnny set up a small speaker and plugged it into his phone. He activated his playlist and designated "Mr. Tambourine Man," by Bob Dylan.

He sang along, anticipating his favorite lyrics toward the end:

"Yes, to dance beneath the diamond sky with
one hand waving free
Silhouetted by the sea, circled by the circus
Sands
With all memory and fate driven deep beneath
the waves
Let me forget about today until tomorrow
Hey, Mr. Tambourine Man, play a song for me
I'm not sleepy and there is no place I'm going to
Hey, Mr. Tambourine Man, play a song for me
In the jingle jangle morning. I'll come followin'
You"

The End.

Nominated "Best Piece of Fiction by an Alabama writer, 2017"

Alabama Library Association

Book 2

Johnny Glass is busy dealing with life. His beautiful girlfriend and band mate, Lucy Whitman, is pregnant—with his baby. Estranged by her parents, Lucy has only Johnny to help her bring a child into the world. The tiny sailboat they have called home for months is no place for an infant. Their Nirvana interrupted, Johnny senses things might never be the same. He has never been more right.

Johnny and Lucy are not alone in experiencing change. Pleasure Island's favorite hot spot for live music and fun—the beloved Flora-Bama, is no longer the tiny, ramshackle honky-tonk locals knew. New ownership and a growing population brought a slew of changes that altered the dive once revered for its spontaneity, overt tackiness and penchant for the unrefined. The quintessential beach bar and ivory island strip loved by all has evolved, prompting locals and old regulars to consider the unthinkable: Seek good times, fun and frolic elsewhere.

Pleasure Island is no longer the quaint retreat. The Mayor of Orange Beach and his developer cronies have unleashed a rash of dubious high rise condo construction projects that threaten to forever alter the gulf coast skyline and way of life. With the help of their powerful allies in the state legislature, new toll bridges and roads are being built to make it ever easier to get to the beach, ensuring that the risky developments will be handsomely rewarded. Despite the obvious warnings, few beach denizens realize their treasured existence hangs precariously in the balance.

Marginalized by his majority stock holding partners and the hardened victim of several past surprise disasters, patriarch Joe Gideon is again in a quandary. Upset with the greed motivating the government's misguided leadership, Gideon feels it may be time to sell out and retire in the nearby haven of West Pensacola, Florida. That is, until he hears of Johnny's newest challenges—and realizes that everything he has worked so hard to create—the beloved Flora-Bama and the faithful community it supports, is certainly worth fighting for.

Johnny and Joe reunite with the familiar cast of local characters to devise a plan to prevent during an unprecedented pandemic and an unforeseen category two hurricane the destructive domino effect from occurring. In order to save the island from certain ruin, they must win the hearts and minds of the locals as well as defeat in court and at the ballot box the energy thieves who will stop at nothing to turn a buck at the expense of their beloved way of life in the name of "progress."

Trouble at the Alabama Florida Line, the much-anticipated sequel to They Met at the Alabama-Florida Line, by Chris Warner, is another romantic, satirical tale seeking to draw semblance to Southern living, art, failed politics and pop culture.

1

Early May 2011
Marina near the Theo Baar Bridge
spanning the Intracoastal Waterway

ohnny Glass eased from his cozy forward sleeping berth without waking his lovely Lucy. She snored slightly, her ivory bosom draped in shiny onyx hair gently rising and falling with each breath. He popped the latch and exited the tiny sailboat's cabin into a thin, pallid veil of morning light, trapping the din of the cooler conditioned air below. The intense shine of a rising scarlet sun pushed through the horizon trees beyond the vast, manmade Intracoastal Canal, where shipping vessels plied protected from the Gulf of Mexico's destructive wrath. Johnny stood tall, his athletic frame straightened, taut arms outstretched. He soaked in the radiant ruby splendor, reflecting.

"I've been here a year," he thought.

"My, how life happens!"

A long, rusted rectangular barge of three identical bleached clam containers linked together by large metal pins was pushed by a puffing white three-story tug boat painted white and lettered black. Under the towering Theo Baar Bridge her presence produced an accordion wave across the still, wide, canal. The cooler air of previous nights was no longer. In its place was an unrelenting humidity that began at sunup and continued until the dark hours of the morning. Summer was upon the island.

Soon the much-anticipated season would start, signaling the annual tourist time that brought families and fun-seeking couples and singles from far and wide to Perdido Key's grainy white shores. Most visited the storied Flora-Bama Lounge & Package Store on the Alabama-Florida Line, as it was a good-time tradition as tried and true as the beach itself. These devout revelers were third-generation born and bred, the progeny of a lesser-known, Bohemian party culture cultivated there during the early 1980s, when Joe Gideon was a budding entrepreneur building a following one customer at a time, honoring the dignity of human beings with a humble offering of music, laughter, friendship and song. This was the Flora-Bama's early, golden years—and they were magnificent.

The iconic place of fun and frolic was infused in these lively people's blood, it seemed, and Johnny Glass—because of the benefits of good fortune, experience and time, understood it all. He was now a "local." He was an accepted part of the extended Flora-Bama family, and particularly, a member of its important creative class— the very people who drove the storied place. He was now one of them; one of the esoteric, lucky few who made a living writing and playing music and making fun, love and memories on the Alabama-Florida Line.

Johnny arrived via Nashville twelve months earlier, on a fateful whim. After an impromptu audition with the owner, Joe Gideon, he landed a gig at the world-famous Flora-Bama Lounge & Package. It was heady stuff for a French Lick, Indiana boy once bent on the elusive velvet neon dream of Nashville country music fame and fortune. Four meager years in the Music City extinguished that elusive pipe dream. He was ready for a change. It was time to move on—and that he did.

Perdido Key, Florida and the Music Mecca of the Flora-Bama gave Johnny a much-needed new start. It was a new mindset; a new band and a whole new life. He met a stunning Southern belle, a dashing buxom, raven-haired brunette with big brown eyes and a soothing voice; and fell in love. He lived on a sailboat with her in a picturesque resort area perfect for making music, memories, a steady living and a host of unforgettable, talented new musician friends, from which they drew comfort and inspiration. At the Flora-Bama, Johnny felt at home away from home; and he was forever appreciative for the opportunity to play there. It was something he thanked Joe Gideon for repeatedly, as for him and

Lucy it made all the difference. They somehow made a living doing what they loved. Johnny felt it was like cheating time, and he often said as much to Lucy.

Johnny and Lucy and their band, Riptide, in short time became one of the local favorites, as the couple's super good looks and real-life romance made them a distinctly entertaining duo. Johnny was excited about the season approaching, as they had just acquired a new player—a hot keyboardist with mad vocal skills—a handsome young fellow named Jerry Boudreaux, from South Louisiana, who had taken the place by storm weeks earlier. Everybody was talking about him, so Johnny figured he needed to nab him and his rare abilities for Riptide before someone else did. It was a great move, as everyone on the island loved "Cajun Jerry" and his enormous musical talents.

"Johnny? Are you up there?" Johnny heard from below. It was Lucy. She sounded distraught.

And then he heard it—again—for the third time in as many mornings. It was the guttural release—the putrid sound and subsequent smell of Lucy emptying her stomach contents into the tiny, makeshift toilet inside the vessel's dank bowels.

"It's a pattern," he thought. His mind raced. He recalled his Aunt Jenny, his father's youngest sister, who lived with his family for a few months when he was young—and she became pregnant. He remembered her similar, pronounced episodes of morning sickness leading to the announcement.

"You might be a father," he told himself. Goosebumps riddled the skin on his arms, his sun-bleached blonde hairs standing straight. He experienced the strange, indescribable deja vu feeling humans often do when they embody the eerily familiar. He opened the latch and jumped onto the floor, joining Lucy at her side in the cramped area housing the small commode. He cradled her lithe, hour-glass physique.

"You okay baby?" Johnny asked. He grabbed a hand towel from a nearby plastic ring and damped the perspiration from her forehead.

"I don't know what it is," she stated. "I guess I've caught something."

"I'd say," Johnny answered, the glinted irony of it all not lost on the bright of him.

Lucy finished and Johnny patted her on the back. She sat with her tiny rear against the wall, straddling the now shut commode. Johnny again used the towel to wipe perspiration beads from her forehead. There was something about the way he said "I'd say," that made her think.

"I am late," she recalled, staring down at her athletic torso. She looked to Johnny, his ruddy face near hers in the cramped area, his thin, muscular torso snaked onto the floor outside the restrictive bathroom quarters, his warm, taut body pressed next to hers.

"I guess I should go to the American Medical Clinic in Orange Beach?" she asked, the fear registered in her voice and face. Johnny sensed the moment and hugged her close, an avalanche of thoughts and emotions thrust upon him. Johnny looked into Lucy's dark, pooling eyes. He saw in them the same cascade of feelings and concerns he was experiencing. He did his best acting job.

"Everything's gonna be okay, Lucy," he insisted, purposely smiling, silently shamed.

He hugged and gently held her, stroking her hair. She clutched him tightly back, wondering if it would be; like he said.

***

Through bent reading glasses Joe Gideon examined his schedule prepared by his assistant, Vonnie. He had a late morning meeting with a decorated local senior and soon-to-be graduate from Foley High School outside the Starbucks at the Tanger Factory Outlet Mall in Foley, Alabama, 35 minutes west of his home in Warrington, Florida, just west of Pensacola.

The young lady, the recipient of hundreds of scholarship offers from universities and colleges across the United States and the world, had chosen to attend Auburn University—Joe's alma mater, in the fall. Joe read a Pensacola News Journal feature about her perfect ACT score and grades, and reached out to her. He explained in a typed letter to her and her parents that he wanted to meet and make a donation to her ongoing educational fund. Despite the rising humidity, the 11:00 a.m. appointment was bearable due to a partly cloudy azure sky.

Joe Gideon sat underneath the timid shade of a large hunter green umbrella outside the stand-alone, wood-paneled Starbucks Coffee store. Moments earlier he purchased a tall coffee with honey and low-fat milk and sought refuge from the misery borne from the rising heat index. His scheduled meeting with the young scholar fell into the realm of the "Random Acts of Kindnesss" campaign he had recently started. It was a simple concept. At a local printer Joe created small white cards with black print that read:

"RANDOM ACTS OF KINDNESS
Do something nice for someone you know or don't know.
Do something nice for someone in your family.
Do something in your community to help a school.
Do something nice for someone who helps others—a teacher,
law enforcement, fireman, or military personnel.
Encourage people who create music, art or short stories and
make the world a better place.
Pass this on so others can enjoy the secret!
Brought to you by Joe G. at the Flora-Bama Lounge & Package
Store."

Joe had the girls in the gift shop and the bartenders and customer service people at the Flora-Bama distribute these Good Samaritan reminder cards to patrons. The program was well-received, evidenced by the fact several found their way into the windows of local bank tellers who taped them on the glass so their customers could read them. One was also on the glass at the toll booth at the Intracoastal Waterway Bridge near the Wharf in Orange Beach. The selfless message was as popular as it was thoughtful, and encouraged altruism on a micro level. The meeting with the young scholar in Foley was one such random act of kindness. Joe intended to make her day a memorable one.

The blonde-haired blue-eyed maiden and her mother approached a seated Joe Gideon. Lauren Smith, the proud product of a middle class family, had never made a B in school. She aced the ACT and had offers from every major university in the country. She chose Auburn, Joe's alma mater, over all of them. From the moment Joe read about Lauren he wanted to meet and help her.

Joe looked up from his IPhone7 and noticed the ladies approaching. He stopped checking emails and placed his phone on the table, volume and face down.

"Good morning, ladies!" Joe said, standing to greet them.

"You must be Mr. Joe!" The mother said, smiling.

"I am Joe Gideon," Joe said, beaming. "Fortunately, I am still a moving target!"

"So nice to meet you!" She replied.

"It is my pleasure," Joe answered. They shook hands.

The young lady offered hers. Joe shook it too.

"I'm Lauren, Mr. Joe," she said.

"Please, just call me Joe," he replied. "So nice to meet you, Lauren! Please, have a seat."

Joe offered them coffees, but they politely declined.

"Thank you ladies for meeting me! I know y'all are likely busy this Saturday morning. You just have a couple more weeks of school, right? "

"Yes Sir. I graduate May 17th!"

"That is fantastic, isn't it?" Joe asked.

"Yes, Mr. Joe, it is!" She said, beaming.

"What do you plan to study?"

"I am going to study English. I will either pursue law or education. I am not sure. I guess I'll wait and see. I've thought a lot about elementary education," she answered, her face a ruddy hue, her smile showcasing her straight, gleaming white teeth. "I love children!" She beamed.

"I was a teacher," Joe said, smiling.

"Really?" she answered, the excitement bubbling in her voice. Joe loved her effervescence. She was so full of hope and excitement about her future. Her unbridled optimism was contagious. He missed seeing that, as he had in his former pupils.

"Yes! I taught high school chemistry and civics in Georgia and California before getting into the bar business. I thoroughly enjoyed it. It is a great way to serve your country and help young people! Teaching was undoubtedly a business asset, as I learned how to communicate with a group of people. I know you will do well, Lauren. You are gifted and have so much to look forward to! It is just fantastic!"

Lauren and her mother smiled and nodded, both blushing.

"I am a 1965 Auburn graduate!" Joe revealed.

"Really?" Lauren responded, smiling.

"Yes—back in those days I sold cold beer to my frat brothers—can you believe the beer distributorship sold me canned beer by the case for cash without asking for a resale license?"

Joe smiled and they all chuckled, reflecting on the lost charm of what was certainly a much simpler time.

"I don't want to keep you ladies…Lauren here is a little something for your educational fund. It's not going to answer all your needs, but it should help. You are deserving of a great education. I am proud of your accomplishments! I am glad to know you and I wish you great success at Auburn, and in life! I know you will be a great teacher, if that is what you choose to do."

Joe handed Lauren a sealed, thick, somewhat heavy white envelope that read, "Lauren" in Joe's cursive handwriting. It contained one thousand dollars in twenty dollar bills.

"Thank you so much Mr. Joe!" Lauren beamed.

"You are welcome," Joe answered, smiling. "You earned it! Please, stay in touch. I would love to track your success!"

Lauren could not resist. She took the envelope from Joe and stood and got close to him. She hugged him tightly with both arms and squeezed, and kissed a beaming Joe squarely on a rosy cheek, knowing well she was a lucky girl.

2

Jacque Buttrell stood erect with colleagues on the roof of the Phoenix West high-rise condominium, Orange Beach's tallest completed building at nearly 375 feet, an obscene, towering edifice dubbed Alabama Towers. At just under six feet, and possessing a lean athletic build, Buttrell wielded a command presence among his counterparts. He wore a baby blue sear sucker suit with prominent vertical stripes and a white Panama straw hat with a wide navy band. He puffed a thick, leafy Cuban cigar while addressing the three eager investors. Below them, an army of construction workers scurried like ants to complete the 26-month construction project, picking up debris, power-washing, landscaping and detailing the unprecedented luxury tower. The building's footprint and silhouette were so large they irreparably altered the beach scene. The raging monolith selfishly blocked out the sun at sunrise and sunset for dozens of smaller condominiums on each side of it. Not only did the structure defy existing height ceilings put in place by the city council, the architecture was considered grotesque and was declared an eyesore and abhorred by the semi-cultured, pretending gentile class in the local Lagniappe Mobile newspaper.

"Gentlemen, my partners and I hit it out of the park with this project…it has far exceeded our profit expectations. Our return on investment has been outstanding. Every unit—except a select handful—has sold. Therefore, we see no reason that our next project—which is bigger—will only yield bigger profits. Market research indicates the demand is there—and growing. The baby boomers have had it gentlemen…they're tired of shoveling snow. They want to come down here and sit in the sun and sip bushwhackers all day long!"

He paused for effect. "And I can't blame them!" He insisted with a sinister smile that matched well his sly countenance, dress and demeanor.

One of the investor guys cracked. He chuckled.

Buttrell laughed heartily, "Can you blame em'? Do you know how cold it is in Minnesota and Wisconsin still?"

The tallest of the three men dressed in snappy sport coats, shined shoes and creased dress pants without ties, spoke.

"I understand you plan to exceed 400 feet on this one…isn't that well beyond the height threshold set by the city council? As I recall there was turmoil about this building going up. An even bigger building should draw more protests. It could create problems. Any setback on a project like this is costly. Time is always money."

Butrell chuckled and sucked on his now spit-soaked cigar. He went hard back into the sell.

"It could. But the mayor runs the show in Orange Beach. The council is just for appearances—you know—to keep the locals happy. I have special permission to move forward. The mayor promised me he will take care of it when the time comes. There's nothing to worry about. It's a done deal. He and I are tight. Donny can handle this. Trust me, gentlemen."

The rounder man smiled from ear-to-ear. The shorter man next to him chimed.

"Sounds almost like a sure thing," he uttered, quickly shifting his girth and weight.

"As long as Mayor Kenner is in office, it is!" Buttrell chuckled. He continued.

"So what do you gentlemen think? Are you in? If you can help us with the necessary financing we talked about, each of you will be rewarded handsomely with a generous return and a premium-priced penthouse suite—one of eight on the building's top floor. The view of course will be identical to this…except better…because it will be even higher up!" Buttrell's index finger pointed toward the ceiling, spiking the chilly, conditioned air.

***

A native of Kiln, Mississippi, Jacque Buttrell was born the eldest son of a son of a soy bean sharecropper. He played football in Starkville before an anterior cruciate ligament tear cut short his college receiving career. The quintessential small-town hero coming out of coastal Mississippi, he met his wife, Peggy, a university socialite and sorority officer, post injury. After the setback he pledged a fraternity and settled into campus life as a student, political aspirant and consummate ladies man.

Eschewing note-taking and studying and possessing a pronounced bent for politics, Buttrell found himself the president of the campus Inter-Fraternity Council and the speaker of the student government association, positions which helped affirm and mold his apparent political skills as well as a penchant for the affections of multiple women. Before leaving Starkville with a degree in mechanical engineering, Buttrell served as the student body president on the SGA and student representative on the prestigious Mississippi Board of Directors that made decisions on important campus matters—like who became athletic director, chancellor and football coach. It was during this formative time that he learned he really liked politics; almost as much as he did strange women; unfortunately, so did his sweetheart, Peggy, as she was conditioned, but not blind.

After graduation Buttrell landed a salaried job running the plant logistics to build airplanes at the Port of Mobile, Alabama and chose to locate his family to nearby Fairhope, a small bedroom community 20 miles from the bustling industrial port city. Primarily a retirement destination at 7,500 people, Fairhope had not yet become a sprawling suburban enclave of young families. Still a postage stamp, its schools were not overcrowded and still performed above the published state averages across the core curriculum. Its roads were adequate based on population. Commute times were reasonable. A lack of congestion and crime made the place enviable as a retirement destination. Unfortunately, this Mobile Bay nirvana was soon upended, like the rest of the bountiful coastal area. Predictably, the predatory developers moved in; and in them Buttrell cleverly saw his campaign financing—the fast money he needed to get elected to the Fairhope City Council, a goal he set his sights on shortly after moving into the hilly, verdant bay side community.

Elected to the Fairhope City Council in 2004 and re-elected in 2008, during his second council term Buttrell became the President of the Coastal Alabama Chamber of Commerce—a de facto business growth group that existed to facilitate and further the physical development of real estate and free enterprise in primarily Lower Baldwin County, Alabama. As Chamber President, Buttrell formed the development connections he needed to make it big in Baldwin County politics. From that point it was child's play to a political animal like him. He got the money he needed to get elected; and more importantly, he and his pals banked millions in subsequent high-rise condo deals he helped put together with his buddy, Donny Kenner, Orange Beach's goofy, likeable and chronically aloof, redneck mayor.

***

Johnny Glass ran west, bare-chested, in cardinal athletic shorts without a tee shirt or shoes against the rising heat index of the early summer sun. The burnt orange disc eclipsed the eastern horizon, glowing amber on its slow and deliberate ascent into a timid pale blue sky. His waxing bare footprints made a predictable trail behind him, washed intermittently by a foaming, flexing Gulf of Mexico.

Sweat rivulets ran like pulsing, clear veins down his taut back, toward a dimpled area covered by his shorts, just above his blood-filled gluteus maximus. His surging rear muscles pumped with precision and refined memory, manipulating the tighter sand full of salt water within the tide's sleepy ebb and flow. The emerald surf was tame in the early morning hours, which for three days a week, was a ritual for the svelte Johnny Glass. He tried to live the elusive Greek adage of, "A sound mind in a healthy body," despite the beach life's omnipresent Epicurean trappings.

Johnny's thoughts drifted from his current predicament with Lucy to his devout Midwestern upbringing. His maternal grandmother and he were close coming up. He recalled a conversation they had on their way to her last chemotherapy treatment, when he was a late teen, before she succumbed to the dreaded disease. At that critical juncture of short time, the thoughtful advice she imparted was never forgotten.

"You should marry some day," she said, unsolicited. The statement startled a young Johnny. He didn't know how to react, as he was too young to think of it. He just drove the vehicle, continuing to their appointment.

"I know it's a little early for you, but in time you will find someone. You will certainly fall in love. You are a handsome, fun guy, Johnny. Now, when you fall in love, you should marry."

She paused. Johnny listened intently.

"If you love someone you should marry and have kids. If you have kids—you will never be alone in old age. This is important. Your marriage may not work—but your children will always love you, Johnny. God knows your mother has been a comfort to me these last few trying months."

Johnny realized what she said was right. He saw the love his mom had for his dying grandmother. He too loved his Grandma and of course, his Mom…and he certainly loved Lucy Whitman. That was not debatable. He needed to marry her, he thought, nearing the end of his run. It was the only thing he had left to do.

"I will need a ring," he thought. "That costs money."

Traversing across the undulating wet sand he thought of his lovely Lucy and their faceless, nameless baby and the new responsibilities a family would bring. Their cramped, on-board living quarters were already a fading memory. They would need new digs—and new gigs—as he knew babies weren't free. There would be a price tag. There always was, he had learned. With that understanding was the added pressure to perform well and make money. But now it was no longer about just him; and that was something he could not stop thinking about, because he knew it would require more of him. He didn't know how they would make it without a little help. They didn't have much.

"Mr. Joe will help us," he thought. "He always seems to have the answer."

Johnny hated to rely so much on Joe—but he was the guy everybody turned to. He was the Mac Daddy of the island—the guy who had decades earlier set their tiny island paradise into perpetual motion. Joe G. had the necessary resources, creativity and connections. He could help make it right—as he had many times before.

Jacque Buttrell exited the Ariel Platinum steam shower in his luxury, 3700-foot penthouse atop the tallest building in Orange Beach, Alabama. The towering, palatial unit overlooked the vast, gleaming, ultramarine Gulf of Mexico. Clad in only a white bath towel clasped at his waist, he faced the bathroom mirror and parted his graying hair to satisfaction. It was actually closer to white, as in the last five years the little remaining darker hair turned gray and the majority of the gray to white. From the towel up he was darkly tan from a recent fishing trip, his taut upper body glowing in stark contrast to the soft ivory Terry Cloth clasping his lower midriff.

"I sure wish we could go down to the Bama' and get a bushwhacker," an inviting, distinctly Southern female voice cooed from the other room. She pronounced sure like "shore."

Buttrell smiled wickedly and spun in place. He darted into the dimly-lit bedroom, where his mistress, Layla, was sprawled prone, buck naked on the California King-Sized bed. With her hair perfectly done, in both hands she held her pinging IPhone. She was busy liking and commenting on a girlfriend's facebook page with a new emoji she discovered minutes earlier. She felt so smart and sassy and empowered on social media—after all, it was where she and Buttrell first "met."

"That's a nice thought but hardly a good idea, baby," Buttrell answered, now standing before her. His gray and white chest hair she called "possum blonde" danced and glistened under the rotating ceiling fan with large, dried, woven palm fronds for blades.

"We don't need any unwanted attention."

She looked to him, revealing a snowy smile. She pulled herself into a kneeling position, exposing completely her voluptuous bare front, and a shoulder-length platinum blonde look freshly updated at the roots. Although she was pushing fifty, Layla remained as striking as ever. She was still the one who shook the room, still the faithful object of every red-blooded man's desires. She was still the irresistible—one had only to ask Jacque Buttrell.

Layla McKenzie Smith Kenner was born Layla McKenzie Smith at the base hospital in Fort Rucker, Alabama, the only child of Frank and Rhonda Smith. Her father, a Master Sergeant in the United

States Army, met her mother toward the end of his two decade-long military career, while she was working in the Peace Corps in Germany where he was stationed. The love affair blossomed and they were quickly married; Little Layla came soon after, along with an early military retirement for her father, who began a second career as a social studies teacher, P.E. and assistant football coach at Orange Beach High School, after his mother passed away and left a small summer vacation cottage to him, her only child.

Growing up in Orange Beach was a water and wonder-filled dream for Layla, as she was seemingly always on the salt, either fishing, skiing, jet-skiing, boating, paddle boarding or sailing. Layla was active in dance and the performing arts and was a standout among the Dogwood debutante trail maids and statewide beauty contest circles. Her starling reputation preceded her during high school when she was crowned the winner of the prestigious state pageant in Montgomery, earning a full academic scholarship to the University of Alabama. After graduation, she returned to Orange Beach and married the son of her father's head football coach—the gridiron legend, Logan Kenner: Donny, the only guy she had ever dated. It was the closest thing to what one would call an arranged marriage in the modern Deep South; although Layla on most days enjoyed being the mayor's wife in their sleepy little slice of paradise. That is, until she was wooed away from it all by her husband's popular friend and business associate, the nefarious Jacque Buttrell.

This was the first time they had had sex—in person, having finally physically consummated minutes earlier their ill-advised, clandestine relationship. It had gone much quicker than she'd hoped; she was unsatisfied, and a little upset over the performance and the subsequent attention she achieved; but nevertheless undeterred, and happy to be there with him, this foreign object of her desire, as risky as it was. The condominium was gorgeous—posh in every way—a breathtaking view of the gleaming Gulf of Mexico below; it was something special she had not experienced. She liked it and felt she could easily get used to it; as if it was something she deserved and did not have.

It began with a random instant message on facebook, from Layla to Jacque. She spotted him, unexpectedly, at the Big Earlvis Show under the big tent at the Flora-Bama weeks earlier, and they

traded knowing glances. Each took a double take and smiled.
Each remembered the look of the other. Eight weeks and several
thousand direct messages later, they found themselves together,
dealing with the not-so-subtle realities of marital deception in a
less-than-private, social media-driven age. They both knew there
could be hell to pay if the proverbial cat got out the bag, Jacque
stating such a revelation would be an insufferable "Pandora's Box."

Before acting against their vows in matrimony, they thoroughly
discussed and contemplated the deception. He was the President of
the Fairhope City Council and the Coastal Chamber—always in the
news. She was the high profile, near perfect ten better half of the
Mayor of Orange Beach, Donny Kenner, who was enjoying a third
term. Kenner traditionally had a steady core of support within the
city, but his strong development stance amidst a growing population
had eroded that once reliable voter base. The many new residents
hoped the development would slow now that they were in town, as
they wanted to protect their investment, i.e. property values and
their life quality. But that was not part of the good ole boy master
plan, and Donny Kenner, after all, had marching orders from his
friends in the Montgomery political pipeline.

Jacque and Donny, fellow Alabama republicans, were friends
and business partners in an ongoing regional real estate partnership
with powerful and rich friends from Montgomery who best allowed
them to use their elected public positions for personal benefit. But
as risky as that was, both Jacque and Layla had insisted on the affair.
The feeling was mutual. They could not resist one another, better
sense and abstinence damned.

"I know darling," she answered his cautionary stance, leaning
forward, reaching and stroking his chest hair with her freshly-
painted crimson fingernails. "A girl can dream, though, can't she?"
She grinned and stared with starry eyes.

"How about I make you a bushwhacker here? I have a recipe in
this cookbook over here that is close to the real thing," he pleaded.
"I have plenty of regular and spiced rum and I have amaretto and
Khalua." He leaned to walk away.

"That sounds delicious!" She beamed. She reached over and
released the fold in his towel, rendering it useless on the floor.

"In just a minute," she added, smiling, pulling him toward her
onto the bed sheet's cool, plush satin.

3

Francis Tripp raked crinkled dried brown and grey leaves on his double lot overlooking Mobile Bay. Broad Live Oaks with thick, gnarled, moss-draped boughs, blooming Bobby Green camellias, pastel azaleas, bursting blueberry, orange and loaded Satsuma trees scattered the hilly, verdant, groomed property that was the area high ground, forming a protruding ridge near Fly Creek on the otherwise hilly, rolling coastal landscape known as the idyllic City of Fairhope, Alabama. The true nature of the place, however, was not nirvana but that instead of a botanical, bayside hedonism, a fact not lost on Fairhope's most persistent, anarchistic gadfly; a former U.S. Marine sniper turned anti-corruption crusader, who by nature and experience, probably knew the place as well as anyone.

Wearing cracked white leather tennis shoes without laces or socks and a cardinal Speedo weenie bikini, Tripp's dark, muscled back was dimpled with sweat that ran in rivulets to the narrower, shadowed, less-tanned part of his torso above his creased rear. A former Marine who saw action in Viet Nam, Tripp's military service was cut short when a rocket-propelled grenade detonated, exploding an adjacent ammo dump, jettisoning him hundreds of feet through the air. When he landed furiously, both shoulders were dislocated. By 2011, 40 years later, Tripp's ongoing Veteran's Administration case file recorded 24 separate shoulder surgeries, and a hefty, unsettled federal claim for unpaid reimbursements and benefits denied. His attorney in the matter, a Yale graduate, and an avowed expert in suing the U.S. Veteran's Administration, was still billing case hours on appeals. Tripp checked his mail daily, hoping to see a settlement.

The dozens of shoulder surgeries would have derailed most men. However, through constant motion, exercise and an unfettered will to continue, Tripp beat all odds and was able to not only function, but thrive, despite the constant aggravation and pain. Nevertheless, the soreness was an everyday reminder of a similar struggle in a much different time, place and circumstance.

The son of a devout military man, Tripp unenthusiastically joined the United States Marine Corps in 1970, in the thick of the Viet Nam Conflict. Fortuitously, he worked a sinecure in South Florida as a whistle-toting lifeguard for a year before seeing combat duty. This first year of military service for Tripp was as unorthodox as it was fun, refreshing and fleeting. Furthermore, the gig fit perfect with his quirky, maverick, Klinger-like personality that questioned the every motive of his sworn military masters.

While lifeguarding, to his enjoyment, and to the grand dismay of his direct superior officer, Tripp supervised with binoculars for several weeks the training of the United States' women's synchronized swimming team as they repeated their lengthy routine to music, sharpening the choreography over an interval of grueling repetition and instruction. However, what drew the ire of Tripp's superior was the fact that the team's coach, a nudist, preferred the girls practice in the nude—along with her full participation, of course. Incredulously, Tripp's heavenly job that summer before seeing combat duty was watching naked women scissor kick upside-down inside an Olympic-sized, outdoor swimming pool. In retrospect, it was only fair, and fitting, as the unrelenting hell that was the jungles of Viet Nam patiently awaited him.

Trained as a sniper, Tripp served and did his job well with respect to his mission and mates; but he did not believe wholeheartedly in the war effort in Vietnam. He was hardly an objector, but his words and deeds outside of his combat service were explicitly not those of a "gung-ho" Marine. He had, after all, a conscience, and a political bent based on dissidence through diligent, civil disobedience. It was a tact he borrowed from his patriotic, academic father.

Born the oldest son of an Army Colonel and college educator in Manchester, England in 1947, Tripp was destined for dissidence. When Tripp was a lad, his Dad, in his post-military career, took a job teaching economics at Birmingham Southern, moving the family across the pond to the nearby suburban enclave of Homewood, Alabama. There Tripp watched his father engage in a regimen of public participation and civic activism that would inspire and frame his adult life's activities.

"I served my country in the knee-deep rice patties of Viet Nam! I didn't fight and get shot at to come home and have to deal with corruption at every level of government!" He repeatedly reminded himself, vowing to make a difference, following the impressive lead his intrepid, service-minded father took. His steadfast efforts were a tribute to his Dad, who perished from a heart attack while protesting a rate increase before the Alabama Public Service Commission. The political stuff was in his blood.

Physical activity was something he equally craved, even at his age. It kept him going strong. He believed fervently in what Albert Einstein said—that bodies in motion tended to stay in motion and more importantly—that time beats at different rates throughout the universe—depending largely on how fast you moved; and because of that, he preferred to keep moving—and therefore cheating allocated time.

Tripp's nearby cell played reggae music randomly from his playlist. The Ziggy Marley number ended abruptly and his phone rang. He stopped raking and looked at the lit up phone's face. He recognized the number as Joe Gideon's. It was a call he was expecting.

"Hey Joe!" he answered, clicking into speaker mode.

"Hey there Mr. Tripp! How's life treating you?"

"All is good, Joe. Staying busy, as usual."

"Vonnie told me you called. What can I do for you?"

"Well, Joe, it's an election year and we've got several hot races we need to win in order to get these scumbag republicans out of office! They're ruining paradise with overdevelopment."

Joe Gideon knew well the rash irresponsibility of the planning departments of the local governments in Orange Beach and Gulf Shores. Having lived and played there long before the Flora-Bama was an inkling, he had seen the area change like perhaps no other. Over time it grew from a small fishing and sleepy family vacation village to a teeming tourist destination for aging baby boomers punctuated by gridlock, congestion and incomprehensible commute times during peak season. The skyscraper condo construction craze adversely brought thousands of more sets of wheels on the road—with no public transportation and an already overloaded road set. A runaway train already too far gone—there was apparently no turning back. The skids toward "progress" were hot and greased.

Predictably, the look and feel of the island was irreparably changed. Sunrise and sunset were different as a result of the increasing footprints, climbing skyscrapers and hauling cranes. The harrowing trend had knowledgeable locals in a collective funk, punctuated by a feeling of utter helplessness and despair. Many could no longer afford to live there due to ever-increasing property taxes. An apparent loss of quality of life was evidenced through ridiculous local commute times during peak season. Some residents were planning to move, or had already fled the paradise they once knew for a place with less hassle. Joe knew well these changes. Those adversely affected were his friends. Many had helped him build the Flora-Bama and were forced to move from the place they helped create. But he understood, from bad experience, the financial realities, and of course, the larger economics in play. It was more than a sore spot for him. He listened intently.

Tripp passionately continued.

"This jackass in Fairhope—the city council president—this guy Buttrell—I call him "Butt Rail." He and his developer buddies are building high rise after high rise on the beach in Gulf Shores and Orange Beach—six in the last ten years; each increasingly taller, and each more destructive to the indigenous landscape and quality of life."

He paused before continuing, steadily raising the tone of his voice. "I got a tip from one of my blog readers that the Orange Beach City Council is gonna okay the largest condominium tower on the gulf coast! They say it's gonna be almost as big as the Empire State Building! It's out of control, Joe! We're gonna wind up just like Destin and Myrtle Beach. We're land-locked. It's a cluster! A total shit-show! We don't have the infrastructure to handle all this growth. I keep telling everybody it doesn't have to be this way. There's a better way of doing things. There's a better way to handle our public affairs."

There was a pregnant pause.

"Nobody seems to get it." Tripp declared.

Joe understood. The politics of his home state infuriated him at times like these. He was more than concerned. He was petrified. He knew what Tripp said was correct. The island had long been on a path to destruction due to overdevelopment. Now, this sad fact was evident. He'd stopped visiting Destin yeas prior. The gridlocked traffic killed the place he once fished with his family and friends as a kid. Orange Beach and Gulf Shores were next. It was the irreversible trend—or so it seemed.

"What do you have in mind?" Joe asked, exhaling, some of his energy escaping with the carbon dioxide.

"I've got several solid candidates I'm backing against the machine. They're fully vetted—none has ties to the real estate development industry. Each is determined to halt the overdevelopment wave and to improve our infrastructure first, through the raising of impact fees. And, of course, they're not bought and paid for by the machine, or its corrupted Baldwin County minions."

The machine Tripp referred to was as real as it was clandestine and mysterious. With nefarious, early-twentieth century origins at the University of Alabama in a dank, fraternity house basement, it was the grand tribunal of the privileged class that handed down a government not for the people, but certainly on the backs of those typified by Alabama standards as the forgotten underclass, encompassing everyone who didn't know somebody in politics— which was everybody outside the privileged coterie operating as one on Goat Hill, that apocalyptic dome masquerading as a capitol in Montgomery.

The machine that ran from Montgomery to the Capstone and to all parts of the Yellowhammer State represented Old Alabama in the modern age, that prideful shadow of the Confederacy that refused to wilt—like an August Alabama sun. As a result of its selfish machinations, the State was deprived of many nice things; and it was an ephemeral reminder that Alabama was the nation's most forgotten swamp; a place that sadly still prided itself on ignorance, racism and a woeful acceptance of second-hand news. A long-time resident, Francis Tripp was on a mission to change that for the beleaguered State of Alabama, and its misguided, subjugated posterity. He knew there was a better way. He was determined to make a difference—to somehow move the bedraggled state along toward its elusive self-actualization.

"How much do you think you need?" Joe asked.

Joe admired Mr. Tripp for having the balls to do something about the problems facing the community. Corruption was rampant. He had long given up on politicians. Most in Alabama were avowed "Christians" who bragged about their weekly tithings, only to engage secretly in reprehensible activities that lined the pockets of associates, friends and family at the expense of the disconnected. It was the Alabama way—and everybody for some strange reason just said "Amen" and went along with the ruse—until Tripp came along. He had really shaken things up—and it was apparent he was doing good things. Joe wanted to continue to help him."

A couple grand would really help us get the word out." Tripp answered. His tireless efforts had created a serious problem for the local representatives of the machine and its Baldwin County bit players, despite their bought and paid for media minions who only wrote puff pieces on their soiled behalf.

Tripp boldly booted "Baldwin County Legal Beagle," an incendiary facebook page dedicated to exposing and eradicating political chicanery. The tag line read, "Political corruption has no place in a civilized society." Tripp religiously attended city council meetings in Fairhope, Gulf Shores and Orange Beach, often speaking to them during their normal, allotted public participation sessions, deftly admonishing them for the wickedness and wastefulness of their crooked ways. Most important, however, was the fact that he used his popular facebook page as a bully pulpit, slamming the compromised players within the corrupted good ole boy network, forcing them to confront for the first time what he called, "The court of public opinion." For this extensive public service Tripp was hated by the ruling class…and nothing made him happier, as he relished his role and the arduous if not impossible task of eliminating public corruption in the State of Alabama—the place he felt time and care somehow conveniently forgot.

"These guys are scumbags, Joe! They fleece the public at every opportunity while claiming to be pious Christians! Jacque Buttrell has his fingers in everything! Not only are he and his pals making millions in beach condo development, but through his various

LLC's he's doing commercial construction work for both the City of Fairhope and Baldwin County! He's double and triple dipping! It's not right!"

"What about the Ethics Commission?" Joe asked.

"What about em?" Tripp answered. "This is Alabama, remember?"

"What do they think about Buttrell's real estate holdings and him getting so much government work?" Joe specified.

"Very little I assume. They're paid to run interference for the machine. They're like a bad cop on a pad."

"Ugh," Joe replied, disgusted. "Okay, I'll mail you a check. Stay in touch, Tripp. Report back. Keep me in the loop!"

"Thanks Joe," Tripp replied. The money was a real boost. It was something he sorely needed, as he hadn't had as many odd painting and lawn care jobs that were the regular cash source he used to pay the bills associated with making the local politicians miserable.

"You're welcome," he paused. "Keep it up! Stay on them!" He added.

"Oh, don't you worry, Joe! Don't you worry!" Tripp replied with a familiar hiss and a grin, his straight, white teeth gleaming, the soft sunlight peeking through the swaying lichen-draped oak boughs overhead, the salt air from Mobile Bay wafting amidst loud clicking swarms of cicadas.

4

We need a larger footprint?" Jacque Buttrell questioned the young architect in coat and tie seated at the work table before him. A large blueprint scroll unraveled and tacked at the corners depicted the massive, unprecedented beach high-rise overlooking the aquamarine gulf.

"It requires a larger base Mr. Buttrell. Since we're going 37 stories we need a wider platform. It's basic building 101. Take the Great Pyramid at Giza, for example. Because of its wide base, it is extremely stable."

Buttrell shifted his weight, watching the enticing gesticulations of the architect. The younger, sharply-dressed man continued.

"By the way, did you know the Great Pyramid was built with 2.5 million separate limestone blocks that weigh between two and seven tons each? With the molded material you could build a three foot wall from San Francisco to New York."

Buttrell looked somewhat bemused, concerned still over pecuniary matters.

"So what does this mean for our project?" He pointedly asked for jaded, parsimonious reasons.

"We redo the plans based on my calculations and revisions." The architect confidently replied. He retrieved a fresh new scroll from a long, sleek, light gray cardboard tube nearby. It was labeled "REDO" in large black Calibri font.

"Damnit!" Buttrell exclaimed. "How much more is this gonna cost?"

***

Lucy Whitman opened the glued cardboard tab on the small rectangular box holding the pre-packaged paper strips. She removed one and tore the perforated seal. She withdrew it from its sleeve and dropped it into the prepared Styrofoam cup containing her warm urine.

A minute later she withdrew the strip, placed it on the center of a cheap, white paper plate on the small utility table inside the sailboat, and waited; watching intently, as instructed, for the appearance of a prominent, thin baby blue line.

Lucy Whitman grew up in scenic Fairhope, Alabama on a shallow, placid and polluted Mobile Bay, the privileged only daughter of a State Senator, Slip Whitman; the eldest son of one of Baldwin County's largest land owners. As a child her father's political ambition and zeal dominated her family life and precluded what she considered "a normal existence." At times during her youth she pined for the regular family life of her closest friends, wanting badly a less-hectic, more genuine upbringing forgone for power's sake.

Lucy's glorious onyx hair, fit physique and engaging smile and presence were rivaled only by her dulcet voice. The cumulative effect of years of formal lessons—and natural talent, Lucy was equipped with what aspiring singers most needed—an enviable set of vocal chords. Not only did she have good range, but her tone was exceptional. Physically-packaged with everything else—she was a natural born entertainer in the making. The sad thing was that her family—namely her father, did not agree with her chosen path. He had made it clear: Under his watch she would not pursue a music career; which of course, ostensibly made the decision for her, as her heart, and not her misguided papa, was in charge.

She thought about her and Johnny being parents. Johnny Glass was the most handsome, talented, sweet, caring, loving man she had ever met. Gentle and kind, she knew he was more than capable of loving, caring for and guiding a child. With her help—they would have a family—if she was pregnant; although she felt she was—and couldn't explain why. She was both mortified and optimistic.

"If I'm not pregnant, it's no big deal," she said to herself, her subconscious mind thinking overtime at fooling herself.

***

Jacque Buttrell stood straight before the Orange Beach City Council. Appearing before the rural beach town governing body as president of the Alabama Coastal Chamber of Commerce, he was spearheading a new litter control program for the area beaches, titled, "Leave Only Footprints." It was ingenious, as it created the bold perception that he and the coastal chamber actually cared about the beaches and the area's quality of life—when of course—they did not, evidenced by their destructive development policies of building high rise after high rise that blocked out the sunrise and sunset.

"Mayor Kenner, honorable members of the Orange Beach City Council, citizens and members of the media, I appreciate the opportunity to speak to you this evening. I promise you I'll be brief..."

Against this promise Buttrell spoke for nearly twenty minutes, finishing with the well-crafted if not blasphemous line, "Our beaches are our area's most pristine and valuable natural resource—they are a gift from God Himself—and we must preserve His bounty, for our posterity."

Buttrell turned the show back over to Mayor Kenner, who switched places with him on the half-sized, portable dais on a folding table attached with an adjustable microphone.

"Thank you, Jacque! We greatly appreciate you and the Coastal Chamber's efforts. Y'all are doing a fine thing here and we appreciate y'all a lot! We will certainly be promoting this here program on our website and social media pages. I have already instructed staff to do so. We here in Orange Beach—I can assure you, will encourage everyone...to leave only footprints on our beautiful quartz sand beaches!"

Francis Tripp was silent during Jacque Buttrell's patronizing speech and Mayor Kenner's obsequious reply. Nevertheless, Buttrell knew he was there, much to his chagrin. Tripp was his avowed arch-nemesis and his absolute worst nightmare. Tripp was the guy who kept him up at night with that ridiculous consumer blog of his. Unfortunately, Tripp was in the audience and Jacque knew that meant he was going to speak at public participation. Buttrell hated the notion, because Tripp would have something untoward to say about him, affirming he was a constant thorn. Nevertheless, like an alpha lion, Buttrell remained stoic, offering not a look of fear, weakness or pain.

The Mayor of Orange Beach, Donny Kenner, completed his address to the smattering of citizens in attendance. In addition to Tripp, there were two other poor souls—an entrepreneur applying for a license to sell liquor who spoke and had it approved, and an older woman with bifocals and silver hair wearing a white blouse and an unbuttoned navy cardigan. The elderly woman was there, like Francis Tripp, to address the council and mayor during their regularly-scheduled public participation segment. At the end of every meeting the council opened the floor for public comments. It was always the last item on the agenda.

Like Jacque Buttrell, the mayor and council members expected Tripp to be there. His reputation preceded him. He was a fixture at their meetings. However, the older woman was a surprise. She was first to approach the dais, now facing the council on a separate table. The politicians watched unknowingly, with careful trepidation and a hint of fear.

The woman in bifocals wore a plaid gray dress. She was short, with a bee hive hairdo. The octogenarian retired to the area 18 years earlier, having fled once and for all the political sickness endemic of the Chicago, Illinois area, where as a younger woman she fought ignorance and greed among a similarly neglectful, spiteful ruling class—the Daley Machine. This was not her first rodeo in the public arena. A graduate of the University of Chicago, she adjusted the microphone and got to work.

"My name is Alice Singer. I live at 222 Paradise Way here in Orange Beach."

There was a delayed pause. She had the council's undivided attention. Her voice was pleasant, belying her message, putting some of the politicians momentarily at ease.

"I moved here in 1994. The place was a postage stamp. It was a nice little town back then."

She paused again, for effect. The council sat on pins. She was a good communicator.

"In those days I could see unabated the beautiful sunrise and sunset. I could access the beach anywhere, and I could get to the grocery store in less than five minutes. "

There was dead silence for three full seconds.

"Back then I actually had a quality of life!" She exclaimed, sharply raising the tone and intonation of her now raspy, tinsel voice, reverberating.

Mayor Kenner squirmed, shifting in his seat from left to right, trying to somehow dodge the indirect accusations. He knew he was to blame. The council was his dog and pony show. The outrageous condo building spree occurred under his watch. For basis points he helped procure construction financing on multiple projects, which indirectly made him an investor/developer. He was definitely getting something in return, which meant he was legitimately compromised—in multiple ways. He wondered again who knew this—other than he and Jacque.

The council, not nearly as invested as the mayor, yet equally culpable, was not amused by the old woman, who despite her age was the pillar of strength and dissent. She turned her focus to her primary foe, looking directly at him, squaring her narrow shoulders.

"And you—Kenner—what a disgrace you are! You tell us with a straight face that you can't 'tell people what to do with their land!' That's hogwash! You cannot by ordinance allow structures over 30 stories! It is preposterous that you claim to be for the people of this community who make Orange Beach their home! You stand here before us—you and Mr. Buttrell here—and you talk about conservation!"

She scowled.

"Leave only footprints?"

She paused.

"Are you fucking kidding me?" She panned. There was a prolonged silence.

Mayor Kenner interjected, "M'am we will not allow profanity! We will have none of that here!"

"Pardon me, Mr. Kenner, but I'm tired of you pissing down my back and tellin' me it's raining!" She retorted. This zinger zapped to life two of the councilmen, one a sweaty man of corpulent proportions with an outdated Beatles haircut; the other a thin man with deep acne scars, a large Adam's apple and a crew cut revealing several nasty head scars.

"Get to the point lady!" The crater-face stammered, pleading.

"I beg your pardon, gentlemen," she stated. She smirked at their reaction and continued.

"What about the footprints of these massive high-rise condos? Are we supposed to just ignore them? So let me get this straight: You want us to worry about biodegradable paper, cardboard and straws while you trash the beach forever, robbing our posterity... cheap dime store hoods that you are?"

The elderly woman felt her age in that moment, her passion getting the better of her. She had not been this worked up in years. Everything in her life had been upturned because of the dreaded developers. All the new people and all their problems came soon after. The quaintness and tranquility she knew was no longer. Strangely, she found herself once again before a governing body complaining about her life quality. Things had for her, come full circle, and she was again reminded of the terminal nature of her existence. She felt weakened. It was time for her to go.

She stared across the dais at the councilmen's blank faces... five dough boys who faithfully did the bidding of their misguided master, Mayor Donny Kenner. She liked what she saw. Each wore a troubled look of consternation—and she sensed a tinge of fear— like they knew they were caught. Each had heard and winced at the citizen rumblings. Things on the island were definitely no longer the same. Overdevelopment was the 900-pound gorilla in the room, a fact not lost on the speaker.

"You guys don't get it! One day you're going to wake up and the town will be screaming at your doorsteps with pitch forks! You are ruining paradise! This is your legacy. You guys are gonna have to own this! This, you will be remembered for!"

She stared hard at Kenner, her piercing gaze unrelenting.

"God help every one of you bastards for turning us out and selling your lousy souls!"

There were no goodbyes. She turned and walked out with an assured gait unassisted, saying nether a word. Only silence followed for the next few seconds, precipitating the opening and closing of the chamber door and the faint echo of the clack of her light, escaping footsteps.

Francis Tripp approached the dais holding a manila folder containing hand-written notes. He adjusted the microphone and spoke.

"Francis Tripp. 585 High Ridge Road. Fairhope, Alabama."

"So you are not from Orange Beach? Do you own property here, Sir?" Mayor Kenner asked, speaking into his microphone in a harsh, condescending tone.

"No Sir," Tripp answered.

"Then why are you here?" Kenner questioned with an authoritative tone.

"Public participation," Tripp answered, matter-of-factly. "Just like the gentle lady before me," he added.

"And by the way—I have to commend her. She really knocked it out of the park!"

Tripp rubbed it in, relishing every moment, knowing the councilmen, Buttrell and Kenner detested his presence. Few locals had the gall to stand before them. Most were too busy keeping up with the Joneses and Alabama football than to follow local politics or speak up at a council meeting to protect their life quality. Besides, the ruling class was known for its vindictiveness. In reality, in Baldwin County, the government could hurt you more than it could help you. One had to be careful, unless they were named Tripp, of course.

Kenner's face turned crimson. His blood pressure spiked. With the female octogenarian gone he could revert. What he did next was wholly regrettable.

"Not you Mr. Tripp! We ain't gonna let you speak! For one, you ain't from here! And two—you're a liar! All you do is print lies and half truths on that Internet blog of yours! We will under no circumstances allow you to speak! Speaking at this meeting is a privilege, not a right, Mr. Tripp!"

Kenner stared and motioned to the tall, broad-chested, uniformed, African-American police chief to do his duty. The chief was quick to move. Moments later he stood behind Mr. Tripp, towering above him.

"Chief Petty, please escort Mr. Tripp out the building!"

Before his exit, Tripp fired off once more, getting in a few choice, last words:

"You are ignoring your own height requirements for density protection. It's irresponsible and destructive!"

Mayor Kenner would have no more of it.

He ordered.

"Chief Petty—remove this man from the meeting and the premises! He is a public nuisance!"

The tall, barrel-chested chief stood quietly behind Mr. Tripp. He knew "Mr. Francis" as a former Marine—and he respected him and his service to the country during the Viet Nam conflict. Moreover, he respected him as a man, as he was standing up to what was still a white, male-dominated machine; and despite its Affirmative-Action-mandated charity toward him in the form of a token sinecure, he knew its corruption remained a challenge for Alabama's next generations—white and black. As he neared retirement, it was something he often thought of, despite his compliant position within the system. He wondered if things would ever improve, if Alabama would one day become more like the rest of the United States and give people a real shot at the American Dream. Because of this, he treated Tripp with kid gloves.

"Come on Mr. Tripp. It's time to go!" He lightly pleaded, being careful not to touch him.

Moments later, he stepped closer, placing his large right palm lightly on Tripp's left shoulder, across the many military operation scars that criss-crossed his skin in raised lesions like lashes from a lightning-fast leather whip. They were a constant reminder of his Viet Nam service, which in turn reminded him of his sense of purpose and conviction for the cause, like that of his departed father.

Trip sensed the chief's towering presence before the hand on his shoulder. He knew it was time to dee –dee out—for now. There would be other fighting days. Tripp turned to the chief, his lone gold ear-ring with a tiny round ruby dangling from a pierced left lobe. He smiled, revealing a straight, gleaming set of pale, veneered incisors.

"One second, Chief. Give me one more second, please!" He whispered. He turned and spoke directly into the microphone.

"I want to say one more thing:"

He paused.

"See ya in court, Donny!"

Tripp turned and jaunted toward the door, the chief trailing him closely until he exited. Kenner clinched his crooked, yellowed teeth and grimaced. He and the members of his kangaroo court muttered and muddled, trying to decipher what had just happened to them.

5

Johnny Glass met Joe Gideon at the Yacht Club across Perdido Key Boulevard from the Flora-Bama. Not only had Joe allowed he and Lucy to stay on his sailboat for free over the past year, he'd gotten them regular live music gigs at the Flora-Bama and other restaurants and bars by introducing them to the owners. In every way he could Joe helped the young couple get a good start on the island. He intended to continue to do so until they no longer needed him, like he had with so many other struggling artists. This was why Joe was so endeared to the local creative class. The entire music and writing community, due to his unparalleled kindness, was indebted to him. Joe had helped everyone out of a jam or two. It's what made him Big Daddy Joe—and the noted barrier island such the hypnotic live music destination.

"What's happening in your world, Mr. Glass?"

"Oh not a whole lot," he lied.

Joe sensed an apprehension in his look, a noticeable downturn in his countenance, and a subtlety in his word and tone. Joe knew better. He probed.

"How is Miss Lucy doing?"

"She's great. Just fine." It was more of the same.

"How many gigs are you guys playing a week?"

"We play Flora-Bama twice a week—on Sunday and Wednesday nights. We play Hub Stacey's on Saturdays and the Reef on Fridays. Mondays and Tuesdays are our weekend. Thursdays are for writing."

"So four nights a week?"

Johnny nodded in affirmation.

On the island musicians made about a hundred bucks a gig. As a result of the meager base pay most if not all sold merchandise and CD's and even tee shirts and coozies and stickers in order to pay the bills. It was a constant, self-deprecating hustle; but it was a must if you wanted to live and play in paradise.

"Aren't you guys getting a new CD together?" Joe asked. "I've heard some of your new songs since Jerry joined the group, and I like them a lot! People have really been talking you guys up!"

Joe searched for the familiar glint in Johnny's jade-colored eyes, that fateful gleam that first drew him to the island a year earlier looking for a place to ply his artful trade. Back then he seemed unstoppable, so talented and fresh; and on a mission; today—not so much, apparently shouldering the natural weight of the world.

"Thanks Joe," he phlegmatically replied, his mind in another place, his concern beyond them, placed somewhere in the puffy cumulous clouds flanking the painted azure horizon.

"Alright, what's going on?" Joe relented. "Has senator Whitman or his wife paid you guys an unexpected visit? Isn't he still in the clink? I know something's bothering you, Johnny."

He paused and added. "You are a terrible liar, by the way."

Joe smiled, trying to ease the situation. The reference to Lucy's disgraced father, Senator Slip Whitman, was a bad joke, as he was serving time on federal charges at Maxwell Air Force Base in Montgomery for stealing a lucrative BP contract to protect Fairhope from the impending oil onslaught stemming from the massive spill. The senator, who ran a retail tractor company and farm, on a fateful whim, decided to go into the oil boom placement and retrieval business. Much to his dismay—it went boom—in reverse, after Francis Tripp got involved in exposing the fraud, which was technically federal monies flowing through state and local agencies, even though it came from the hefty bank account of the misguided British Petroleum Corporation.

Johnny looked at Joe and looked away. He had been on his own for five years. His Mom and step Dad were still living in French Lick, and it was times like these he wished his real dad was around instead of being an infantry casualty in the First Gulf War in Iraq, in 1991, when Johnny was three; although he hated feeling sorry for himself.

"I think Lucy's pregnant," he said, getting it out there. He felt somewhat relieved. The catharsis helped to calm him. He breathed loudly in and out, and repeated. He felt his blood pressure stir. He whizzed out another prolonged, deep breath.

Joe listened. He paused before answering.

"What does she think?" He quipped, trying to make light of a heavy moment.

Johnny rolled his eyes and flashed a tiny grin.

Joe smiled when he spoke, his eyes full of light. "Johnny, even if she is, it's not the end of the world. Hey—it's gonna be okay!" He assured Johnny. But he could see the concern. Johnny wore it like a funny hat.

"But we live on a sailboat, Joe. We're honky tonk musicians! We can't raise a child like that! This is a game changer!"

Joe admired Johnny. He thought much of his art, but he also liked Johnny the person. He was part of the extended Flora-Bama family now, and that meant he would be treated as such.

"You know what's interesting, Johnnny?" Joe asked, leaning back, folding his arms. Johnny focused on his ruddy, stubble-filled face; and his projected positive, confident demeanor—like he had it all figured out.

"What's that?" Johnny replied with a wispy smile, anticipating something good from Joe's altered posture and gaze. He sat up in his chair in anticipation.

"Vonnie contacted me yesterday about putting her house off Innerarity Point Road up for rent."

Johnny perked up.

"It's a two bedroom." Joe smiled, pointing his right index finger into the air.

***

Inside the sailboat Lucy withdrew the submersed paper wick from her still-warm urine and placed it on the paper towel on the counter to dry. Within seconds a thin baby blue line appeared. She grabbed the paper strip and waved it wildly in the air, trying to somehow shake the noticeable, damp azure color from it. However, the skyline hue was as unshakeable as the situation was irrevocable. The verdict was in.

After feverous shaking, she looked again. It was darker, the line more pronounced than before. The point hit home. The trembling slowly subsided.

"I'm pregnant," she thought, accompanied by a flood of

contradicting emotions. "A baby!" She imagined, thinking vaguely of a child that would look like her and Johnny. She thought of its precious, cherub-like features, its warmth and the insatiable, unforgettably fresh, new way a newborn intrinsically smells.

"How beautiful!"

She reconsidered. "How will we pay for everything?"

Staring at the solid, thin baby blue line, she had never been so happy to be scared, or scared to be happy.

***

The color blue has a story as fascinating as its bountiful, elusive hue. While blue is omnipresent in our natural world, comprising the vast oceans and the sky, anthropologists and linguists contend the word for blue did not enter the English lexicon until the middle nineteenth century, following red, orange and yellow, the higher frequency colors on the spectrum. It seems early humans were color blind—and because of this—had no concept of the color, much less a word to describe its non-existence.

The human eye has three color sensors. Each picks up red, green and blue. These are "true" light primary colors. In paints, dyes and inks, however, it is different. Mixing is instead done subtractively, where the primary colors are magenta, yellow and cyan.

The first blue pigments were made from rare minerals such as lapis lazuli, cobalt and azurite. Blue dyes were made from plants; usually woad in Europe, and Indigofera tinctoria, or true indigo, in Asia and Africa. Today most blue pigments and dyes are made through a synthetic, chemical process.

Over 6,000 years ago modern humans developed blue colorants. Lapis, a semiprecious stone mined in Afghanistan, was coveted and prized by the Egyptians, who were mesmerized by the mineral's bright blue color. Also called "true blue," lapis lazuli first appeared as a pigment in the 6th century and was used in Buddhist paintings in Afghanistan. It was renamed ultramarine—in Latin: ultramarinus, meaning "beyond the sea" when the pigment was imported into Europe by Italian traders during the 14th and 15th centuries. Its deep, royal blue quality was highly sought after among artists living in Medieval Europe.

It was at this time that an Egyptian word for blue emerged, proving the Egyptians were an advanced society accomplished in realms other than monument building, stargazing and honoring their dead in careful preparation for the active afterlife.

Considered the first synthetically produced color pigment, Egyptian blue was created from ground limestone mixed with sand and a copper-containing mineral, such as azurite or malachite. The result was an opaque blue glass which was crushed and combined with thickening agents like egg whites to create a long-lasting glaze. In the early 21st century, it was discovered that Egyptian blue glows under fluorescent light, making coated ancient artifacts more recognizable.

The Egyptians used their blue in ceramics, statues and to decorate pharaoh tombs. The popularity of their dyes spread throughout the world, finding favor with the Persians, Mesoamericans and Romans. However, they were expensive; a luxury only royalty could afford. Thus, the color blue remained rare to the masses for many centuries; though it slowly became popular enough to earn its own name in various languages.

Blue was for the wealthy, as it was considered as precious as gold. Only a few artists with money had access to the hue. Baroque master Johannes Vermeer painted Girl with a Pearl Earring. It was reported he so loved ultramarine that he forced his family into debt. Blue remained expensive until a synthetic ultramarine was invented by a French chemist in 1826.

Costly to use in paintings, blue was cheaper for dying textiles. Unlike the rarity of lapis lazuli, the arrival of a new blue dye called "indigo" came from a crop by the same name produced across the world. Its import shook the European textile trade in the 16th century, catalyzing trade wars between Europe and America.

Sir Isaac Newton, inventor of the color spectrum, believed the rainbow consisted of seven distinct colors to match the seven days of the week, the seven known planets, and the seven notes in the musical scale. Newton championed indigo, along with orange, though many other contemporary scientists believed the rainbow had only five colors.

While the nineteenth century saw innovations in cobalt, cerulean and Prussian shades, in pursuit of the color of the sky, 20th century French artist Yves Klein developed a matte version of ultramarine he considered the best blue of all. He registered International Klein Blue (IKB) as a trademark and the deep hue became his signature between 1947 and 1957. Klein once said of the elusive color, "… blue has no dimensions. It is beyond dimensions…" Klein believed his blue could take the viewer outside the canvas.

The story of blue as a color for everyday man began in 431 A.D. The Catholic Church color-coded the saints, and Mary, Mother of Jesus, was given a blue robe. The blue Mary wore became what is now known as "navy blue." Because Mary stood for innocence and trustworthiness, navy was seen in a positive light. Navy was adopted by militaries and police to convey trust.

When reading through ancient Greek texts, historians have noted strange color descriptions. In the Odyssey, Homer makes hundreds of references to white and black, but colors like red and yellow are sparingly mentioned. The color blue, it turns out, is never mentioned. Instead, descriptions like "wine-dark" are used to describe blue items such as the omnipresent sea.

The word "blue" did not exist in Greek times. It seems this color was barely distinguished from competing neutral shades like white, light and dark. You can read every ancient Greek text and you will never find a word for "blue." It was not important enough for reference.

Even as the English language developed, blue took a backseat to other shades. The first color words to appear in English, and most other languages, were words for "white" and "black." Next, red, the color of wine and blood appeared, followed by yellow and then green. Blue appeared last.

Blue is rare in nature. Most people do not have blue eyes; blue flowers do not occur naturally without human intervention; and blue animals are rare, as blue birds and blue jays live in isolated areas. The sky is blue. Or is it? One theory suggests that before humans had words for blue, they actually saw the sky as another hue. This theory is supported by the fact that if you never describe the color of the sky to a child, and then ask them what color they think it is, they often struggle to describe its hue. Some describe it as colorless, or white. It seems that only after being told the sky is blue, and after seeing other objects labeled blue over a period of time, does one see the sky as blue.

Additional support for this theory comes from studies of an ancient Nambian tribe that lacks separate words for the colors green and blue. When shown a set of squares, 11 of which are green and 1 of which is blue, members of this tribe cannot identify the single blue square from the green squares. Thus, it seems that since there was no word or even a concept for the color blue, early humans did not notice it.

This aloofness to the color blue is a powerful notion that can be applied to other aspects of the human existence. For example, Alabama citizens are historically so intrinsically uneducated, so patently obtuse, so blissfully unaware and less-evolved than their American citizen counterparts living in more progressive states, that they fail to realize they live in a democracy where the people rule, and are wholly deserving of all the rights and privileges afforded under the U.S. Constitution, the same ones deprived them by their churchgoing, hypocritical civilian masters who have no intention of improving their mean, perilous, undeserved plight. Theirs is a sordid story seldom told; one purposely forgotten by the ruling class—not unlike the color blue. Francis Tripp was bent on correcting their unfortunate plight.

6

Johnny and Joe drove to Vonnie's tiny wooden cottage on Garcon Street off Innerarity Point Road. Innerarity Point and its adjacent Innerarity Island, once an ancient peninsula, extended from the Gulf Beach Highway near the Baar Bridge, three miles to the West, ending with a peaceful, hilly residential island replete with fantastic views of surrounding waters. On one side were dolphins group hunting mullet in Perdido Bay; on the other was the man-made Intracoastal Canal, a constant parade of sport fishing boats, pleasure cruisers and commercial shipping vessels, tug boats and barges moving heavy freight. Named after John Innerarity, a former explorer and noted area pioneer, the eclectic, funky enclave reminded many of the Florida Keys and its subtle penchant for the simple, easy and unrefined. The little wooden house off Innerarity was the quintessential starter home, if there ever was one for Johnny and Lucy.

Joe opened the front door with a key left under a potted plant perched on the front porch ledge and replaced it. He let Johnny in and followed him. The house was furnished, albeit dated. It was neat and clean, the layout adequate based on their humble needs.

At only 1080 square feet the freshly-painted beige house was diminutive, yet was still more than twice the room on the sailboat. Moreover, it had a quaint backyard with a sealed wooden deck and an overhead trellis infused with blooming jasmine, honeysuckle, heirloom jade and wisteria. Various and miscellaneous items of folk art adorned the yard in a funky beach museum of sorts. These were odds and ends Vonnie collected through the years living on

Perdido Key. Some she bought, some she reclaimed, some she was given or found. All of it she revered.

A faded and withered old wooden wire spindle used as a table for potted flowering plants showcased scarlet carnations, a rainbow of gladiolas, running marbled cream and jade ivies and vine-ripe cherry tomatoes. In their center was a groovy sun dial.

Johnny had never lived in a house other than the one he grew up in. This one would be "his." It would be for him and his new family, he prided. He thought about what Joe asked, about what Lucy thought, regarding her pregnancy.

"I wonder if she went to the clinic?" he thought.

***

Minutes later Johnny met Lucy back on the sailboat, an aging 32-foot double fiberglass hull that housed their cramped sleeping quarters, tiny head, mini appliances and few material possessions; it was the dank space they had made a happy, humble home for the last year. On his walk down into the vessel, he noted it felt different, for some strange reason. It was unexplainable—another déjà vu— his second in as many days. As he dropped into the hatch in his peripheral vision he saw splashes of magenta, peach and pink dot the western evening sky, signaling the day's end.

Seated Indian style on the made bed Lucy pretended to read from her Kindle app on her phone. The din of the dark cabin was punctuated by a damp coolness and the incessant, rhythmic hum of the laboring window unit. Johnny was glad to see her, as she had been on his mind the entire day.

"Hey Sweetie!" Johnny said, pushing himself into the dimly lit forward sleeping berth that filled the ship's narrow nose. The tiny, slow-leaking AC unit attempted to cool the unorthodox resting quarters. He hugged and kissed Lucy on the cheek, lips and forehead, like he always did. He grabbed her dominant hand and held it tight with both hands. He brought the other hand up, squeezed and kissed her clasped hands in his, stared into her deep brown eyes and smiled.

"How was your day?" He asked, flopping himself onto the padded sleeping and sitting area next to her.

Lucy pushed the book of baby names she was reading under the covers before Johnny sat down, just after she'd heard him enter. He was now on top of it. He felt it and reached underneath the covers and withdrew the paperback. He examined the catchy, inexplicable cover.

"Names for Your Baby."

Lucy noticed the shocked look on Johnny's face—and said nothing. There was a prolonged moment of silence between them. She feared his full reaction.

"So it's official?" He questioned, his olive eyes pooling.

A nod was all she could muster, looking down. Johnny tilted her head up with a gentle index finger under her chin.

"I love you," he said, the intonation and tone of his voice rising in the quiet moment. "Everything's gonna be just fine, Doll. Joe and me went and saw Miss Vonnie's place today. She's putting her little house up for rent. It's a tiny two-bedroom, but a Shangri La compared to this! It's got a sweet deck and a big back yard! It's really pretty. I think you're going to like it."

He smiled, pearly whites gleaming, cheeks flush with color.

Lucy beamed, her rosy complexion glowing like the breaking evening sky. She imagined watching a toddler in the backyard, amidst the breeze, barbecuing supper and watching a marmalade and magenta sunset together—as a family. She experienced a rush of new endorphins.

"Oh Johnny!" She squealed, crying happily. She hugged him close. "I love you, too."

They managed to save a little money during the prior twelve months since Joe let them live rent-free on the sailboat, paying only the utility bill in his name. They had a little over three grand between them in savings. It was enough to pay the first and last month's rent, with a little left over for things they would need in the new place, like service deposits, incidentals and the like. Johnny had already done the math. They could make it work. It was liberating.

"How much is rent?" Lucy asked, excited about the prospect of having a home. She was beyond ready to say goodbye to the sailboat.

"Joe said she wants a grand a month. First and last month's rent to start."

She grinned, imagined decorating a baby's room, a crib, and a rocker, and stacking little baby toys. She had never felt this way. It was magical—and she loved it. Filled with the courage and promise of a thousand twinkling stars, she beamed.

"Oh Johnny! I'm so excited! I'm so scared at the same time—but I am so excited!"

The two hopeful hearts hugged tightly, their fears and concerns eased by the warmth of their embrace and the stoic, solemn promise of the near future, unrealized; as they had alas made it this far.

7

J acque Buttrell met with Mayor Donny Kenner for breakfast at Hazel's in Orange Beach, the one off the beach road in the Rouse's parking lot. It was a popular eatery, frequented by locals and tourists. It was also the place where years earlier the former Alabama Football Coach Mike Brice spoke to the Orange Beach Sunrise Red Elephant Club—a popular Crimson Tide breakfast booster group, before heading to Destin for the annual SEC head coaches meeting where he unwittingly hired an unscrupulous Cajun prostitute. The clever hooker got him loaded on Jack Daniels charcoal filtered whiskey and stole his cash, jewelry and credit cards. That was not all. While he snoozed off the booze she ran up a $2,000 hotel room service tab—much of which she boxed, bagged and conveniently left the hotel with. That wasn't the worst part.

Of course, the sordid Southern story revealed made national news, and within days the imbroglio forced the resignation of the newest and perhaps dumbest, Alabama Head Football Coach. This happened before Brice ever coached a game at the Capstone. After Brice's successor was hired and in place, it was revealed that the questionable lady of the evening responsible for the coach's downfall was named "Thibodeaux," a fact not lost for laughs on the LSU Tiger fan base. As an asterisk, Brice finished an auspicious 0-0 as head football coach at Alabama—which means they'll never call him a loser, for scoring.

Kenner ordered eggs, lightly-buttered toast and black coffee. Butrell preferred pancakes and bacon and juice. Professionally dressed in their preferred beach attire of designer fishing shorts, collared, pressed sport shirts and leather sandals, they faced each other across the enamel two-top. A framed, autographed photo of a smiling former head coach Mike Brice wearing the beloved crimson and white hung on the wall behind them. Kenner leaned forward before he spoke.

"What's the word from Montgomery on the beach road extension? Have you heard anything? I've got buddies asking if the deal's gone through." Kenner asked.

Buttrell chewed his food in small bites and sipped his steaming coffee before speaking. He quietly contemplated the question as well as how often the Mayor had sex with his wife—particularly over the last few heated weeks.

"It's a done deal," Buttrell began. "I spoke to the governor yesterday and she said the Senate is finally in line with the whole thing and the two-cent gas tax to pay for it. If we can get the Speaker to come to terms we'll bring the bill up for passage next week."

"And that's gonna extend the Beach Expressway another 56 miles north to I-65, right?" Kenner asked.

"That's right. It's gonna make it a lot easier to get to the beach for folks who normally come down on I-65—which is just about everybody in the Midwest who doesn't have the money to fly!" Buttrell smiled, impressed by his own logic.

"Well then I guess it's time to bring up the new beach tower before the council. Anyone can plainly see there's a growing need for more condos—the tourists are a comin'!" Kenner stammered with a wry grin. Buttrell laughed along knowing the project was indeed a done deal—and that his friend Kenner was blissfully unaware he'd made him a cuckold.

***

Barry "Strick-9" Strickland lounged in a padded lawn chair on his weather-polished wooden pier. It was a shaky, above-water structure attached to the deck of his ramshackle, tin panel hut on placid Old River, a few paces from the bustling Yacht Club Restaurant. A red and gray-bearded fellow of nearly 70 years, he ate cold boiled peanuts from a clear Ziploc bag and gripped his tight gin and tonic in a red Solo cup as he awaited his favorite part of the day.

He ran his fingers through his graying stringy, shoulder-length auburn hair as he cooled off and reflected on the day. His trimmed, liver-colored beard was a stark contrast in his appearance, but it gave him a certain distinctive look; his leathered skin the drench of a thousand scotch and middle American whiskies.

The story behind the nickname "Strick-9" was as interesting as the character he had become as a 30-year island denizen. To his credit, Barry told everyone the same moniker-related yarn.

"It was some really great acid—that turned out to be some really bad acid," Strick-9 explained with a great first line, gesticulating wildly with both hands. The story was consistent. He never wavered, as strange as it was.

"We thought we had taken some of the best acid out there. It was great. We were happy, loving life, seeing sounds, hearing and smelling colors; the whole nine yards of fun—it was super groovy man," he recalled. "Until the Strychnine kicked in! Apparently somebody got the bright idea to lace the stuff with rat poison—supposedly to give you that speedy, nasty, shaking effect. Some liked feeling like that—but not me! I was shakin' like a cat shittin' glass! Although, a couple of the boys loved it! Most, like me, had a hard time with it that night; but the nickname—Strick-9—unfortunately stuck!"

Like the peculiar story behind his name, Strick-9's legend grew over time. Flora-Bama patrons wanted pictures with him and his books. A self-proclaimed, "shitty dime-bag novelist," Barry managed to pen a pair of half-hearted tomes titled, "Tales from the Davenport," a whimsy, flimsy read with noteworthy local historical fascinations, and a decent novella, "Black Beard's Revenge," which garnered a smattering of publicity and a dash of literary praise from the local media gatekeepers, who tabbed it a "distinct artistic contribution to area history and lore…" which was of course, alright with Barry, as it helped weekly book sales on the back deck near the oyster and tent bars at Flora-Bama and on the weekends at his shack on the water behind the Yacht Club.

Beloved by his patron fans and musician friends, Strick-9 was one of the unique characters Joe Gideon insisted made the island the vibrant, zany, carefree atmosphere it was; and of course, the Flora-Bama the revered quintessential roadhouse adored by so many, that ephemeral memory factory and vortex of fun on the Alabama-Florida Line.

***

In a seeming rush and a momentary green flash the amber dot dipped low in the burnt orange western sky, touching the steely horizon, signaling the end of another early summer day on the Key. It was a natural phenomenon and spectacle Barry had witnessed and enjoyed many times under similar conditions—a gorgeous sunset on placid Old River—but the precipitating green flash he had seen maybe a handful of times.

"Wow!" He thought, amazed at his good fortune. "Lucky me! The green lantern returns!"

It was moments like these that gave him solace. As silly as it seemed, Barry felt like a millionaire. He was the one who lived the beach life—not those city people who worked like dogs for the man all year to keep their condos up and down the highway so they could use them maybe once or twice in a blue moon.

"I've now seen the green flash a handful of times! Most don't even know what it is! I live at the beach..." he reminded himself, paradise not yet lost on the boast of him. "Ahh...what a life!"

A green flash across the sun, which occurs more at sunset—but can also occur at sunrise —is a rare phenomenon where part of the sun can be seen suddenly and briefly changing color. It lasts only a second or two—which is why it is called a flash—as the sun changes from red, or orange, at sunset.

The green flash is viewable because refraction bends the sunlight. The Earth's atmosphere acts as a prism, which separates light into its various colors. When the sun's disk is fully visible above the horizon, the different colors of light rays overlap to where each individual color cannot be seen by the naked human eye.

When the sun begins to dip below the horizon the colors of the spectrum disappear one at a time, starting with those with the longest wavelengths to those with the shortest. At sunrise, the process is reversed, and a green flash may occur as the top of the sun peeks above the horizon.

The remaining dull light of the day was now short, within ten minutes. Brad Masterson pulled his shiny new Ford F-150 pickup truck with all the bells and whistles to the conspicuous front step of the deck leading to Strick-9's lopsided shanty. It was a faded crimson hard plastic milk crate he'd gleaned from the Yacht Club, another of the island's many offerings for the ever-resourceful Strick-9.

Barry heard Brad pull up. He looked over his shoulder and saw his round bifocals and smiling face. They'd known each other for 20 years. Brad, a successful local architect, designed dozens of homes on Ono Island and was friends with the Flora-Bama owners, having worked with them for many years. He designed the recently-completed Flora-Bama rebuild post-Hurricane Ivan, making it much larger than its former inglorious self, while somehow still maintaining a semblance of the over tackiness that had made it the quintessential beach dive bar and honky-tonk. However, lately, Brad had been particularly busy.

In the short time since the completion of the Flora-Bama rebuild, Brad designed three restaurants for the Flora-Bama Corporation. Across the Gulf Beach Highway from the Flora-Bama, the Yacht Club was built first; the Ole River Grille, next door, the refurbishment of a former failed bar, followed. Unbeknownst to Barry, the third restaurant project—perhaps their boldest yet, was the reason for Brad's impromptu call.

Brad enjoyed Strick-9's keyboard playing during his many years on the island and knew him as one of the more colorful, creative characters who made the Flora-Bama so special. Brad parked his truck and cut the engine. Strick-9 was standing now, still smiling, against the backdrop of a jaw-dropping scarlet, dusky, burnt-orange sky. He waved Brad over, out of his vehicle, to join the spectacle. With trepidation he exited and shut his truck door, locking it with a quick click of the chirper.

"This ain't gonna be easy," he thought. Driving over he'd considered his words.

"There's a right way to do this," he thought. He was still upset the Flora-Bama asked him to break the news to Strick-9, who he knew simply as "Barry." They could have and should have done it themselves, he felt. "I guess that's why they pay me the big bucks," he reasoned.

The Flora-Bama principal, along with his partners and stockholders, like any business person in charge, was motivated to recoup his initial investment; and then some. He wanted to build a third restaurant on Old River; exactly where Strick-9's shack sat unfettered for years. This meant Barry's shanty would be razed in order to prepare the construction site. To Brad, the hollow thought of Barry not living there was difficult. He hated this, as Barry was as much a part of the place as anyone, and was beloved by all.

Barry Strickland came to the Flora-Bama in the early 1980s, at a time when a young Joe Gideon was really making a name for the place. He'd grown up in Pensacola as a bass player and keyboardist for various teenage and college-aged bands that traveled along the gulf coast. He was talented and knew the songs and had played so many gigs illegally as a teen with a fake I.D. that by the time he was 18 he had worked nearly every one horse juke joint and dive bar from Pensacola to New Orleans that would pay and/or feed him and his band. And he and his buddies had a hell of a time doing it!

Strick-9 hated to be reminded of it, but he was the last remaining vestige of Boys Towne, a designated area of land near Old River behind the Yacht Club that years prior Joe land-granted to performing musicians and songwriters to park their slightly loved trailers, RV's and campers. As long as a player had a regular, paying gig in the Flora-Bama music rotation they were allowed to flop for free in Boys Towne. Barry took full advantage of this deal for nearly 40 years…living rent-free, playing a regular gig and running sound at the world-famous Flora-Bama Lounge & Package; what some might consider a "dream," much less a dream job. In retrospect, it was quite the heist—like money for nothing and chicks for free—because the property where Barry's shack sat on Ole River was worth millions.

As a pioneer of the creative class of musicians who haunted the hallowed Flora-Bama stages, Barry was considered a "new-age hippie" by some and an absolute legend by anybody who'd hung around the juke joint for a considerable period of time. His reputation preceded him. Barry had a wild, psychedelic bent and a penchant for the nasty when it came to women. It was not that he liked nasty women as much as he liked getting nasty with them. Barry wrote dozens of funny songs, most of which were about the crazy things he had actually done! His trademark line was: "You can't make this shit up!"

Brad figured at worst it had been a noble run—nearly 40 years living free on the Key. Who could say that? It amounted to a small fortune in unpaid rent. However, Brad knew Barry would have a hard time relocating. It was unlikely he would be able to afford the luxury condo, the Mediterranean, next door to the Flora-Bama—or anywhere else nearby. The rents were too damn high. He lived a waif's existence. Flora-Bama paid him a pittance for putting up the weekly music schedules on the walls and doors and for running sound during the day. Any money he had left over from his meager Bama paycheck and book sales was passed along to his daughter, and her two small children, his grandkids, in the form of money and gifts. Oddly, in a pinch like this, he could be forced to move in with them, which was unthinkable; and he could forget the caretaker role, as he wouldn't be able to continue living there—which meant he would lose his job and income at the Flora-Bama. His life would never be the same.

"That might kill Barry," Brad pondered. Regardless, he knew Barry was looking squarely at a huge lifestyle change, because his bosses were intent on building a new restaurant. Before he settled into the task, he wondered again why he had to be the bad news bearer.

"How's it goin' brother?" Barry asked, lifting his half-finished, clear-fizzing cocktail into the air. "You've been away for a while."

"All's good, Barry. I've been busy with a slew of new projects. It's great and all—I love the money, don't get me wrong—but I just don't seem to have the "Leisure Time" I used to back in the day!"

Brad Masterson was an Auburn graduate, like Joe G., and a master at laying it on thick. He was making a clever play on words.

Strick-9 and his songwriting pal, Barry Brown, a.k.a. "Downtown Barry Brown," formed an occasional duo known as "Men of Leisure." They wrote and sang funny, raunchy numbers for rich rednecks across the South. They traveled for birthday parties, reunions, wedding receptions and other gatherings where people wanted lively, less-predictable entertainment.

Years prior, Brad hired the Men of Leisure for his older brother's retirement party in Montgomery, Alabama. It was a stupendous hit. Brad's extended family and friends raved about the good time they had when the Men of Leisure from the Flora-Bama performed just for them.

"Ha! That was a blast! Me and Brown enjoyed that gig! Your family's a hoot!" Strick-9 replied. "How's your brother doing? Enjoying his retirement? He told me he was gonna do some serious fishing…"

"He's fishing a lot now," Brad answered shortly, seeming preoccupied.

"Good." Barry answered, sensing something was awry. There was a lull in the conversation, until Barry blurted.

"What's up, Brad? Give it to me," he presciently demanded. He'd seen this type of thing before. This wasn't his first taffy pull.

Brad gritted his teeth and swallowed.

"Get it out!" Barry demanded. "Let me have it."

"They wanna build another restaurant," he said, his tone somber.

Barry didn't reply. The lot his shack sat on was worth ten million dollars. It was the last vacant parcel of land within what was now the vast Flora-Bama compound, ranging far and wide on both sides of the beach highway. He had dreamt of losing his little slice of paradise. The revelation—the nightmare, was surreal.

"Right here," Brad added, pointing to the area where he parked.

Barry's few detractors on the job these days were a group of young bucks running sound—guys who were jealous of his unbelievable free rent deal. After all, they couldn't afford to live on the island. They had to drive to and from work. Over the last couple of years since the new owners took over these punks had badgered him that it was "just a matter of time until they put up another condominium…"

As it turned out, they were nearly right; but it was something else.

"They want to build a 250-seat barbecue restaurant," Brad blurted.

Barry liked barbecue.

"Memphis or North Carolina style?" Strick-9 quipped.

Brad laughed out loud, surprised by the pithy, humorous retort. "You know you'll have to move, right?" He implored.

"Of course I know I'll have to move, damn it!" Strick-9 retorted, his blood pressure spiking.

Brad responded with a chuckle, trying to make light of the tricky situation. "I'll help you figure something out, man. Don't worry about it!"

The next few silent moments were punctuated by a bending mauve and magenta sky, yielding to the dwindling light of the day's close, that fleeting time where everything seemed gentle and copacetic—even though it really wasn't.

"I bet if we talk to Joe he'll have some ideas. It would be great if you could stay living close by," Brad injected. "I mean, you're one of the oldest living musicians from the original Flora-Bama cast!"

"Me and Jay Hawkins!" Strick-9 replied. "He was here before me! Jay's still around! What a fricking badass—what a legend!" He declared, trying to deflect any deserved glory or praise.

"I'll give Papa Joe a call and we'll see what we can do." Brad stated. "He's always got an answer."

"Thanks brother." Barry answered, staring off into the distance, into the dark, thin veil of humidity in the fading light. He got up slowly to see Brad off.

"Hey Brad," Strick-9 called.

Brad stopped and turned and faced him.

"Yeah man?"

"No hard feelings, brother. I know you had nothing to do with all this. It's just the way of the world these days."

Brad appreciated the gesture by Barry. In his weakened, humbled state, he had thought of him. He promised himself he would do what he could to help him. He would talk to Joe as soon as he could, as promised.

"You've got a few weeks until construction starts, so that's a plus," Brad added, standing inside his open door. "I'll get back to you after I talk to Papa Joe! Hang tight, Barry."

Strick-9 straightened his body tight and silently saluted, mimicking a military man. Brad drove off with a wave. Strick-9's posture reverted and he retired for the evening, resolved painfully that it would be one of his last on Perdido Key. He had a difficult time grasping the concept. He took a warm shot of Fireball and shot-gunned a cold canned Coors Light beer; he then hit the rack, not before dreaming of his younger days on the Key when there weren't so many condos; when Joe still had the place; and when everybody from the patrons to the workers and the songwriters and musicians had so much fun together during and after hours; and when happenings on the island weren't so busy, touristy and commercialized. It was a much simpler time. It was the best of times.

And these, undoubtedly, were the worst of times.

8

F rancis Tripp sat smiling before his favorite lawyer. Tripp wore creeping cardinal running shorts, the kind that ran high on the thigh, worn leather sandals, and a white beefy tee shirt that read, "San Pedro, Belize" in black lettering. His left wrist bore a large brass African fighting bracelet bearing many scars. A thin gold ankle chain rested on his right shin and a matching gold rope necklace hung from his darkly-tanned shoulders. He sat back in his chair with his legs crossed in the air-conditioned legal office in the Baldwin County seat of Bay Minette, a block off the circular courthouse square. His white bangs lifted gently up and down under the ceiling fan's oscillations. The small gold pendant earring in his right ear wobbled slightly when he spoke.

"I've got em' this time!" Tripp stammered, pointing into the air with an index finger. "They've really done it! What a bunch of morons! You ready to go to court, Greg?"

There was no appointment. Ever the impromptu, Tripp called on his way over, knowing Greg would be there, as he was a creature of habit. His attorney, Greg B. McMakin, a balding, somewhat reserved but more than capable counselor, sat behind his desk with both feet on the floor. Greg was an Auburn grad, but attended the University of Alabama Law School since Auburn lacks one. Nevertheless, he still pulled for Auburn annually in the Iron Bowl. It was a family thing. They were eaten up, like so many, with the indomitable War Eagle spirit.

McMakin wore an early look of consternation, along with a pressed sport coat, and a buttoned-down, gray collared shirt without a tie. The top two buttons on his shirt were unfastened. A steaming cup of coffee sat before him and in Tripp's steady hand, recent compliments of his secretary.

McMakin was a sloth without coffee. He hadn't taken any yet. He also knew Tripp well enough to know he was harmless—just strangely motivated—and equally sincere. He got it, though. He even thought he understood Tripp, as he had known him a while. He had twice represented him in court, winning both cases against the City of Fairhope and the Baldwin County Commission. Tripp was actually a good client—and here he was—yet again, before him… apparently with another legal case for the making.

"I'm listening," he answered, sipping the aromatic brew made from fresh-ground beans in a French press.

"I want to file a federal lawsuit against Mayor Donny Kenner in Orange Beach."

McMakin was not fazed. He wore an expressionless look. He sipped his coffee with sugar and placed the cup on the round ceramic holder before him on the mahogany desk. It was the kind with a small heating element designed to maintain drink temperature.

"And I want to see his wife naked," McMakin quipped and paused. "And we both know THAT ain't happening!"

Tripp chuckled and wondered at the same time. "I haven't seen her. I have heard she is very attractive, however."

McMakin looked him squarely in the eyes. "Are you serious?"

He paused, looked away and returned his gaze.

"She's an 11."

"Really?" Tripp answered. "What's she look like?"

"Imagine a real-life Barbie doll."

"Aye-yie-yie!" Tripp stammered. "Makes my teeth hurt just thinking about it! I need to get out more."

"Go to Flora-Bama on Fridays for the Big Earl show. You'll see her there, along with Kenner. They're regulars." Tripp made a mental note. He liked Big Earl. He had one of his CD's Joe gave him. He thought it was hilarious. He loved the song, "Eating corn and watching porn," one of Earl's more popular diddies.

"What happened?" McMakin asked, his steaming java kicking in.

"I went to the last city council meeting in Orange Beach. I've been before and spoken to them. You know the drill. They're out of control with their beach high-rise development. There are already too many wheels on the damn road! Especially at peak season!"

Tripp paused, shifting his weight in the padded leather chair, gesticulating.

"I waited to speak at public participation. When it was my turn to address the council, Kenner denied me. He had the big black police chief—a guy I like by the way—he was just doing his job—escort me out the building."

"Huh?" McMakin asked. He sat up straight and his eyes widened.

"Rewind! Tell me again exactly what happened!" He demanded, increasing his volume and tone.

Tripp repeated himself, emphasizing that he was denied his Constitutional right to free speech under the First Amendment.

"So Kenner had you escorted out and disallowed you to speak during a recognized public participation session?"

"Yes. He also said that citizens speaking at their council meeting is a "privilege and not a right."

McMakin's mug wore an incredulous look. He sat back in his chair and stared momentarily at the wall behind Tripp.

"The city council proceedings are videotaped. They are accessible online." McMakin stated. He sat up straight and swiveled to his keyboard. Within a minute he found the embedded meeting video on the city website and had queued it to the end during the public participation segment. He turned the large horizontal screen toward Tripp and played the sequence.

After the video was done, corroborating completely what Tripp had stated, McMakin sat back in his chair. He rocked and smiled. Then he thought of something. He tracked to the beginning of the public participation sequence, before the old lady spoke. He let it play and saw that Kenner verbally opened up the floor for public participation, thereby making it an open public forum. Based on that alone—and the fact it was on videotape—meant that the case was open and shut—prima facie—and was definitely a free speech denial case.

"What do you think?" Tripp asked.

"I think you're right!" McMakin answered, grinning in anticipation.

"About what?"

"I think you've got their ass! This is serious! This case is ripe for federal court. From what I just saw on video you were absolutely denied your American right to free speech under the Constitution! This is a classic prima facie case. At face value the defendant(s) will be held liable. In other words, after we file suit that you were denied your constitutional rights, it will be considered so until proven otherwise untrue. He paused and his countenance shifted, sitting back in his chair. He rocked and pondered, staring again off into the large oil landscape on the wall depicting a field bursting yellow Black-Eyed Susans, tall, bent grass the color of peas in the foreground and a solitary, Spanish Moss-weeping Live Oak in the background.

"I heard some things about Kenner recently that I refused to believe—that he was involved in illegal activities and was in big with the developers up and down the beach. I guess I just didn't want to believe it. Anything's possible but the guy before him—Mayor Musso—went to prison for being on the take from developers. I never thought I'd say this, but it may be true about him."

He continued after a breathing moment. "But this type of third grade behavior makes me wonder what Kenner is really up to. Because this looks to me like you have really pushed his buttons, and he does not want you on the record any more than you already are."

Tripp smiled. "Greg, do you know how good you make me feel? I didn't think anyone was paying attention to me." He burst out laughing.

"This guy has too much fun with this stuff," McMakin thought, watching Tripp writhe with laughter in the leather chair before him. Tripp settled down like an adult and spoke.

"I've given Kenner and Buttrell more crap than a Shrimp Festival port-o-potty! The last six weeks on the Tripp Report I've done at least one update on Buttrell and more than one on Kenner. The series is called, "You Don't Know Jacque," fully exposing him, and of course, his pal Kenner."

Tripp paused, and added, "Jacque is Jack in French."

"I know," "Greg answered, raising his eyebrows, even though he'd studied Spanish at Auburn.

Tripp continued. "Kenner and Jacque Buttrell of Fairhope are tight. Buttrell is basically the Machine representative for Baldwin County and his ties to real estate and development are as significant as they are lucrative. Word is Buttrell, operating under a veil of anonymous LLC's set up to do national and international business in various states across the union, has built with the help of his many investors, over a half dozen high-rise condos in the last eight years. They are making a fortune. It's sickening! Traffic during the season is now a slow crawl! We can't even see the beach anymore in some spots! And to add insult to injury, they outlaw locals from the beach now! It's all private—yet the beach itself is a natural public resource—or at least it should be. It certainly used to be!"

McMakin listened intently. He was an area native, and while he was financially successful and friends with many of the developers exploiting the demographic shift for real estate gains, he didn't wholeheartedly agree with what was happening. Like most, he had reservations, but little say in the matter, as he was not political, except for the regular contributions to the Republican Party Machine apparatus, and to his local Baptist preacher, whom he somehow equally trusted.

Tripp realized his concern, tracking the subtle change in his countenance, voice and posture.

"And what you heard about Kenner is consistent with what I've heard." Tripp stated.

He paused for effect. "He's dirty, Greg."

McMakin accepted it. "After hearing all this, I'd say there's a good chance he is. He certainly seems like someone who has much to hide—treating you the way he did. It was not advisable under the law."

Tripp sensed there was something else. "What else have you heard?"

McMakin thought carefully. He answered, "My wife Debbie is best friends with Kenner's wife. We have a condo at Tourquoise in Orange Beach and we get together with them there every now and again."

"My condolences," Trip offered.

McMakin stared familiarly at the wall behind Ripp's head—and then focused, turning directly to him.

"She's my wife's friend. She seems like a sweet girl. I am not a fan of Kenner. He can go pound sand as far as I'm concerned!"

Tripp sensed there was more to tell.

"So you'll sue him for me?"

"Absolutely!" Greg emphasized. "After all, that's what I do! The wife will just have to get over it. This is a slam dunk—and it involves the Constitution. The fact that it's on tape is golden. They have no out. Ultimately the City is liable. It's all there on video!"

"The big eye don't lie!" Tripp declared, beaming. "That's what I like about you Greg—you're a principled man."

Greg blew off the compliment with a shrug, amazed that Tripp somehow had brought him another solid case—one that was likely to pay off handsomely. As a practicing attorney, the fact Tripp had become a rainmaker fighting the proverbial bad guys warranted further his varying concerns of rampant political corruption plaguing the area. As Tripp's lawyer on now three cases against local governments, he was now seriously involved in the noble fight to upend the Machine—even though he donated to it. He wondered where it could and would go, as Tripp was capable of anything. This third case, however, was different. It would cause him some grief at home and on the golf course, not to mention in the court ante room. He did not waiver, reminding himself he was getting paid—which was all he really cared about. He left the idealism to his clients.

"Okay, I'll draft the filing and email it to you in the morning. This should be an easy one."

"Sounds good," Tripp stated. He stood and offered his hand. McMakin shook hard.

"One more thing," McMakin added.

"What's that?" Tripp asked.

"Contingency?"

"Sure, why not?" Tripp replied. "How about 70-30? You get 70 and I get 30."

McMakin stuttered. "That's a bit much, don't you think?"

"No." He flatly answered. "It's fair."

"How is that?" Greg inquired. "I'm listening."

"Nobody seems to get me. I thought you did." Tripp paused and smiled ear-to-ear, ivory incisors shining. "Look Greg—this is not about money—it's about justice. It's about doing the right thing. I am the person who has the balls to stand up to these cretins. No one else does. I just want to win. You can keep the bulk of the money. Just draft the filing. I'll look for it in on my computer in the morning."

Tripp knew Greg was a good, capable attorney—and more importantly—one not opposed to suing anyone if he could make a buck.

"Good enough," he replied. "70-30 it is." He stared expressionless at his client.

Before Tripp exited he stopped and abruptly spun in place. He reached into his pocket and handed Greg a navy blue business card with white lettering. He turned and left his office.

Greg looked to the shiny card with white lettering. It read:

Francis P. Tripp
Equal Opportunity Non-Partisan Political Goad and Shit-Stirrer
336-989-7845
Seeker of Truth and Justice
Defender of the Downtrodden
Environmental Protectionist
Anti-Corruption Specialist
Political Whistleblower
United States Marine Combat Veteran
Afflicter of the Comfortable
Comforter of the Afflicted
Http://www.TheTrippReport.com
Http://www.BaldwinCountyLeagleBeagle.com
Email: Francis@theTrippReport.com

McMakin twice shook his head. He looked from the card and stared blankly at his favorite oil painting, flabbergasted, like he had just seen a UFO; and there was no denying it.

9

ayor Donny Kenner reached for his cell. He fumbled it and dialed Jacque Buttrell. He was so mad he was shaking. The Orange Beach City council meeting ended and Buttrell rushed out, late for a rare dinner date—with his wife, Nancy. Kenner was worried; and wanted to talk to him, but missed the short window to speak to him because he had to urinate. Buttrell was already driving west to downtown Fairhope, the site of his dinner reservation, when his phone buzzed. He saw it was Kenner, his business partner and husband of his mistress.

"Yo! What's up Donny?"

"Can you believe that asshole, Tripp?"

"Donny I told you already—don't let him get to you! Don't let him get under your skin! He thrives on it. Just ignore him! I know it's not easy, but please, just don't pay him no mind! When you do you are playing to him. Don't react to him. This is important!"

"I am trying Jacque but he's such a bastard! People ask me all the time if I've read this or that from his stupid blog on the Internet. Do people really read that bull crap?"

"Donny—listen to me!" He paused and lowered the tone of his voice so he sounded calm. "Let it go. He has no power. We have the power."

"Okay, okay, man," he relented, sounding apologetic, yet still stirred.

"By the way," Buttrell added, "It looks like the Senate is gonna introduce the new infrastructure improvement plan for the State of Alabama. I've gotten wind of what's in it."

"Really? Is it good for us down here in Lower Baldwin County?"

"Is a four-pound robin fat?" He cockily asked.

Kenner chuckled, breathing hard through his mouth. "I heard there were concerns we wouldn't get the full funds requested by the Gulf Coast Chamber."

"Nah, word is it will be fully funded to original plan and they will build not two but three new bridges across the Intracoastal, which will only increase access and improve hurricane evacuation to and from Orange Beach and Gulf Shores, opening up more ways to and from the island. It's gonna be a lot easier to get here!"

He paused briefly. "And it looks now like they're extending the Beach Expressway on a diagonal path to the north to just below Montgomery. The Alabama Department of Environmental Management says it'll shave close to 20 minutes from the drive down. It's gonna be a big deal for beach tourism—our own lil' gold rush!"

"Sweet!" Kenner proclaimed. "I can almost smell the condo cash!"

There was an awkward moment of silence.

"Speaking of funding," Buttrell added, seizing the moment, "We had to get more money for the new high rise because we had to enlarge the footprint since we decided to go up so high. It's all good, though. The investors approved another $1.2 million for the redo. It's a full go."

"Super!" Kenner replied, excited to hear the great news. He had his eye on several new toys: An offshore sport fishing vessel with three fancy, duel four-stroke engines and a pair of fast Sea Doo jet skis. They didn't come cheap. His plan was to flip the condo he had coming and spend the cash on water sport gadgets and travel.

"I'll be ready to expedite the approval process with planning and zoning and the council. Just let me know, Jacque!"

"Awesome Donny!" Buttrell thanked him, knowing he had to keep Donny close—for obvious reasons. He had always been concerned about him running his mouth, but he sensed Donny knew nothing about him bedding his wife, as he had no reason to. He had to keep it that way.

"And don't forget about my gulf view penthouse condo you promised!" Donny reminded.

"Don't worry about that, my brother! You're all set!" Buttrell assured him, knowing by Donny's excited voice and tone that he and Layla were still golden. Donny had not a clue.

Contingent upon the closing of the new skyscraper deal was a free unit in the high rise—one facing the water, for Mayor Kenner. The plan was to have it secretly deeded to Kenner's Laurel, Mississippi-based, Gulf Coast Living, LLC, so as to not cause unwanted political problems or concerns. As far as he and Buttrell were concerned, the citizens and the media were on a "need to know" basis regarding their engaged beach development, and they figured if they needed to know, they would tell them—long after they had ruined the quality of life of the place once called paradise.

"Alright Jacque, thanks again! I'll talk to you later this week. We need to get things rolling in the right direction for final approval."

"Good enough," he replied before hanging up. He pulled into the restaurant parking lot looking forward to the cocktails more than the quality time and dinner with the ball and chain.

***

The day after meeting with Greg McMakin, Francis Tripp checked his personal email and reviewed the filing draft for the United States Federal Court in Mobile, Alabama. He suggested a few stylistic changes and agreed that they should sue for a healthy, six figure amount to help in the eventual negotiations. McMakin noted in his email that he doubted Kenner and the City of Orange Beach would allow the case to proceed to court, which meant they would surely come to their senses beforehand, and settle. By asking for more money it gave them a better negotiation starting point.

Tripp sent the return email to Greg and drafted a press release regarding the federal court filing. In the release he embedded a link to his Internet Web Page "The Tripp Report," listing the complete text of the filing and the amount they were suing for. Later in the afternoon he learned via text message from Greg that he had indeed made the filing, in person, in federal court. On that signal Tripp sent the press release to every news agency in the state, after of course posting the link to the filing and the live video of the Orange Beach City Council meeting in question on his companion facebook page,

"Baldwin County Legal Beagle," for good measure. In doing so he had created another firestorm. He was giddy.

After pressing the return button on a $200 ad buy on facebook boosting the post, Tripp celebrated his small success. He felt great, as he again—in yet another instance—held the upper hand against the vaunted, supposedly untouchable, Baldwin County political machine.

"I'm comin' for you, Donny Kenner!" Tripp said out loud to himself, lighting a half-smoked Cuban cigar, reveling in the sheer pleasure, excitement and fun of it all, gladly reminding himself that they had picked a fight with the wrong damn Marine.

10

Johnny and Lucy drove east over the Theo Baars Bridge and turned left on Innerarity Point Road. They drove a half mile and turned left on Garcon Street and parked in the driveway where Vonnie's bottle-green, late model Toyota Celica was parked, reflective silver sun shade on the dash.

Vonnie was expecting them, as they had called earlier and confirmed she was home, and that they would be there shortly. She peeked through the thin beige curtains in the front windows and saw their arrival. She walked to the door and opened it, greeting them.

"Hey you two lovebirds! How's it going?" She asked.

Johnny and Lucy exited Johnny's truck and walked toward her.

"Hey Mrs. Vonnie!" Johnny answered. He hugged her and stepped aside. "Have you met Lucy?"

"I have not!" She stated. "Hello my love," she said, wrapping her arms around her. Lucy hugged her back. Johnny thought of adding, "The mother of my child," but decided better.

"I heard the good news! Joe told me!" She squealed.

"Ugh," Johnny thought. He was a little embarrassed—because they weren't married. It was a technicality, but it was something Johnny had thought much about over the last couple of difficult days. He hoped the new digs would help his mental state. So much was happening now for him, and the pregnancy wasn't exactly planned. He felt immature and irresponsible; and that was the source of his discomfort. He figured he'd be in a better financial position expecting his first child. This wasn't the way he drew it up.

"I'm so excited for you!" Connie squealed, shaking both fists up and down like she was running in place.

"Lucy I have heard so much about you!" Connie stated. "Joe says you have the loveliest voice! I need to hear you guys one of these days. I never go out anymore."

Lucy replied, "Oh that's so nice of him and you to say Mrs. Vonnie! Thank you so much!" She smiled, her gleaming teeth a stark contrast to her shiny onyx mane. Her smooth, pale skin shined, highlighted by a rosy complexion and a glowing, cherub-like grin.

"And he also said you were gorgeous—and he wasn't kidding! My goodness, I cannot wait to see the child!" She motioned with both hands toward Lucy's belly, which still did not bear signs of pregnancy.

"You are so sweet Mrs. Vonnie! Thanks." Lucy replied.

"When are you due?" She asked.

"Christmas!" She smiled, grabbing Johnny's warm hand for assurance.

"Oh, how wonderful! Let's go inside! I'll give you the nickel tour." She insisted.

The tiny house was spotless. The small living room contained a sofa, coffee table, love seat and a dated flat screen TV. The kitchen was circa 1985 but functional, and of course much more so than the sailboat, which had only a single hot plate and a mini fridge. The sliding window above the kitchen sink sprayed white sunlight across the worn countertops and into the living area. To the left was a small wooden circular table with four matching chairs sat between the living area and the back door, obviously the dining room. To the right of the layout were two small bedrooms. There was one on each side of the single full bathroom—a master and a guest bedroom, which would be perfect for the baby.

"There's not much to it, but it's comfortable and easy to keep clean," she said, leading them further on their cursory tour. "But this is where I spend most of my time, guys." She opened the back door and stepped outside, Johnny and Lucy following.

The plain wooden hurricane fenced backyard was a botanical joy. A large, flowing trellis was the centerpiece, in which everything radiated from. A rowed vegetable garden was nearby, with tomatoes, cherry tomatoes, cucumbers, bell peppers and even a couple of tiny corn stalks. Wisteria infused the tangled trellis in a blend of lavender and light, providing marbled shade to the area underneath. Flamingo-colored azaleas and pastel camellias bloomed along the fence and there were bursting ivory Easter lilies in small pots adorning the edges of the covered area. A hand-made hammock was strung diagonally between two of the support beams and there was an old tire hitched to a rope swing for those inclined. It hung from the gnarled bough of a shady live oak that grew twisted and at a 45-degree angle from the gritty, sandy, ancient island soil.

"Oh Johnny," Lucy cooed. "This is so nice…and relaxing!" She imagined playing with a toddler there, against the kaleidoscope of shadows dancing across the grassy backyard sand.

By now Johnny was lying supine in the hammock, his hands placed firmly behind his head, swinging side-to-side in the gentle intracoastal breeze. His face wore a contented smile.

"I dig it baby! I dig it!" He announced, his hands in the air for emphasis. "Mrs. Vonnie, when can we move in?"

Johnny withdrew a sealed envelope from the back pocket of his jeans. It contained cash for the first and last month's rent.

"Oh boy!" Vonnie squealed. "I wasn't expecting this…but I guess we can start on the 15th and thereafter the rent will be due then, on the 15th."

"That's in two days!" Lucy blurted excitedly.

"Oh, and the place comes furnished," Connie added. "I'll be living in my R.V. on my waterfront property on Perdido Bay, just down the road off Bob-O-Link by the Point Restaurant. Y'all are welcome anytime! We'll have to catch dinner and music at the Point—they have a bluegrass band that plays every Friday—or we can cook out and watch the sunset. It is gorgeous off the bay—so many pretty colors!"

The place Connie had on the bay was the remnants of Hurricane Ivan, a category 4, Cape Verde (Africa) storm that passed directly over the Key. Joe G. at one time owned the property, which included a narrow boat slip and a tiny, wooden three bedroom home. The unrelenting rain, wind and fatal storm surge of Hurricane Ivan in October 2004 razed the simple structure. Joe later sold Vonnie the vacant lot for a song. In time she erected several small indoor-outdoor structures, an outdoor shower and a workplace for her stained glass art projects.

She continued, "Of course, I am certain you won't want all this old stuff I have in the house, so just let me know what you don't want me to leave here and I'll get it out for you."

Lucy was so excited. She wanted to leave the stirring confines of the sailboat months ago, but Johnny relented, insisting they should save their money and take advantage of the deal they had from Joe. Now, with the money they needed, they were ready to move into their own place. She quietly walked back into the house while Johnny and Vonnie signed the lease paperwork. She entered the guest bedroom—which would be for the baby, come December. She imagined nursing their infant in a rocking chair, playing with him or her; and amazingly—having a family and a place of their own.

***

Two days later Johnny and Lucy moved their few belongings into their new home. Johnny could tell Lucy was happy, as all she did was smile, her rosy complexion preceding her.

"You're glowing again," he cooed. They lounged together in disbelief, sprawled on the plaid sofa with big square cushions, still trying to comprehend the newfound luxury of the tiny, two-bedroom home that was now theirs—with a baby on the way.

"We have so much room!" Lucy exclaimed, gesturing with open arms.

"Certainly more than before!" Johnny replied.

"Mr. Joe was so nice to tell us about this place! And to let us stay in his sailboat for free all those months…"

Johnny anticipated something. She continued.

"I was thinking sweetie, that we might…"

"That we might what?" He timidly answered.

"Name the baby after Joe."

"Josephine?" Johnny answered with a smile.

She slapped his chest lightly with an open hand and they laughed and hugged one another like there was no tomorrow.

11

Joe Gideon sat half naked inside a small, chilly, rectangular patient room in downtown Pensacola. Wearing only his trousers, he was in the middle of a medical checkup, seated before the similarly aged general practitioner wearing a traditional, long white physician's coat, an indigo button-down business shirt and matching dark Perlis tie. The light gray-haired fellow with round, wire-rimmed spectacles, Jim Solace, a Harvard graduate, went with Joe to Pensacola High School, part of the Class of 1960. In those days they hunted ducks on Goat Island before it was ever thought of being called "Ono." That was before the Pass Bridge was built in 1962, connecting for the first time Alabama and Florida, when Perdido Key Boulevard ended precipitously at the Reef, that subtle bend in the road past the long approach to the first Theo Baars Draw Bridge over the Intracoastal. It was a much simpler time—long before the monolithic high-rises and zany beachgoers were even a notion; long before the cut-throat politics; even long before the Flora-Bama.

"You seem to be doing fine, Joe." The earnest doc commented, listening through the ears of the stethoscope, placing the cold metal receptor lightly on Joe's bare chest.

"Your heart sounds good. Blood pressure is fine. You could lose a little weight and exercise more, but that's just about all of us—including me."

"Yeah, no kidding!" Joe joked, poking his buddy's protruding gut with an extended forefinger.

"I guess I'm no better off thanks to you!" Joe kidded. "Though the last couple of days I've really felt my age, Jim. I've got a dull aching in my chest, neck and shoulders; and yesterday I started a light cough. I'm not completely wrecked—I'm still getting around, but I'm just so tired. I just don't feel like myself."

"Take it easy old friend," the Doc joked. "You've still got plenty of time on the planet. I want to see you again next week—unless I see you again first at V. Paul's downtown—he has done a great job with the place in such a short time, hasn't he? Everybody loves it!"

"He has," Joe commented on the popular new Italian Restaurant their longtime friend and business associate had recently started. "I am extremely proud of his efforts. Such a nice place!"

V. Paul worked for Joe years as an accountant at the Flora-Bama, learning much about controlling costs, the impact of music on mood and setting and the importance of paying attention to the dignity of each and every customer. At V. Paul's, menu prices were considered a value, a talented piano player in a tuxedo entertained the evening crowds and V. Paul, always sharply dressed, was there nightly, making the regular rounds to speak to dining guests, just as he had seen Joe do so artfully at the Flora-Bama for over three decades.

"I am impressed with what he has done in such a short time." Joe added. "I will likely see you there again. I think the food and ambiance is fantastic! I had the veal and meatballs a couple of weeks ago."

"Excellent! I hope so. It's always great to see you, Joe."

"Likewise. Same here, Doc."

"Alright then, I'll talk to you later. I've got other patients."

Joe's cell phone, which sat on the table nearby, next to his removed shirt, lit up. He had it on silent. He noticed "Brad Masterson" on the face. He answered.

"Hello, Joe here."

"Papa Joe how's it going today?" Masterson asked, talking fast.

"Excellent! Just finishing a medical checkup downtown...the Doc here swears I'm still a moving target!"

***

Brad Masterson was by chance in downtown Pensacola when he reached Joe by cell. He suggested they meet for an early lunch. Joe fasted the afternoon and night before and felt like a light snack was in order. They met at a funky place on the water on the way back to Perdido Key, a water-based haunt called the Oar House, which had deftly entertained the Navy Point and downtown denizens for years, in spite of its nefariously clever namesake.

They sat facing each other at a high top table, the pallid sun clawing its fiery ascent into the eastern sky, the humidity and heat index already spiking, placing a damp hold on everything settled. They made their order with the waitress after she filled their glasses with ice cold lemon water from a sweaty glass pitcher and placed their silverware wrapped tightly in thin white paper napkins before them.

"Have you heard about the third restaurant?" Brad asked.

It was news to Joe.

"No, I haven't." He retorted. He found himself increasingly in the dark regarding such matters, which was expected, given his level of ownership.

"Where are they putting it?" Joe asked.

"On top of Strick-9's hut, near the water."

"Down there on Ole River?" Joe asked.

"Yep." Brad answered. He was silent for a moment. He watched Joe's face for a reaction.

Joe grimaced and looked away.

"It's a 250-seat barbecue joint." He added.

"Of course," Joe stated. He stared at the moored shrimp boats lining the harbor, their long, grass-colored nets hoisted high, like a brown pelican wing-shading her chirping nest.

"So Strick-9 is gonna have to move." Brad started, saying nothing else.

"I reckon so," Joe said. He could see Brad's concern. He thought ahead, remembering something.

"I'll take care of it, Brad," he said, smiling.

"Really, Joe?" He asked, incredulous.

"I will. Have you spoken to Strick-9 about this?"

"I have. He seemed pretty bummed."

"Wouldn't you be too?" Joe replied with a commanding scowl, looking at Brad like he was nuts—and certainly insensitive to his plight.

12

Jacque Buttrell rode the speedy elevator to the penthouse atop the towering beach condominium high-rise he and his cronies built. A phallic monument to his power and hubris, it was where his mistress, Donny Kenner's smoking hot wife, the First Lady of Orange Beach, Layla Kenner, was already naked and supine, waiting for him in the posh, dimly-lit master bedroom suite.

It had become a weekly Wednesday afternoon ritual. Jacque's wife, like the fawning media, knew nothing of the penthouse condo, as it was listed under an obscure LLC known by an esoteric few in the practicing accounting and legal trades. They arranged their schedules for an after-lunch rendezvous within a two-hour time frame. On this Wednesday Layla had already been waiting for him for nearly 35 minutes—quite the window—and she was not a happy camper.

She heard his key turn in the lock. The front door to the spacious condominium opened. His loud leather dress shoes clopped on the imported stained tile floor.

"Jacque?" She called. "Is that you?"

He said nothing. His footsteps grew heavier as he approached her location. With one hand he loosened his tie, with the other he removed his coat and tossed it onto the padded leather furniture.

"Jacque?" She repeated.

The bedroom door flew open, followed by a horizontal Jacque Buttrell. He went airborne and landed next to her on the massive bed.

"Boo!" He yelled, doing his best to startle her. It worked.

"You asshole!" She screamed, relieved it was indeed him, and not someone who could compromise what was now an ongoing, extra-marital affair.

"What?" He loudly complained. "I was just kidding around!"

She was mad about him being late. He was supposed to be there early. He promised.

"You said you would be here on time!" She pleaded. Plus, he was more distant lately, as they could only chat through facebook messages, as they could not risk texting or calling one another.

"Baby I was on the other side of the county for a meeting in Bay Minette! Traffic on 59 was a nightmare! I did the absolute best I could!" He argued forcefully, pleading.

"But you didn't make it like you promised!" She stewed.

"Well maybe I will just have to make it up to you…" He relented, moving to kiss her.

She pulled her face away from his puckering lips.

"Things aren't the same!" She relented, pulling the cool, silky covers to her warm bosom.

He didn't like the way that sounded.

"What do you mean?" He asked. "What is wrong?"

"We never talk anymore!" She complained. "I feel like you don't even care about me!"

"Layla, we are both married!"

"That's not an excuse, Jacque! I still deserve to be treated with a little respect! I will never be taken for granted!"

Jacque didn't like the way this was going. He had never seen Layla like this.

"Who's trying to take advantage of anyone?" Jacque asked, ignoring that his wife was not there to defend herself, or her vulnerable reputation; and for that matter—neither was her Mayor-husband.

***

Cindy McMakin waited in the driver's seat of her air-conditioned white Cadillac Escalade with dark tinted windows, white leather interior and polished chromed magnesium alloy wheels. Her earlier manicure-pedicure and deep tissue massage was rejuvenating. She sat upright, alert in sunglasses, beige tennis outfit and a tennis visor in the parking lot across the beach road, opposite the tallest condo tower on the Gulf Coast, a sun-blocking obelisk devoid of aesthetics. She had secretly followed her best friend, Layla Kenner, when for the third time in as many weeks she'd cancelled their regularly-scheduled tennis match. She knew something was up with Layla, despite her laconic refusal to say anything when prompted. On that day her curiosity got the best of her, forcing her to investigate, to trust her intuition.

Cindy and Layla had known each other for years, going back to their cheerleading and debutante days at Orange Beach High School. They both attended the University of Alabama and pledged the same sorority. Predictably, they returned home and married well, both meeting their future husbands at the Flora-Bama Big Earl Show. So when Layla went silent on her, she figured something serious was going on. Curious about her friend's deception, she decided to play detective.

Having tailed her from a careful distance from the entrance to her neighborhood, minutes earlier she watched Layla turn into the dark shade of the massive, dank parking garage and disappear inside the bowels of the monolith. Layla had given her a different excuse for each successive absence—and none matched this action by her close friend.

"What is she doing?" She thought, concerned. "She said she had a dental appointment today. I doubt there's anyone cleaning teeth in the building."

***

Johnny Glass and Jerry Boudreaux worked on a new song inside Jerry's one-bedroom Orange Beach apartment at L'ai Lani, next to the gated and manned entrance to Ono Island, a couple miles west of the Flora-Bama on the Gulf Beach Highway. They worked on a new number Jerry originated. He had the music—they were just trying to get the words down. Like old washers, nuts and screws from a cloth-covered Mason jar, they tried different words to complete Jerry's well-crafted lines that told a simple story. After a couple hours, they sang the new tune for the first time, much to their enjoyment. It gave them the special feeling of satisfaction that comes from being creative and productive. In theory it was self-expression for profit—which was alright by them, nevertheless elusive.

"How's things with you and Dawn?" Johnny asked. Jerry had stepped away from his keyboard stand to smoke a cigarette, which was against the rules of the complex. Nevertheless, he opened the kitchen window and lit the Camel Light, much to his relief. His face wore a wide smile after the exhale, his dark, wavy Cajun hair wafting in the window breeze, his straight teeth gleaming.

"Good…she's up at Auburn. We still talk. We went to a couple ball games together last fall and she's been here twice since, so, I guess it's my turn to go visit her. I don't mind. I like Dawn. Like we say down in Louisiana, "She's good people." He smiled even wider, and when he did it furrowed his thick brown beard. It was contagious.

Johnny chuckled. "That she is, my Cajun friend!"

Jerry took a long drag from his cig and threw it out the opened window. He exhaled in the same direction and closed it, returning to their work space. Johnny continued his line of thought.

"How's them boys—your frat brothers—they still with her friends—those hot twins? And what about that super hot one? My goodness the tanning oil girl…she's gorgeous! I heard your boy from Baton Rouge got smart and married her!"

"Those twins are psycho, man! That didn't last. But yeah, Dan and Sunny just got married, man. They eloped. That was a good move on his part, I told him, because weddings are all for dough. My mom used to plan em' for people. It's a complete racket!"

The point was not lost on Johnny.

"Let's go over it again," Johnny encouraged. "The song," he clarified.

He strummed the chords and they went back into the number, refining it further. When they were done he voiced his satisfaction.

"We'll have to try it out tomorrow during our ten o'clock gig on the deck stage after Big Earl."

Jerry nodded and lit another smoke, heading for the window.

***

Cindy and Greg McMakin enjoyed cocktails at their beach condo. They invited Mayor Kenner and his wife, Layla—Cindy's best friend, but they were unable to attend due to a prior engagement.

"I guess Donny and Layla had other plans?" Greg asked, turning the steaks and twice-baked potatoes on the outdoor grill. They relaxed on the balcony perch overlooking the aquamarine gulf against a scarlet sunset where the horizon transected a bright, slinking orange disc.

"I imagine they do," Cindy answered, lightly rolling the white wine in her glass, contemplating. "Layla has been distant lately," she added. "I'm wondering if she and Donny are having issues?"

Amused by her word choices, Greg replied. "Issues?"

"Oh I don't know, Greg. It's just a hunch. She's acting weird. We used to play tennis every week. That ended a few weeks ago."

"You think she's seeing someone else?" Greg imagined.

"I'm not saying that. I don't know that. I just know she's no longer playing tennis with me like we did and she has been giving false excuses for her absences."

"You've caught her in lies?"

"Yes. More than one."

"And what else?"

"More than once I've seen her go into the parking garage of the big condo they built down there in Orange Beach—you know, the one tabbed the largest in the history of the gulf coast."

Greg twitched at the realization. "A rendezvous perhaps?"

"Perhaps." She replied. "Thus my concerns. What an absolute mess if true."

13

Barry "Strick-9" Strickland sat comfortably on the trusty, dusty davenport inside his drafty, makeshift home perched on the edge of Ole River behind the Flora-Bama Yacht Club. It was just after nine o'clock and pitch dark. It was a pleasant Thursday evening. The air was cool for that time of year, not yet the warm wet blanket of August. Things had settled in at the nearby restaurant and bar. The local kids had not been let out of school for the summer, precipitating the onslaught of vacationing rednecks the place was widely known for. They had only a week left, however. In a matter of days their release triggered an inexorable wave of frenzied, beach-bound Southerners, Midwesterners and revelers bent on a joyful, music and libation-filled reprieve. Barry knew they were coming, as sure as the massive life changes on his horizon. Things were about to get real for Strick-9; and he felt the pressure of it all weighing on him like a massive sword of Damocles. It was not a pleasant feeling. Like he often did, he chose to temporarily avert it; and self-medicate.

Barry placed two pieces of wheat bread on a thin paper plate inside a dusty brown, round, plastic paper plate holder. He pasted crunchy, no-name peanut butter with a bald, wide, wood-handled knife on both slices and put them back on the paper, butter side up. He retrieved from a Ziploc baggie four small pieces of psychedelic mushrooms, grown in the basement of a bona fide hippie he knew in West Pensacola. The guy was legit—Barry knew him; he was a former horticulturist and professor at nearby West Pensacola University. He could attest from experience that these were some of the best recreational mushrooms on the planet, fun buttons he labeled, "smoother than a baby's ass."

A psilocybin mushroom is one of a polyphyletic group of fungi containing various psychedelic compounds, including psilocybin, psilocin, and baeocystin. When ingesting these commonly found "liberty caps" some people experience feelings of euphoria, extreme happiness and laughter; some get an energy burst. An unlucky few experience paranoia, acute anxiety and helplessness. Everybody feels something, and it largely depends on their outlook, mental acuity and the cumulative effects of their unique life experience. It also helps to have tolerance.

Barry placed the small dark brown shroom pieces on the middle of the spread peanut butter—getting some on each half. He smashed the two pieces together, making a sandwich. With a long, thin knife he cut the square diagonally in half and ate a quarter in two bites. He chewed his food. He washed it down with a swallow of tap water from a red Solo cup. He placed the quarter sand back on the plate, along with the other half. He would tend later to it.

Barry poured a shot of cinnamon-flavored Hot Damn and quickly took it. He chased it with a small Styrofoam cup of ice cold water he'd prepped. He pulled a canned Modelo from the fridge and cracked it, taking the first sip just as fast, shot-gunning the rest, tilting his head far back to facilitate beer flow. He lit a deftly manicured, aromatic, hand-rolled cigarette and took several puffs, blowing the smoke in concentric circles in a lip-puffing, filling the small living quarters with a sweet, pungent smell. He damped out the number and placed the remaining end with others like it in a large box of wooden match sticks nearby. He cracked the window, letting in the steady north breeze with the help of the open doorway. He settled into the davenport and propped up his feet, enjoying the moment, however fleeting; taking careful solace in the buoyant late spring night air.

Minutes later, like an angelic specter of vertical light in the still darkness, Joe Gideon approached Barry's shanty. The front door was propped open with a large rock. It was eerily quiet. The street lamp above provided ample, but not bright light. Joe proceeded with caution onto the creaky deck.

"Barry?" He implored, trudging to the dark, open threshold. "You in here?"

Barry awakened from his light slumber on the faded and tattered sofa. In a deepened state of relaxation, he recognized Joe's voice. Joe was the guy who had given him his start at Flora-Bama…nearly 40 years prior. He'd worked with him for many moons before he lost control of the beloved watering hole due to unforeseen natural and financial disasters. He wasn't expecting him, but was certainly glad to see him, as they had not talked much since the new owners took over.

"Joe!" Barry exclaimed, his position still supine. He sat up. Joe faintly recognized him and was relieved.

"Oh hey man. I wasn't sure if you were in here. Sorry if I woke you!"

"No problem, Joe. I was just relaxing, is all. Enjoying this pleasant evening…"

Barry looked to Joe in the doorway. The light from the street lamp above cast a tiny shadow that preceded him. In Barry's altered state Joe looked beamed in from a spaceship. It was surreal and hazy—Joe looked like an angel—sent from heaven… standing in the threshold of his doorway. He wondered if it was real, given his buzzing, tingling head. He focused his eyes on the glowing figure before him, squinting.

"Mind if I come in? Can we turn on a light or two?" Joe asked with a contagious chuckle.

Strick-9 snapped into motion, everything in strobe. He stood and flipped a wall switch, illuminating a lone, dull 40-watt bulb without a cover screwed into the ceiling. Dull light filled the cramped room. Barry motioned to a padded sitting chair for Joe.

"Please, have a seat, Joe. It's great to see you, man!"

Joe sat and looked at Barry. The lines on Barry's forehead were pronounced, his hair a fanciful nest, his eyes—conspicuously bloodshot. He looked rough—but he'd certainly looked worse.

"I heard you got some tough news," Joe said, his voice shifting in tone. "Things sure seem to be changing fast around here these days."

Joe loudly exhaled.

Barry looked to Joe with puppy dog eyes. "They're making me move," he said. "I don't want to, though. I've got nowhere to go, except my daughters' place, and I don't think that would work long-term."

Barry looked away, embarrassed.

"I know." Joe said, reassuring him. "That's why I'm here."

"Is it time for me to move?" Barry asked.

"Not now. Not tonight—anyway. Well, maybe!" Joe said with a surprising smile.

Barry's face wore a look of curiosity, like an unsure gambler, or that of a child contemplating the veracity of the tooth fairy, the Easter Bunny or Santa.

Joe noticed Barry seemed sluggish—almost sloth-like in his words and motions. Everything was slightly off. But that's how Barry was; Joe wasn't alarmed, it was just an observation. Joe was used to working with creative characters. They came with peccadilloes and Barry was no exception to the rule. Joe got along with musicians because he helped them so much and cared for them, but also because he didn't take himself too seriously, and realized the importance of the team concept where everyone worked together to create the world-famous honky-tonk roadhouse. It was a heart-driven philosophy that had worked for him and the storied place for nearly four decades.

"Good." Barry replied. He wanted a final answer. "How much longer do I have here?"

"Not long," Joe answered, scanning the room, taking stock of the dearth of furniture, small appliances, box fans, electric blankets and space heaters, humorously acknowledging to himself that it would indeed be an easy move.

"Barry I am here to tell you that you are being relocated." Joe insisted, standing for emphasis.

A petrified Barry stared at him. His face bore a cold, strange look—like that of a terribly confused child. "But where am I going?" Barry asked, his voice rife with fear. His coveted life on the island hung in the balance of Joe's words.

"Not far," Joe answered, matter-of-factly, his tone lowered. Joe raised an index finger.

Barry's wan face wore a bewildered look. He said nothing. He feared the end. He bowed his head in defeat, just as the mind-titillating powers of the shrooms were kicking in. He closed his eyes and saw fireworks in reverse; an open gulf oil tanker explosion and a blazing hellfire conflagration unabated. He saw wolves with red mouths running through the trees and a baby doll with its head cut off torturing a sleeping child in a shit-soaked diaper. It was tormenting. He was about to fully lose it in front of Joe. He opened his bloodshot eyes and stared at his harbinger, unknowingly.

"I purchased a sizable sport fishing boat yesterday. It's right outside, here, at the marina. You probably noticed it." Joe smiled.

Barry's drooping eyes perked up, conspicuously. White sparks danced in his blinking consciousness. He focused coolly on what Joe said, not fully comprehending. There were several moments of silent thinking, his synapses firing, relaxing and recharging. "A fishing boat?" He asked himself. "Sounds familiar," he vaguely recalled. He remembered a rather large vessel being towed into place the day prior. It was the last open slip at the marina—right outside his front door. When he saw the impressive floating behemoth he figured it was the plaything of some rich asshole.

"Barry?" Joe asked. "Are you there? Hello?" He waved a hand in front of Barry's stoned face.

Barry snapped out of it, emerging from his self-induced fog like a sea turtle from shallow sand.

"Yes! I'm sorry, Joe. I'm a bit preoccupied this evening, it seems," knowing well the blistering liberty caps were the reason for his skittishness. He was starting to peak. He could feel it, the gentle wave.

Joe stood and walked back through the threshold, standing just outside the shanty, in the faint light of the street lamp hanging paces away. He motioned with one arm to the massive marine vessel, a 68-foot Buddy Davis fishing outfit with three bedrooms, three baths, a full kitchen and a nice living area with a host of favorable amenities that included a dishwasher, a trash compacter, Wi-Fi Internet and a 70-inch big screen television. There was even a desk with an apple computer equipped with a large monitor.

It was a bit much in terms of a fishing boat, as it would require maintenance—but that's where Strick-9 would come in, Joe figured.

From the dock the boat looked to Barry more like the millionaire plaything he earlier recalled instead of his new home on the drink. It was heady stuff, and frankly a bit surreal for him, in the heightened moment.

"I figured you might want to work a trade with me for rent," Joe said. "I'm gonna need someone to look after it and maintain it for when we take it out. But of course, that'll only be every now and then. Diesel fuel for this thing is ridiculous. But I think it will be fun to make a go of it every now and again."

The boat was paces away from the shanty, moored to the dock with a large, winding, cleated rope, alongside several other fishing craft of the same class, yet smaller. The stark juxtaposition of the two living quarters was startling. Barry stood beside Joe. He stared at the impressive craft, in all of its glory. Brand new the boat was well over a million dollars. He thought of himself living on it, which was difficult, as its luxury was so foreign, so unfamiliar. He pinched himself.

"Ouch," he thought. Joe explained.

"It's of course a little bit bigger than what you're used to, but the timing is right. Johnny Glass moved off the sailboat I had at the marina near the Baar Bridge. I wanted to sell it, but a friend who owed me money offered me a deal in trade I couldn't refuse. He offered me this boat for a song if I deeded over the sailboat. He moved to Isla Mujeres, off the coast of Mexico, to run a hotel and no longer had a need for the fishing boat. But, he was in the market for a sailboat—and he owed me a bunch of cash from a bad land deal we were in on together. To make a long story short—I now own this boat—and I need you to live on it and take care of it, Barry. Can you handle it?"

Barry imagined living on the fancy fishing boat, which to him, seemed like socks on a rooster. He looked from the boat, back to his tiny dwelling, and back to the expensive fishing craft. He smiled ear-to-ear, realizing that Joe was really there—that this was not a dream—and that he was indeed moving out of his place…just a few feet over—onto what to him was a floating mansion. He didn't have to leave! Once it fully registered with him, he couldn't believe it. He thought for a moment he was tripping—and he was!

"Holy shit!" He thought. "This is a game changer!" He beamed.

A wave of newfound energy overcame him. He was euphoric. He felt a supreme rush. No longer would he have to use the toilet at the Yacht Club. No longer would he worry—about anything—ever again!

"Of course I can, Joe! Of course!" Barry answered, still dazed, despite the fantastic revelation. He hugged Joe and stammered toward the dock, stepped onto the craft, and boarded his new home over the gang plank.

"Here, take a look inside," Joe insisted. "Here's the key." He threw Barry a tiny orange float with a single key on the end. "I'm gonna get a sip of water from your tap in the sink," Joe said. "I'm thirsty."

Barry didn't object to the drink of water, as he was bent on seeing his new digs. He didn't reply. He ventured eagerly onto the craft and entered through the cabin door with the key, disappearing from sight into the posh living quarters below.

Moments later, Joe exited Barry's tin-roofed hut with a red Solo cup in one hand, and unbeknownst to him—a quarter of a peanut-butter and magic mushroom sandwich in the other. He saw Barry exiting the cabin, coming back out onto the deck of the boat. Joe chewed as he spoke.

"Not too shabby, huh? I figure we can comfortably sleep six easy, maybe eight." Joe said, chewing. "We should be able to spend a couple nights on the salt if need be."

"Shit—you could spend a couple of weeks out on this thing if you had enough fuel," Barry commented. Barry saw the red Solo cup; and Joe eat what looked like the other half of his magic mushroom sandwich. He gulped, fearing the obvious, his heart racing. His buzz fluttered with his rising and falling blood pressure.

"Oh shit," Barry thought. "That's likely a double dose."

Joe saw Barry noticed. "I hope you don't mind," Joe blurted. "I love peanut butter, and I was in need of a light snack. I've been fasting lately, trying to drop a few unwanted pounds like my doc advised."

"Not at all," Barry smiled. "My pleasure, Joe…my pleasure… Look, why don't we go back inside and sit down a while and you can tell me more about the boat and what I'll need to do. How about a rusty nail? I recall you have a fondness for them."

"Indeed!" Joe answered. "What a delightful idea!"

Barry and Joe G. cracked a large bottle of Johnny Walker Red Scotch Whiskey and laughed and reminisced until the wee hours of the morning drinking one of Joe's favorite cocktails—the often-forgotten, always trusty, Rusty Nail. A traditional, potent concoction that surfaced during the failed American temperance movement of the 1930's, the libation was made popular by the glittering "Brat Pack" of the 1960's. Originating at the famed "21 Club" in Manhattan, New York, the potion consists of 3/4 ounces of Drambuie and 1.5 ounces of Scotch Whiskey, garnished neatly with a lemon peel. The "old man's drink" it is often called, is as curiously strong and metallic as its legendary namesake, capable of instantly sprouting chest hair to those willing and in the proverbial know.

Barry and Joe talked about the new vessel, its many modern capabilities and where they could first go fishing once it was tuned up by a mechanic and outfitted for sport. They joked of the fun it would be to talk some pretty ladies into taking a joy ride around the island, and perhaps even an overnight fishing trip or two, if they were so easily inclined. The rusty nails went down easier than expected and their conversation and laughter turned predictably from fishing the ultramarine salt to their early, super fun, busy days together at the Flora-Bama, when the island was more isolated, and the Flora-Bama was in its bright infancy—an esoteric Bohemian sub-culture on the precipitous rise.

Feeling the moment, Joe reminisced, "When I first started at the Flora-Bama I worked so many hours I often missed sleep. I remember it was right at a year that I had owned Flora-Bama, and I scheduled a deep sea fishing trip with friends to celebrate the milestone. I was so tired I never wet a line—I just slept in the cabin the entire time—exhausted. I worked myself to the bone—but it paid off! And it was great fun! So many interesting characters used to come around back in those early days. It was just incredible!"

Joe felt great. He was having a good time with Barry, having saved him from his dire predicament. Barry was in a celebratory mood, his cheeks above his thick, curly, gray, orange and brown beard ruddy with excitement. Joe valued Barry as one of the mainstays that made the Flora-Bama. Joe was glad he could help him out and return the favor of thirty-plus years of dedicated service to the loveable pump house on the Line. The rusty nails were going down easily, and the many memories they conjured through conversations were so vivid—so real, Joe thought. To him, it was a singular, enjoyable experience.

"These rusty nails are fantastic!" Joe blurted.

"Damn straight!" Strick-9 replied, offering his red solo cup into the air with a hellish grin.

Joe met him in the middle with his red Solo cup. They toasted.

"To many great years on the Key!" Joe saluted.

"Indeed!" Barry exclaimed. "And here's to many more!"

"Indeed!" Joe mimicked, sipping the manly, biting concoction.

There was a moment of silence before Barry spoke.

"Joe, I have to say something."

A seated Barry placed his drink on the table and rested his hands on his thighs.

"It's been over thirty-five years since I got here. And when I did, I couldn't believe what I found! There was this place where the owner cared about musicians and songwriters—not only about us making bills—but about us as people—us as human beings."

Barry paused. He got a little emotional. He was peaking.

"You go out of your way to respect the dignity of people, and that's a great thing, Joe. That's what sets you apart from the other guys. You always made us musicians feel like we were an important part of the Flora-Bama family. And I think that's what made it so special—everybody loved working here so much because of the unique, creative, family atmosphere you created.

And it was built on love. Thanks man!"

Joe was flattered by the emotion and the message.

"Thank you, Barry. That means a lot to me that you feel that way."

In addition to the inherent opportunity costs of foregoing a predictable nine-to-five schedule, a regular, dead-end job or a salaried career with health care benefits and a 401k, the overall "costs" of being a creative person are many. There are the late nights and early mornings. There are the many associates but few true friends; and because they forego a normal life like everyone else and do not work a normal job, they are misunderstood and generally seen as slackers by those who do. Predictably, creative people are destined to be single, unless lucky enough to find a mate who understands their unique pursuit and lifestyle. They are married to their craft.

People of course in general want their creative friends to do well—but not better than them—that wouldn't be fair—to them. Because of these things many artists live a life of solitude, as people usually pity or envy their quintessentially American, brazen, iconoclastic pursuit of self-expression, happiness, fulfillment and financial success. They are jealous of creative people who make a living doing what they love. On top of all that, musicians' life spans are on average 25 years shorter than the average person, meaning the noble pursuit of their craft is an early death wish. Stew on that the next time you hear original music and don't tip.

The noted, late author and "Gonzo Journalist," Dr. Hunter S. Thompson, aptly stated, "The music business is a cruel and shallow money trench, a long plastic hallway where thieves and pimps run free, and good men die like dogs. There's also a negative side."

Joe Gideon knew this sad truism better than most. He had outlived many of his former players. Accordingly, he proudly assumed the role as the living "Patron Saint of songwriters and musicians," and by look, word and deed he was the undoubted difference maker in terms of keeping the Flora-Bama's lifeblood— its indispensable talent base—its amazing songwriters, singers and musicians, together and working in harmony to entertain the patrons. It was Joe G. who selflessly went the extra mile for others to keep his dream alive. These were the finer, omniscient points of his art not recognized.

Joe and Barry carried on well into the early morning hours, with Joe and him reminiscing of good times gone by. Joe told the story of how in just his second year at the Flora-Bama, when he was 37 years old, in the fall of 1979, an unexpected natural phenomenon led to an impromptu party.

"It was the summer of 1979, right before Hurricane Frederick ravaged the gulf coast and opened up this entire area to condo development. It was a warm summer night. I remember early on seeing that it was a clear night and that the moon was exceptionally bright, but we were fairly busy and I was having fun with the customers as usual, and didn't really pay much attention to what was going on outside. Around 9:30 p.m. or so, somebody came running in from the beach into the bar. Back then we didn't have a boardwalk leading to the water. There was only soft sand, so it took longer to walk or run to the surf.

"The guy was breathing heavily and pleaded with me to go back with him to the water, to see how beautiful it was at the beach. He was wildly enthusiastic, to the point that I couldn't say no; so I followed him. As we neared the water I saw how bright the night sky was. The moon appeared larger than normal, like a piece of cheese, and it was as clear a night as I had ever seen. Moreover, more remarkable, at the water's edge, about ten yards out into the gulf, was a phosphorescent glow that I will never forget. The abundant phosphorous in the water had formed a mysterious green-lit glow, making for an unbelievable sight along the water line as far as the eye could see toward the east or the west. It was surreal.

"My friend and I quickly ran back to the Flora-Bama. Upon our return I got on stage between songs and commandeered the microphone. I told everyone in the bar—about two or three hundred people I'd guess—that they had two choices: 1) they could go home; or (2) they could come skinny dipping with the rest of us in the Gulf of Mexico. I explained that I would be providing the beverages.

"Minutes later, after grabbing several cases of cold beer, about a hundred or so of us jettisoned our clothes, and were innocently naked, enjoying a beautiful night, skinny dipping and chicken fighting in the surf like giddy school children. It was wonderful, and I can still remember the way the water strangely glowed that beautiful summer night. For the next couple days people returned to reclaim their clothes they had gladly left behind."

14

Mayor Donny Kenner reported to work around 8:30 a.m., at Orange Beach City Hall, one of a modest set of buildings that formed the Orange Beach municipal complex between Canal and the beach road. He exited his parked cream-colored 2011 Hummer Hum-V with dark tinted windows jacked three feet off the ground with an expensive, custom-built suspension system. He was walking toward the double front doors of City Hall when the process server appeared—seemingly out of nowhere. He was bushwhacked.

"I have something here for you, Mayor," blurted the middle-aged, burly, bearded figure with dark hair and skin. He looked Indian or Middle Eastern. He wore pressed slacks and an expensive dress shirt and plaid dark sport coat, his scuffed dress shoes a contrast to his exceptionally dapper look.

He handed the opened folder containing the subpoena to Mayor Kenner. The mayor reluctantly accepted it, understanding the legal process now in motion.

"I need you to sign here, please, Sir." He insisted, holding a clip board with a tiny, perforated receipt. Kenner signed and took his half of the confirmation. The process server evaporated like a midday summer drizzle; as quickly as he came. Kenner looked at the heavy envelope in his hands. He was scared to open it.

As he contemplated its disturbing contents he thought about that royal pain in his ass, the undeniable, unshakeable, Francis P. Tripp, of Fairhope. He knew he was behind it. He recalled Tripp's final words at the city council meeting—the promise that he would "see him in court!"

"Damnit!" He yelled, startling everyone in his office. It was already a different kind of Friday.

That afternoon, during the "Freaky Friday" edition of the Tripp Report on the Internet page and facebook, Francis Tripp announced that Mayor Kenner had been served legal papers to appear in Federal Court in Mobile, as he was being sued by him, Francis P. Tripp, for violating his fundamental right to free speech protected by the First Amendment to the United States Constitution. Tripp explained that he sued, at the direction of his attorney, Greg McMakin, who instructed him that his case was more than ripe—and was what smart lawyers called, "Prima Facie," in that his case would be considered winnable "at face value" on its inherent merits.

The early scuttlebutt to the filing in federal court was that Tripp had the City of Orange Beach by the short hairs, and that given what happened, the City would have to settle to avoid further financial encumbrances or embarrassment. Of course, all this was on Mayor Donny Kenner, as he was the one who disallowed Tripp to speak during public participation. He was the guy who had him thrown out the meeting. He was also the one who insisted months earlier that all Orange Beach City council meetings were videotaped, an eventual costly fait accompli for the brash, self-serving coastal Alabama politician.

***

Joe Gideon awoke on the comfortable King-sized bed with satin sheets. Temporarily unaware of his surroundings, he found his glasses nearby and scanned the walls adorned with round windows.

"I'm on the boat!" he gathered, remembering he decided to crash there instead of driving home in the early morning hours. After a bit of self-coaxing, he managed to get upright and walk over to Barry's riverside cottage, across the plank connecting the mini-yacht and the tiny dock where his shanty sat. When he crossed he noticed his reflection in Barry's front window. He laughed to himself when he saw his hair stood high on his graying head in a matted Mohawk.

He knocked on Barry's door, realizing it was easily eight o' clock, as the sun was already making its slow, deliberate, fiery ascent in the eastern sky. As he waited, he again felt a tightness in his chest, and strange pains across his shoulders, neck and back—like he had the flu—or something.

A minute passed before Barry opened the door, after considerable rumbling.

"Good morning," he said to Joe, turning back around to sit on the couch. Barry wore plaid boxers and a tee shirt. He looked like he had been welding without a helmet.

"We stayed up kinda late, didn't we?" Barry asked, rubbing his swollen, aching head.

"That we did. I'm feeling it, too!" Joe answered, rubbing his chest. "I feel like a truck hit me!"

Barry also felt beaten. Dehydrated, he poured himself and Joe a red solo cup full of water from the tap.

"Thanks," Joe said, eagerly sipping, hoping it would rehydrate his still-working system, despite its age and avid use.

"We didn't drink that much," Barry quipped.

"This doesn't feel like a hangover." Joe muttered. On his way out to his truck he stated, "Thanks for the water. I'm gonna hit the road. By the way—the king sized bed in the boat master is wonderful. You may want to move on board soon. It's definitely an upgrade to your single bed here. There's more room and the mattress is a Sleep Number."

15

It has been said that art decorates space and music decorates space and time. At the iconic Flora-Bama Lounge & Package this adage is ephemerally on display, a thriving, pulsing kaleidoscope of music, laughter, libation, libido and song for the bold, the faithful and the willing. The people who frequent the Flora-Bama—those intrepid souls who come back for an untold second or third time and more—are a special breed. These professional revelers know how to have fun, many having weaned themselves on the bushwhackers, redneck smut, bare nipples and cold draft beer the place made a way of life in a wholly unique, far away corner of the maddening world. None of these amazing people apologize for anything—and they shouldn't have to.

Not since the pet rock has ingenuity met opportunity quite like the conjured circumstances set in motion by Joe Gideon at the Flora-Bama. The place was as legendary and lasting as its humble originator. Joe, God bless his soul, somehow got everyone, much like Twain's affable Tom Sawyer, to paint the fence and happily pay him. Although ingenious, it's much easier said than done. Think about that the next time you get a bright idea to make money. After all, there's certainly many a slip between a cup and a lip, and the bar and entertainment business is certainly no exception.

***

A balding, graying, distinguished-looking Big Earl stepped into the glaring white circular light of the deck stage wearing khaki shorts, a crisp, white tee shirt and cheap, rubber flip-flops. The beefy tee read, "I Pooped Today" in capital bold brown lettering. Earl stood silently before the thirsty, adoring, packed crowd of die-hard Southern rednecks and devout Midwesterners already tweaked on cold beer, whiskey, red wine and hard cider. Flanked by his talented band comprising keyboard player, Stan "The Man" Walker, drummer Preston Stanfill and trusty bass player, Mark Laborde, it was the beginning of a third and final set—the last leg of a four-hour weekly tour that transported patrons happily to another place and time for the unadulterated, vastly understated, always underwear-optional, "Big Earl Show."

If there was a bona fide star of the five-star honky-tonk it was Earl the Pearl Roberts. His zany act on Friday and Saturday nights at 5:30 was the stuff of legend among multi-generational Flora-Bama fans and was rivaled only by Sam Morgan, the lively, unorthodox daily bingo caller, in terms of customer popularity. With over 20 years of experience playing music at the Flora-Bama, Earl had made hundreds of dollars—and nearly just as many friends on his way to island stardom and a revered place in local and Redneck Riviera entertainment history. His dubious reputation preceded him.

After testing the hot microphone, Earl tested the crowd.

"I talked to one of the last snowbirds on the island today." Big Earl explained to the smiling drunken lot staring up and down at him from all around. A horseshoe of grinning faces hung above him from the top floor observatory, like impatient, laugh-starved, thirsty Indians, listening intently.

"The old boy told me: 'I got some advice for ya' on birth control.' I said, 'Oh yeah?'

He said, 'Yeah…the rhythm method is good for about 90 percent.' I nodded.

…and the pill is only 95 percent effective.' He added.

I nodded again. I knew about this from experience. And then he said:

'But the man bun is 100 percent!'"

The place erupted in raucous laughter, cackles and applause, providing the perfect segue into Earl's newest number, "You Ain't Gettin' None Cuz You Got a Man Bun!" The crowd gyrated in willful anticipation.

Earl crooned:
"Well he's shaking his ass on the dance floor
He's looking good and that's for sure
It's Friday night, he just got paid
But the boy ain't gonna get laid
Because he's got a man bun
He ain't gonna get none
He ain't gonna get someone in bed
With that shit settin' up on his head
He's been tryin' all afternoon
But he ain't gonna pull the poon
He ain't gonna get none
Cuz he's got the man bun
He worked all night
To get it right
He piled it high
Nice and tight
But tonight he'll still be going home
And having sex alone
Because he's got the man bun
He ain't gonna get none
He ain't gonna get someone in bed
With that shit sittin up on his head
He's been tryin all afternoon
But he ain't gonna pull the poon
He ain't gonna get none
Cuz he's got the man bun…"

Johnny Glass, Lucy Whitman, and Jerry Boudreaux strode into the teeming Bama Dome as Earl played the tune known by adoring fans as "the Man Bun Song." For the other hapless bystanders who somehow found themselves before the deck stage at the iconic honky-tonk, the time was well spent—as they were imminently less serious, infinitely more useless and ultimately geared for having more fun. They laughed—and laughed heartily, at Earl's ridiculous shtick. Each fellow entertainer took a belly full of giggles with their drink, easing into the working evening with a permanent smile on their eager faces, knowing well their time on stage was nearing.

"Oh-my-God!" Lucy stammered, one hand on her still-flat tummy. She wore dark stretch denim jeans and a cream-colored sweater that accentuated her natural beauties. Her onyx hair glistened like angel's wings in the manufactured light. There was a certain glow about her that was undeniable. She had an aura as she cradled her Shirley Temple with a cherry garnish.

"He's fricking nuts!" Johnny interjected, laughing terribly next to Lucy, his right arm wrapped snugly around her, his left clutching an ice cold Coors Lite.

"This is hysterical," Jerry quipped, lighting a smoke. "My Dad would get a big kick out of this shit!"

Jerry grabbed a round of drinks for the band. They would finish the Big Earl Show as guests—enjoying the music, laughter, libations and song until it was time to trade places with him and perform in the 10:00 p.m. to 2:00 a.m. slot, some of the busiest hours at the Bama' in terms of drinks served and patron time made.

Francis Tripp sat in full observation, donning shorts, flip-flops and a white cotton muscle shirt at the center of the rail running across the balcony atop the Bama Dome. Long ropes transected the large open space before him. Along these transecting lines were as many sizes, shapes, colors and styles of brassiere one could imagine, an everyday reminder of the adult business that occurs there on the regular. The unpainted plywood walls were plastered with a quarter million scribbled signatures, aphorisms, adages, dirty limericks and phone numbers of the lonely, overworked or the simply lost. Pennants of the 14 Southeastern Schools adorned the rafters, along with a bright orange Tony Stewart #20 in white lettering, and the license plates of a hundred colorful, old, departed souls. Brightly shaded alcohol advertisements plastered the place like the midday sun. The lingering smell of spilt beer wafted in lieu of air freshener throughout, a reminder of the many recent good times gone by. The anticipated end to a long week, Tripp relaxed and felt the palpable electricity in the air. It was Friday night at the Flora-Bama; and like most everyone else, he was almost tight.

Tripp sipped a chilled double shot of Patron straight up with an ice water and lemon chaser. He enjoyed Big Earl's showmanship and could not help but notice the stunning brunette near the stage. Tripp had no idea who the raven-haired beauty was, but he was sure he wanted to know the one with the shiny onyx hair. She had a distinctive way about her.

"Quite the looker," he noted, shifting his gaze across the large, muddled area below. Halfway through the drink he scanned the room, looking for the usual suspects. He recalled his attorney, Greg, saying that if he wanted to see Donny Kenner and his gorgeous wife—he had to look no further than the Flora-Bama deck stage on Friday nights for the Big Earl Show.

To his surprise, he spotted his attorney—Greg—dressed casually in shorts and a plaid, collared madras shirt, and an accompanying pretty lady near his age that had to be his wife, wearing a maize sun dress and matching sandals. Much to Tripp's pleasure, following Mr. and Mrs. McMakin was Mayor Donny Kenner and his stunning wife, Layla.

Over his old man physique Kenner lazily wore a five o' clock shadow, a lime and white Hawaiian-style shirt over a nearly-matching muscle tee tucked into white bathing shorts without a zipper, and worn sandals. Overshadowing the mayor's sloppy appearance was the presence of the platinum blonde bombshell on his arm. Much like she did her overachieving husband, Layla outshined every female within a few hundred miles. Hardly appearing her age, her body was still tight, still supple, still the sought after female form that drove both men and women—absolutely crazy. She wore a one-piece white cotton dress that gripped her thin, shapely female form, and unbeknownst to most—only a pair of matching ivory sandals. She was exquisite in every way—a stark comparison to the rest of the Southern ladies there; but alas, it was not a fair comparison. It never was. Layla was in her own league.

"Oh my God, shoot me now!" Tripp pleaded to himself when he laid eyes on Layla, his right hand clutching his heart like Red Foxx. "Aye yie-yie!" He repositioned his eyeglasses. He looked hard—but saw no panty lines. His blood pressure pulsed. He seethed.

He drew his knuckles to his mouth in a fist and clinched his teeth hard. "Damn!" He marveled. "What the hell is she doing with him?" was his first reaction. On the ten-scale he felt she was a solid eleven. Having traveled and lived around the world with the military and for business, Tripp had seen his share of beautiful women; and having lived in Lower Alabama for 20 years, Layla was by far the most gorgeous. She was the one percent, as far as he was concerned. He felt his blood pressure spike a second time.

"Jesus," he said to himself. He flicked and clicked his fingers. "Goodness gracious."

The two couples found their way to the cordoned section to the right of the main stage and sat around a small round table in a tiny U-shaped booth facing the music. They settled in as Earl addressed the lively, growing, chattering crowd before him.

"Everybody I want y'all to welcome our mayor here in Orange Beach—Mr. Donny Kenner, and his lovely wife, Layla—my neighbors. Let's give em' a round of hearty applause folks!"

The crowd came alive, clapping and hollering, prompting the mayor and Layla to briefly stand and wave.

The couples watched the rest of the Big Earl Show and socialized when the first act was over, while the Sexual Biscuits took a break. Everyone planned seeing Johnny and Lucy and Riptide afterward. Word of Lucy's pregnancy had spread fast across the tiny community, spurring the First Lady of Orange Beach, Layla Kenner, to purchase a gift certificate for baby items at a local gift shop. Layla had the typed, pre-paid present in her purse in a large pink envelope lettered, "Lucy." When she spotted Lucy with Johnny she went straight to her, leaving Donny and Greg and his wife in the booth.

As Layla broke from the pack to shower Lucy, Jacque Buttrell and his wife, Patty, slipped through the hanging vertical visqueen strips designating the pedestrian Bama Dome entrance. They stopped in the middle of the dance floor, underneath a large air conditioner vent blowing cool air, not far from where Lucy and Layla hugged and made small talk in a nearby wooden booth. Buttrell did not see Layla when he entered, but he knew she and her husband would be there, as Layla had facebook-messaged him so earlier. He was to be on his best behavior. They could ill afford any errant looks, words or deeds; or lest be compromised.

Jacque Buttrell and his wife of nearly twenty years in every way that evening looked like a successful Southern couple. Jacque wore shiny fishing shorts, designer leather sandals, a starched silk Tommy Bahama sport shirt and matching gold rope jewelry adorning his neck, right wrist and left ankle—along with a solitary gold wedding band and automatic gold Rolex on his left wrist. Over her ivory skin and matronly figure Patty wore a hideous, form-fitting white jumper with an embossed floral print, and matching orange heels. The ensemble lacking the gaudy jewelry of her husband was dull and frumpy next to the younger, more tanned and shapely ladies in attendance, hardly the perceived perfect match for the bronzed, athletic, command presence of her handsome, high-profile husband, the possum-blonde, silver-tongued devil, the macho condo man from Mississippi, Jacque Buttrell.

Patty wasn't always so disinteresting. A former soccer player at State, she was once in tremendous physical shape. Two kids, a straying husband and local politics in a fishbowl had run her emotionally and physically ragged, an apparent hidden price tag of a pretentious life serving the beguiled Lower Alabama population. Compounding her predicament was that she realized her husband was no longer eager to physically couple with her; a painful fact she knew pointed to larger, more destructive problems within their long-time, embattled relationship.

From his cat bird seat Francis Tripp finished the first shot glass of chilled Patron and ordered another from the roaming waitress carrying a small circular tray filled with drink orders and empties. A trained observer, he took particular notice of Buttrell, as he was the most obvious of the usual suspects in attendance, and seemingly the shot caller as of late, despite the fact it was the City of Orange Beach and Mayor Donny Kenner he was suing for violating his First Amendment rights under the U.S. Constitution. While he could not make out what Jacque and Donny were saying after they greeted one another, he watched their body language for subtle clues to the content of their conversation. He wanted to stay ahead of them. He found it compelling that they were apparently such good friends.

The Mayor of Orange Beach saw Jacque approach the stage.

He met him and Patty on their way up, high-fiving and hugging them in seriatim.

"What's up y'all? Y'all ready for some bushwhackers? I've already got my credit card down at the Lotto Bar. Order what you want and tell Big Phil, ya hear? Good to see y'all! Oh Patty you look terrific tonight! What a lovely outfit!" He lied.

"Oh thank you, Mayor!" Patty replied, sounding surprised. She did her best to play along, knowing him as a supreme shit talker.

She didn't feel comfortable in her own skin, much less the hideous, restricting jumpsuit. She had gained weight and nothing fit her anymore. She feigned a smile and a gush, having mastered the social technique during the last few difficult years. The suggestion of heading to the bar sounded divine. Repeated trips would be necessary to get the evening through.

"I'm gonna head on over now!" She responded, trudging in the general direction of bushwhackers, her preferred number for the evening.

"Jacque what do you want from the bar?" Patty asked. He was busy hugging and shaking hands with Mayor Kenner and Big Earl's roadies.

She repeated. "Jacque? What would you like to drink?"

He heard her the second time.

"What? Oh—give me a double vodka tonic with a lime! Thanks baby!" He answered, beaming from the glad-handing he was engaged in.

She hurried off without saying a word, disappearing into the stirring crowd of misplaced rednecks, damn Yankees, spring breakers and mischievous snowbirds turned locals.

"What's up pal?" The Mayor asked Buttrell.

"All's good. Are we gonna be ready this week? Can we run the new tower project by the planning commission? I say we hit hard and fast—like the Germans. Hitler was right you know--you can't stop a blitzkrieg!"

Mayor Kenner grinned. Having skipped his college lectures and slept through high school history lessons, he knew nothing of Hitler, other than the obvious fact he was German. What did he care? He lived in Alabama, home of the 14-time national champions, the Crimson Tide! He pulled hard on his Jack Daniels and Coke and spoke, in awe of Jacque's education and intelligence. To him, he was polished and savvy. He was the guy who was gonna make him rich—his golden parachute! Jacque was the answer to his financial concerns, his gourmet meal ticket for possibly decades to come—or so he believed.

"I told you buddy—it's a go! It's always a go for you, Jacque!"

Buttrell liked the sound of it. Everything was kosher. He imagined fat stacks of high denomination bills, extended trips to

Europe, junkets to Vegas, Cabo and Belize…expensive water toys—and unbeknownst to the Mayor of Orange Beach—with a seriously upgraded wife—in all, a nefarious, dangerous plot. Unfortunately Kenner knew nothing of it. He was a sitting duck.

Layla and Lucy made it to the right of the deck stage and joined everyone frolicking, waiting for Big Earl to return for the final set. All the ladies hugged Lucy and kissed her cheek in congratulations for her pregnancy. Johnny watched the outpouring of affection and it made him a bit uneasy, as it reminded him of the added responsibility he had not only to Lucy—but to their family. He thought of an infant and shuddered; he slowly shifted his weight, determined to do right. "I'm gonna need to marry that girl," he thought for the first time, finally realizing the obvious.

Big Earl and the band made it through the hanging vertical visqueen strips and strutted back onto the well-lit stage, on the way up high-fiving their roadies, ardent fans and complete strangers. They readied their instruments and prepared the sound for the evening's final set. Everyone in the area right of the stage, the preferred section designated for friends of the band, waited patiently for the finale, the triumphant, thundering climax to the Big Earl Show. The end was always the best part—not only did Earl finally quit playing silly songs to make room for younger, more talented and better-looking artists, but he and the band always finished with an epic, huge, white boy CRAP, which was an acronym for "country-rap" according to Big Earl. It was a fateful, country gold combination of the hip hop smash, "Apple Bottom Jeans," coupled with the incomparable "Uptown Funk," in an extended, long play setting, with Big Earl and Stanley Walker on keys doing the constant ad-libbing, rapping and singing. The catchy number was a mix of down home country and urban ghetto rap, making an interesting impromptu set that drew everyone shaking on the dance floor. The anticipated ending was always—like the Big Earl Show—funky, different and fun, with enough impromptu to make it lively and interesting.

In an unlikely bonus, a 79-year old woman from Chatanooga threw her Double D brassiere over the rope transecting the Bama Dome; she then popped and moon walked like a young Michael Jackson for an adoring, screaming, titillating, mostly redneck crowd. Everyone took notice as she flashed her large, sagging boobs for fun. The party, as usual, was on full tilt.

A smiling Francis Tripp paid careful attention. He watched Mayor Donny Kenner and Jacque Buttrell interact with one another, noticing they knew each other well, as they were in each other's ear as they spoke, in close proximity to the other, meaning their conversation was intended for them and only them.

Big Earl interrupted the silence. "I want to dedicate this next song to my neighbor and friend, the Mayor of Orange Beach—Mr. Donny Kenner. Donny, I don't want you to take this personal."

He paused.

"I would never make anything personal, by the way. I'm not like that."

He paused for effect, and continued.

"This is about the people—the people who live here; and our treasured way of life."

He paused again.

"It's absolutely not personal. "

Earl looked to Donny. "You know I love you, right?" Earl asked.

Mayor Kenner perked up and moved away from Jacque Buttrell, ending for the moment their budding real estate conversation. He smiled and stared at Big Earl, standing front and center on the deck stage, a column of white light engulfing his thin, crisp silhouette.

"Mayor Kenner, we are friends, right?" Earl implored.

Mayor Kenner nodded, blushing. "Yes!" He yelled, looking to the stage. "I love you, too, man!"

"Well then, I don't want you take this the wrong way or anything, but this song's for you. I wrote it for you and that piece of shit city council of yours for building too many damn condos on the beach!"

Mayor Kenner stared in disbelief. He wore a look like a boy who had been squarely stomach punched and kneed hard in the forehead by a much larger, tougher girl.

"That's right! I said it! There. I had to get that out!" Earl stated. "It feels good! I'm gonna tell you right now we got too many fucking condos on the beach!"

Earl raised the intonation of his voice at the end for added effect. Much to the Mayor's continued dismay, Big Earl proudly sang the new diddy—"There's too many condos on the beach!" to the delight of the adoring crowd. Everyone could relate to it. It resonated.

"Condo's here! Condo's there! Motherfrickin' condos everywhere!" Earl stammered. "I can't even take my bitch…they've made it out of reach…There's just too many fricking condos on the beach!"

When the little number was done several Orange Beach residents in the crowd whistled and cat called to the mayor, voicing their approval of the song—and their absolute disapproval of the massive condos being built, the large construction cranes an ephemeral reminder of the "progress" being made. The mayor could only eat the criticism, as there was no escape. He just sat there and listened, taking it, like the half man he was.

"There's too many fricking condos on the beach, Mayor Kenner! Stop it!" Said a random Big Earl fan.

"Yeah, Mayor! Enough is enough! We can't see the God-damned beach anymore, Kenner!" Chimed a second.

"Yeah give us a break! Traffic is a royal nightmare!" Another added, with vitriol. It was evident the unbridled growth and sprawl was killing the area known for relaxation, fun and frolic.

Mayor Kenner hung his head. He looked up and saw an equally concerned Jacque Buttrell, who was lost in thought, wondering how they were gonna bring up the new condo tower project if everybody was pissed about them overbuilding the beach. Jacque winked at him, giving his best sure and confident look—but it was a total acting job, and Donny knew it. There would be trouble. Both sensed it— and both knew it. Donny felt it in his gut. He was certain a war was brewing—and that he had no choice but to fight, and he knew they would be perceived as the bad guys. It was a game changer—there was certainly a new perspective on things. He could feel it.

The mood at the Flora-Bama was upbeat and fun and neither Jacque nor Mayor Kenner wanted to spoil the good time. They avoided addressing the obvious with each other, despite their mutual concerns. Each stayed with their significant other until the Big Earl show ended.

After the show Big Earl's roadies cleared the stage, making room for the Flora-Bama sound crew so Johnny and Lucy and Riptide could take over. During this time Jacque saw a window of opportunity. Mayor Kenner was outside the Bama Dome talking to constituents, crawfishing about island growth. Not wanting any of it, Jacque slipped away from the heated conversation.

He had consumed four double vodka tonics and was feeling the normal effects. He noticed Layla standing alone near the stage, while he was waiting for Patty to return from getting a drink and taking a visit to the restroom. There was no one watching, as far as he could tell. The deck stage room was mostly clear of people he knew. Jacque was careful not to face Layla. Instead, he moved in next to her, shoulder-to-shoulder, speaking out of the corner of his mouth.

"Hey hot stuff," he muttered under the fill music playing over the sound system. She was busy looking at her phone when he approached, so she didn't see him. His voice startled her, but it was a pleasant surprise.

"Oh hey!" She answered, blushing brightly. She looked around to see if anyone was watching. They were good—or so she thought. She too was buzzed. She was glad to be able to talk to him in the open. These moments were rare.

"Having fun this evening?" He asked.

"Not really," she answered, wanting to. He sensed it in her body language and in her gaze. "Maybe we could get together Sunday afternoon? I told Patty I'm going to play golf at Peninsula. We could meet at the condo." He offered.

"We are supposed to go to go to a fundraiser I think. I'll message you. I'm walking to the bar. I so wish I was going home with you instead! Ta-ta for now, honey bunch!" Layla whispered. She squared her shoulders to him, blew a kiss over the cup of her right hand, turned and strutted toward the Lotto Bar. Jacque watched every tilt of her hips, every sway of her gorgeous, model-like physique. He really felt the white liquor now and it was all he could do to resist her. Patty would soon be ready to go. Instead of lovely Layla he was going home with the hag. He vowed things had to change. He couldn't go on living like this, he convinced himself. He deserved better. He would have her—as his. Somehow he'd make it happen; he'd make it work; he promised himself.

From his perch on the top rail Francis Tripp finished another chilled Patron with a lemon chaser, his third in as many hours.

Relaxed, he reviewed his hand-written notes. He smiled. The white quilted bar napkin in front of him bore a single scribbled cursive note: "Buttrell has a Layla problem."

Tripp served as a sniper in Viet Nam. During that time he learned everything he needed to about human beings and what they tell you non-verbally with their movements. On one occasion he stayed frozen in one spot for nearly two days, waiting on the equally adept enemy sniper to compromise his position with an errant move. The enemy revealed his position by allowing his knee to become visible, granting Tripp his own "Wounded Knee" combat moment. After the successful shot, when the enemy tumbled into plain view, he waited for his comrade to come and rescue him and pull him to safety. Tripp shot him too, doubling his quarry.

In this civilian matter, Buttrell and Layla were unaware of Tripp's presence. They never saw him watching them plainly from above. The body language, eye contact and blown kiss at the end pointed to a definite physical chemistry between the two. Tripp thought they made a nice-looking couple.

"Too bad they're both married to other people. " He thought, another inconvenient truth.

***

Big Earl placed his padded black guitar case in the back of his silver Toyota sedan and opened the driver door. With keys in hand, his right leg was in the car when Mayor Donny Kenner appeared before him, breathing heavily. Kenner placed a hand on the car's hood, steadying his weight. He raised the other and gesticulated.

"What gives Earl? Why the business with the song? What—what—did I do to you?"

Earl wasn't in the mood to be serious, but it was a serious situation. He was at a breaking point. The way he said you was like an Et tu Brute' thing—it was passive aggressive—and belittling, as Earl had publicly backed every one of Donny's political campaigns, going back to the beginning. He had even done a series of folksy facebook live interviews for the mayor. But things had changed. It hadn't gone like he said. Nirvana was interrupted. On the island, the imminent future loomed large. Everything was completely in disarray—SNAFU.

"Donny, will you please shut up for a second?" Earl implored.

"Okay," the mayor relented. His labored breathing subsided.

"In a week the kids get out of school. Do you know what that means?"

"The season starts." Kenner answered.

"Exactly! And you know what it means for me and Jenny? It means there's gonna be 10,000 fricking cars and trucks and motorcycles and campers and motor homes clogging the two roads we use to get around! I live on a dog leg that has one way in and one way out! During the season I can't get out my neighborhood because of the snarling traffic! It's so bad I have to either take a golf cart on the sidewalk or a boat—which is really a dinghy, to get here to the Flora-Bama! It's screwed up. You and that council and your developer buddies have put too many people on the island! This is real, Donny! I'm not making this shit up! I'm not the only one affected by all this bullshit! All your bullshit, by the way!"

Earl pointed directly at the mayor for effect, punctuating the moment.

Donny stood, taking it in, as difficult as it was. He grimaced and swallowed. His stomach grumbled. He wanted another drink. He was at a loss for words. He selfishly wondered, "How in the hell are we gonna get this new high-rise through the planning commission and the council if everyone in town is pissed about perceived overdevelopment?" He was stuck on that salient fact.

Earl impatiently waited for a reply. He got none, so he continued.

"So yeah, I wrote a song about it! It's just a diddy. Big deal. That's what I do. I make fun of stuff writing silly songs. But I do hope people think about what I'm saying sometimes, you know? The sad thing is there's nothing funny about paving paradise, Donny. One day you'll realize that—but it's gonna be too late, I'm afraid. Unfortunately, I just don't think you get it."

"I had no idea, Earl," Donny managed, disingenuously.

Earl stood with his right leg in the car, his left still claiming purchase on the dusty, bleached clam shell-covered lot. His long-time friend stood slumped in the dull evening light. Earl thought he appeared different—like he didn't really know him anymore. He thought of the derogatory term: "politician."

"You do now." Earl quipped. He paused for effect.

"Mayor."

Earl slid into the driver's seat, turned the ignition and the lights. He drove from the dank parking lot toward home, heading west down the hazy Gulf Beach Highway into the sleepy, nostalgic Southern anachronism turned retirement destination: Baldwin County, Alabama, where unbeknownst to the new Midwestern baby boomer residents, the rights of most are subjugated for the greed and control of the connected few. It was the Alabama way. Retire at your own peril.

Kenner had a Eureka moment. He knew unequivocally moving forward—and there was no turning back—that there would be hell to pay. He and Buttrell would be going to war with the locals—the very people he purported to represent and care about. Paradoxically, he realized he and Buttrell had painted themselves into a corner. Not only was he facing the impending wrath of the Orange Beach citizens, but also Tripp's Federal lawsuit over denying him his right to free speech. He felt like things were beginning to get away from him, as this was not what he and Jacque had planned. He feared a grand reprisal; a sting; and a precipitous fall from grace. On this jutted track, these things were inevitable.

"Shit." Donny Kenner said to himself, standing alone in the faulty white light of the flickering mercury vapor lamps above. A light humidity laced the night air like a wet handkerchief. He felt a chill and walked back inside, heading straight to Phil for a final call and to settle his hefty credit card tab at the Lotto Bar.

On his drive home to Fairhope, to avoid the Orange Beach cops, Francis Tripp went the back way through Lillian, down rural Alabama Highway 98 and took the beach expressway through Summerdale down County Road 32. With his suburban windows down he smoked blended tobacco through a corn cob pipe, blared Ziggy Marley and thought of the sheer avarice that motivated the actions of Jacque Buttrell and Mayor Kenner; as well as the feckless way the lovely Layla Kenner bounced and strutted after blowing Jacque a kiss.

16

A gainst better judgment and a host of local citizen detractors who spoke vehemently against it, Mayor Kenner and the Orange Beach City Council met, heard from Jacque Buttrell the many merits to growth, development and new building and voted in the largest high-rise development in area history, ushering in what the astute typified as "the death knell of Orange Beach." The monumental vote was seen as an egregious slap in the face of the beach citizenry that still cared, and as a result their stirrings and huddled, vocal contemplations were rife and sundry. People were talking action—something had to be done; something had to give.

***

On Sunday Lucy accompanied Johnny on his early morning trip to nearby Johnson beach. Named for the first African-American from Escambia County to perish serving as an American soldier in the Korean War, Rosamond Johnson, the state-protected recreation area was a short ride from their tiny cottage off Innerarity over the Theo Baars Bridge. Parking was always easy and there was quick beach access once you did. It was an area known more by locals than tourists, reflected in its tidiness and idleness.

The silver-orange sun crept across the steely horizon as Johnny stretched for five minutes in the sugar soft sand, warming his mid torso, calf, leg muscles and arms in a series of light calisthenics. At 73 degrees and low humidity, running conditions were ideal. Lucy sat Indian-style, reading, nearby, enjoying the peaceful early portion of the day. He finished his limbering routine and kissed her lightly on a puffy, rosy cheek. She smiled, as radiant as ever.

"Gonna run twenty and I'll turn and come back. See you soon!" He voiced, checking his digital wrist watch before scampering off. He quickly assumed a steady, positive gait. A set of consistent pock marks followed him like his stubborn shadow down the water's whispering, ebbing edge.

Lucy's attention faltered. Her eyes left her Kindle app momentarily, allowing her to notice a half-submerged, sun-bleached sand dollar, only paces away. She put her phone aside and crawled on hands and knees and knelt before it. She snatched the pale round, wafer-thin object with two fingers and held it lightly in her left palm, admiring its symmetry. She remembered a trip to the beach she and her Grammie—her father's mother—took when she was four or five years old. On that occasion her grandmother showed her that if you break open a sand dollar you always find five sets of angel's wings or what some people like to call "doves." Every sand dollar—if broken apart, yields these five little white sets of wings.

Startled by the beauty of the fond early memory with her now departed grandmother, Lucy grabbed the sand dollar with two hands and firmly snapped it in half. Careful not to lose any of the jagged, glistening material inside, Lucy emptied the expected five separate "angel doves" into her left palm. As she marveled at their uniqueness and symbolism, she couldn't help but think of her mother, her incarcerated father, Johnny and her—and their baby.

Her irascible, overbearing father had been in the federal pen for many weeks, the first few of a lonely, humbling, multi-year sentence. She wanted to call her mother to clear the air—and possibly rekindle their severed relationship. Her Mom was alone now, free from the dominating influence of her father's lack of conviction. She figured she could use a call. It had been months since they'd spoken. She picked up her IPhone and perused her contacts. She pressed "Mom" and her number dialed, lighting up the screen. She hit speaker and the dial tone sounded above the waves crashing lightly in the foreground. Her mother answered on the third ring.

"Lucy?"

"Yeah, it's me, Mom," she said, nervously.

"How are you?" She asked, sounding overjoyed and excited to finally hear from her—her only daughter.

"I'm pregnant."

***

It was a bad idea. But they did it anyways—like people often do. The problem was Jacque and Layla had grown out of their weekly clandestine routine of meeting at the safe place of Jacque's posh condominium overlooking the gulf. They longed for more zeal—a little more excitement—more passion. They brazenly took Jacque's 95-foot marine vessel out for the first time. It was a massive Versilcraft marlin fishing outfit, retrofitted for lengthy, deep water tours. Refurbished and repainted, it was a cool $1.8 million, purchased through one of his different LLC's operating outside the State of Alabama. His downfall was parking the massive craft behind the yacht club in order to buy four ice cold bushwhackers for himself and Layla. Those bushwhackers, as it turned out, cost Jacque much more than the forty bucks spent on them along with the tip.

Jacque and Layla tried to cover their tracks. They knew the risk. He boarded the boat on the Intracoastal inside a large, roofed storage facility, where it was kept year-round. He picked up Layla at a nearby small boat launch used mainly for jet skis, kayaks and canoes, that rarely was busy.

Jacque took them east around the big, man-made sand bar created where the Intracoastal Waterway connects with the turbulent, blue-green Gulf of Mexico, the path all local fishermen took to get out on the salt. They rounded the sand bar and motored slowly back towards the key in the shipping channel in the middle of the waterway, under the Baar Bridge and turned west and headed to the Flora-Bama Yacht Club. Jacque pulled into the first spot available, next to Strick-9's new fishing boat, in front of his old, water-logged, now-vacated water-side shanty. Jacque asked Layla to stay in the cabin—but she followed him momentarily onto the deck, hugging and kissing him in plain view of Strick-9 from his singular vantage a few feet away, for just a few dangerous moments—and just like that she and Jacque were seen; and quickly made, despite Layla returning forthwith to the concealed cabin confines, as instructed.

Strick-9 sat comfortably inside the cabin/living area, legs crossed, cocktail in hand, in a steering room with a spectacular, tinted view that allowed him to see out but no one else to see in. Layla and Jacque had no idea anyone was watching them from that intimate, insider angle. Both thought they were protected by the cover of the surely empty boats on each side from onlookers, as they thought they were hidden. They were mistaken.

"Interesting," Strick-9 thought to himself. "The mayor's wife is with another man." As he watched Jacque and Layla kiss playfully in the shade of the boat, he was reminded of how things aren't always how they appear at first glance—that there are always complications, always inequities in this tangled, lost, dark and unforgiving world we live in. He remembered that he too had experienced infidelity from a straying woman. It was a bummer to him, the way people often mistreated one another.

"I wonder how many people know about this?" He said to himself. "Other than me?"

***

On Sunday afternoon after church at Flora-Bama under the big beige tent outside Johnny and Jerry Boudreaux got together at Jerry's place to work on a couple new songs they had started. Johnny told Lucy he'd be a few hours and would be back around five for dinner on the grill. He planned to cook fresh red snapper, sweet potatoes and cob salad—one of their favorites. His departure gave Lucy a window of opportunity she anticipated.

Lucy met her mother at Wolf Bay Lodge in Foley, a long-standing family restaurant known for its impressive salad bar, buttery hush puppies and delightful, home-made desserts. She got there early— at a quarter to one, for their one o'clock meeting; but her mom was already there, dressed smartly, seated at the bar, a clear glass of Pinot sparkling before her.

Her mother wore what she had earlier to church—a beautiful, conservative orange and white polka dot summer dress and a white sun hat befitting a matron—even a somewhat single one as her. Her husband, Senator Slip Whitman, was in the federal clink serving a prison sentence for stealing a lucrative floating boom contract during the economic tragedy of the BP oil spill. Though his case was on appeal, he would be away for many months, and she was struggling settling into her new, "temporary life." Still vibrant and attractive, she had started taking calls from barely married and single guys in the community aware of her unique "situation." To her flattering surprise and dismay, many of them were friends of her husband; but of course—she liked the attention.

Lucy entered the restaurant and made a bee's line for her mother, who was seated with her back to her, checking her phone. Lucy wore a simple, ruffled white summer dress lined with pink lace along the neckline. Her flats matched an ivory straw hat, designer purse, earrings and bracelet; she showed no signs of being with child. She was as apprehensive as she was anxious.

"Hi Mom," she said as she appeared beside her mother and removed her sunglasses, revealing tears welling in her big brown eyes.

The forlorn mother stood and hugged her child and pulled her close, still seated. Lucy leaned into her. The hug felt good. She missed her perfume, her confidence—and she didn't blame her for her father's transgressions. If anything, her mother was a victim. Nevertheless, her troublesome father was no longer around—at least for now.

"Let me look at you!" Her mother said, smiling. "You look wonderful!"

"No signs of a baby—yet!" She added, unable to resist, looking her up and down.

"I'm only a few weeks along, Mother!" She whispered. "Goodness."

"Where are you living? Please tell me you are not on that awful sailboat! Lucy you just cannot do it! Please!"

Lucy found humor in the fact her Mom agreed with her about the sailboat.

"We have a house, Mom." She blurted to her mother's pleasant surprise.

"Really, now?" She answered with a wry smile. She took a quick sip of the golden-white wine.

"Yes," she beamed. "We live on Innerarity Point off Garcon Street. It's a tiny, wooden two-bedroom. We're renting it from a friend of the guy who started Flora-Bama, Mr. Joe Gideon. It's small but it has all the space we need and a wonderful back yard where the baby will be able to play. There's a nice breeze off the Intracoastal in the afternoons. It's really cute and I can't wait to decorate the baby's room!"

"What color will it be?" Mom asked. "Pink or blue?"

"I want a little boy...but I think Johnny wants a baby girl," she let on.

The bartender stepped in and provided Lucy with lemon water and her mother another light golden colored glass of Pinot Grigio, which was a surprise to Lucy, who never knew her mother to drink away from home.

"How are you, Mom?" She asked in an altered tone. "How are things without Dad?"

Her mother was embarrassed. She looked away and sipped her wine before replying, trying to cope with the humiliation, the bitterness, the shame. And that wasn't all.

"It's not easy," she managed, sipping the nectar-colored flute. "I'm awfully lonely."

Lucy felt for her mother. She knew she was facing a difficult challenge alone. She wondered how her parents' marriage would fare over the prison sentence. With good time her father would likely be out after a couple years or so—but that seemed like an eternity to Lucy—who calculated her baby—boy or girl—would be walking before her father's eventual prison release.

"How are your friends? Are they helping? Do they provide support? What about Miss Annabelle and the other tennis ladies? Do y'all still spend time together?" Lucy asked.

Her mother took a deep breath and sighed. "It's not like it used to be, honey. Everyone has ostracized me and your father over his conviction. It's like we've been cut off from the community. I wrote your father the other day that I feel like we should consider putting the house on the market and moving to Mountain Brook or Vestavia. I just don't think it will ever be the same, here, especially when he gets out. It's probably going to be worse. "

She paused.

"I fear ahead there will be many tough decisions." She relented.

***

The study of economics has been called the science of decision-making. Education, in theory, should enable people to better understand themselves and the world around them; and to thereby make better decisions, putting core values first; plotting, contemplating, readying for the long, steady journey of a successful life. However, the conception is debatable.

Success in life has been called, "Doing your best," or "the self-satisfaction that comes from knowing you gave your best." But to some, success must be measured, quantified, even promulgated for everyone to see. To these timid souls, success is a zero sum game—a sorry, glinted collection of ill-gotten gains; a silly race to impress with money, luxuries and stacked toys. These material glory seekers are the vain energy thieves of our time; and they are led by the elected officials, our politicians.

The ancient political axiom attributed most often to Lord Byron, that "Power corrupts, and… absolute power corrupts absolutely," is a reminder of the inherent weakness of men—even in those well-intended souls, in their zeal to serve the public by running for and holding public office. Often their true intentions are as masked as they are misguided, as a fortune awaits the bold and determined politician.

In the forgotten State of Alabama, once you become an elected official you are part of an elite, white male-dominated, hunting club. You are paid to do nothing outside the wishes of the machine and you get a generous stipend to run your empty political office back home. When the legislature sobers up and convenes you get a healthy per diem, hollow social status and unlimited paid expenses. There are also the secret lobbyist perks, a continuing legal charade with more semantics than a late night with good liquor and old friends. The City of Montgomery, that forsaken, drab, shoddy place of public business replete with its garish capitol building, is aptly named "Goat Hill," that proverbial plantation overseer of a gangly, denuded human morass known as the State Legislature of Alabama. There is also a blasphemous side to the fall.

Alabama's Christian conservative coalition of Grand Ole Party members may piously attend church on Sundays, but their deplorable actions when no one is looking is what truly defines them; which is why one should always be skeptical of do-gooders, church-goers and even the well-known, so-called philanthropy. That is because both the church and the government contain bad actors, human beings inherently incapable of doing what is right. These are the hypocrites—the people who say one thing and do another; and throughout the world these miscreants are as common as head colds and rainy days. It is for that reason Francis P. Tripp thrived in his singular role, as his firm stance against public corruption found constant purchase; strangely, like in the jungles of Viet Nam, he was again perched prone with his rifle, camouflaged and focused; all from a new moral high ground. His vantage was clear.

Just because it's legal doesn't mean it's ethical. What's wrong is wrong even when everyone else is doing it. And finally, people rationalize bad behavior so they can live with their weaker selves. This was especially so amongst Lower Alabama's most privileged lot of entitled, crooked politicians. It was a sordid story of greed, one as old as time itself. Francis Tripp was not only fighting compromised public officials—he was fighting history, because the State of Alabama didn't become a swamp overnight. It was an ongoing, intergenerational plight—like overt racism, ignorance, the Ku Klux Klan and winning football. It was unfortunately omnipresent—and lasting.

***

The following Wednesday, Joe Gideon showered at home and laid down for a nap. When he woke he still felt awful, as he strangely had for many days, and he finally decided to call his doctor, like Vonnie had been insisting. He left message with Jim Solace's secretary that his symptoms of light chest pains, labored breathing and fatigue had persisted, but were now worse. She returned his call and said that the doc was with a patient and would get back to him.

"I can't remember feeling this awful," he said to himself, settling down in his robe in front of the big-screen high definition television, a large black remote with colorful buttons in one hand, his IPhone in the other.

Minutes later his cell phone rang. He looked at its face: It conspicuously read: "Big Earl." Joe took the call. "Well hello there Earl. How's the world treating you these days?"

"Things are okay, Joe. I wanted to talk to you about something important. You got a minute to talk?"

Joe sensed the necessity of the call. He sat up on his sofa, listening.

"Of course, what's up?" He asked, wanting Earl to continue.

"I've decided to run for Mayor of Orange Beach and of course, I'm gonna need your support. I'm sick and tired of all the condos going up, Joe. I am disgusted! The Orange Beach Council and Mayor Donny Kenner are out of control! We can't continue to live like this! Traffic is a nightmare and our quality of life is disappearing faster than our beach access. So, I am doing something about it. I'm going on Monday to sign up and qualify for Mayor of Orange Beach. Will you support me? It's gonna take a little money and I don't have much."

Joe was stunned, but he quickly recovered, energized by Earl's unbridled enthusiasm for the cause. "Absolutely you can count on me! We will hold fundraisers and I will network on your behalf! Public service is important and I am proud of you, Earl. I know you're upset. I share many of the same concerns you have—this has been going on for a while now, as we both know."

He paused and had a Eureka moment.

"Look, I want you to get in touch with somebody—someone who can really help you. His name is Francis Tripp. He lives in Fairhope. Talk to him and then get back to me and we'll get a meeting together and start building your campaign committee. You can count on me as treasurer. Get a pen and paper and take down his name and number."

17

Francis Tripp was bent on learning more about his local adversaries. In that vein, he felt it necessary to make another hour-long drive east on a blue bird Friday afternoon to the world-famous Flora-Bama to listen to good music and to see what was happening at the storied meeting place. Cirrus clouds painted the pale azure sky in narrow white strokes. A cool breeze whispered through the Suburban truck cab, making for a pleasant journey. Tripp was buoyed by thought of having another Don Julio chilled 100 percent agave tequila, or two. Maybe he would get more intel on the corrupt mayor and his lovely, possibly straying wife? Maybe he would again be surprised. Maybe he would get lucky, he thought, waning optimistic—his libido assured.

Like many men, Francis Tripp enjoyed an interesting if not dubious personal life, all things being relative. Although he still lived with his second wife, and mother of his daughter, they had been divorced for many years. The separation was necessary due to Francis' constant political wrangling. By severing marital ties he protected his family from legal recourse, insulating them—and himself. By signing over his stake in their estate on behalf of his daughter, he was worth little to nothing. He definitely wasn't worth suing. There was nothing there, as his full disability check was untouchable by law. Tripp's monthly government assistance payment stemmed from his shoulder injuries sustained in Marine service in Viet Nam and the dozens of required surgeries since that troubled time. Despite his age and the severity of his wartime maladies, every appendage below the shoulders still worked—and quite well, a credit to his daily rigorous exercise routine.

It was late June now, the irrepressible coastal heat a constant, like Alabama political corruption and ephemeral vice; the beach air hung heavy with sun, sand and sweat, the vacationers still bent on cheating time and place, the excitement at the exalted pump house Alabama-Florida Line, almost palpable; a typical summer Friday evening at the Bama it was; a sure promise of a good time by the willing, ready and able in the proverbial know.

Tripp wore a killer tan, cologne splashes and a faded blue bandana tied around his neck; a white, collared sport shirt, faded ruby running shorts and worn leather sandals. He drove scenic Alabama Highway 98 east to the Florida Line. He crossed the Lillian Bridge and headed south along Bauer Road before turning right and heading west on the Gulf Beach Highway, over the Baar Bridge, and the last five quiet miles through the state park preserve, past the towering Eden Condominium, back to the edge of Alabama, just inside Florida, to the revered, raucous pump house on the Alabama-Florida Line.

As he parked in the pock-marked white clam parking lot at 5:30 p.m., he noticed Layla Kenner in a tight white dress that accentuated her supermodel physique. She and her unsuspecting husband, Mayor Donny Kenner, stepped out of their white Cadillac Escalade with large spoked wheels and graphite windows into the bleached shell parking lot, their feet crunching the white clam shells. Kenner wore white shorts, sandals and a baby blue silk button down, neatly starched and pressed; a large gold rope chain hung from his neck. There was electricity in the air. Tripp sensed it, as did his idling biorhythm.

"Aye yie-yie!" Ripp muttered to himself, staring at Layla, again futilely searching for panty lines. "I bet you a million dollars Buttrell is gonna be here!" He said to himself, parking. "If he ain't—he'll be wishing he was! That's some serious candy! My goodness!"

On the other side of the lot, Big Earl exited his Toyota and carried his acoustic guitar in a large black case with a carrying handle. It was adorned with various band stickers and graffiti he collected during a semi-successful 25-year entertainment career. Tripp made him immediately. Their paths crossed on the way to the joint entrance.

"Hey—you're Big Earl—aren't you?" Tripp asked, smiling ear-to-ear, pale incisors flashing. His blonde-graying hair danced on his head in the salty gulf breeze, making him appear much younger than his age.

"That's right," Earl smiled and laughed, not yet playing the evening part. He wore jeans, sandals and a white beefy tee that read in bold black letters, "Your Mom was Here." An arrow below the lettering pointed to his zipper. Earl stopped and placed his guitar case in his left hand and offered his right hand to Tripp. Tripp gripped it and they shook.

"I'm Francis Tripp. I drove over from Fairhope. I'm a fan." He proudly stated.

"Thanks man, nice to meet you." Earl chuckled. He thought the name sounded familiar. Tripp explained.

"A year or so ago Joe Gilchrist gave me a CD of yours. I like Joe a lot—he's a heck of a guy. The CD gets played quite a bit. In fact, I think my little sister who lives up in B-Ham stole it when she was down here after we were playing it on the water! She had to have it and shared it with her book club back home and I think every one of them have been down here with their husbands to see your show. I'm looking forward to it."

He paused.

"This is my first time seeing you." He smiled in a pearly glow.

"Poontang on the Pontoon!" Tripp howled, raising two closed fists high above his head, beaming. "My God! The first time I heard it I thought it was my long lost theme song!"

Big Earl belly laughed, leaning back and rubbing lightly the top part of his tummy. "You know, I didn't remember at first but now I do, Joe Gideon told me I need to talk to you, Mr. Tripp."

"Really? About what?" He asked, looking serious. Joe Gideon was a trusted friend and supporter—definitely one of the good guys.

"Well, I've decided to run for Mayor of Orange Beach!" Earl stated, rocking somewhat as he spoke, shifting his weight from one leg to the other, swapping the guitar case to his other hand.

"Really?" Tripp asked, beaming. "Are you serious, man?"

"Serious as a heart attack! This overdevelopment has to stop Mr. Tripp. Orange Beach is about ruined. If we keep building high rises we're all gonna have to move! It's hard to bear."

"This is terrific!" Tripp stammered. He couldn't believe it. A local celebrity wanted to run for office! He pulled a card out of his wallet and handed it to Big Earl.

"Here's my contact info."

Earl placed it in his wallet and reached into his guitar case and retrieved a brand new CD wrapped in cellophane. He handed it to Mr. Tripp.

"Here—here's my new CD. Enjoy it on the ride home—and be careful—watch out for the cops. They're terrible here in Orange Beach. That's another thing I'm sick of. Everybody around here's gotten so greedy. It seems we're all a mark these days."

"I know—it's why I run the back roads, through Lillian."

"Good call!" Earl answered. "It's great meeting you. Enjoy the show Mr. Tripp! Have some fun!"

"I will—give me a call early next week and we'll talk about everything. I look forward to it."

"You'll hear from me," Earl answered matter-of-factly.

Tripp could not believe his good fortune. He went back to his truck and stowed the free CD Earl gave him, looking forward to listening to it. He strutted into the Flora-Bama and made a bee's line to the back bar near the tent—the one with the view of the stage and the beach. His spirits buoyed, he ordered a chilled dark Patron and took in the soothing sea breeze and the party happening before him.

***

Mary Whitman pulled into the cratered parking lot adjacent to the Flora-Bama, a piece of prime real estate not dissimilar from the moon's surface. She found a spot closest to the beach, against the chain link fence. She checked her matronly look in the mirror. She had done her makeup at home, but that was an hour ago—or more. Despite her own doubts, she looked great for her age. There were a few wrinkles and a gray hair or two here and there, but she still turned heads. A former track star, she maintained her physical fitness throughout adulthood. She could still wear all her old clothes and she looked nice, if not conservative, in her khaki shorts, sandals and light, collared, buttoned down Polo shirt.

Lucy told her to meet them under the tent, where they were playing the early evening slot. Mary made her way through the gift shop and paid a $5 cover charge, had her hand stamped "over 21" and found Lucy and Johnny on the tent stage setting up for the six o'clock show. Mary was somewhat apprehensive about being at the Flora-Bama, as it was her first time at the storied haunt. Through the years she heard horror tales of the unsavory types of people who frequented the famous dive bar; she nevertheless looked forward to seeing the kids perform. She had never heard Lucy sing outside their home, and was eager to. She even packed an overnight bag, like they suggested. She wondered if she would need it.

"Mother! How are you? You made it! We are so glad you're here!" Lucy squealed.

"Hey Ms. Whitman!" Johnny called from the back of the stage, waving. "Thanks for driving out to see us!"

"Please Johnny, call me Mary." She insisted, hugging Lucy now beside her.

"Mom sit up here in front, at this table," She motioned to a wooden picnic table. Her mother walked to it, placing her purse on its weathered top. She had the full view of the stage.

"Here Mom," Lucy insisted, handing her mother a small rectangular card, what looked like a business card. Her mother took it and looked at it, squinting at its small print.

"It's a free drink card!" Lucy blurted. "Have one on the house!"

"Why thank you!" Her mother answered, thinking of a crisp, chilled pinot.

"The bar is right over there," Lucy pointed in its direction.

***

It was 5:40 p.m. Francis Tripp sat at the wooden, boxed outdoor tent bar on a sturdy metal, padded barstool, sipping straight chilled agave tequila, looking forward to the Big Earl Show, which was about to start inside the Bama Dome. He half-sipped the shot glass beaded with condensation, slurping the clear, cool white liquor between his teeth and gums. He enjoyed the burning cold sensation and temporary shortness of breath it brought, followed by a lowered blood pressure and a quick beating of his heart; all familiar trappings. A slender, shapely woman walking toward him got his attention. It was Mary Whitman, in a gait as sure as the sinking summer sun.

She walked to the bar and stood next to Mr. Tripp. With a smile the bartender asked for her order.

"Pinot Grigio please," she answered, smiling back. She handed the bartender the drink card, and two one dollar bills—for a tip. The bartender returned with the small plastic bottle of wine, unscrewed the cap and poured its contents into a clear plastic cup, placing the two dollar bills into a large plastic pickle turned tip jar, half full of quid. "Thank you!" the bartender, a tanned, handsome young man with a man-bun, answered.

"You're welcome!" Mary replied, taking the cup of wine and napkin into her tiny hands. She sipped the powerful nectar, lowering its level in the glass, making it easier to handle. She took another for good measure. Tripp noticed.

"Come here often?" Francis Tripp provocatively asked, obviously hitting on her. He saw no wedding ring.

Mary looked to her right. She noticed a smiling blonde-haired Tripp, and a half-consumed shot of what looked like Tequila before him, amidst the lime wedges and napkins. His dark complexion belied his light colored hair, shirt, bandana and bright white smile. She felt for her wedding ring that wasn't there.

"Never!" She laughed. "This is my first time here! I've lived in Alabama all my life and I can honestly say I've never been to the Flora-Bama!"

"Well, don't worry!" Tripp retorted, liking her energy. "What goes on at the Flora-Bama stays at the Flora-Bama!" He chuckled. She thought it was funny; it reminded her of the famous Las Vegas line.

"Oh really?" She asked, smiling, playing along. She took another sip of the wine.

"That's right!" Tripp said. "Nobody says a thing! Nothing."

"I like secrets," she added, grinning.

"Where are you from?" He asked. "I live in Fairhope. I drove up for the Big Earl Show. I have never seen him in person—I've only listened to his CD's. He's great!"

"You're from Fairhope?" She asked.

"Not from Fairhope. I live there. There's a big difference."

"I'm in Point Clear," she responded, which was an unincorporated area down the bay road.

He smiled as he watched her. She liked the attention. She liked the way he looked at her. She thought he was a handsome—and harmless, older man.

"My name is Mary," she offered her hand.

"My name is Francis," he replied. "But Mary, you can call me Paul." He grinned, reciprocating, lightly shaking and squeezing her diminutive hand.

"Let's go over here and see the Big Earl show. He's starting in just a minute."

Tripp stood and led Mary by the arm upstairs to the balcony where they found two seats overlooking the center stage. He ordered another shot and a second cup of wine for Mary, and they settled in for the beginning of the Big Earl Show.

"My daughter is playing outside with her boyfriend under the tent," Mary explained.

"Oh really? What's the name of the band?" Tripp asked.

"Rip Tide," she answered. "They start at 6:00 outside under the tent. I don't want to miss a song! So we can only watch a couple of numbers here and then we have to get back out there! I have to see my baby, Lucy, sing!"

***

Joe Gideon watched Fox News from his upstairs lair at the old brick ranch house off South Loop Road in a swampy, rustic plot spanning 40 acres. The drab, inconspicuous, dilapidated place was built in the 1980's on the flat, soggy lowlands of the area adjacent to the back base entrance dissected over the years by the creep of the massive base infrastructure. He focused on the Fox News broadcast, enjoying a bowl of homemade vegetable soup, squarely cut cheddar cheese and wheat crackers. The news lead was as sharp and biting as the prepared snack. Shepard Smith's tanned, shiny face marked the opening:

"The President of the United States is set to address the nation this evening in what is being called an emergency announcement over the public health and welfare of the United States citizens."

He continued. Joe's attention riled; he turned up the volume with the large remote.

"According to sources close to the White House, it appears that the country will be moving into an unprecedented lockdown period. Moving forward after Sunday, all bars and restaurants, churches and schools are ordered closed. This is a difficult measure—one cited for the greater good—as a way to fight this dreaded Heineken virus."

Joe was stunned. He placed the steaming bowl in front of him on the coffee table. He turned up the volume again, disbelieving.

"Heineken virus?" He asked himself. "What the hell?"

"Again, as of midnight Sunday, all bars and restaurants across the country will be closed. The Center for Disease Control is asking citizens to give them 'two weeks to flatten the death curve.' So it looks like for the next 14 days the country will be in an unprecedented lockdown state. Again, it is only for two weeks. The government is asking for just 14 days."

He paused. A paper is handed to Smith, who is still on air. He reads the directive.

"And another breaking tidbit...this just in...it appears that along with the lockdown order, is a face mask mandate. Everyone is strongly encouraged to wear face masks to fight the spread of this dreaded Heineken virus, which has already taken the lives of thousands. We repeat: A mask mandate will be in effect, going forward, after Sunday, in addition to the lockdown order prescribing the closing of all schools, churches, restaurants and bars."

Joe stared aimlessly at the thousands of tiny TV pixels comprising the big bright screen before him and wondered, "How are the people who work at Flora-Bama going to survive?"

***

Francis and Mary listened to the first two songs of the Big Earl Show—a couple of diddies titled, "Get out of the Left Lane you stupid S.O.B." and "Made Love to Your Sister at the Motel Six." Francis thought they were hilarious, but Mary—not so much. He could tell she wasn't thrilled.

"Let's head back outside and check out Riptide," he insisted.

"Let's," she enthusiastically replied. They stood and made their way downstairs and back outside. When they reached the picnic table where she had placed her purse, Mary noticed it was gone. She looked to the stage. Lucy saw her and called out, "I have your purse, Mom! I was wondering where you were when you didn't come back! It's safe up here."

"Thanks honey!" She said. "Mr. Francis and I checked out the other act."

"Well hello Mr. Francis!" Lucy waved, smiling.

Francis obliged with a wave and a smile of his own. He recognized Lucy as the attractive brunette he'd spotted a few nights before. They settled in at the picnic table in front and the show began. Lucy and Johnny took turns singing, alternating during the first set. Francis was impressed.

"They're really good," he said. "Your daughter has a lovely voice."

"Thank you!" Mary answered.

"She's beautiful too," He added, attached to a pregnant pause. "Just like her mother."

Mary blushed. "Well, everyone has always said she favors her father, but I'll take the compliment. Thank you!"

Tripp saw an opportunity. "Where is her father?" He asked, presuming they were divorced in the absence of a wedding ring. The two cups of wine she finished provided courage in a difficult situation. She took a deep breath and exhaled.

"He's in prison, she said. "He stole a BP contract for $750,000 intended for boom protection for the oil spill, and was sent away." She looked away, ashamed.

Tripp was silent. He was shocked. He noticed the resemblance of Lucy's misguided, incarcerated father, feeling somewhat sorry for her—and her forlorn mother. "Unreal," he thought. "This is Whitman's old lady!" A million thoughts raced inside his swimming head.

"So you are Mary Whitman?" He asked, sounding understanding.

"Yes." She answered, unaware that Tripp was her husband's anathema.

***

It has been said that music is the balm that heals the ache of a forlorn heart. There is unequivocal evidence that music and humans share a special harmony in our universal existence. Artful vibration has the power to raise our level of consciousness, to stir us to action and even to heal us. In antiquity, healers used vibrations and frequency—music therapy—to improve and maintain physical and psychological health. They learned that various music frequencies can affect brain areas, including those regions associated with emotion, cognition, sensation and movement.

For example, 528Hz is referred to as the "miracle" tone. Its therapeutic application was proposed by Dr. Leonard Horowitz. He believed that 528Hz is the median of all mathematical calculations of music. Horowitz stated that 528Hz is the "frequency of love," and that is the epicenter of all good things, and that music filtered out through this frequency could greatly improve our existence and plight; even repairing damaged DNA.

Another essential and effective frequency is 432Hz. Music tuned to this frequency is softer and brighter, giving us greater mental clarity and insight, while falling easier on our ears. Meditation music tuned to 432Hz is relaxing and harmonious for the body and mind. 432Hz works at the heart chakra and influences positively the spiritual development of its listeners, increasing joy and relaxation simultaneously. 432Hz is also more closely aligned with the geometrical Phi ratio, which is 1.618, the universally accepted blueprint for nature on which most natural processes are based upon, like how your hair knows how to grow, how your body knows how to synthesize proportionally so you appear human, and how trees and plants know how to photosynthesize so that each leaf receives the proper amount of water and sunlight, enabling it to exist. Phi is also known as the divine proportion, the ideal mix humans attempt to approximate to every single day of our lives.

18

Lucy and Johnny finished their third set under the tent around 9:30 p.m. in time for the Jenna McClelland Band, a real up-and-coming group of youngsters that had been making waves, to set up for the final gig of the night, in the 10-2 slot. Lucy was hungry and she and Johnny suggested to her mother and Mr. Francis that they hit Hub Stacey's on the way back home and grab a bite. Mary was certifiably tipsy from several glasses of pinot, while Mr. Francis had had his share of tequila shooters. They both could have used a light snack to even out.

Francis was still stewing on the obvious fact that Mary was a married woman in a most unusual predicament; he had not yet fully processed the unlikely coincidence of it all—how incredibly small the world often seems; nor had he divulged that he was the sole whistleblower responsible for her husband's incarceration—and that he still lived with his ex-wife. Despite their apparent attraction to one another, he knew these were obstacles to Mary and him eventually hooking up. He resigned to himself, as always, that these things were never easy, but that this particular ascent into the foggy unknown—even to a seasoned dog like himself, seemed more complicated than imaginable, possibly much more trouble than fulfillment and fun. Nevertheless, he pressed on, his libido and adventurous side, the guider of him.

Hub Stacey's off Innerarity Point Road was crowded, as usual. Johnny Barbado and the Lucky Dogs were wailing on the porch, where guitar riffs and cold beer competed with the steady Intracoastal breeze to cool off the locals bent on relaxation, stellar eats, good vibes and interesting company. Johnny and Lucy and Francis and Mary ventured inside, into the air conditioning, where it was quieter and they could better have a conversation amongst themselves. They found a booth, ordered waters with wedged lemon and settled in. The early part of the conversation revolved around the breaking news concerning the impending national Heineken virus lockdowns and the strange mask mandate—and whether or not they would be enforced by the local government officials who relied on the tourist tax dollars to pay their bills. After that, the conversation turned more personal, if not predictable.

"Y'all were great tonight," said Francis. "I'm sure you hear it often, but you're talented. I was impressed. I had a lot of fun listening and watching you two perform."

"It was terrific!" Mary added, beaming with admiration and pride.

"Thank you so much!" Johnny answered. "That's nice of you to say." He smiled and looked to Lucy. "We've been playing a lot lately and I think it's paying off."

"I'd say," Francis added, smiling bright.

Lucy smiled in return. She looked to Francis and prodded, noticing the absence of a wedding band on both of their fingers. She wondered what her mother was up to; and more importantly— what he was up to.

"Mr. Francis do you have a family back in Fairhope?"

"I do." He replied. "I have a daughter and an ex-wife. My daughter is married with two kids. They live right down the street which makes me a very lucky grandpa!"

"That's wonderful!" Mary interjected.

"I have pictures of them here in my phone," He bragged, retrieving them. "This is Ezra and this is his sister, Delilah. They're five and three years old…and they love my pancakes!"

***

After finishing their meal at Hub's Johnny and Lucy and Mary announced it was time to return home to their cottage just down Innerarity Point Road. Before they left Francis and Mary had a quiet moment together in the bleached clam shell parking lot, under the weeping Spanish moss of the diminutive, salt-soaked live oak trees that scattered the late evening scene.

"Mary I had a great time hanging out today." He said. "You are a lot of fun. Maybe we could do it again sometime—maybe we could get together in Fairhope."

It had been a long day. Mary was tired but she was buoyed by his words.

"If you are so inclined." He added, smiling optimistically.

"Maybe so." She smiled in reply. She looked over her shoulder and saw Johnny and Lucy in their vehicle, waiting. It was a little awkward.

"How can I get in touch with you?" She asked.

He retrieved his wallet. He pulled out his card and handed it to her.

"Give me a call and we can get together." He stated. "Good evening Mary."

He leaned in and kissed her lightly on the cheek, giving her a final scent of his cologne.

As he walked away, Mary looked quickly to see if the kids saw the kiss; and then read the unusual, navy blue business card. After connecting the dots, she looked up, astonished, as his faded blue suburban left the parking lot ahead of a gray dust plume.

***

Joe Gideon met with his assistant, Vonnie, inside his home office off of South Loop Road in Pensacola. She had a box full of Flora-Bama masks, the simple surgical kind with yellow Flora-Bama classic font emblazoned upon them.

"I hope this is what you wanted, Joe. It's all they had."

Joe envisioned the bright advertising idea after he saw the mask mandate announcement on TV.

"I think these will do just fine. We might as well promote the Flora-Bama if we have to wear these darn things!"

"Oh I forgot, the doctor called." Replied Vonnie. "He said to come in this morning and he would see you right away."

"Oh good," Joe answered. "I have to figure out what's wrong with me."

A Flora-Bama mask-wearing Joe Gideon sat patiently in the cold doctor's office patient room, waiting on his long-time friend, Jim Solace, to give him the news. He'd spent the last two hours providing blood and urine samples, as he still felt strangely awful.

The patient room door swung open and in walked Dr. Jim. He did not wear his usual smile. Instead, he wore a look of concern, one closer to consternation and dismay.

Joe noticed. He anticipated a stern answer to his stinging health problems.

"Joe, you have tested positive for the Heineken virus."

Joe's worst fears were realized. He imagined a slow, and painful death, changing completely his normally upbeat countenance.

"But I don't want you to worry about it!" The doctor insisted. The doc moved into action. He grabbed a prescription pad and filled it out quickly, scribbling his illegible signature at the end. He retrieved a light green surgical mask from his white coat pocket and looped the elastic bands firmly around his ears, muffling his voice.

"You are going to be fine, Joe. I am prescribing hydroxychloroquine, baby aspirin, and zinc. Take all three as directed and you should be fine in a week or so."

He handed the prescription to Joe.

Joe was somewhat relieved. The doc seemed overly confident.

"You are my first Heineken virus patient! I corresponded with a European colleague in Spain who has been highly successful with this treatment mix. Just take the zinc and hydroxychloroquine as recommended and two or three aspirin a day for pain and discomfort and you'll be back to normal in a week to ten days."

Joe perked up.

"So that's it? I'm not gonna die?" Joe implored, "No thanks to you, of course!"

"Joe, the rumors of your demise have been greatly exaggerated." The doc smiled.

Joe grinned from ear-to-ear.

***

"The attorney for the City of Orange Beach called me yesterday." Said Greg McMakin, inside his office. "They are ready to settle."

Francis Tripp beamed, sitting before him in creeping running shorts, sandals and a smudged white muscle shirt; a large, steaming cup of coffee hooked in his calloused right hand.

"How much are they willing to pay?" He asked.

"They've offered fifteen grand." McMakin replied, smiling, knowing he had barely lifted a pen for a ten grand commission.

"No way! Tell them sixty!" Tripp replied, matter-of-factly. "They know they're in trouble!"

"They will never pay sixty." McMakin answered, seeing his easy money drifting away.

"I know that; but I want at least thirty—because I have to pay you 70 percent, and I'm going to use the money against Kenner in his re-election campaign!"

McMakin relented. "Okay, I'll give them the counter offer and we'll see how it goes."

"They'll come around," Tripp insisted. "They have no choice. They can't let this go to court!"

"You think Kenner will have competition? I doubt he will." McMakin replied, obviously in the dark.

Tripp smiled enthusiastically and nodded, in total affirmation. Before donning a black mask and exiting, he uttered, "You can bet on it!"

19

The following day McMakin called Tripp with news that the City of Orange Beach had offered a check for thirty grand in a knee-jerk response to his hefty counter offer.

"Ah hah! I told you Greg! I told you they'd come around!" He stammered into his cell.

"Are you good with 30 grand?"

"I'm good with it!" Tripp replied.

"All right then, I'll let them know. We should have a check in the next couple days. The city attorney told me he would cut it now if we would agree to settle. I reckon they want this to end quickly."

"Too bad for them," he replied.

"What do you mean?" Greg asked.

"Oh I'm just getting started," Tripp replied, reaching for a fresh cigar.

"That reminds me," Greg replied. "There's a confidentiality agreement—you can't talk about the settlement on your blog or anywhere else. You have to keep quiet."

Tripp laughed. "Tell them to cut the check."

***

On Monday a mask-wearing Big Earl followed through on his promise and qualified to run for Mayor in Orange Beach, posting the $50 cash fee required with his signature and proof of residency.

The City Clerk was shocked when Earl walked in wearing a white mask that conspicuously read "Big Earl 4 Mayor in large block red font.

"I'm here to sign up to run against Donny," Earl stated without hesitation. He was quickly and politely accommodated by the clerk.

Before Big Earl left the building the clerk had texted Mayor Kenner that he had competition in the upcoming election. She had agreed beforehand to tip off the mayor on any candidate signing up, but never thought that there would actually be anyone brave enough to contest him, as he was seen as omnipotent in the tiny gulf side village, even despite his unpopular leanings toward the condo developers. The electronic message sent to Mayor Kenner was as brief as it was alarming:

"Mayor—Big Earl just signed up to run against you!"

The clerk was specific. "Big Earl" was exactly how he signed his name on the ballot requirement, which meant that the name that would appear on the ballot on the day of the election—September 26th, would be "Big Earl" and not his formal name, Earl Roberts. This was as funny as it was practical, for Earl, as his stage name was well-known and certainly more recognizable than his real name, which meant it would help his chances and lower those of his adversary—incumbent Donny Kenner.

***

Joe Gideon's cell phone rang. He was propped up supine in his usual spot on the couch on the second floor of his ranch home off South Loop Road, easing into his Heineken virus prescriptions as the doctor ordered. Much to his surprise and happiness, he was already beginning to feel better. He found his cell phone under a thick wool blanket, donned his glasses and looked at its face. It read: "Francis Tripp." He took the call.

"Hello there Mr. Tripp! Good to hear from you! How are things in your world?"

"Things are moving fast, Joe! I just picked up a check for nine grand from my attorney, Greg McMakin, for settling out of court my federal law suit against the City of Orange Beach for denying me my constitutional right to free speech! I think it's time to call a meeting, because I just read online on the Orange Beach website that Big Earl—like he promised—signed up to run against Donny Kenner for Mayor! I like our chances, Joe! Donny Kenner is as dirty as a shrimp fest porto-potty and I can prove it! He's in deep with the developers! Him and Butrell from Fairhope both are. I know they are!"

Joe sat up straight against the back of the sofa, his left leg brought up in an upside down V position, his left hand on his knee, his right clasping his cell phone on speaker mode. His head swam in thought. He knew Earl intended to run, based on their earlier conversation. The nine grand was a total surprise, and he knew it amounted to serious ammo for the impending political battle.

"Wait a minute, you got a $9,000 settlement from the City of Orange Beach?"

"Yes Sir!" Tripp answered.

"Well, well, well…" Joe began. "I guess it is time for a meeting. I tell you what, let me reach out to Big Earl and a couple of other local characters who can help and we'll set a meeting by the end of the week. We'll lay this thing out and figure out our strategy. This is certainly looking promising."

Joe paused.

"Just to get a bead on how you feel early on, what do you think about Earl's chances?" He asked.

Tripp replied, "I'd say 50-50, considering Big Earl's popularity. If we can get the media to cover the race and reveal some of Kenner's developer dealings, then I think it could be 60-40 in Earl's favor, but that's gonna be the crux of it—we've got to get people to see Donny's bad news for Orange Beach—and that's going to be tough, considering he's their favorite son. His Dad's still a legend because of football."

Joe agreed with his careful line of political thought.

"Alright Tripp, I'll be in touch within the next couple of days. Sit tight."

"Right on, Joe. Lemme know."

***

Joe returned his focus to the big screen TV where he caught the evening news segment showing Jacque Butrell speaking to the Alabama Legislature's afternoon enactment of the n ew gas tax to build toll roads and bridges considerably shortening the route down Interstate 65 to Orange Beach. While Joe liked the idea of more patrons possibly visiting the Flora-Bama, he also knew well that the energy thieves in Montgomery had their grimy sights firmly set on erecting more debilitating high rise condos, which could have a counter-acting and disastrous effect in terms of quality of life lost. He knew Kenner and Butrell were pals. He knew Tripp was right. He knew it was time for him to act.

Earlier that year, Joe had quietly contemplated selling out to his partners, tired of witnessing up-close what he thought was an excruciating demise of Orange Beach and Perdido Key. Now, he was resolved to fight back—hard. He picked up his cell phone and dialed Brad Masterson. Brad picked up after the second ring.

"Brad—hello there—could you meet me at Strick-9's in a couple of days? I'm planning a meeting and I'm thinking I'm going to need your help again…"

20

After hanging up with architect Brad Masterson Joe got a call from singer-songwriter Johnny Glass. It seemed Johnny was in the neighborhood and wanted to stop by. Joe welcomed the visit, as he had not seen Johnny in weeks. He wanted to get a first-hand update on how he and Lucy were making out in their new digs off Innerarity Point Road, how Lucy was coming along, and how life was in general for the two would-be parents, as he knew that was challenging.

Minutes later Johnny let himself in downstairs and yelled up to Joe.

"Anybody home?"

"Who's there?" Joe implored.

"It's Johnny!" He yelled, removing his Flora-Bama mask.

"Johnny! Come on up! I'm just watching TV. Grab us a couple of bottled waters from the fridge before you make it up here, will you?

Oh—and wear your mask—I have the Heineken virus. You'll just have to keep your distance."

The two settled in, a careful six feet apart, on separate, opposing couches, making small talk about the many weird changes occurring in their little world tucked far away from the maddening crowd. The Flora-Bama had surreally been shuttered for several days, per the national mandate, and Johnny and Lucy were now both living on unemployment—like the rest of the Flora-Bama workers and musicians—out of necessity to stay alive. The Florida unemployment website was overwhelmed at first, as a result of the avalanche of forced benefit seekers, but it had caught up after crashing numerous times during its first few busy days. Most if not all of the shift workers and musicians and songwriters had gotten through and enrolled after repeated futile attempts, their lives successfully upended. Joe talked about how the BP oil spill and past hurricanes and his financial problems had threatened the Flora-Bama in the past, but that he had never imagined a pandemic shuttering the revered honky tonk.

"So you guys are doing okay?" Joe asked. "Are you able to meet all of your needs? What about Lucy? Is she able to go to the doctor for regular checkups for her and the baby?"

"Yeah, we're fine, Joe. Since Lucy and her Mom started talking again she's been getting money from her to help with prenatal care. She likes her doctor. She's had regular visits. Things are looking good for the baby. It should be here around Christmas. Everything else is good. We just wish we were still playing gigs. Lucy is starting to show now and it's unlikely she'll be going back to performing if this lockdown thing lasts more than a couple of weeks like they're saying."

"Who's saying it's gonna last longer than two weeks?" Joe asked unapologetically through his mask.

"Everybody," Johnny replied, looking incredulously at Joe over his mask, his green eyes piercing above the lettered cloth. "Pretty much everybody in the media."

"Really?"

Johnny shook his head up and down in firm affirmation, maintaining a willful stare above the fraying navy blue cloth mask.

"Ugh," Joe managed, thinking of the dire economic consequences that awaited them. There was a moment of silence. Joe sensed there was something else on Johnny's mind, something they'd not yet talked about, something other than the negative.

"So I guess you didn't come here to talk about the Heineken virus." Joe stated. "What else is going on?"

Moments later Johnny cleared his throat and spoke, by the hardest.

"Mr. Joe, I hate to ask you for any more help. You've been so good to us. You really have."

He paused. Joe listened.

"But I want to do the right thing here and I need a little money in order to do it. I swear I will pay you back fast—as soon as I possibly can. I'll get another job on the side until I do," he added.

"What is it?" Joe asked. "What is it you want to do?"

Johnny pulled off his mask, so Joe could see his youthful, handsome face.

"I want to marry Lucy. But I need a wedding ring. Nothing too expensive; something simple and pretty; something she'll be happy with. Just something she'll be proud of."

He paused.

"I visited the downtown pawn shop off Palafox Street today. There's a nice little ring I can get for just under a grand. If you could lend me a dime I'll pay you back in a few weeks, I promise, Mr. Joe."

Joe felt sorry for him and his predicament. On the other hand, he was proud of Johnny. He had done everything he intended since coming to the island on a fateful whim. He'd found a gig in paradise—actually multiple gigs. In the process he unexpectedly found love; and a family. Now he was in the throes of a pandemic and the clip of a fast-changing, non-discriminating world. His life had changed irreparably. Everyone's lives had. In spite of the tumult, he was still trying to do good—the best he could. It was more than admirable. It was the right thing, to help him.

"Of course I can lend you the money, Johnny. Because I know you'll pay me back."

Joe pulled out a blank sheet of typing paper from a nearby folder. He placed it on the coffee table with an ink pen. He gestured to Johnny as he spoke.

"Write out an IOU for $1,000. Date and sign it. Pay me back when you can. I know you're good for it."

He paused. Johnny went for the paper and pen as instructed, completing the task.

"Thanks Mr. Joe"

"Thank you Johnny. I'm proud to know a stand up guy like you."

Joe reached into a nearby bank envelope resting on the cluttered coffee table before him, thick with hundred dollar bills. He removed the pack of Benjamins and counted ten, crispy Federal Reserve backed notes. He handed them to Johnny. He hesitated—before handing him another. Johnny took the cash and counted out eleven bills.

"There's one too many here," he asserted, looking oddly to Joe for an explanation.

"I did that on purpose—an early wedding gift!" Joe said with a peaking smile that broke the faint edges of his mask.

"Thanks Mr. Joe! I'll never forget this." Johnny said.

And neither would Joe.

***

Mayor Donny Kenner and Jacque Buttrell met for breakfast at Hazel's Nook in Orange Beach, their regular eating and meeting spot. They wore their standard dressy beach attire of shiny fishing shorts and starched, collared short-sleeved designer sport shirts, gaudy gold jewelry, expensive, Swiss-engineered, automatic watches, sandals and cologne. They also wore tired looks of festering consternation, a sure reminder of their preoccupation and concern with the precarious con game they were playing with the locals. Pretending to be men of the people while screwing the people was a difficult tight rope act—especially for the crippled and the compromised. It required a special dedication of the mind and a particular, willful abandonment of the heart. Each player was being fully tested, their wits fully exposed. Neither was doing well with it.

"Who put Big Earl up to this?" Buttrell asked, chewing his eggs and toast, his tanned brow furrowing an angry look.

"I don't think anybody did," Kenner replied. "He confronted me a few weeks ago saying he was tired of all the high-rise development. He was bitching about the traffic and all that jazz. I guess he's just fed up—like most everyone else on the island."

There was a hollow ring to the mayor's voice, like he had already resigned himself to losing re-election to a crooning comedian he once called a friend. Buttrell, however, would not allow it.

"Wise up Donny!" Jacque insisted. "You're still going to win this race!"

"How are you so sure?" He questioned with a jaundiced eye. "Big Earl is stronger than new rope! Early polling by Southern Strategies out of Montgomery has him at 95 percent name recognition. I'm at 71—and I'm the mayor! All Earl has to do is sing and tell jokes. He can promise anything or nothing. Nobody's gonna care! Me? I have to answer for all the condo development! Plus—I had to pay Francis Tripp 30 grand to settle his federal lawsuit challenging me on not allowing him to speak at the council meeting. He hasn't said anything yet—there was a confidentiality clause written into the settlement—but I'm afraid of him. The guy is fearless and he and that blog of his will be a huge problem leading to the election. There's no way around him. He's the 900-pound gorilla in the room!"

Buttrell finished chewing and spoke, his face contorted in ruddy anger.

"You cut Tripp a check for 30 grand?" He asked.

"Not me—the City Attorney did. I had no choice. He had us. I disallowed him free speech at an open forum. It was either pay something now or pay more later and go through a nasty trial with unwanted negative media attention right before the election."

"Jesus H. Christ!" Butrell complained. "He's gonna use that money against us!"

"There was nothing I could do, Jacque. He had us!"

"That son of a bitch!" Buttrell proclaimed. "How can we get to him? We have to neutralize him somehow!"

"I don't know! You tell me! You're the one who said not to worry about him—about us having the power! Well he scares me Jacque! The son of a bitch is crazy!"

They both continued their breakfast, chewing and drinking coffee. After a few silent moments, Buttrell spoke.

"What's his weakness?"

"I don't know much about the guy," Kenner replied. "I just know he's on a mission."

"Who's his attorney?"

"Greg McMakin. He's a friend—at least I consider him a friend. I'm sort of upset about it. I'm losing friends as fast as voters these days."

"Well ask him why the hell he's helping Tripp sue you! He owes you an explanation if he's a friend!"

He paused. "I know someone who can find out more about Tripp." Buttrell added.

"What are you thinking?" Kenner asked.

"A private dick. We can get one to look into him and Earl. Gather intel we are unaware of on both adversaries. From there we can formulate a plan on how to win—how to defeat them. This is war, Donny. All is fair."

Donny twitched nervously. He thought of the trite, "love, war and politics" line. Buttrell was upping the stakes—big time. He was now conflicted—big time. Donny didn't give a flip about Tripp. He loathed the guy—and he feared that silly blog of his. But he still liked Greg McMakin and Big Earl—he actually felt sorry for them. Even he knew the island was on the fast track to hell in a hand basket—he just couldn't see past the easy money. The conflict of interest was real to him now, in multiple ways, his selfish interests be damned.

"Then do it," Kenner insisted. "We can't afford to lose. If we do we lose our cover for all the deals we've made; and plan to make. If that happens, then they'll run us out of Baldwin County for good, and that's just the start of it."

Buttrell cracked an eager smile, scraping and finishing with a fork and butter knife the last morsels of his early meal.

"Don't worry—I'm on it. I know what to do." He assured.

21

Joe Gideon, Francis Tripp, Brad Masterson, Big Earl and Barry Strick-9—all mask-less, met on Barry's new floating house, the luxury fishing vessel parked behind the Flora-Bama Yacht Club. Barry's shack next door had been emptied, readied for impending demolition in a matter of days. Only a few odds and ends hanging from the tattered walls remained; the storied, dated ephemera and hanging detritus from more than three decades of decadence and fun crashing in Boys Towne across from the world-famous honky-tonk lounge and package store. It was a legendary run.

Joe took center stage, standing in the cramped living room of the comfortable sport vessel, the other gentlemen seated around him on the white leather couch, padded barstools and matching chairs adorning the posh, comfortable recreational space. The air conditioner purred in the background, cooling and removing the thick moisture from the humid outside air, making it pleasant inside the tinted, luxury cabin.

"Gentlemen, I appreciate each of you taking time out of your busy schedules to join us here today. As you know our world has undergone considerable turmoil these past few months and years. The energy thieves in Washington and at home seem more empowered than ever. It seems like we're living in the twilight zone; I keep telling myself. If it's not an oil spill, a financial crisis or overdevelopment, it's a pandemic—and the apparent overreaction from it—the unfortunate negative economic impacts caused by the lockdowns and the ridiculous mask mandates. All I can say right now is that I'm thankful we haven't had another hurricane, or we might all be goners!"

There was a grumbling among the cheap seats in affirmation.

"Don't even think of it! Don't want none of that!" Big Earl insisted. "Nope—not gonna do it! Forget a hurricane!"

"Yeah—that would be icing on the shit cake!" Barry interjected. "That's the absolute last thing we need right now—a hurricane!" Barry had experienced several hurricanes—and they were all terrible experiences he'd rather forget.

Joe continued.

"Well, we're here to talk about doing something about our difficult situation. We, as citizens, must try and deal with this. And we are trying to do something, as we must, to make a difference. This is why we are here."

Joe paused for effect. He scanned the tiny quarters, eyeing each friend.

"The old adage says that all politics are local. And because of that, it is important that we have good candidates from our community to vote for. Without good people you have a system without hope. So, when Earl called me and told me he was planning on running for mayor—I was excited, as he's got as good as a chance as anyone to unseat Donny Kenner—a guy I feel has more than worn out his welcome these past couple of terms. Overdevelopment, I fear, has irreparably changed the area I once saw as an easy-going getaway for those who were tired of the hustle and bustle of the unforgiving, dreaded real world. For years we strived to be a place where folks could come and enjoy themselves and leave everything behind. Sadly, all that stuff—the trappings of civilization, are now here—it's part of us; and it's sickening."

He paused. His audience, transfixed, was as silent as it was somber.

"So we're here today to talk openly and come up with a plan to defeat Kenner and get Earl elected so that we can hopefully buck the trend. I figure as long as we still care, there's hope!"

He paused again. Each man in attendance listening wore a look of admonishment and self-pity. Each wondered how it had gotten so bad. They shared Joe's concerns. They were finally trying to wrap their head around the conundrum—that thing nobody wanted to deal with all these years. The thing they feared.

"And with that I'll turn it over to Earl—our next mayor here in Orange Beach."

Joe motioned to Earl and sat down on the couch next to Strick-9. There was a smattering of applause and a wolf whistle by Brad. Earl stood and addressed the group. Tripp listened intently. Earl wore shorts, flip-flops and an indiscriminate, plain white tee shirt and an Arkansas Razorback Hogs baseball cap. He was his normal, jovial self; but seemed determined, in a way other than achieving laughter from his audience.

"Like Joe, I too appreciate each of you coming here. I will definitely need your help to win this race! Donny has the money and the connections and of course, he's the incumbent, so it's going to be an uphill battle. But, I'm better looking, can sing and play better and likely have more friends than him since he's been more concerned with building condos than taking care of the city; so there's that!"

There were several chuckles that bounced around the wheelhouse. Earl continued. He withdrew a folded sheet of paper from his pocket and read from it.

"Here I have a short list of campaign promises I'm going to offer the citizens of Orange Beach. I thought I'd share them with you fellas."

He read aloud:

"Number one: Free bushwhackers and bingo for all housewives between one and four o'clock—along with free, on-site babysitting and taxi cab service to and from home and the Flora-Bama."

Joe and Tripp laughed heartily, as did Barry and Brad.

"Number two: No more damn condos on the beach!"

He paused. They laughed together again.

"That's all I got so far. I told you, it's a short list."

"I think it's perfect," replied Tripp. "You make em' laugh and then remind them of the most important issue—overdevelopment—and its negative effects on quality of life. It's the most important issue because it's the one most tied to corruption. Kenner and his pal Buttrell and their Montgomery cronies are making big bucks at the expense of everyone in Orange Beach—while pretending to care."

"How do you know this? How do you know they're corrupt?" Brad Masterson asked, intervening. "I mean, it's one thing to say it, but can you prove it? We need proof in order to say it with conviction—to make it stick. By recorded votes we can prove they've supported development—but how are they corrupt? We have to prove they're making money off of new development; that they're benefitting directly from these legal votes allowing it to happen."

"These guys think they're slick," Tripp replied. "They operate under anonymous LLC's registered in other states. Their construction partners do the financing work for them and kick them back the money after they get their proposals passed by the planning commission and city council and the buildings are built—often not to code or recommendation. Kickbacks come in many forms. They are creative. Sometimes they get cash. Sometimes they get property in the form of condo units that they quickly flip. It's not easy to trace this stuff. But—we do have their voting records, like you said. You're right—we need proof they're making money off the building and sale of the condos they approve—that they're involved in that aspect—not just the political passage at the planning commission and council levels. So yeah—you're right—we need proof of their involvement and obvious benefit."

There was a sullen moment.

"How about a sex scandal?" Barry asked without provocation, grinning dastardly.

Joe answered. "What do you mean?" His eyebrows lifted.

"I mean, what if we could prove there was some hanky-panky going on?" Barry countered defensively.

"That'd be good too," Tripp answered, knowing well he needed ammo for the court of public opinion—and that negative campaigning worked best. "What do you know that we don't, Barry? But remember—it's the same standard—Brad's right—we need proof!"

Strick-9 smiled. "Well, I don't have Polaroids, but I saw the mayor's wife the other day on a huge boat parked right here next to this one. It was a damn yacht—probably 90 feet. At first they didn't see me. She was on their back deck in a tiny black bikini having a martini and making out with another guy—and I'm positive it was her; and it was definitely not her husband hugging and kissing and groping her."

Tripp leapt to his feet. "Wait a second! Was it this guy?" He exclaimed. Using his smart phone, Tripp searched the Internet for an image. From DuckDuckGo he showed the head shot and collage of related pictures to Barry. Barry grabbed the phone and held it closer to him. He pulled his glasses up from the lanyard where they hung and squinted through the bifocals, holding them just right.

"Yeah—that's him!" Barry confirmed. "That's definitely him—it's the same tan and the same gray hair. Same build. What's his name?"

"Jacque Buttrell. He's the President of the Fairhope City Council and the Coastal Chamber of Alabama—the local champion of the growth movement. He's the face man for the builders and developers."

"Oh yeah?" Barry retorted. "Well, he's jabbing the mayor's wife as far as I can tell, so how's that for a face?"

Joe grimaced.

"It was definitely her, too!" Barry continued. "There's only one Layla! I was sure of it. That body of hers is incredible, man!"

"Damn, I'd like to see that in a bikini!" Tripp interjected.

"Let me tell you what!" Barry confided in disbelief. "Wooiee! That's some hot stuff!"

"Well I'll be," chimed Big Earl. "The mayor is not only a sellout—he's a cuck!"

Brad laughed heartily.

"A cuck?" Barry asked, in the dark.

"Yeah—a cuckold," Brad explained. "Somebody else is doing his wife—obviously like he can't. Donny ain't taking care of his 'bidness' so somebody else is!"

"Ahh…" Barry imagined, giving closure. "I see. You learn something every day."

"Now look guys we don't need to go this low. I don't think it is right to bring Donny's wife into it." Joe insisted, wanting it not to be a gutter fight, trying to maintain some semblance of citizen decorum.

Tripp countered, "Joe, if you're in public life, if you hold elected public office in the U.S., you need to remember that you are held to a higher standard of judgment and accountability. It's called the

Public Doctrine. Basically, if you are public official your life is an open book."

"But not his wife's!" Joe defended his position. "I don't think it is right."

"Well Joe," Big Earl began, "If he isn't taking care of business, I figure it's his problem—and not ours." So, on that I agree with you."

He paused.

"But also, if he's not taking care of business in that area, there's a good chance he's not taking care of business in other areas equally important—and I think the people have a right to know about that kind of a thing."

There was another pregnant pause. Trip continued. "And of course, I think Donny has the right to know that his supposed best friend and alleged business partner is slamming his wife—don't you?"

"You're damned right he does!" Yelled Strick-9, laughing. "That son of a bitch will thank us for it!"

"Oh my God!" said Brad. "This is gonna be a total shit show! I guess Tripp will just put all this on his Internet blog? Straight to the Tripp Report...am I correct?"

"Well of course!" Tripp answered. "Why not? It's free speech, remember? Don't we still live in America?"

Everyone laughed heartily, except for Joe.

"We may not ever need to make it public," Tripp predicted, smiling wryly at Joe, trying to assuage his scrupulous concerns, trying to placate him and his good intentions.

***

Johnny and Lucy sat in a booth at Fisherman's Corner Restaurant, a dilapidated, makeshift wooden, screen-porch building under the Theo Baar Bridge on the eastern side of the Intracoastal. Johnny had conspicuously asked Lucy out on a date, and she was wily suspicious. Although, Fisherman's Corner was their favorite—Creole Italian seafood, and only a few hundred yards from where they lived. They were both dapper, Lucy wearing a bright-colored yellow print maternity dress, her shiny onyx hair and puffy scarlet lips in stark contrast. Johnny wore beige slacks, a button-down,

V-neck short-sleeve and dark brown cowboy boots. His slick hairdo was an impressive waterfall pompadour, gelled to perfection. To anyone, they were a lovely young couple, the veritable portrait of hope and promise; something singular, something special; something approaching unforgettable American iconography and folklore.

"This is so nice, Johnny, us being able to get out and enjoy a meal. It's been tough staying in all the time because of the pandemic. We needed a break."

Johnny felt the ring box in his right pants pocket. His wallet held the eleventh hundred dollar bill Joe gave him, the other ten having secured the important symbol of matrimony. He had thought about this moment many times. He knew he had to get on his knees in order for it to be official—or so he believed. It just seemed that way to Johnny. Everything he'd ever known told him he needed to kneel, in respect, in deference to her.

"I know, right, baby? I mean, I am all for staying safe and all, but these lockdowns are not easy. After a while, people need to be able to go on with their lives. I'm tired of the masks already, to tell you the truth. They said give us two weeks and we're going on two months now. Also, why can people cram into Wal-Mart but not church or a bar? It really makes you wonder."

The elderly waitress took their drink and food orders. They chose shrimp and grits with a fried calamari appetizer, splitting the sizable entrée. Johnny ordered a Jack and Coke while Lucy sipped lemon water and only briefly smelled Johnny's liquor, which she had chosen to refrain from. Johnny felt like it was the right time. He pretended.

"I need to go to the men's room," He stated, sliding to his left in the booth, standing to leave.

Johnny instead stood in place for a second and looked to a seated Lucy, her face aglow in the amber evening light. Johnny retrieved the box from his right pants pocket and as he pulled it in front of him he smoothly genuflected, landing precariously on one knee. Lucy's countenance shifted. She went from contentment to surprise and from surprise to utter joy, as Johnny opened the tiny box, revealing the solitary, sparkling, little diamond set in gold.

"Lucy, will you marry me?" He proudly asked, catching the attention of the four-top table across from them.

Lucy began to cry while smiling. She nodded up and down, cradling first his face to her bosom and tummy; and then the gleaming ring between her tiny hands.

"Yes—I will marry you, Johnny. Yes!"

She pulled him close to her warmth once more and he kissed her on the cheek and then firmly on her puffy, radiant lips, across a searing smile drenched in tears.

22

Armed with new and incriminating intelligence he intended to fully weaponize, the next day Francis Tripp placed a phone call to Fairhope Council President Jacque Buttrell's office. He left a message on his public voice mail for him to please call him, that it was important. He called the Mayor of Orange Beach's office as well, leaving a similar message, asking for a return call, stating he had a pressing matter he needed to discuss. He was busy while he waited.

Trip sat at his computer in his self-proclaimed war room—a dank office space with a tiny window unit and a space heater he maintained in the back yard of his sprawling, assiduously landscaped property. The radiant, window-laden structure was outfitted with a dual computer panel and two large monitors in full display, quite the impressive, technological set-up. He began typing.

The Tripp Report Website and Facebook Page Update Francis Tripp drafted was a real doozey. The title read:

"Mayor of OBA, a Developer, & Fairhope City Council President Jack Buttrell, also a Developer/Adulterer/Kickback Artist, Caught in Fraud Scheme to Enrich Themselves"

The body of the typed message followed:

"It is important to note for my faithful readers and supporters, the citizens, that I maintain a 24-hour, seven days a week Tip Line at the TrippReport.com. This conduit has been a valuable information source in the past and remains so. This week, via the "Tip the Trippster" email tip line on my web page, I received startling new information that the mayor of Orange Beach, Donny Kenner, is apparently unable to sexually satisfy his wife to the point that she must go out and sleep with other men, namely Jack Buttrell, Fairhope City Council President and President of the Alabama Coastal Chamber, a noted business growth and building coalition. It is unfortunate that this information must be made public. It doesn't have to be this way. There is after all, a better way for us to handle our public affairs.

It is also unfortunate there are those who are elected to serve the people but who instead turn on those very people, serving instead themselves and their empowered acquaintances. Donny Kenner and Jack Buttrell abuse the public trust in every way when they act as de facto developers and builders of high-rise condos and pretend as elected officials to simultaneously support and protect the quality of life of the citizenry they simultaneously dupe. These guys are terrible. They are liars at best and thieves who have stolen your community with empty promises, treachery, bribery and dishonesty. Each deserves a cold, windowless jail cell."

He finished the update by imploring each citizen to contact both public officials via provided email links that went directly to their public accounts, along with the final, overriding directive and action call:

"Get Involved. Stay Active. Have a Voice. Vote."

Tripp emailed the Tripp Report draft to each of the men in question, blind copied in plain view on the electronic receipt. He stated he was going to go public the next day if he did not hear from them both, and that he expected a call by noon tomorrow—or else. He also told them not to talk to one another. Now it was just a waiting game. As he hit the send button on the incendiary email Tripp got a giddy feeling like a kid who got away with something he should be duly punished for. He admitted he enjoyed it all too much, but this was not easy work, this vital slog he was involved in; and he reminded himself that it was important to relish the good days in battle along with the small wins, as they were hard-fought and few, in the grand scheme of things—in the larger scope of the war against the machine, as Tripp was a former Marine, and a trained warrior—and overall—wholly different from the average citizen.

***

Jacque Buttrell drove his black SUV with super-size mag wheels, curb finders and dark tint fast down Highway 59 from Foley to Gulf Shores, late to a meeting with the mayor of Gulf Shores about a new condo and restaurant development at the foot of Highway 59, a historic area where the main beach-bound artery met the gleaming Gulf of Mexico in a conspicuous T. An impromptu decision to play morning golf put him off schedule. The itinerary change delayed his call to the private detective he wanted to hire to fully investigate Francis Tripp and Big Earl. After lunch, he had more pressing matters; and the task was again delayed.

The successful young owner of the Hangout planned a large hotel, condos, retail and restaurant space in the new development venture, which would further the backdrop of the annual alternative music festival bearing the same name that occurred in late spring. The mayor wanted to introduce Buttrell to the innovative mixed use project, feeling he could help with it, given his vast development acumen and experience, his reputation preceding. The mayor also wanted more development in Gulf Shores like Orange Beach was getting.

When Jacque saw the email from Tripp titled "In Your Best Interest TO READ ASAP" he opened and read it forthwith, while driving. He was so upset by what he read he pulled onto the shoulder of the road, nauseous, sweating, heart palpitating. He again read the email. He became furious—and then scared, as he knew moving forward Tripp had the firm upper hand—and that Donny was no longer his business partner and/or partner in crime. He also knew that he and Layla were done. Compromised fully, there was little wiggle room. For the first time in a long spell Jacque felt lonely and forlorn. It reminded him how he felt when he knew his football career at State was over due to injury.

"God damn it," he said to himself, hating what his miserable life had become as a result of the pursuit of greed and power through unsound choices. He knew he had brought it all upon himself.

***

Mayor Donny Kenner sat inside his office at Orange Beach City Hall. After reading Tripp's email he physically gagged. Clammy, he contemplated suicide by gun shot, but quickly chickened out and caught his hurting, spinning head. His eyes watering, he composed himself and tempered his anger toward his straying wife—and then more appropriately, focused and stoked it for Jacque—the man who royally betrayed him and took what was lawfully his—his proudest, if not most forgotten possession—his gorgeous bride, Layla. Donny wanted to kill the unforgiveable bastard interloper, thinking again of his rifle or gun—with the trigger cocked against the ear of one Jacque Buttrell. He tried to stay calm and think things through. Any rash decision could be the end of him. He sat still as a statue in his padded leather chair, contemplating his few available options.

"Who will I call first?" He wondered. "Tripp or Buttrell?" He hated Tripp less, he admitted to himself, and was reminded of the adage—the enemy of my enemy is my friend.

Francis Tripp knew that for Buttrell and Kenner this was one of those unenviable situations. He realized he had the two of them—quintessential politicians, in an untenable jam. In Layla's infidelity he had the perfect bargaining chip—the one thing Mayor Kenner could not allow known—above all else. If it was ever leaked that the mayor's wife was making a cuckold of him, it would all be over. Kenner would have no hope as he would be socially emasculated and a political eunuch, not to mention—an embarrassing cuckold. The two went hand-in-hand. Donny saw clearly he had to push to keep this quiet at all costs; and he realized that he had much less to lose than Jacque—as it was Jacque with the notable banking and developer buddies who were making them rich through secret LLC's.

Kenner surmised he was only guilty of voting and swaying the council to vote for Buttrell's projects, as the cash, gifts and favors he'd received as perks for playing ball came from Buttrell himself—and no one else, making Jacque, and not him, the bigger fish the feds would want to fry if all this came out. If he had to, Donny imagined he would rat out the son of a bitch if necessary, but he knew most of the questions would be for Jacque, given the arrangement. Also, he knew Jacque had done dozens of deals with other municipalities. These reasonable thoughts gave him solace. He knew well these were uncharted waters for both of them and that he needed to look out for himself. Donny picked up his cell and dialed his attorney friend, Greg McMakin.

"Hey Donny," Greg said answering the phone. "What's up?"

"I need your help. I know you represent Francis Paul Tripp..."

***

Mayor Kenner phoned Mr. Tripp's number. Tripp picked up promptly on the third ring.

"Francis Tripp here," He spoke into the phone, after pressing the green button.

"Mr. Tripp, this is Mayor Donny Kenner."

Tripp put the call on speaker. "Hello there, Mayor Kenner. Thanks for getting back with me so quickly. I appreciate the attention and the respect."

Mayor Kenner didn't like his tone. In fact, he hated it. But he didn't have a choice. He was now operating under Tripp's rules. He realized this.

There was a noted pause, before Tripp again spoke.

"Have you a lawyer?" Tripp asked. "Have you spoken to counsel?"

"I have." The mayor replied.

"Who might that be?" Tripp asked.

"Greg McMakin," he answered, provoking a slight chuckle from Tripp.

Donny continued. "Mr. Tripp can we meet somewhere, maybe—just me and you?" He asked through the cell phone placed face up on his desk, speaker turned on.

Tripp preferred being on the phone. It helped his steady cause. He had no reason to meet anywhere. He was in complete control.

"We don't have time for that, Mayor Kenner. It's time for action."

Kenner was mortified. He was silent, but knew Tripp was right. He was completely compromised.

Trip continued. "I am so glad you called me first, Donny. I have not yet heard from Jacque. You don't mind if I call you Donny, do you?"

"Of course not."

"Good, Donny. Look, I need for you to do a couple of things. Understand that I am calling the shots from now on. "

He paused.

"I need for you to help me bring Jacque in. Jacque is in more trouble than you because he has the big money ties. He has used you in all of this—and you let him. I am sure you now understand this, but of course, it's too late."

There was another pregnant pause. He moved in. Donny, silent, listened.

"But you can save yourself, Donny. You have the opportunity to make the best of a really bad situation; but you have to agree to do what I say and if you do, that rat bastard who stole your wife is going to take the big fall for all of this, instead of you. You are in the perfect position to talk to the Feds and get clemency. Jacque is the one directly connected to the bigger fish—the people much higher up on the proverbial food chain, the ones with the real money and the power. Jacque is the bigger player here, the one with multiple LLC's, and he's the one who will take the fall—not you; you're in trouble, but if you do as I say you'll get the lesser of it. I promise you that."

This all sounded great to Donny—especially the revenge aspect. He'd pose as the unfortunate, spell-bound, victim of the fast-talking Mississippian, Jacque Buttrell, Fairhope's biggest imported disappointment—the newfound poster child for political bad acting, the next victim in a long, drab line of broken Alabama politicians, the exact anathema of what he once pretended to be while campaigning. But alas, there was no time or rhyme or reason left for pretending, only time for pain, reflection and sorrow if you were Jacques Buttrell or Donny Kenner, their lives upended, their families shattered, their careers dashed—all for the sake of money and power.

"I will gladly do as you say," Mr. Tripp. "I just want all this to end. I want my wife back. I'll talk to the Feds."

Donny shared Tripp's hunch that the Feds would go easy on him if he rolled over on Buttrell—especially if Tripp was involved; he sensed, like his attorney, that Tripp would be an asset for him moving forward, in this painful, surreal process they were setting into motion. Tripp was astonished at how easy Donny came around.

"Excellent, Donny. You are doing the right thing. Give me until tomorrow. Do NOT talk to Jacque. I will speak to him and get back with you in 24 hours. I will call you tomorrow at this time—at 4:00 p.m."

Tripp hung up on the call and checked his phone. Using an application he downloaded, he recorded the call between him and Donny. He opened the app and played the saved file. When he heard the beginning and confirmed it he smiled from ear-to-ear.

Trip knew Alabama is a one-party consent state, meaning that it is legal to record a phone call as long as one of the participants is aware they are being recorded. Given this, the file was legal, as it had been recorded with Tripp's consent. Tripp texted the audio file to the FBI agent he had worked with before on the Senator Whitman conviction, the one he would soon be calling to confirm a new investigation and bring closure to law enforcement relative to the developing situation, so they could take over.

***

Jacque Butrell twice phoned Donny Kenner's cell phone, five minutes apart. Twice in a somber tone he left a message for him to please return his call. Twice he waited with no answer. He felt hopeless. He dialed Tripp's number and waited.

"Hello Jacque." Tripp said, answering the phone, recognizing the number. It was Jacque's personal cell, he remembered, from the look of it. "So glad you called."

Buttrell was frozen. He was afraid to talk. He shook with fear, perspiring.

"Good afternoon Mr. Tripp." He managed.

"It is for me," he stated, "Not so much for you, though, Mr. City Council President."

Tripp reached for a cigar and lit it, rolling the tobacco between his tanned fingers as he puffed cylindrical rings into the semi-cooled air inside his office, his white incisors gleaming in the cascading natural light.

"This is the deal, Buttrell. This is how it's going down. Listen up."

Tripp pulled hard on the stogie, the nicotine flowing through his teeth, over his lubricated gums and the tip of his rabid tongue, neatly exhaling.

"You are going to resign as President of the Fairhope City Council and you will not seek re-election. You will make a statement to the Feds, as they will be contacting you. I will be calling the United States Attorney's Office in Mobile later today, setting up a meeting for Mayor Kenner to talk to agents about an ongoing kickback scheme involving you, him and the Orange Beach City Council and Planning Commission to overdevelop the beach and further the interests of your bag men.

"Okay," he replied. Like before, Tripp was flabbergasted. He couldn't believe his good fortune. Both of them were rolling over passively. He wondered if they'd talked to each other.

"And most importantly, in all of this—Jacque—nobody finds out about you and Layla Kenner. It ends here. This is your only saving grace, Jacque. As far as you and she are concerned, it never happened, okay? Layla will not be dragged down by all this. She and Donny will deal with their mistakes and their marriage on their own. You will not say anything about the tryst moving forward. Deal with your own problems and don't create anymore for yourself or anyone else. Tell the truth. It will serve you, Jacque. The Federal Correctional System is set up like that."

Tripp had worked with the Feds before. With information provided by Tripp the FBI successfully indicted and prosecuted Senator Slip Whitman in Fairhope, Mary's disgraced, incarcerated husband, over the theft of the BP oil boom contract. He had already experienced success in that esoteric realm. It now preceded him, instilling fear in his every good ole boy detractor associated with the machine.

"But Jacque," he continued. "You also get a chance to go out like a man—with some semblance of tact and respect, giving hope to what will patiently await you on the other side. If you fully cooperate I can see the Feds giving you a break, down the road. You may have to give up a few of your higher associates, but I surmise you will be out in seven years tops, with good behavior, possibly sooner. I've seen it before."

"And again, I'm giving you both—you and Donny, a chance to get out of this honorably. Keep the love triangle stuff out of it. It will be a lot easier to deal with for everyone's families. This keeps your dirty laundry in check, and prevents everyone from forever seeing you in an imperfect light. Don't make it worse. You've already screwed the people enough. Don't completely screw yourself. Keep your word. It's all confidential from here on out. Remember that. If the love triangle stuff comes out—it's a Pandora's Box. The media attention will be ten times worse, I can assure you."

Seven years didn't sound so bad to Jacque. He imagined at least 15 to 20 in every best-case scenario he contrived. Navigating by uneducated imagination the pitfalls of an indictment and then a federal criminal trial and sentencing was horrifying. He felt foolish. He needed to lawyer up. Realizing the propensity of the moment, and the large amount of money he would need for a decent attorney for a wretched situation like this, he checked his back balance on his computer and thought of the best attorney his dirty money could get.

"Mr. Tripp I am going to need expert counsel. I understand what you're saying and trying to do, but I'm going to need a little time. I have to look at this from a legal standpoint."

"I'll give you one day. Call me tomorrow by 2:00 p.m. I'll be waiting to hear from you. Do not jerk me around, Buttrell. I can and will go public if need be. I will rock your world in a keystroke! Remember that."

***

The next day Jacque met with an attorney, a white collar criminal specialist with experience trying cases at the federal level. The would-be counselor required a $100,000 signed retainer check before the meeting ended, if they were to move forward in the representation arrangement. Afterwards, an anxious Jacque Buttrell called Francis Tripp, wanting to talk.

The prior afternoon, Tripp, after ending the call with Jacque, contacted the FBI in Mobile and emailed them documents related to the case against the two corrupted Baldwin County public officials, along with his taped phone conversation with Buttrell. The FBI was waiting to hear from him at the close of the following business day, as to what the next step in the process would be based on feedback from the primary subject, Jacque Buttrell.

"What's the plan, Buttrell?" Tripp asked. "You've lawyered up, I presume?"

"Yes, I have an attorney."

"Well, who is it?"

"Frank Levin."

"Alright, well what does Furlough Frank suggest?"

"He asked me to ask you if you've spoken to the Feds yet."

"I have spoken to the Feds." He replied. "They are very interested in talking to you."

"Okay," he muttered. "I'll sit and talk with them—with my attorney present, of course—I mean, I want Frank to be there."

"Alright then Jacque. I'll make the call. What's the best number for you? This one?"

"This number is fine." He answered.

"Alright. Good enough. I'll be in touch." Tripp finished, ending the call. He phoned the FBI agent he had spoken to the day before and gave her Jacque's cell phone number and the green light to contact him.

"He's ready to talk," Tripp emphatically stated. "He told me so himself."

Buttrell's attorney agreed with Tripp, wholeheartedly, that the Feds would cut him a nice deal if he agreed to discuss and name others' involvement in the high-rise real estate schemes. Buttrell's bigger problem was the sheer number of deals he'd done in Baldwin County—he needed to keep that quiet, as he didn't want to have to do any more time than necessary, given he was allegedly fully cooperating. The game, according to his counsel, was to minimize guilt and live to fight another day. Levin agreed completely that not talking about the affair was important as it helped diminish the rumors regarding his and Donny's sudden resignations and surprising legal revelations admitting guilt in a kickback ruse. A story about two crooked politicians repeatedly lying to their neighbors was dull compared to the same story with a forbidden love triangle. The latter, more salient, titillating fact was what was more concerning, as it would drastically alter the media coverage of their crimes and ultimately, their lives and that of their families and friends. It would also mean more jail time.

Jacque was instructed by his attorney to stay quiet, to talk to the feds exclusively about the two projects in Orange Beach, give them a name or two and be reconciliatory and cooperative toward letting the process play out, meanwhile staying cool, never mentioning the affair.

23

The following day, Jacque Buttrell voluntarily interviewed as a potential defendant with the FBI in their offices in downtown Mobile, Alabama. Francis Tripp was there with the precinct's top brass watching and listening to the interview on recorded closed circuit television pumped into an adjacent room. In an effort to save his skin, Buttrell, with his attorney present, surprisingly gave up three names of men he said had been instrumental in the two high-rise condominium projects. He said that these men were what he called "the big money getters"—the guys who raised the capital needed to build; and that they were the ones who pieced the job off to others who helped rent and sell the units, of course always keeping a large share in the stake.

The FBI used its vast, computer-driven information network to investigate the men named by Buttrell. Preliminary results indicated these bad actors were from the Birmingham and Montgomery, Alabama business circles, and were known developers and bona fide movers and shakers within the state political community, having donated large to the campaign of every major republican player in the state legislature. Each had ties to business and industry, with a particular, recent bent toward real estate development in Lower Alabama, particularly the Gulf Shores and Orange Beach areas. The men together were listed as principals or equity investors in 38 LLC's spread across Florida, Alabama, Mississippi and Louisiana.

***

Big Earl met with Francis Tripp and Joe Gideon at the Yacht Club across from Flora-Bama. They found a semi-private, shaded area under a taut red tarp stretched flat with nylon cables cinched with metal fasteners. They were there to talk campaign finance.

"How's the campaign coming along?" Joe implored.

"It's humming," Earl replied. "The feedback has been positive. I've been talking to a lot of folks standing outside Publix supermarket in Orange Beach. The manager lets me stand outside the front door in the mornings and greet people. If they seem supportive I give em' a bumper sticker or a mask—or both."

"Thanks for helping me, fellas. I've already spent four grand on my credit card for the Big Earl 4 Mayor masks, yard signs, push cards and a web page. Oh, and I also ordered the bumper stickers."

"That's a great way of getting exposure," Tripp stated, impressed. "Keep it up!"

Tripp retrieved a blank envelope from his pocket. He pushed it across the wooden picnic table to Earl, who opened it. It was a check for $7,000. Earl was stunned. Trip could tell by the disbelieving look he wore.

"Pay off your credit card and order some radio and newspaper ads—maybe even some tee shirts," Tripp suggested. "I'm using the other $2,000 I got from Orange Beach to promote the Tripp Report and your candidacy on my pages thru facebook boosting. You should get some serious exposure from that. I have over 40,000 followers."

"I have a donation for you also, Earl," Joe added, handing over a signed check for $1,500. "I've encouraged friends to get in touch and make a donation. Hopefully they'll come through for you. Although It seems everyone is leery about being on the record against Donny."

"Yeah, you must report these donations with the Secretary of State," Tripp added. "That's important."

"I'll get that done," Earl assured. "Speaking of donations, does anyone know an Alice Singer from Orange Beach?"

"No, why?" Joe asked, after contemplating.

"She sent me a $400 check!"

Tripp smiled from ear-to-ear, ivory incisors gleaming, recalling her from the Orange Beach city council meeting.

A riled up, no mask-wearing Big Earl kicked off his Orange Beach mayoral campaign on stage inside the Bama Dome, to a packed Friday night house of horny, humbled, hell-bent revelers sick and tired of the political status quo. The lockdowns, the masks, the corrupt government actors and condo developers—everything weighed heavily on the local populace. Something had to give—and Earl was seemingly their big way out. Earl was hotter than a white hot pistol; and that was the one clear thing that Friday afternoon at the Flora-Bama. The place was buzzing with the news of his mayoral candidacy.

Barry Strick-9, with Joe and Brad's help, serving as Secretary of the Election Committee, phoned a list of locals in the days leading to the campaign kickoff, asking them to attend the Big Earl Announcement Show, explaining that there would be complimentary drinks and finger foods under the back tent before the spectacle took place in the Bama Dome. Barry was assured by the overwhelming, positive response to the news Big Earl was running for mayor of Orange Beach. There was palpable excitement regarding Earl's candidacy, and it was contagious, Barry thought, having talked to two dozen or more voters, all saying it was time for a much-needed change and that Earl would do a fine job as mayor.

As strange as it was, everyone in Orange Beach was happy with the concept of Big Earl being the city's chief executive, as it was the ultimate act of defiance by a tired and defrauded citizenry and actually a good investment, as Earl was smarter and much more savvy than people gave him credit for. The buzz around town among the old-timers was that he would do a much better job than Donny. So it was easy getting a few hundred people from the community to pack the Flora-Bama for Earl's formal entry into local politics, which was as strong as a statement the upstart candidate could have hoped for, as he knew thereafter that he had the locals on his side—too many of them came out to show their support for him. So many good people stepped up and stood up, and were counted. It was an amazing turnout for Big Earl and the greater Orange Beach community.

Unsolicited by the committee, the excited participants passed a tip bucket around for the campaign and raised an amazing $3,430 in cash. Earl couldn't believe it, looking across the smiling, adoring throng of friends and supporters, ready to hear him speak, sing and perform. Buoyed beyond belief, Earl for the first time actually saw himself winning the election and being sworn in as mayor of Orange Beach—even if Donny didn't step down like he supposedly promised—like Tripp revealed in a recent phone conversation. "I can likely win this thing regardless!" He imagined.

As Earl led into the diddy, "No more condos on the beach!" he thought of the current mayor and that rat fink Buttrell; and wondered if they would follow through with law enforcement, as planned, while everyone else remained quiet. Tripp told only Earl and Joe about his dealings with the mayor and Buttrell, and asked them to maintain strict secrecy regarding.

The Friday night Big Earl Show Earl chose to kick-off his campaign was near the middle of September, a week later than he wanted due to scheduling snafus, less than two weeks from the day of the election, when everyone had to leave the house and vote for their candidate.

An early afternoon weather bulletin quietly and unceremoniously mentioned there was a formed hurricane in the Gulf of Mexico, and that Lower Alabama and surrounding areas were within the immediate area of concern, within the proverbial cone. Hurricane Sally was her name, and she was a category one storm, barely an organized blip on the coastal zone radar, as cat ones are not as edifying as a Cat 4, like Hurricane Ivan, 16 years earlier, which devastated Perdido Key. Those who stayed for Ivan's wrath swore they'd never remain for another named hurricane, as it left them mindful of their violent nature and awesome destructive power. To those coastal dwellers in the know, hurricanes were nothing to mess with. If one was coming, it was time to go somewhere else.

Strick-9 saw the Friday weather report and recalled riding out Hurricane Ivan 16 years prior. He vividly remembered being miserable, riding out the typhoon in the Silver Moon Package Store and Lounge, without power and amenities for over two, long weeks. He did not want to do that again, and he felt that Joe jinxed them in the cabin that day when he mentioned a possible hurricane. "It's sure to happen now," Barry thought.

On Saturday the storm intensified further and Barry decided he would drive the boat north and find a place upriver to stay, far away from the beach, where a hurricane feasts on the coast, like a lion does hapless prey. Barry was also concerned about his new home. He wanted it out of harm's way; and Joe was happy to hear he was going to take care of it, and himself, by fleeing the vulnerable coastal zone. He, on the other hand, preferred to stay, thinking it would surely miss them.

Joe and the other guys, against better judgment, remained. Tripp stayed in Fairhope, Big Earl and his wife stayed in Orange Beach. Joe stayed at his place in West Pensacola and Brad stayed at his place off Innerarity Point Road. Those who did not flee experienced one of the area's most destructive and lasting hurricanes, one that saw the eye of the storm sit over Perdido Key for a devastating 36 hours, flooding the barrier island and furiously wind-whipping its many condominiums and beach homes up and down the strip, buckling power lines and littering the black top, divided highway with fallen electrical lines, light and power poles, drowned vehicles, sheered building material and flying debris. When the power failed that early Monday morning around 4:00 a.m., upon landfall, flood surge waters had risen over four feet on the Ole River side of the island, inundating hundreds of vehicles parked in areas once thought safe from a flood surge, as they had never seen such a spectacle. Ivan, 16 years prior, was a different type of hurricane—one that brought little in terms of inland flooding borne from surge. Ivan, in contrast, was more of a raging wind, wave and heavy rain event, in comparison.

Hurricane Sally was an Atlantic hurricane, the first to make landfall in the State of Alabama since Ivan, a category four storm, in 2004; coincidentally on the same date. The eighteenth named storm, and seventh hurricane of the active Atlantic season, Sally developed over the Bahamas on September 10. On September 11th she was designated a tropical depression, which made landfall at Key Biscayne, and strengthened into Tropical Storm Sally that afternoon. On September 14th, a reformation into the center of the convection occurred, and data from hunter aircraft showed Sally intensified into a strong Category 1 hurricane and later into a

Category 2 hurricane, making landing near Gulf Shores, Alabama, on the 16th, with maximum sustained winds of 105 miles per hour. The storm weakened after landfall, becoming a remnant the next day.

The vast area between Mobile, Alabama, and Pensacola, Florida, took the brunt of the storm, with widespread wind damage, storm surge flooding in coastal areas, and over 20 inches of rainfall. Several tornadoes were spawned from the long-lasting, swirling vortex. Damage from Sally was estimated at $7.3 billion.

Anyone who stayed was treated to a difficult few days. While the devastation wasn't as vast and permanent as Ivan in 2004, Sally was nevertheless destructive, especially to the key itself—exposed to the full brunt of the storm's unbridled fury and a surprising flood surge, the southernmost tip of civilization was in a most vulnerable and awkward survival position, as it is surrounded by water.

The quick rise in gulf water on the Old River side of the Key was what wreaked havoc on island residents, along with the nearby denizens of Ono Island, as anything on or near the water was adversely affected. Wooden piers and wharves were toppled like Tinker Toys by the fast-rising currents. Water crafts not properly moored drifted off with the fast-moving, rising tide, only to never be seen again by their owners. Many vessels properly moored for the event were nonetheless sunk when the piers and wooden pilings they were latched to were decimated by the angry, high-running tidal surge. Few families escaped the swelling gulf's vitriol, as many had parked cars outside their homes and in closed, lower level garages, which were all enveloped by the irrepressible rising flood waters. It was not uncommon for a single family to lose three vehicles and a boat—or two, in the tumult and grimy aftermath of the indiscriminate storm.

It took a day or two for flood waters to recede to the point where people with working cars and trucks could enter the area and assist the needy. Residents began reclaiming their property in the best and most fastidious manner. They removed every inch of wet sheet rock from their ground level structures so that any transfer of dangerous, sickening mold would be stopped. They gathered flood-ruined items and placed them on the beach roadside for pick-up. Power trucks with ascending buckets and hard-hat wearing, working men descended on the island from every possible direction and roadway and the massive effort to rebuild paradise began, albeit slowly.

The arrival of the hurricane put an end to the regular media cycle, just before the U.S. Attorney's Office in Mobile was readying to send out a press release related to the confessions and arrests of Jacque Buttrell and Donny Kenner. The pressing, inclement weather and its painful aftermath became the only news for almost a week. In the tumult the U.S. Attorney's Office returned to its offices by Wednesday, six days out from the scheduled Orange Beach municipal election. They sent out the press release as the first order of business, barely making headlines across the area, as the media was still bent on covering power outages, gas shortages and a timeframe for the return of normalcy. No one was worried about a looming municipal election. And strangely, for a spell, no one cared about wearing masks and the long-continued lockdowns.

Tripp persuaded Kenner and Buttrell to sign statements saying they were resigning from public office and would not be seeking re-election. Tripp offered that this was being considered strongly by the court as an act of contrition by the perpetrators, demonstrating their will to atone for their sinful ways. It was the information Trip funneled to Earl, letting him know that he had nothing to worry about, because Kenner's name would soon be stricken from the ballot once he tendered his full resignation and fulfilled his promise of not running for re-election; and that happened on Thursday evening, of that same week.

Mayor Kenner, in a short, apologetic letter and speech to the City Council, resigned his post and announced he would not be seeking re-election. Jacque Buttrell followed his lead, resigning in a press conference of his own outside the Fairhope Municipal Complex. The two men were no longer politicians, yet remained political figures, as they would serve moving forward as a glaring example of what can happen to you as an elected official when you tempt fate, time and circumstance—and in this instance, consumer advocate Francis Paul Tripp.

When Francis saw the news releases picked up on his online news feed, he picked up his cell and dialed Big Earl and told him the news. Since he and Donny were the only two who qualified, Big Earl was now the mayor-elect of Orange Beach, Alabama—which was heady stuff for a country boy from Dardanelle, Arkansas, as Earl, theretofore, represented the stilted hopes and dreams of the beguiled and battered beachside community. He was no longer just an entertainer. He was a bona fide public official, as the person on the ballot opposing him, was now officially no longer on the ballot. Even if no one voted for Earl, he would still be sworn in as Mayor of Orange Beach.

In the municipal council races, three candidates challenged sitting city councilmen in Orange Beach, and on Tuesday, Election Day, each won over the incumbents, giving Big Earl a new council to work with once everyone was sworn in. Joe invited everyone to Flora-Bama for a celebratory open bar under the back tent. Tripp and Strick-9 were there, as was Brad Masterson and of course, a beaming Joe, who was extremely happy the way things turned out, that all matters were able to be settled without things getting personal, and any more ugly than they already had. The hurricane had been a huge and destructive surprise on par with the pandemic, but the political win was a salve that seemed to heal all wounds. Everyone was extremely hopeful and upbeat.

"They asked me to say a few words tonight..." Earl started in at the microphone on a pedestal on stage. "I am extremely happy with the outcome! Woo-hoo! We did it!"

There was lively and raucous applause for over a minute. Earl continued.

"I understand I am the first mayor of Orange Beach ever to be elected by default—without a single vote cast for him! I am so proud of that, y'all! I just can't tell you how proud I am of that! Yesiree! Good things are coming, folks! Not just free bushwhackers and regular bare titty sightings, either!"

There was a smattering of chuckles, rapid applause and a lively string of cacophonous cat calls. The crowd fired up its favorite, now go-to chant; in perfect unison they sang, "No more condos on the beach! No more condos on the beach! No more condos on the beach!"

"And yeah—no more damn condos on the beach!" Earl yelled, pointing to everyone in the crowd. "There ain't gonna be no more of that crap!" He paused. Joe joined him by his side, as did Barry, Brad and Tripp, everyone ecstatic in victorious applause.

"Thank you again! Thank you very much!" Earl finished. "Everybody have fun and be safe!"

After Earl finished speaking to the jubilant crowd, Joe caught up with Tripp, who was enjoying a chilled tequila shooter and carrying on with everyone during the victory celebration. Jay Hawkins was almost done setting up to play the tent stage, and everyone was looking forward to the start of his musical show.

"Tripp I haven't had time to catch up with you, but I just wanted to thank you for what you've done for this community. Through unwavering commitment you've done everyone on the island—everyone in Baldwin County really, a great service." Joe said.

"No worries, Joe."

"No—let me finish," Joe interrupted, insisting. "I may have sounded critical of your, let's say, deliberate approach to unscrewing all of our political problems, but I can assure you—I am extremely happy with the outcome and the way it all went down! I am also especially thankful it didn't get ugly with respect to others involved—which we know had great negative media potential for everyone; and finally, I am just thankful for the quiet, positive outcome. This has made a huge difference—and that's what we set out to do, in the first place. It is truly a new day here at the beach, and well, you're largely responsible for it, Mr. Tripp. You and Earl, that is," he said, smiling. "Thank you! And thank you for serving our country in Viet Nam."

"You're welcome, Joe!" Tripp thanked him.

Joe pulled from a nearby table a plaque he had made for Tripp. It was wooden and varnished with an attached brass plate that read: "To Francis Paul Tripp: For his unwavering, unselfish and unbelievable public service to the people of Fairhope, Orange Beach, Baldwin County, Alabama and the United States of America."

Francis read the plaque and swallowed hard. "Thanks, Joe—this means a lot—I'm gonna hang it proudly on the wall in my office along with my Marine memorabilia!"

Joe and Francis firmly shook hands and smiled in congratulations, the local photographer/publisher for the Mullet Wrapper, Fran, taking their picture.

356

24

The following morning Francis tackled the large monument of hurricane debris piled across his sprawling, beautifully landscaped property at the end of High Ridge Road in Fairhope. He was loading large limbs, sticks and clumps of leaves and matted detritus onto a large trailer bound for the county dump, when his cell phone rang, interrupting his Ziggy Marley Pandora playlist. His cell face lit up. He did not recognize the showcased ten digits.

"Francis Tripp," he breathed into the IPhone, still in the steady rhythm of his work.

"Hi Francis!" The familiar female voice sounded. "This is Mary!" He smiled.

"How are you?" She asked.

"Hello there, Mary! Fine! How are you? Did you fare well in the storm? I wondered how you and the kids made out, if you stayed or if you got out in time. It has been a difficult few days. I stayed and I've been without power since landfall and I still have tree material everywhere. Fairhope must have lost 10,000 trees!"

"I am fine and so are the kids. We were scared and drove to Birmingham to be with my sister during the storm. We came back to an awful scene. The kids' house on Innerarity is fine but my place is a wreck. It's awful! I still have stuff everywhere out here on the bay! I don't know what I'm gonna do. No one is available apparently to ride out here and help. All the tree contractors are taken right now, according to my neighbors. They've called everyone."

"You know, Mary, I am finishing up a load here with this trailer, and I will be bringing it to the dump shortly. How about when I'm finished there I come out and take a look at your property and see what's needed to be done? I could even get a few things out of your way today. I'll bring a chain saw and some other things in case we need them." Tripp said.

"That would be great," she answered. "What time do you think you might get here?"

"Give me about an hour," he said, checking the time. "I'll call and confirm."

Chewing on a cigar Tripp went inside and grabbed an overnight bag with two pairs of shorts and a couple of tee shirts, his passport, an unbroken half gallon of agave Tequila, his chainsaw and an oil-mixed red metal fuel can with a spout from the shed. He placed the various items in the back of the Suburban before heading to the dump.

***

Tripp made it to Mary's off Highway 1 on Mobile Bay. He had all of his tools and the trailer so he immediately got to work. He removed several large limbs from the yard, using the chainsaw to make them easier to move and handle. By the time he was done, Mary's front yard, once cluttered with storm debris and detritus, was green and clear again, the picture of tranquility against the idyllic backdrop of a placid Mobile Bay. Tripp, soaking in his own sweat, leaned against the back end of the loaded trailer and removed his gloves. Mary from the porch, with a perspiring pitcher of lemonade, called to him.

"Francis, why don't you come and enjoy a glass of lemonade before you run off?"

Tripp and Mary found themselves alone for the first time. Mary was impressed with his physical fitness and strength. In a few hours he had done a ton of work in her yard that few younger men together could have achieved. She thanked him for the work, reminding him that her neighbors said no one was available for the job.

"Gosh Francis, you worked for over five hours. How much do I owe you for all this? I can't believe you got all those trees out of here!"

"Don't worry about it, Mary."

"No, I insist on paying you."

She reached for her nearby purse, and removed her billfold.

"It's not necessary, Mary." Francis insisted.

"But you still have to haul all this to the dump. That's another hour of work!" She forcefully replied. "No, here's $500. I insist. Most tree services would have billed me a grand."

After finishing his glass, Francis set it on the coffee table before them. She clasped five crisp Benjamins in her extended hand.

"First of all—I'm not taking any money from you." He said. He paused and continued.

"Secondly, it's okay if you call me by my middle name." He paused. "In fact, I'd prefer it."

Mary smiled. "Sure, what's your middle name?" She asked.

"Paul," he answered.

"Sure thing, Paul." She answered, beaming.

"Have you ever been to San Pedro, Belize?" He asked—out of nowhere. It was somewhat of a shock. To Mary, in tone and intonation it sounded like an invite—like he wanted to go that minute. She was surprised, yet strangely undaunted.

"No, I have not." She answered, resolutely.

"There's a red eye that leaves at 10:30 tonight out of New Orleans. We can catch it and be in Belize by morning, having breakfast on the beach. I'm a certified scuba dive instructor. I built a resort on San Pedro back in the 1970's, when the place was a postage stamp. Back then there were 400 people on the island. Everything came by boat. No Internet. The island had one phone. Life was slow. It was like Robinson Caruso."

He paused, having her full attention. It sounded romantic.

"San Pedro sits on a coral reef. I'll show you how to dive, how to use your breathing apparatus and show you many things you've never seen. We could even dive the amazing Blue Hole—I've been there over 30 times. I've actually flown there a couple times by helicopter. Once I brought a British film-making crew there to see a 35-foot Tiger Shark. They couldn't believe it. They got some incredible footage. The shark was massive with huge spots—a gorgeous specimen."

Mary interrupted him.

"I'll go," she replied. "What will I need to bring?" She intently asked.

"As little as possible. A swimsuit or two. We can shop when we get there."

"Okay then, Paul." She smiled, giving in. She emphasized his preferred middle name.

"I'm gonna haul this load to the county dump. Afterwards I'll come back and clean up and we can hit the road. It's two and a half hours to the Big Easy."

"I look forward to the ride," She answered.

"As do I," he replied.

25

Two weeks later, two days after Francis and Mary returned from San Pedro, Belize on an unexpected island jaunt, Johnny and Lucy were married behind the Flora-Bama, against the backdrop of the undulating, indigo Gulf of Mexico and the muse of a marmalade setting sun, amidst a select group of family and friends. Johnny's buddy Jake was there with his girl, engaged. Jerry Boudreaux was there with his girl, down from Auburn. Lucy's best friend from high school was there, as was her well-tanned Mom and Mr. Francis, who looked like a colored person he was so dark. A barefoot Joe Gideon was there, in khaki shorts, light shirt and a dark coat with no tie, along with a well-dressed Miss Vonnie, in an attractive, plaid ladies' pantsuit of her own.

The orange-brown sun faltered in the autumn-winter sky; a cool, steady wind blowing from the north. Sea gulls sailed below the few low-hanging cumulus clouds and squawked above the chalk looking for what might be an easy meal from those gathered conspicuously on the beach. It was a momentous occasion.

Johnny wore a black suit with a gray shirt and a thin black tie, his hair slicked back and tight, parted, no pompadour. His satin black dress pants were rolled to his knees and he was barefoot, like everyone else in attendance that fair, breezy afternoon. Lucy looked like an angel in white, with long, tight arm bands and a puffy, flowing trail and a light veil that shielded her eyes. Even at this late date, at a full seven months pregnant, she only slightly showed she was with child. They were, as always, the lovely young couple. The Flora-Bama Pastor, Dan, a devout family and church man, gave the honors.

After the short, spirited ceremony, everyone piled under the tent and enjoyed beverages and finger foods and live music performed by a host of Flora-Bama players donating their time for the formal celebration of the marriage of their favorite entertaining couple, Johnny and Lucy. Jake played a couple of tunes solo, followed by Jerry Boudreaux on keys and then by Ken Lambert, the first player hired at the Flora-Bama, who sang a couple of old tunes for the young lovebirds and Joe, who asked him to come and play for Johnny and Lucy's sake. One of the tunes Jerry played was the new number he and Johnny had just finished.

In between sets Joe offered a toast to the young newlywed couple, gathering the attention of everyone under the sprawling tent, drinks in hand. Joe ceremoniously raised his cup.

"I hereby offer this toast to Mr. and Mrs. Johnny Glass—two of the finest writers and players and singers we have had here at the Flora-Bama and really, simply two awesome people we are proud to call friends! Best of luck to you—and your family, now and in the future! And remember, be kind to one another, have fun and most importantly, always remember…that the principle business of life is having fun!"

The End.

Epilogue

After their confessions to federal prosecutors and press releases announcing their formal resignations from public office per the agreement with Francis Tripp, Donny Kenner and Jacque Buttrell agreed to meet at the beach near the T down by the Hangout in Gulf Shores, as Donny finally returned Jacque's many calls. They intended to meet to sort things out between them. Donny knew he had the upper hand, given the circumstances, and didn't need to meet with Buttrell; but he did, for selfish reasons.

Donny parked and saw Jacque sitting on a bench near the large, manicured green space at the public park. He approached. Jacque stood to greet him, offering his hand. Donny, only feet away, tackled Jacque, pinning him on the ground in a helpless, supine position, using his extra girth to control him; and proceeded to bludgeon his tanned face with his fists. After a severe beating he stood and spat on him; and he silently walked away. Jacque thereafter went into hiding, as it took weeks for his two black eyes, broken nose and jaw to heal. They never spoke again.

The feds were kind to Donny. Convicted for bribery and racketeering, the judge sentenced him to 30 months in the minor security federal penitentiary in Montgomery, on the grounds of Maxwell Air Force Base. Jacque was not as fortunate. The higher ups on the food chain he fingered were not happy with him snitching them out. In retaliation they revealed knowledge of his many other dubious real estate deals, which brought in kind, more charges; and of course, stricter sentencing. Jacque got 18 years at a federal facility in Texas for his part in the ongoing scams. With good time, and the completion of a drug awareness course available to all federal inmates, each perpetrator was eligible for release in half their allotted time, which meant Donny would be out in about a year and three months, while Jacque would do closer to ten years, if he behaved.

Strick-9 continued living on his new floating home docked behind the Yacht Club on Ole River. He penned another novella, "The Weather Cannon," which drew considerable praise, consternation and criticism among readers, and set up a table near the back of the fishing boat on dry land and sold his three books and a kids' coloring book to curious tourists and die-hard locals, sometimes while surreptitiously enjoying the bountiful effects of the liberty caps he was so fond of. He maintained his beard, and his penchant for telling it like it is, further endearing him to those who encountered and knew him.

Francis Tripp and Mary Whitman continued seeing each other, but as her husband's release date from prison approached, their relationship was strained. Torn over the decision of divorcing Slip and staying with Tripp, she said she needed time to contemplate. A month before his release, Slip, inside the penitentiary, was served divorce papers drawn up by Greg McMakin. Francis and Mary flew to Roatan, Honduras to celebrate her newfound freedom. Upon their return they moved in together into a condo at Eden they purchased, just east of the Flora-Bama, after Tripp's ongoing case against the United States Veteran's Administration—the longest of its kind in America, was finally settled—for seven figures. Tripp continued his uncivil war against the machine, ramping up his efforts through improved technology and talent with the bounty the windfall brought. He remained the most-hated person in Baldwin County among the power-broking elite—even though he lived in Florida.

Brad Masterson continued his busy work as an architect on Perdido Key and abroad, and began his lifelong dream of writing a fictional screenplay set on the island, with the help of a local screenwriter and novelist. The screenplay, titled, "Mamou" was covered by Creative Artists in Beverly Hills and made into an award-winning musical involving scenes from the Flora-Bama, Mobile, New Orleans and of course, the esoteric Cajun Mardi Gras enclave of Mamou, Louisiana. He met a lovely Cajun girl on the movie set and purchased a condominium in the French Quarter, splitting his time thereafter between Perdido Key and the Chart House, his unofficial office located just off the House of Bourbon on the corner of Chartres and Bienville.

Big Earl was successful at slowing the condo craze but he failed miserably at delivering free bushwhackers and babysitting services during the afternoons at Flora-Bama, a setback he admitted, apologized for and wholly regretted when speaking to the public. Earl served only one term as Mayor of Orange Beach, explaining that he was giving up the political post for some other crazy person, so he could return fully to what he loved most: An amazing life of leisure, laughter and song, playing his legendary Friday and Saturday night gigs at the world-famous Flora-Bama.

Lucy Whitman Glass gave birth to Josephine Earline Glass on December 25, 2011, at Thomas Hospital in Fairhope, Alabama. The bouncing baby girl was a blessing to everyone and everything thereafter changed for Johnny and Lucy, who adored their new parenting roles as much as they did their rosy, loveable cherub, Josephine. Johnny and Lucy continued their creative pursuits on the island, having fun making music and new friends, living the lives they loved and that other people so envied. When they needed a babysitter they dropped Jo-Jo off at Grandma Mary's, where she and Paul were always willing to watch the lovely, vivacious one, who like her parents, was blessed with a musical bent, which brought them great joy and entertainment.

Joe Gilchrist fully recovered from the Heineken virus and shared his antibodies by frequently giving blood. He remained the favored Flora-Bama patriarch and the Samaritan everyone counted on for guidance, leadership and charity. Buoyed by Big Earl's election and the progress made with the local planning commissions towards easing development pressures through impact fees and improving public transportation with an off-road island trolley service, he was optimistic that their quality of life on Perdido Key would continue to improve. He expanded his random acts of kindness program and reminded people whenever he could about the importance of being nice to one another and planning to have fun in life, making the most of our time on the planet. "After all," He would say, "This is the best life I've ever lived!"

Chris Warner is a double graduate of LSU in Baton Rouge and holds a doctorate from the University of New Orleans.

He is the author and publisher of over 20 books, including "Bushwhacked at the Flora-Bama." He lives in Perdido Key, Florida. Visit his website: chriswarnerauthor.com